RELUCTANT QUEEN

RELUCTANT QUEEN

TUDOR HISTORICAL NOVEL
ABOUT MARY ROSE TUDOR,
THE LITTLE SISTER OF
INFAMOUS ENGLISH KING, HENRY VIII

Geraldine Evans

SOLO BOOKS NORFOLK ENGLAND

RELUCTANT QUEEN

This paperback edition published by Solo Books in 2014
Previously published as a digital book by Geraldine Evans
ISBN-13:978-1495255595
ISBN-10:149525559X

Solo Books
N Walsham
Norfolk NR28 0DZ

Publisher's Note: This is a work of historical fiction. Although attempts have
been made to describe character traits where known, this novel is a product
of the author's imagination. Real locales, events and names are used where
known, but occasional artistic licence has been utilised in order to make for
a better reader experience.

Book Layout ©2013 BookDesignTemplates.com
Cover:
http://commons.wikimedia.org/wiki/File.OMarie_reine_de_France.png
/selfpubbookcovers US PD-1923
Ordering Information: Order via www.amazon.co.uk / www.amazon.com

Dedicated to those in my family with special birthdays in 2014: Andrew, Alex and Aimee. Best wishes to all of you.

FOREWORD

Although this is a work of fiction, the principal characters in the novel actually existed in the sixteenth-century though some are sparsely documented in historical records.

All those depicted were real people whose lives were closely interwoven with that of my 'Reluctant Queen', Mary Rose Tudor. I have endeavoured to adhere strictly to the dates of actual events.

Most conversations are of necessity invented, but a proportion of Mary Rose's words are her own as noted by contemporaries.

RELUCTANT QUEEN

BOOK ONE

CHAPTER ONE

'No, I won't marry that feeble, pocky old man,' Mary Tudor stormed at her brother. For all that twenty-three-year-old Henry was the elder and had for five years been King of England, Mary was determined not to submit to his entreaties.

'Now, sweetheart.' Henry bent from his great height and coaxed, 'You know nothing about him. Louis, the French King may be no young stripling, but they say he's very rich. He'll be kind and loving, I doubt not. You will learn to be fond of him in time.'

'I will not,' Mary insisted. Louis was old and sickly; fifty-two to her eighteen. The thought of marrying such an old man appalled her. Henry was all sweet reasonableness now, but Mary knew that would soon change if she continued to defy him. Since becoming king, Henry had rapidly grown used to having his own way; *he* had not sacrificed himself on the marriage market. Instead, just a few months after their father's death, he had speedily married Catherine of Aragon, their brother Arthur's pretty young widow, ignoring their late father's advice. It had been a marriage made, at least, in part, for love.

Mary didn't see why she should not also marry where she would, as rumour had it their sister Margaret was determined to do. Now nearly twenty-four, Margaret had set her

1

heart on marrying the young and handsome Archibald Douglas, Earl of Angus. Just fourteen, Margaret had married their father's choice of King James IV of Scotland eleven years earlier, carrying with her the forlorn hope that this marriage alliance would bring to an end the interminable wars between England and Scotland.

Forlorn hope it had proved. For Margaret had been widowed just the previous year when King James had been killed fighting Henry's army at the battle of Flodden. Mary had no doubt that Henry's present wish to use her for a similar, unnatural alliance, this time with France, would prove equally fruitless. Had he not been long allied with the Emperor Maximilian and King Ferdinand, the father of Queen Catherine? And although they had had a falling out after Henry had discovered Ferdinand had made a secret truce with the French, Henry would revert to the long-standing Hapsburg alliance in a second, rendering vain her sacrifice in marriage to old King Louis. His naming of Louis as 'The French King' rather than the 'King of France' was further proof of how unnatural such an alliance would be. Henry considered himself the rightful King of France. He longed for his own Crécy and Agincourt. Only the previous year, he had led his army against the French and had captured Thérouanne and Tournai.

Mary felt she had sacrificed enough for her brother's ambitions. He had caused her to be spurned by young Prince Charles of Castile, the Emperor's grandson and Catherine's nephew, to whom her father had betrothed her six years earlier. Now he wanted to replace this match with one far more distasteful to her.

But between her brother's alliance-swapping, Mary had fallen in love, just like her sister. Mary knew that if she wished to copy her sister's example she must hold out against her brother's demands. It wouldn't be easy. But when she thought of the unheroic figure of Louis XII, the old French invalid whom everyone laughed at, her determination to defy Henry grew stronger.

'You know where my heart lies, Henry,' she reminded him now. 'Where it's lain these many months, whilst you've been toying with Castile and its prince.' Mary's gaze narrowed accusingly. 'Where's the magnificent dowry jewel they sent our father, but perched in your hat, brother?'

Henry's small mouth tightened, before he gathered in the reins of his temper and tried more sweet reason. 'As you say, King Louis is old and sickly and has been for a good long while; any marriage couldn't be for long. Think of the honours and riches that would be yours and you could be free in a year or less. What's a year when you're only eighteen?'

'No, Henry, I'll not be persuaded.' Mary smoothed her gown and tried some sweet reason of her own. 'Surely I could be permitted to please myself, as you did.'

Henry's lips were now a thin line. His skin flushed up and he shouted at her. 'This is foolish talk. I'm a man, Mary and a king. You're only a princess and princesses must dispose themselves where duty, not the heart, lies.' Henry's gaze turned longingly towards the window, for the day was fair. Mary, too, wanted to be out in the warm sunshine instead of cooped up indoors arguing with her brother. She hoped Henry's love of pleasure and hunting would persuade him to give over trying to browbeat her. But this hope was a vain one. Even as she thought it, Henry dragged his gaze from the

3

window and stared so consideringly at her that Mary realised he was about to try another tactic.

'Do this for me, this once,' Henry pleaded, 'and when Louis dies, as he will, and that no doubt right soon, you may choose your own husband afterwards. On this you have my word.'

Mary stared broodingly at him. Much as she adored this handsome giant of a brother, she had learned to be wary of Henry's promises and this one had a too-ready air about it. But he had given his word on it, she mused. His offer weakened her resolve. Given Henry's determination to have his own way in all things this might be her best chance to attain her desire and marry Charles Brandon. But the repugnant necessity of first marrying the sickly Louis invaded her mind and would not be ignored.

Mary's thoughts turned this way and that while the silence lengthened. How could she bear to let the old French king fondle her, couple with her, when all her senses craved only the touch of Charles Brandon? Yet, it was true that Louis was sickly, liable to die ere long, as Henry claimed. Perhaps his poor health would allow him nothing more intimate than a formal bedding with her for the sake of convention.

If she could trust her brother's promise she might soon be able to go to Charles freely. Upset, confused, wishing to be left in peace to consider what she should do, Mary was startled from her reverie by Henry's angry voice.

'What more do you want, Madam? Most girls do not need to be cajoled into marriage. They're told whom they are to marry and they marry them.'

4

Henry's handsome face was flushed with a right royal temper and Mary knew he had taken her silence for willfulness. Now, he towered threateningly over her and for the first time, Mary felt something of that fear that her brother's rages so easily engendered in others.

'I've been too indulgent towards you, Madam, too easygoing. You'll come to your duty, sister, or perchance, I might have to find a teacher, one not as kindly as I.'

Mary, with her own goodly share of royal temper, now forgot Henry's promise, his kingly majesty and her own wavering doubts and flung back defiantly at him, 'Perhaps you should do that, brother, for I'll not wed him else.' Turning on her heel, Mary fled from the chamber, her steps echoing up the passageway, mingling with the sobs she could no longer hold back.

Thomas Wolsey, the king's almoner, stepped from behind the curtained doorway. 'That was not well done, Your Grace,' he chided. 'Your sister may be a sweet and loving girl, but she has a certain spirit. She should be gentled into agreement, for love of you and for the sake of the French alliance. Chivvying and harrying is not the way with her.'

Henry's gaze narrowed and he stared hard at Wolsey. But Wolsey, aware that his young king valued honest counsel, was emboldened to continue. 'With the help of Princess Mary's friend, Mistress Popincourt, and our obliging French hostage, the Duc de Longueville, we've advanced the match this far; perhaps we should encourage them further. Mistress Popincourt is mighty friendly with your sister. Let her use her soft words at every opportunity. 'Tis my belief, Your Grace, that between her and de Longueville, they'll sway your sister to the match if we make it worth their while. De Longueville is kin to His Majesty, King Louis. He will, I'm sure, be doubly rewarded for providing the old King with such a lovely young bride. He will also get his freedom if he helps to persuade your sister to the match.'

'What of Jane Popincourt?' Henry asked. 'What reward for her?'

Wolsey gave a sly smile. 'From what I understand, Your Grace, she has had her reward from de Longueville - a tarnished reputation. They have conducted their liaison with little discretion. For her, the gleam of gold will be carrot enough, but no further payment should be necessary. She will, I doubt not, expect to accompany your sister to France, but that is something I would counsel against, Sire. We do not wish your sister's good name to be joined with such a wanton's at the French court.'

'No, indeed. But Mary will expect the girl to accompany her. They've been friends since childhood. If we are to get her agreement to the match it would be wise not to upset her on this matter.'

Wolsey had already given due thought to the question of Jane Popincourt and as a natural diplomat, he had quickly found the obvious solution. 'What need is there for us to upset her, Your Grace when others can be persuaded to do it for us? Our Ambassador, Worcester, has only to whisper in King Louis' ear about Popincourt's morals and His Majesty would, I'm sure, see to the rest. Princess Mary is young and innocent; he will want her to stay that way. He admires virtuous behaviour in a woman, so we may surmise that he dislikes the opposite. I think, Sire, we can safely leave King Louis to do our refusing for us.'

'You may be right in what you say, Thomas. It would seem Mistress Popincourt has already led my sister astray, putting romantic notions of love in her head when there should be naught but duty, making her pert and disobedient. I like the idea of Louis banning Mistress Popincourt from accompanying Mary's train. He who makes the rules must also take the blame.' Henry's laugh boomed out. But the laughter was quickly replaced by grim determination, as, with his little eyes narrowed, he vowed, 'we will try the gentle option first to get Mary's agreement to the match, but if she is still hot against it, we will need to use more ungentle methods.'

Mary raced into her bed-chamber, long, golden hair flying behind her, and threw herself, sobbing, on her bed.

Lady Guildford, her governess, came up to her, tutting at such unseemly behaviour. Mary's 'Mother' Guildford, in whose charge she had been placed since the death of her own mother, was all calm reason. 'What's to do, my lady? What's to do? Get up, child, you'll crush your gown.'

'Whatever is the matter, Mary?'

Through her sobs, Mary heard the concerned voice of her friend, Jane Popincourt, but she didn't answer her. Eventually Mary's sobs subsided and she sat up on the bed, her lovely face a mask of misery.

'Now, madam, will you tell me what ails thee? Have you a pain? I'll send for the physicians.' Her Mother Guildford bustled to the door, but Mary called her back.

'Nay, Mother. This is a pain which no physician can cure.' She raised her tear-stained face. 'My brother wishes to wed me to old King Louis of France.'

7

'Surely he's not looking for another wife?' Lady Guildford asked. 'He's buried two already. Besides, 'tis well known he's too old and sickly to get himself any sons. They say he only clings to life to spite Francis, his son-in-law.'

'But what riches you would have, Mary,' Jane cajoled. 'Think what your trousseau would be for such a marriage. It would make the one for the Castilian match look like a pauper's rags. To be Queen of France - 'tis a magnificent honour for any girl.' Jane's soft French accent turned the words into a honeyed caress.

Mary was not to be comforted. Sunk in misery, she caught the look of dislike her Mother Guildford cast towards Jane. But Lady Guildford was a stern and pious woman and thought her worldly friend Jane a bad influence. But then she had been a great friend of Mary's equally pious paternal grandmother, Margaret Beaufort. Together, with her father's sanction, they had ruled the court, over-riding Mary's meek and gentle mother, Elizabeth, whose only duty was the getting of sons. She had done her duty in that as in everything else. Indeed, she had done her duty so well that she had died, worn out from child-bearing, but a short while after giving birth yet again. The baby, Catherine, had also died.

Fresh tears filled Mary's eyes as she thought of the gentle countenance of her dead mother. Now, apart from Mary, there was only her brother, Henry and her elder sister, Margaret left out of the brood of babes her mother had borne. Her father and grandmother were also long dead.

The atmosphere at court had changed markedly after her brother Henry had replaced their father as king just before his eighteenth birthday. And although gaiety had not replaced piety – for Henry was devout – there had been so

8

many balls and banquets that it had seemed Henry couldn't run through their father's carefully accumulated wealth quickly enough.

'If you did marry him, my lady, it could not be for long.' Practical as well as pious, Lady Guildford repeated Henry's soothing words. 'An old and sickly man and a young, lively bride is a sure recipe for an early funeral.'

Although she knew it was sinful, Mary couldn't help but be cheered a little by this and she asked curiously, 'Is King Louis very sickly, Mother?'

Lady Guildford nodded. 'He's been sickly these many years. They say he retires to his bed at six of the clock every evening. Even the king's cocks and hens tarry later than His Christian Majesty.'

'My brother seems very keen on this marriage,' Mary confided. 'Surely, if he loved me, he could have found a more suitable match for me?'

'Would that someone would arrange such a match for me,' Jane commented. 'You'd not find me weeping and thinking on the age of the groom.'

'You'll be lucky to find anyone to marry you, madam,' Lady Guildford told her tartly. 'Your indiscretions with the Duc de Longueville are all over the court.'

Jane gave a careless shrug. 'What care I? Mary will take me to the French court with her and find me a rich husband.'

'There's many a noble lady ahead of you in the queue for a rich husband,' Lady Guildford waspishly reminded her. 'Why should you think you would be permitted to go to the French court?' Suspiciously, she demanded, 'Unless you and de Longueville have been plotting while you indulged your lusts?'

'I don't know what you can mean,' Jane retorted.

'Do you not? Can it be that you and de Longueville have decided that the best way for him to achieve his desire to return to France is by persuading the king to marry Mary into that country?'

Mary saw that her Mother Guildford's shot had hit home. De Longueville had been one of the French nobles captured by her brother's forces the previous year at Thérouanne. In his eagerness to return home had he persuaded her friend Jane to betray her? The possibility upset her and Mary remained silent while she listened to the continuing exchange.

'A marriage alliance with France would be an ideal way for a prisoner such as de Longueville to return home,' Lady Guildford continued thoughtfully. 'Maybe taking his mistress with him into the bargain?'

Mary found her voice and demanded, 'Jane, can this be true?' Mary looked reproachfully at the girl as she saw confirmation on Jane's face.

'For all your plotting, madam, I doubt you'll get your way. Do you think King Henry will want his little sister's name sullied by association with yours?' Lady Guildford upbraided the unrepentant Jane. 'And from what I hear of King Louis, he's turned very pious in his old age—he wouldn't countenance any immorality at his court. Or loose women either.'

Jane's expression turned venomous, before she flounced from the room. Lady Guildford snorted after the departed Jane before she took a hairbrush and, after bidding Mary to come and sit on a stool set before the glass, she began to smooth the brush through Mary's disordered hair. Waist-length, and golden, it was one of her greatest beauties.

10

'You know, my lady,' Mother Guildford remarked, 'perhaps there is something in what that wanton says about this French marriage.'

'Not you, too, Mother,' Mary protested. ''Tis enough that my brother should harry me, without you start—'

'Hush, child. There are worse fates in this life than marriage to an old man.' As Lady Guildford smoothed the brush through Mary's hair, she told her, 'King Louis divorced his first wife for her ugliness. He couldn't abide her near him. His second, Queen Anne, he was supposed to be fond of, though she was on the plain side too. Do you not think that a young beauty like yourself would fare better than either? He would be ready to fall at your feet if it would please you, I vow, having first decked you in costly rubies and diamonds.'

Despite her fears, Mary smiled to hear the devout Lady Guildford speak so. 'It is not like you to talk in so worldly a manner, Mother.'

'I can be as worldly as necessary when it is for the good of my little maid. I have taken the place of your mother and grandam, and must think of your best interests, as they would.'

'And would it be in my best interests, think you, to marry a man so old, with creaky joints and gouty limbs? What of love? What of romance?'

'Foolish notions for a princess, as I'm sure your brother told you. Both your mother and grandam married for duty, though I'm not saying love didn't come. You should put such thoughts out of your head for I know none of high rank who were permitted to marry for love.'

Mary, about to remind her of the love-match that had formed the basis of her own Tudor dynasty, remained silent as she recollected how that love-match had ending. The marriage between Catherine, Henry V's young French widow and her own paternal great grandsire, Owen Tudor, the Welsh gentleman of her guard, had been a secret one, ending in tragedy with Owen eventually clapped into prison and Catherine forced to retire to a convent where she had died at an early age. Such was not the future Mary wanted for herself and Charles Brandon. So, although she brooded, Mary said nothing when her Mother Guildford told her she would submit to her duty, as many before her had submitted, and that her brother, for all his gay charm, would see to it that she did so.

Mary knew it was useless to speak to her Mother Guildford of love and passion. Like Henry, it was clear she thought the match an excellent one. But Lady Guildford was old. Piety was her passion. And neither she nor Henry would have to endure King Louis' shameful fumblings. Beneath her lowered lids, Mary's blue eyes darkened. But as Lady Guildford continued to pull the silver-backed brush through her silken hair, Mary's mind quietened. And as thoughts of the future were so distasteful, she cast her mind backwards, to the carefree days of her childhood at Eltham which she and Henry had shared; their sister, Margaret, long married and in Scotland and Arthur, Prince of Wales, in his own establishment. Henry, as second son, had been destined for the church until Arthur's early death altered his prospects. Mary had always found it impossible to imagine her tall, adored, handsome brother a man of the cloth. He exuded too much of the love of life and its many pleasures for that. Henry had basked in her adoration and loved her the more for it, far more than he had ever loved their elder sister, Margaret, who, once betrothal to King James of Scotland, had delighted in queening it over them.

Mary wished she could remember more of her mother; but she had died shortly before Mary's seventh birthday and all she had was an impression of soft arms and a gentle voice crooning lullabies. Her father, a thin, solemn man with a careworn face, she could remember more clearly. He had arranged the 'great match' for her with the young Prince of Castile. She could still remember the betrothal ceremony held at Greenwich with the great throng of nobles and clerics. Her betrothed, or more probably his grandsire, had sent her the brilliant jewel in the form of the letter 'K' for Karolus, made of diamonds and pearls, which Henry now wore in his hat. She had been proud of the jewel and had loved to show it off. It had an inscription on it, which, with childish notions of love, she had taken to her heart— 'Maria had chosen the good part, which should not be taken from her.'

But it *had* been taken from her. The marriage had been due to be finalised this year, despite her lately wayward-leaning heart. Her father had paid her dowry of 50,000 crowns, but had cautiously demanded a pawn for the money. Mary could still remember his delight when his demand had been met and a magnificent cluster of diamonds worth twice the dowry sum had been sent. But then her father had died. And although he had left her her dowry, in the form of the diamond cluster, when he became king, Henry had taken a great fancy to the jewel and refused to part with it. Mary had been left with nothing, not even her Castilian Prince who had repudiated her after many months of wrangling and recriminations.

And now her brother proposed another, even grander, match for her. But Mary's taste for grand marriages had turned to ashes. She had only to look at those of Catherine and her sister, Margaret, to know they often brought misery and humiliation in their wake. Had not Catherine, Henry's queen, suffered near-destitution for seven years after the death of her first husband, Arthur? Her misery only alleviated when Henry became king and married her. And owing to her faithless husband's 'fatal weakness for women' Margaret's marital humiliations had been without number. Such memories strengthened Mary's resolve to marry Charles Brandon. She wanted only to live in peace with her beloved. She must find Charles and persuade him to declare himself. Surely Henry, who could be sentimental, would relent when he realised how great was the love of his sister and his bosom friend.

Before, caution had made Charles reluctant to claim Mary's hand, but the time for caution was past. Unless he wanted to lose her to old Louis, he must speak out. She must find the words to persuade him to it. The alternative didn't bear thinking about.

CHAPTER TWO

Mary looked back down the Dover Road at the snaking tail of the royal party, its last third obscured by the dust kicked up by the horses' hooves. She wished her fast-approaching future could be as easily obscured. But they were nearing the end of the leisurely seventy-mile journey through Gravesend, Rochester, Sittingbourne, Faversham and Canterbury, which had given her ample time to consider what awaited her at journey's end. Soon now, they would reach Barham Down and Dover Castle.

In spite of the choking dust, the courtiers were gay. But why shouldn't they be? It was a beautiful day. Her brother, who rode a little way ahead, had got his way and was merry. And when her brother was in an ebullient mood so must be the rest of the court. Mary didn't share their gaiety. Even the glorious weather didn't lighten her mood. Although it was already October, all along the roadside the flowers still bloomed; everyone said they couldn't remember such a year for flowers — lovely, wild, deep pink thyme, purple, fragrant lavender, sweet, white, creeping chamomile — all nodded their salute in the slight breeze created by the passing of so many riders.

The peasants in the fields stopped their labours and gazed, open-mouthed at the bejeweled courtiers as they passed, the sun glinting off their finery. Even Mary had to admit that none in the party could match the magnificence of her brother. At twenty-three, Henry, who stood head and shoulders above most of the courtiers, was broad-shouldered and handsome. His loud laughter rang out frequently. Mary saw him glance back to where she rode with her sister-in-law, Queen Catherine, saw his smile fade as he took in her woebegone looks. Mary knew she didn't look her best. The only member of the party who looked more wan was the five months' pregnant Catherine.

Henry turned his horse around and waited for them to come up to him. 'Marry Madam, you look as though you were riding to your funeral instead of to your husband,' he told her as he twitched the reins and pulled his horse into step with theirs. 'King Louis will not like your glum looks, I swear.'

'Perhaps he will repudiate me, then brother, like the Prince of Castile,' Mary replied pertly. 'She glanced at Catherine for support. Catherine had been delighted when she had been betrothed to her nephew, the Prince of Castile and had not been pleased when the match had been replaced by the one with Louis. But Catherine was a dutiful wife and did not criticise her husband in public, so she said nothing and Mary turned back to Henry.

'Anyway, Henry, did you not tell me that marriage is a serious voyage on which to embark? Surely, then, I must leave smiles and other inappropriate and frivolous things behind.'

Henry's rude snort told her what he thought of her answer. He wheeled his horse about, gave him the spur, and galloped back to his friends, where loud laughter soon once again drifted back. She was glad to see him go, for although her words had held a soft defiance, in truth, she had had enough of arguments. Henry had her unwilling agreement to the French marriage and must needs be satisfied with that and not also seek to ease his conscience.

Mary felt Catherine watching her, sensed the sympathy and armed herself against it as she had armed herself against her brother's reproaches.

'You won't find it so bad, Mary,' Catherine tried to console her. She was speaking from the purely personal view, Mary knew; politically, she would never be reconciled to this French match. 'I understand that Louis, though old as you say, is likely to be kind. Resign yourself to it, child and a lot of your unhappiness will be eased. I know 'tis hard at first to leave your home, but try not to fret too much. It'll only increase your sadness.'

Catherine's accent, her tiny body wearied by heat and pregnancy, was more strongly Spanish than ever. Shamed by her sister-in-law's stoicism, Mary reminded her, 'But sister, you married young men. First my brother, Arthur, and then on his death, Henry; a handsome, manly man I have to say, though he be my brother.'

'Youth and handsome looks are not everything, Mary. For all my husband's fine face and figure, we can't get us a son.'

Mary glanced at her sister-in-law and her mound of a stomach. Poor Queen Catherine had already suffered several previous pregnancies, all but one ending in either miscarriage or a stillborn child. The longed-for son had tragically died at seven weeks.

'This time you'll bear a son that thrives, I trow,' Mary tried to console Catherine, 'a prince as strong and handsome as his father.'

Catherine put a brave face on her plight. 'It is what I pray for daily. But you are right, Mary. I will concentrate my mind on happy thoughts of sons.' She gazed up ahead, at Henry's broad back, and winced as, in his youthful exuberance, he challenged one of the courtiers to a race. The pair galloped off in a heavy cloud of dust through which Henry's whoops of delight drowned out the coughing fits of those left in his wake. 'I would please my husband.'

Henry didn't like sad looks, as Mary had recently had reason to know. He thought, rightly in her case, that they hid discontent and lack of obedience. As for Catherine, though Mary knew well how mightily she sought to please her husband, the queen would be twenty-nine in December. Wearied by pregnancy, she looked every year of her age. Although Catherine's skin retained its admired pink and white colouring, the youthful prettiness Mary remembered had faded. Henry, by contrast, was still a young man, his boisterousness accentuating even more the five years between them. Mary was afforded a glimpse of how Louis, her much older husband, might feel when he came off worse in a similar comparison. But the spurt of compassion for Louis was brief. Louis had had a choice in the matter. Mary tried again to comfort her sister-in-law. 'But you do your duty,

Catherine. No one could have tried harder to provide Harry with an heir.'

Catherine's smile failed to show its usual serenity and Mary had a glimpse into the other woman's soul. She hurriedly looked away, not wishing to witness such pain.

'Tried and failed,' said Catherine softly. 'Such failure is not regarded as a virtue in queens. But you, Mary, you are lucky in some ways. Oh, I know you don't agree with me now, but perhaps in time you will. You are to marry an old and sickly man, past worrying about heirs. You won't have to suffer the pain and loss of repeated failure as I have.'

Though that was small consolation to Mary, she admitted she might have been wed to a lusty and possibly long-lived prince and should count her blessings. There was still hope that she and Charles would eventually be able to marry.

As they rode on along the dusty, potholed roads, Mary's thoughts went back through the weeks that had led her on this journey. After alternate soft and harsh words from her brother, her friend Jane's cajoling, joined with the Duke de Longueville's persuasive attentions, she had given in, wearied by it all and wanting it to end in the only way, as she had known in her heart all along, that it could end.

Once she had agreed to the match, many glittering balls had been held in her honour. Given no time to brood or reflect, she had been whirled through the weeks to her marriage, held in August, in that palace of bitter memory, Greenwich. The Duc de Longueville, acting as Louis' proxy, had put the bridal ring on her finger. Mary's colour rose as she remembered the bedding ceremony after the banquet.

She had been undressed by her ladies and put to bed and there, before the assembled court, her proxy husband had climbed into bed with her, one leg naked out of his bright red hose. The marriage announced consumated when he had touched her body with his bare leg.

Mary shivered in spite of the heat of the day. King Louis, old as he was, would no doubt expect to do more than touch her with his leg. Although she had yet to set eyes on her husband he had already managed to upset her. After being assured on all sides that Louis would be eager to please her she had never thought that his first action should be one he must know would upset her. She had assumed that since the choice of husband was not hers she would at least be allowed to choose which of her ladies would accompany her. It had seemed little enough to expect.

But Louis had thought otherwise, though he had delayed the messenger who carried the unwelcome news that Jane Popincourt, her childhood friend, wasn't to be allowed to accompany her to France, until after the proxy marriage ceremony. Although Mary still felt that Jane had betrayed her by plotting with her lover, de Longueville, believing de Longueville to have put the marriage scheme into Jane's head, Mary had forgiven her. Besotted, Jane had simply wanted to please him. Now, instead of the glittering future she had hoped for, she had lost both Mary and her lover.

Mary had counted on Jane's company to lighten her hours at Louis' dour court and she had asked Henry to intervene. But as he had explained, she was now married to Louis and was his responsibility. Henry had suggested she should try charming her husband into changing his mind. Doubtless, he meant she should play the harlot in order to get her own way. The far more knowing Jane had tried a similar ploy. It had gained her nothing. Perhaps if she had held out Henry would have come round. But Mary had felt hounded into giving a hasty assent which Henry had seized upon. After that, there was no going back. It was too late to wish she had been stronger. Now she had all the time and peace in the world to regret her momentary weakness.

If only Charles, her love, hadn't so skirted around the subject and hedged them in with ifs and buts and maybes that their love had been doomed before it had a chance to take wing. She had pleaded with him to declare himself, sure that together, they could have swayed Henry, but he had refused, his low birth and his fear of what her brother might say and do to him for having the temerity to aim as high as the king's sister, put forward to placate her.

Mary's gaze flew again to the front of the train. Henry, some of his ferocious energy burned off by his gallop, was once again in fine fettle, laughing and enjoying himself as he knew well how to do. But thwarted, Henry wasn't such a merry companion, as she knew to her cost. Mary dropped her gaze to her bridal ring. Louis' bridal ring and thought of might-have-beens. She and Charles, her lost love, had had a last meeting in a quiet part of the palace gardens. Charles had plucked roses for her to try to cheer her, red and white roses for Lancaster and York, the two rival arms of her family whose warring had largely ended with the marriage of her parents, Henry of Lancaster and Elizabeth of York. He had

kissed her and they had plighted their love, using their secret language of love, as the red and white blooms tumbled
from her arms.

Mary had felt herself drunk with love, but Charles, twelve
years older, and more cautious, had restrained her abandon,
pushing her from him in spite of the longing in his eyes, in
spite of the ardor that heated her body. Wretched, she had
taunted him. 'Do you not truly love me, then, Charles?' she
had asked. 'How can you let us part like this? Do you not care
that soon old King Louis will kiss me as you now kiss me?
That he will take what should be yours? I offer myself to you
yet you spurn me.'

He had tried to comfort her. 'Mary, sweetheart, try to understand. You know my situation. I can offer you little as yet.
You are the daughter of a king, whereas I am merely the son
of a lowly knight. How could I dare marry you now?'

'Lowly knight he might have been,' Mary replied. 'But he
was a valiant one. If he had not sacrificed his life to save my
father on Bosworth Field, there would have been no kingship
and none of these royal marriages, either. My brother might
remember how much our family owes to yours and give you
your due.'

'But sweetheart', Charles had protested, 'the king, your
brother, gave me the Dukedom of Suffolk February last past.
Doubtless he considers he has now given me my due and that
I should not look for more.'

'It seems you would rather please my brother than me.
You cannot love me as much as I love you or you would not
give me up so easily.'

'I would please both of you, if I could. You must know
how I long for you. How can you think that I do not?'

She had clung to him then, thinking he was weakening,
but he had only pushed her away again and told her not to
torment him. 'It appears I must find restraint enough for
both of us. What do you think your brother and his Council
would do to me if we were discovered? Let us only bide our
time. Your brother is right, Mary. Old King Louis is not a
well man. You must marry him since you have agreed, but
it'll not be for long, I swear. Only be patient, sweetheart, be
patient, and do your brother's bidding this once and he'll be
tender towards us later. Have you not his promise? Our position will be that much stronger in the future for giving him
what he desires now. We must just be patient and trust the
king.'

Mary had protested. 'I would have one sweet memory at
least to look back upon to make the waiting easier to bear.
Must I beg you to love me?'

'Nay, sweetheart, please do not. I'm not sure I'd have the
strength to resist, for resist we must. You know it as I do.'

Dismayed, with an ache in her chest and a throat so tight
she feared it would choke her, denied even one memory of
their passion to warm her in France, Mary said, 'If you won't
ask my brother for my hand, I hope you will at least kiss it —
and me — goodbye.'

'Not 'goodbye', he insisted. 'Only 'au revoir'.

'We cannot be sure it is not 'goodbye' in very truth and
that forever,' Mary reminded him. He said nothing. 'Very
well. 'Goodbye' or 'au revoir', whichever it is to be, I bid you

farewell.' She held out her hand, her manner distant, as if she was already moving away from him.

It disconcerted him for a moment, she saw, for he quickly seized her hand and kissed it as fervently as she could wish, before he raised his lips from her hand to her mouth and kissed that more fervently still. Mary threw her arms round his neck and pressed her body down the length of him. If she couldn't take away with her the memory she wanted, she could at least leave a lasting memory of her with him. She felt his body give a lusty response and began to caress him.

But Charles tore himself away again. His breath ragged, his voice hollow, he said, 'By the Mass, Mary, I pray you do not do this to me. The king, your brother, would cut me to collops if he caught us.'

Mary gazed at him from eyes made languid by love. 'We won't let him catch us, then. I can get one of my maids to hire us a private room at an inn and we can—'

Charles turned away from her and the temptation she offered. 'I cannot,' he told her. 'I dare not. You know I dare not.'

Anguished, she gazed at his broad back. 'Some men dare much for love,' she taunted. 'Abelard loved Heloise so much, he—'

He turned back to her then. 'Aye, sweetheart. And look what happened to him. Would you have me gelded, as he was?'

Haste had made Mary choose a poor example. His words served to sober her, too. 'No, of course not. You are right. I'm sorry.'

'Let us part as friends, so we may come together as true man and maid.'

'Maid no more if Louis does his duty.'

'We must then pray that age has gelded *him*.'

Mary, who had never realised how much pain could be brought on the wings of love, whose very heart ached for love of Charles, and whose body rose up in revolt at the thought of Louis, said a heartfelt, 'Amen to that.'

Mary came back to the present and the choking dust of the road. She mustn't think of it; each time she did, her stomach heaved. There would be no more stolen kisses. She was on her way to her ancient husband and she must try to resign herself to it. Resign herself too, to the fact that her love would be taken as of right, rather than given freely as she had wished.

A shout went up and broke the chain of her thoughts. And as she looked up she could see the mighty stone walls of Dover Castle in the distance. One of the largest castles in England, built high on the cliffs, it dominated the town and had served England well through many episodes of invasion. Mary was struck by the irony that the latest role of the castle would be to hold her fast in its keeping till she sailed for France on the morrow.

The last of several long days that had begun at dawn, was winding down to its nadir as the royal party clattered through the castle's magnificent gateway. Mary's head now beat in tune with her heart and as soon as she had climbed wearily from her horse, she begged leave of Henry to retire. Thankfully, he was more than willing to bid her wan face adieu and she was able to escape to the chamber allotted to her.

The bedding, under the circumstances of her imminent departure, was rather makeshift, but somebody had at least put a pallet bed in the room and, after being relieved of her head-dress and gown by one of her attendants, Mary sank on to it and settled back on the cool pillows. She didn't expect to sleep as her mind was too troubled. Besides, her Maids of Honour entered the chamber then, chattering like so many argumentative magpies, excited by the prospect of travelling to France. Mary couldn't bear their excitement and turned her head away. Along the corridor, she could hear Lady Guildford sternly rebuke another of her ladies before she bustled in and banished the rest from the chamber so Mary could sleep in peace.

Her thoughts drifted and she fell into a light doze, her dreams filled with pictures of an ardent Louis, all scrawny limbs and drooling, toothless red mouth, pursuing her around their bedchamber. She wasn't sorry to be wakened from such a dream by the crack of thunder overhead. Immediately, lightning raced across the sky, lighting up the room.

The warmth had vanished from the day. A chill struck her as she climbed from the pallet and she shivered. Lady Anne Grey, daughter to her cousin, the Marquis of Dorset and one of the ladies who were to accompany her to France, was sitting by the window, quietly reading by the light of a candle and Mary asked her, 'What hour is it?'

'Tis after five of the clock, Your Grace.'

Mary had lain for an hour, but didn't feel rested; no doubt worn out by the necessity of making sure that, in her troubled dreams, Louis didn't catch her. But at least her headache had subsided to a dull throb.

Anne closed her book and summoned the other ladies. Mary submitted to their ministrations as they prepared her for supper. All her gowns were packed, so she must climb back into the one she had worn on the road. But while she had slept, her ladies had seen to it that the dust had been brushed from her gown and head-dress, her jewels burnished till they shone once more. Now, with her hair brushed, her skin perfumed, and her head-dress fixed on her head to shut in her dreams, Mary took a last, lingering look at her reflection in the hastily set-up glass. She hoped her brother wasn't feeling too hearty, as this evening, she felt as hard put as the ever-pregnant Catherine to match his energy. Mary turned away from the glass and with a resolution that was new to her, she walked to the door and descended for supper.

The day had turned sultry and the hall was suffocating, a heat made worse by all the hot, sweaty bodies of the courtiers. Mary spotted Henry, his auburn head easily visible above those of the admirers that always surrounded him and she made her way across to him.

He saw her and made space for her beside him. 'Well sister,' he remarked, 'you are in better looks than when we arrived. Have you rested?'

Mary nodded. 'Till the storm woke me. Think you it will delay my departure?' Hope entered her voice at the prospect. Henry noticed, of course, and immediately crushed it.

'Nay, sister, 'tis only a squall. Tomorrow will dawn bright and clear, you'll see. Your departure will not be delayed.'

Swallowing her disappointment, Mary forced herself to murmur, 'That's good. I'm sure Your Grace has much urgent business awaiting you back in London. I'd not like to delay you.'

Henry was not deceived. He chided, 'Nay, sweetheart. Don't sound so tragic. I'd not abandon you here in Dover to await clement weather.'

Her brother's voice was soft and he was at his most charming. He had always loved her well, Mary knew. A love she suspected had sprung from her patent adoration of him as a little girl when she had followed him around like a puppy. It was only her recent defiance that had caused a breach between them. Mary realised how much she would miss him. Perhaps he was thinking the same of her for Henry could be a sentimental man. She put her arm through his and drew him away from his boisterous courtiers to a relatively quiet corner of the hall. He didn't resist.

'Henry,' she began.

'Sweetheart?' he prompted.

'Henry.' She stopped again.

He tilted his handsome head on one side and looked enquiringly down at her. 'Come, Mary, 'tis not like you to act the coy maid. Ask what you will and if I can grant it I will.

You know well I would be happy to please you. Apart, that is, from—'

He didn't finish. He didn't have to. Mary knew what he meant—apart from the French marriage. She cleared her throat and tried again. Her words fell over one another in her nervous rush. 'You won't forget your promise, Henry, will you?'

Henry raised an eyebrow and demanded loftily, 'Think you I am in the habit of forgetting my promises? I am the king .You have my word. Did you doubt it?'

Although Mary was quick to deny it, she *had* doubted. Much as she loved Harry the brother, Henry the king was a different matter. The needs of policy came before affection for his little sister. If she were left a widow in France, he wouldn't hesitate, if policy demanded it, to push her into another loveless state marriage. Still, she reminded herself, she had extracted a repeat of the promise, and she must needs be content with that. Now she smiled up at Henry, again entwined her arm through his, and said, 'Come, Henry, let us into supper.'

They walked through the body of the hall and up to the dais. Henry signaled to the minstrels to play and a sweet, haunting tune filled the hall, accompanied by words telling of the sorrows of lost love. Its poignancy was particularly apt and Mary's eyes stung with tears. Henry must have noticed, for he immediately banged a huge fist on the table, making everyone jump. The musicians stopped with a discordant jangle.

'Must we have that tormenting dirge?' Henry demanded. 'Play something merry, for the love of God. This is a happy occasion, not a time for tears and lamentations.'

After a hasty conversation, a far more lively air sprang up. Satisfied, Henry settled back in his chair and reached for one of the many well-laden platters that formed the first course.

The cooks had done well in the limited time, but then, with the nomadic nature of the court as it moved from palace to castle and back to palace again, they had plenty of practise. Henry, ever one to enjoy his food, began to fill his vast appetite with relish. But he still had time to notice that Catherine was toying with her food and he chided her. 'Come, sweeting, you're setting Mary a bad example. She'll need all her strength for the journey tomorrow. Eat up, both of you, eat up.'

Catherine did her best, though Mary knew her sister-in-law's morning sickness made mealtimes a battle to be endured. Mary, too, began to eat, though her stomach, too, was in a state of rebellion.

But Henry was pleased to see them eat. 'That's better. I like to see hearty appetites about me. Hearty appetites breed hearty sons, my dear.' Henry glanced at Catherine who lowered her eyes at his reproach.

At last the meal, with its endless courses, was over. And Catherine and Mary, having eaten sufficient to satisfy Henry's demands, received no further chastisement. The trestles were cleared for dancing. The sky had darkened considerably during the meal and the candles had all been lit. They guttered in the draught of the increasingly stormy evening, their flickering gave a now-you-see-me, now-you-don't, quality to those congregated there, lighting up a face, then shadowing it as the candle flame favoured another. Mary closed her eyes in an attempt to capture the picture in her memory for the uncertain future that awaited her on the morrow.

'Your Grace?'

Mary's eyes flew open and she found the Duc de Longueville kneeling at her side, still playing proxy husband. He bowed. 'You look sad, Your Grace,' he said. 'New brides are often filled with uncertainties. 'Tis unfortunate that Jane isn't here to cheer you. She would tell you of the glorious future that is now yours and would soon have you smiling.'

'Truly, I would be glad of such comfort,' Mary admitted. 'But King Louis—my husband,' she forced the words past her lips, 'as you know, forbade Jane to come.' According to Lady Guildford, Louis reigned over a pious court. He wouldn't relish the presence of the wanton Jane. Even so, Mary felt it was such a little thing to ask of her new husband. Especially as, if Louis were as unwell as had been reported, he would surely spend much time on his knees seeking absolution with eternity looming and would be poor company.

The Duc de Longueville wasted no time in suggesting she speak for Jane at the first opportunity. 'I miss her too,' he said. 'Perhaps, when we see him, we could both try to persuade King Louis to alter his mind. He has a kind heart and will want to please you.' He smiled and changed the subject. 'But His Grace, King Henry has demanded happy faces tonight. It seems a shame to waste such lovely music in melancholy thoughts. Will you honour me with a dance, Your Grace? Your last dance in England before you dance at the French court.'

Mary, who usually loved to dance, wondered how much opportunity she would have for such pleasures with Louis ailing. And tonight, although she didn't feel much like dancing, the music was infectious and she sensed Henry's lowering frown, so she gave de Longueville her hand and they took the floor. She knew they made a handsome couple, herself so fair and the tall de Longueville so dark, as they made the graceful movements of the pavane.

Mary, all her senses tonight especially acute, caught some of the whispers from her Maids of Honour as she and de Longueville danced past.

'Tis a shame,' one murmured. 'To think she's destined for a dried-up old man. What will gouty Louis do with so much beauty? She'll likely kill him.'

'But think what she's gaining,' murmured another. 'Honours and riches seem a fair exchange for the fondling hands and limp manhood of the French King.'

Some of Mary's younger Maids looked tired after the long hours on the road. They couldn't retire till Mary did, but Mary, determined on making her last day in England endure as long as she could, danced on with a feverish gaiety, as if she never wanted the evening to end. But Henry was pleased with her at last. She caught his look of satisfaction as he took in her cheeks flushed with exertion and not a little wine.

But there was to be an early start on the morrow to catch the tide. Henry would not allow sluggish bodies and even more sluggish heads to delay matters. Soon after, he called an end to the evening's festivities. Reluctantly, Mary followed her ladies as they lighted her to her chamber. Tomorrow would come all too soon. The next time she opened her eyes it would be to see the dawn of the day that would bring an end to all familiar things.

The storm still raged over the night sky as her ladies readied her for bed. It didn't auger well for the voyage. In spite of Henry's determination that tomorrow would be clear even her brother couldn't command the weather. With this happy thought to comfort her, Mary finally slept.

CHAPTER THREE

Mary woke to the sound of rain lashing the windows. It had finally come; the day she had dreaded. But she was given no time for morbid fancies, as her Mother Guildford bustled into the chamber. Mary had expected her to chivvy her from the bed, but after curtseying and bidding her good morning, Lady Guildford's next words immediately cheered her.

'Though, as you can no doubt hear, the weather is not so good. You might as well abide in bed awhile. You'll not leave today. The king, after stomping about the castle calling on all the fates in his wrath, is up on the keep hoping to see a break in the sky.'

Reprieved, Mary rejected Lady Guildford's suggestion that she stay in bed for a while, and flung off the bedcovers. She wanted to enjoy all the hours of her unlooked-for bonus. Dressed, she hurried down to the hall to find out what was happening. The sight of her brother gave her answer. From his pursed lips and heavy pacing, the view from the keep had failed to please.

'Cheer up, Henry,' she called as she approached. 'Are you not glad to keep me with you for one more day? Will you not miss your sister as much as your sister shall miss her big, handsome brother?'

Henry turned at her words. 'I might say the same at seeing you up so early. Are you so eager then to leave us all?'

'You know the answer to that, Henry. I have no desire to sail to France. I would remain here, with you and Catherine.'

'You know that is impossible, sweetheart. You must go to your husband. He is anxious there should be no delay. He feels he has been a widower too long, I think.'

Mary could only wish Louis found more joy in his solitary state. And as she was the one expected to remind him of the pleasures to be found in the marriage bed, she had no desire to provide passion's prod. Her joy at the reprieve the weather had provided had gone and she crept away to find some of the solitude that Louis was so keen to spurn.

The storm raged on, and Henry raged with it. It seemed the fates now wished to keep Mary in England, for the bad weather continued, day after day, making departure impossible, till, finally, Henry's limited patience snapped. He set watchers to signal any lull in the storm so she could depart.

Loud voices dragged Mary from sleep to a room still night-dark. After a moment spent wondering where she was and what was happening, she remembered. Immediately wide awake, heart thudding, she realised what all the noise portended.

The door to her chamber was thrust open and Lady Guildford hurried in, her hand cupped protectively round a wildly flickering candle-flame. She was followed by Mary's Maids rubbing the sleep from their eyes.

'Come, your Grace,' said Lady Guildford. 'The king has decreed the weather is favourable. He has ordered our immediate departure. You must get dressed at once.'

Mary protested. 'But it is the middle of the night.'

'It's nearly dawn,' Lady Guildford corrected. 'And your brother's patience is at an end. We must go now. There's been a lull in the storm and he says we must make haste and get away before it passes over.'

Mary had not anticipated being harried from the country like an importunate guest who had tarried too long. And what if the lull was a brief one only? She could drown, her ladies and Mother Guildford with her. An imp of humour told her that at least the embrace of Neptune, the Roman god of the sea, would save her from that of Louis. But that would mean she would never enjoy those of her love. And if she had little else to look forward to, she still had hope that sometime, somehow, she and Charles would be together.

But there was no time for brooding. No time even for a long round of goodbyes. Mary scarce had time to dress before she was bundled down to the ships like a fugitive from justice, hair half-brushed, head-dress awry, the shock all the greater because with the delay she had half managed to convince herself that the day of departure would be continually put off until Henry relented or Louis, the husband everyone told her was so sickly, died.

The wind still howled, despite the lull that Henry's determined optimism had claimed. The rain poured down in torrents. The dirty sea looked as if it had a grudge against her; its huge waves rocked the fourteen anchored ships of the flotilla that would take her and her attendants to France.

Mary shivered. Could Henry really mean to make her set sail in such weather? It seemed he did, for he strode about the quayside, issuing orders left and right. Mary picked out the tiny figure of Catherine with its precious burden thrust before her. She looked as bedraggled as Mary as she made her way towards her. They both stood, silent and watchful as the terrified horses were chivvied into the hold, their whinnying over-ridden by Henry's furious roars as the weather once again threatened to upset his plans.

But finally, it seemed, even Henry was satisfied. He strode to where they were huddled with the Maids of Honour, his countenance plainly declaring that if Mary were to display as much reluctance to embark as the horses he would lash her up the plank as he had lashed them. But before Henry could say or do anything, Mary roused herself sufficiently to remind him once again of his promise. She knew it was her last chance to place a troublesome thorn in his ever-prickly conscience and she meant to make the most of it.

He was brusque with her. His patience, both with her and the weather, at an end. Now he wanted only to get her away. 'Yes, yes. I gave you my promise, did I not?' he demanded gruffly.

But Mary was determined to press him on the matter. His promise was too important for her to allow him to get away with such a testy repetition, especially since, on reflection, his original promise had seemed but lightly given. 'Please don't be vexed with me, Henry. This is a sad time for me. Do not make it sadder still.'

It seemed, at that moment, the fates decided to hit Henry, too, with the realisation that he might never see his little sister again. It made him tender. He clasped her in a great bear hug, gave her a loving kiss and repeated his promise solemnly enough to satisfy even Mary's doubts.

After a little, Henry released her. Mary embraced her sister-in-law. Eleven years her senior, deprived of babes of her own, Catherine had often acted as a stand-in mother to the young Mary and they had a deep affection for one another. Now, as their eyes met, each saw sadness reflected in the other's. They had both suffered so many partings and losses already; brothers, sisters, parents, all either dead or far distant and unlikely to be seen again, thoughts made more poignant by this latest parting. It was too much for Mary. Although she had been determined to remain dry-eyed, soon, both their faces were wet and not only with the rain. Even Henry's eyes looked suspiciously wet.

But her brother's sentiment concealed a stronger resolve—determination that they would not miss the tide. It was, Henry claimed, the first break the weather had shown since they had arrived in Dover. Though, as Mary gazed at the heaving seas, she failed to see any sign of the break her brother had claimed. She was about to remark on it, but he waved her words away before she could speak, as though he guessed their content. Henry threw a warning glance at his wan-faced queen and persuaded Mary into the arms of her ladies, who after guiding her up the gangplank, hustled her below. Her brother must have warned them to keep a fast hold on her. Mary could almost discern the voice of Henry at its most ferocious, warning them they would be held to account if aught went awry. Their grip as tight as a babe's swaddling clothes, as if all feared she might yet make a bolt for it, there was no escape. The gangplank was lifted and, denied even one last glance at Dover's familiar, towering white cliffs, Mary's little flotilla set sail, taking her to France and her aged husband.

The ships of Mary's escort had barely cleared the harbour before the weather closed in again. The little ships were bobbed and tossed on the angry sea like so many corks in a tub and Mary was too ill to attempt a last look at the home she was leaving behind even if the rough weather had permitted it.

The storm played with them for so many hours that Mary and her ladies, wretched with seasickness, wished only for death, their hastily-donned finery glittered incongruously in a cabin with a floor awash with seawater and vomit. Lady Elizabeth Grey, another of Mary's cousins, started up a nerve-ragged wail that they were all going to die, until Lady Guildford staggered her way across the cabin and roundly boxed her ears. After that, the only sounds were the howl of the wind, the ominous creak of the ship's timbers and the retching, the endless, painful retching that rendered the air of the tightly-shuttered cabin foul.

Lady Guildford set the ladies to praying for their salvation. Their voices, in between bouts of sickness, followed hers in the traditional plea of those in peril on the sea:

'Our Lady, Virgin Mother and star of the sea,
port of our salvation, save us in this our hour of danger.'

The chanting voices went on, becoming lower and more despondent. But, at last, their prayers were answered, for not long after they finally faded, the shout: 'Land ahoy', filled them with joy at the realisation they would live after all.

But the joy was speedily followed by gasps of fear as the ship bumped heavily aground. A seaman, water cascading from his hair, his surely inadequate clothing plastered to his skin, staggered into the cabin and told them, 'Ladies, we're stuck fast on a sandbank. But we're near the harbour mouth of Boulogne. Make your way up to the deck, if you please, and you'll be taken off.'

Mary and her Maids needed no second bidding. Lady Guildford and Mary led them up on deck, assisted by a swarm of sailors. Behind her came Mary Boleyn and Anne Grey, Elizabeth Grey and Mary Fenes, Mistress Anne Jerningham and Jean Barnes and the rest, followed by Mary's equally-bedraggled gentlemen. The deck settled at an odd angle and it was only with difficulty that they reached its uncertain sanctuary. The rain lashed at the decks, making the boards treacherous and Mary and her ladies clung desperately to each other and whatever other handholds they could find.

Mary learned that three of her fourteen ships had made it safely to harbour; she could see them, already at anchor. There was no sign of the rest and Mary prayed they had made it into some other port. As they watched, a flotilla of little boats set out from the harbour. Green-faced and trembling, Mary was lowered into the first of these with several of her ladies. They had reached nearly to the shore when the boat, swamped with water, threatened to capsize. Sir Christopher Garnish, one of Mary's most gallant gentlemen, strode out from shore, in waist-high seas and plucked her from the boat. He carried her, high in his arms, till he reached the shore and could deposit her safely. Mary thanked him gravely for his courage in daring the waves to rescue her.

By this time, Mary and her ladies were in a wretched state. Their clothes were soaked with seawater and vomit, their hair hanging in rats'-tails down their backs. Mary was in no condition to meet the deputation of nobles and clerics, led by the Duke of Vendôme, who waited to receive their new queen and her train, and after a few perfunctory greetings, they were conducted to a nearby lodging where they were able to dry themselves and their belongings and rest after their terrible ordeal.

Shortly after, Mary was brought news of her flotilla. Although the rest were safe, the 'Great Elizabeth' had been lost at Sandgate, close to Calais, and four hundred of the ship's complement of five hundred had perished.

Disconsolate, Mary brooded on this tragic start to her marriage. The deaths of so many with their sins unpurged, weighed heavy on her conscience. Perhaps, if she had been bolder in her resistance to Henry's demand that she marry Louis, these men would still be alive, their widows and children not left bereft. She feared it was an ill-omen that presaged greater sorrows.

Rested and restored to health, Mary was still subdued when she set out with the rest of her party on the journey to Abbeville—and King Louis.

The weather continued damp and chill and Mary and her ladies travelled in litters and wagons. Henry had spared no expense on Mary's litter; of cloth of gold, embroidered with gold lilies in wrought gold, it ostentatiously proclaimed that while Mary might be the new Queen of France, she was also the sister of Henry—a Henry, moreover, determined to impress others by this display of wealth. And while, on the back and front were French lilies, they shared the honours with the parti-coloured roses of York and Lancaster, the two horses which bore the litter trapped in like manner. Mary could only hope her behaviour, when she met King Louis and his court, would prove a match for such splendour.

In deference to their recent travails, they approached Abbeville in easy stages. The Duke of Norfolk, riding beside Mary's litter, took it upon himself to point out places of interest along the route. And as they approached the north east of Abbeville, close to the village of Crécy-en-Ponthieu, he reminded her that, one hundred and fifty years before, her ancestor, Edward III, had defeated the French at the Battle of Crécy. And, in 1066, from the village of St Valery, the glorious conqueror, William, had sailed to invade England.

Mary, her nerves stretched taut as lute strings, had scant interest in his anecdotes. Finally, even Norfolk that bluff soldier, noticed her distraction and fell silent. Shortly after, he took himself, his battle tales and his horse back to the head of the column.

They were within a few miles of Abbeville when a party of riders approached. Norfolk rode back to tell Mary that they were led by Francis, the Duc de Valois, King Louis' son-in-law and the heir-presumptive to the French throne.

Mary studied him with curiosity. Francis was tall like her brother, but all likeness between them ended there. The French heir-presumptive was swarthy and, given his lusty reputation, had a suitably huge priapic nose. Francis was Louise of Savoy's only son and she was said to be very ambitious for him. They must have thought, given Louis' increasingly poor health, that it was only a matter of time before Francis stepped into Louis' shoes. What must they think now? For the Louis they must have thought halfway to the grave had instead climbed from his deathbed and made of himself a bridegroom. If Louis managed to father a son on her and thus destroy Francis' hopes of succeeding... Mary shuddered at the thought and its implications for her future. How he and his mother must hate her.

Mary had naturally felt some trepidation at meeting this Valois heir-presumptive, a trepidation made worse when she remembered what her sister-in-law, Catherine, had endured at the hands of the two ruthless kings: her father and father-in-law. The thought did nothing to relieve Mary's growing anxieties. But, to her astonishment, Francis proved to be charm itself. After bowing low and trailing his expensive hat in the muddy road, he approached her and made a pretty speech welcoming her to France. Tall, dark and sardonic-looking, Francis, while far from conventionally handsome, with his long nose and devilish looks, carried himself with such a confident, rakish air, that these could be discounted. He enquired after their voyage and threw up his hands in horror to hear of their ordeals and the loss of the 'Great Elizabeth' and so many men.

He gazed at the golden-haired Mary in her matching golden litter, the light of admiration in his eyes and said, 'But, Madam, surely not. You all look so blooming. How the sea dared to toss such loveliness about I can scarce comprehend.'

After her recent dalliance with a watery grave, Mary felt a little hysterical. She gave a nervous, girlish giggle. Lady Guildford, who had little time for flowerily-worded compliments, couldn't restrain a snort.

Francis ignored her and addressed himself solely to Mary. 'I shall expect Cardinal Bayeux to chastise such an impudent sea strongly in his next sermon.'

'I'm sure the Almighty knows what he's about,' Lady Guildford told Francis, piously. 'And we're here now, safe enough, my lord, so there's no need for any chastisement.'

'Come, come, my lady,' Francis chided, to Mary's amusement. 'Even the Almighty shouldn't get away totally unscathed for such unseemly behaviour. I shall demand *two* such sermons from my Lord Cardinal and I'll even listen to both of them and not sleep a wink, I promise you.'

Used to respect and deference, Lady Guildford tutted some more. Even Mary's father, King Henry had consulted her opinion—yet here was a young man of no more than twenty summers, who looked at her with a lazy insolence and cared not a whit for her or her opinion. Mary guessed Lady Guildford feared trouble with the Maids of Honour at the French court if all the young men had such free and easy ways as Francis. She began to understand why the flighty Jane had been excluded from accompanying her.

Francis turned his attention back to Mary and begged her to walk a short way with him as he had something of importance to tell her. Mary nodded and tried to ignore the fascinated stares of her ladies, like so many inquisitive Birds of Paradise, in their bright plumage of silks and gold brocades.

After he had assisted her from the litter, Francis took her arm in a familiar fashion. At her surprised expression, he merely commented, 'Are we not now family, Your Grace? And you my mother? We should be comfortable together. Come, let us stroll. The day has brightened somewhat and the air will put some more colour in your pretty cheeks.'

Mary blushed at this and lowered her eyes. Francis might be her new son-in-law by her marriage to King Louis, but he was over-familiar considering they were strangers. She rescued her arm from his and strolled a little way before looking back at the cavalcade. It was certainly impressive. After her ladies, some on palfreys and others in carriages covered with

gold brocade, came more running footmen and yet more palfreys, all trapped in gold brocade and murrey velvet. Bringing up the rear were 200 English archers, the first division
in doublets of green satin and surcoats and belts of black
velvet, with shaggy red and white hats, the second division
wore black doublets and shaggy white hats, while the third
division wore black with grey hats. But even such a spectacle
of colour was insufficient to distract Mary from Lady Guildford's stern visage, and she knew if her behaviour was insuf-
ficiently modest she would have to endure a lecture.

Francis saw the direction of her gaze and laughed. 'She is
something of a dragon, I think, your old guardian, is she
not?'

'She can be a little stern at times' Mary admitted. 'But
she's fond of me and would guard me from any harm.'

'Still, my lady mother, you are now a wife. Perhaps the
time has come for the fledgling to try out her wings, hmm?'
The ardor in his gaze as it swept over her body discomfited
Mary. Perhaps he noted this, for he simply took her arm
again and resumed their stroll. 'The King has planned a little
surprise for you,' he confided. 'A silly game that men like to
play on their brides. Oh, it is nothing very terrible,' he assured Mary. 'He merely wishes to see the bride of whom he
has heard so much, without all the formality of an official
meeting.'

Mary had been warned to expect this. Hadn't Catherine
been 'surprised' by an 'informal' meeting of her father and
Arthur on her arrival in England as a young bride? Louis

would be anxious to verify his Ambassador's report as to her looks and figure.

'He will 'accidentally' happen along whilst out, ostensibly hunting, in the best romantic tradition,' Francis went on. A contemptuous little smile hovered over his sensuous lips as he told her, 'Don't be fooled. King Louis does little hunting nowadays as he suffers from the gout. You must act as if surprised to see him. It is a delightful game he plays, nothing more.'

'I must thank you, my lord, for giving me warning of this,' Mary replied. And although she had no interest in such foolish games, she gave the expected response. 'I must return and make myself presentable for my husband. I would not like to meet him for the first time looking less than my best.'

'You could never look anything but lovely,' Francis told her. 'I swear my father-in-law will fall in love with you at first glance. He's already half in love with the thought of you. He's never had a beautiful wife before. His first wife, Jeanne, was so ugly he couldn't tolerate her near him, so he divorced her. And his second wife, Queen Anne, my late, lamented, mother-in-law, wasn't noted for her beauty either, though at least she wasn't a complete cripple and managed to provide him with children. Claude, my wife, is the eldest. You will meet her when we reach Abbeville. She is a trifle indisposed at the moment, but I ordered her from her bed so she could give you a proper greeting.'

'You should have left her to rest,' Mary told him. 'I would have come to her chamber to meet her. I wouldn't want to cause her distress if she is unwell.'

'She's well enough to leave her bed to formally embrace her new mother,' Francis insisted. 'The demands of etiquette brook no other course.'

'Even so, I hope we will become friends.' Mary, conscious that she might need all the friends she could get at the French court, wondered how many must resent her arrival?

Claude, too, must be set on disliking her. How could she not when she would be aware of the dangers Mary posed to her and her husband's hopes of succeeding her father?

'You will find Claude very gentle, obedient and most loving towards you, I promise,' Francis reassured. 'Indeed, the whole family is ready to love you, including myself and my mother.' Hand on heart, Francis bowed and smiled winningly at her.

'Thank you, my lord,' Mary murmured, while she thought she might need some persuading of Louise of Savoy's love for her. She must be furious at this marriage.

'Call me Francis, please. I beg of you, let etiquette be no bar to our friendship at least.'

Mary was a little unnerved at the way Francis' gaze kept sweeping over her body and suspected it would be wise not to be too friendly. But it would be churlish to deny him this, so she replied, 'Very well, Francis. Now, I had better return to Lady Guildford. She will be fussing herself to distraction.'

Indeed, Lady Guildford was imperiously striding about, collecting up stray, giggling Maids of Honour and chivvying them back to the litters and wagons, lest they be guilty of any breach of French etiquette with the young noblemen accompanying Francis.

He and Mary had strolled back, and Francis said to Lady Guildford, 'I've returned your chick to the coop, my lady, safe and sound and a most charming chick she is, too.' He bowed low, then sauntered off to his companions, who greeted him uproariously.

Lady Guildford turned her back on their goings-on and said to Mary. 'That young man is very insolent, taking you off like that alone. I'm sure King Louis will not like it when he hears.' Testily, she enquired. 'And what was this great secret that he had to tell you, my lady, that he could not disclose in front of your guardian?'

'Nothing of any great moment, Mother.' Mary told her what Francis had said about Louis intending to 'accidentally' meet her on the road. Although Mary felt that Francis could be a dangerous young man, his arrival had unaccountably cheered her. Unfortunately, it had done little for Lady Guildford's peace of mind.

'Of no moment,' she now exclaimed. 'Of no moment, you say, Madam? It's a good thing I'm here, my little queen. I had half expected some such foolishness. These men and their games. They don't realise the trouble they cause. Come, my lady, get into the litter. You must change into a more suitable gown for this 'surprise' meeting.'

Mary allowed herself to be chivvied back to the litter, stripped in its cramped confines and dressed in a gown of cloth of gold on crimson so heavily plated with goldsmith's work that she could hardly move. Imprisoned in such an armour-like outfit, with a shaggy hat of crimson silk perched in a jaunty manner over one eye, as she was assisted with difficulty onto her white palfrey, Mary felt more as if she were about to ride into battle than to meet her new/old bridegroom. The animal, unaccustomed to bearing such weight, staggered awhile till he adjusted himself to his suddenly burdensome mistress. Then the party set off again.

The Maids of Honour were becoming more excited. Mary could hear their chatter behind her and knew that Francis had won at least one heart. Now, they all craned their necks for the first sight of the royal 'hunting' party. However, it wasn't till the Duke of Norfolk, back in his earlier role of guide, told them they were approaching the Forest of Ardres, that they encountered King Louis. As the king and his party approached over a wide plain, Mary discovered Francis at her side once more. In between increasingly intimate sallies that wholly ignored etiquette and completely discomfited Mary, he identified each of the king's companions for her. She struggled to concentrate as she tried to commit the names to memory.

As was the fashion when kings and queens appeared in public together, King Louis was dressed in a short riding dress of the same stuff as Mary and looked even more burdened than she by the weight of it.

Expected to dismount and pay homage, Mary struggled to get herself and her cumbersome gown to the ground. Louis, seeing her rising embarrassment, begged her to remain mounted. Mary, only too glad to obey him, doffed her hat and kissed her hand at the king, supposing the equally encumbered Louis must sympathise with her plight.

Louis must have taken this for encouragement for he brought his gleaming Spanish mount with its barb of cloth of gold and black satin in chequers close up to Mary on her palfrey. She almost backed away, but then, remembered this was her husband and she must not. He had the right to do whatever he pleased. After a few whispered words spoken so softly that she failed to understand them and was unable to give an appropriate response, Louis threw his arm around her neck and kissed her soundly. Startled, conscious of the sardonic looks of Francis, Mary blushed, which brought a delighted laugh from Louis.

He turned to his noble companions and cried, 'Well, my lords, what think you of our new Queen? Is she not exquisite?'

Although the cardinals of Auch and Bayeux kept their expressions pious, the admiring stares of de Vendôme, the Duke of Albany, the Count Galeazzo di San Severino and the rest of the nobles echoed their enthusiastic words for Mary's delicate skin and golden hair. And as they gazed from her back to the gouty Louis, Mary could imagine the ribald comments they would exchange in private as they speculated whether the king's manhood would be up to the challenge she represented. Louis' lustful expression warned her that he intended to do his best to rise to the occasion. It was not a pleasant thought.

Louis turned back to Mary, grasped her hand and kissed it. She could feel drool on her skin and had to force herself not to snatch her hand back.

'Lucky for me, my beautiful Mary, that I happened to be out this way hunting. To think I might have taken a different route and missed you.' Louis shook his head in wonder at the fates' sudden kindness and smiled at her.

In her dream, Mary remembered, Louis had been toothless. In reality, he was not entirely so, but what few he had were black with decay. She suppressed a shudder at his remembered kiss and just stopped herself from wiping a hand across her lips. She was Queen now. Louis' Queen. She must, somehow, find the strength to endure his embrace.

'I feel, my lady, you and I shall be happy together. Do you not agree?'

What could she say? Bemused, Mary surveyed her decaying and creaking bridegroom. Louis was bent over slightly in the saddle, as if his heavy robes were altogether too much for him. Perhaps they were, for he looked sick unto death. His face was pasty, his lips gummy. 'Yes, Your Grace,' she murmured, forcing the unpalatable words past suddenly dry lips. Mary glued a smile on her face and assured him. 'I'm sure we shall.'

Louis seemed satisfied by her stilted reply, for he bowed and after exchanging a few more pleasantries with her, he turned and greeted the Duke of Norfolk, Dorset, Surrey, Ruthall, Lord Herbert and Docwra, the Prior of St John of Jerusalem. Mary took the opportunity to unglue the forced smile and find a more natural expression.

Louis and his party left them shortly after. Mary was relieved, for her new husband's appearance had shocked her. She had rather taken it for granted that the tales of Louis' ill-health had been exaggerated by Henry to encourage her to agree to the marriage. He seemed like a corpse already. Spiders seemed to have crawled under her skin and set to weaving their webs, as she thought of bedding with him. How could her brother have done this to her?

Francis rode up to her. His expression more sardonic than ever, he seemed amused at her barely concealed distaste. He enquired familiarly, 'So, what do you think of your husband, Mother? Do you like his handsome looks?'

Mary hid her distress as best she could, looked him boldly in the eye and said she liked them well enough.

Francis studied her with a gleam in his eyes and set about interrogating her. 'Are you not curious about your bridegroom? Do you truly have no loving bride's questions to ask about him? His likes? His dislikes? His little foibles? Surely there must be something you wish to ask, Mother?'

Mary realised her lack of questions had been more revealing of her true feelings than any words. But she was determined not to satisfy Francis' seeming desire to obtain some foolish indiscretion from her. She temporised by asking, 'I understand from the Duc de Longueville that the King is not robust and keeps early hours. Is that so?'

Francis nodded. 'The king's health has been poor for a long time. He's been near death several times, but has always somehow pulled through.' His expression rueful, Francis went on. 'But even before his ill-health, the court of King Louis has always been on the dull side. And then, with the death of Queen Anne, court mourning made it even more so.' He gazed at her with that unconcealed admiration that was beginning to unnerve Mary and added, 'But now that you are here, my pretty Mother, I will do my best to enliven it. You'll not want to spend half your time sewing with the late Queen's ladies. You'll want to be gay and with your beauty, the king will be able to deny you nothing.' Francis smiled roguishly. 'The court is certainly going to be more interesting than it was.'

Mary felt her delicate skin flush, which only seemed to amuse him more. He noticed Lady Guildford approaching, pulled a face at Mary, bowed and made his escape.

'What a to-do, my lady,' said Lady Guildford as she came up. 'I've been trying to get your Maids of Honour in their places so we can move off, but it's a hopeless task, I vow. Let's get you settled back in line and it might bring the rest to order.'

As they rode back to the procession, Lady Guildford must have noted Mary's gaze follow the departing Francis because she asked, 'What's the matter? What did his insolent young lordship want with you this time? Not more important secrets?'

'Nay, Mother,' said Mary as she quietened her palfrey and watched her esquires organise themselves at the head of the procession, followed, two by two, by the Duke of Norfolk, ambassadors and other noblemen all wearing their enormous costly gold chains. After the nobles came Garter King at Arms and Richmond Herald with eight trumpeters in crimson damask and macers with gilt maces surmounted by a royal crown to remind the world, and Mary, who scarcely needed reminding, of her raised status. 'He was simply telling me about the court. King Louis' health is worse than we had expected. Indeed, he looked sick unto death, do you not think?'

Lady Guildford's features took on a more downward aspect. 'He's not long for this world, my lady, mark my words. We must hope there's no delay in getting you crowned.'

Mary concentrated on the still-forming processing, hardly knowing whether to be pleased or sorry at the news that she might emulate Catherine by becoming a widow shortly after becoming a bride. In front of her the two grooms in their short doublets of cloth of gold and black velvet each led a palfrey, followed by two other palfreys ridden by pages. Mary waited till these last had settled in line before she said, 'Perhaps he's not as sick as he looks? He kissed me heartily enough, I'll trow.' A shiver ran through her at the memory. 'He must be able to do his husbandly duty else why trouble to marry me at all?'

As Mary's running footmen fell into line at their side and the pages on the two large horses that bore her litter, drew up behind, Lady Guildford warned, 'Just let the king cause no delay in the ceremonies, or it's his funeral and not his official wedding we'll be attending. And yes, Louis may have kissed you heartily enough, but I saw the effort it cost him. It looked to me that it was only the weight of his garments that kept him on his horse. And for such an 'ardent' groom, he didn't linger long. I don't suppose he dared in case he outraged the conventions and fell at your feet—not with love, but sickness.'

W hen the procession eventually got moving. Francis again attached himself to Mary, etiquette forcing Lady Guildford to retire and join the other ladies behind Mary's empty litter. As though determined to disconcert her, Francis charmed Mary anew so that she forgot the anxiety his frank appraisal had caused her earlier.

'How many broken hearts did you leave behind you in England, ma petite Mère?' he asked. 'Such beauty as yours makes men mad.'

Mary, having failed to lure her love, Charles Brandon, from the paths of sanity and caution, forced a lightness into her voice lest the teasing Francis should suspect her secret. 'Why should I have left any broken hearts behind me, Francis? It is Frenchmen who are famed for their love of romance. The men of England pursue worldly ambition with greater zeal than affairs of the heart.'

'Then that cold and wet island of yours must surely have weakened their manhood. They should be ashamed to leave such a lovely lady without amusement. We will have fun together, you and I,' he promised. 'Now you are truly French, we must teach these churlish English the importance of l'amour.'

As he said this, Francis grasped her hand and kissed her palm with such a lover-like intimacy that Mary drew back in alarm. Francis' expression hinted at feelings far deeper than his playful words implied. But he was French, she reminded herself. Such gallant, but meaningless flirtations came as naturally to them as breathing. He was young , simply testing how far she would allow his familiarities to go. It was up to her to set the boundaries. Perhaps the sternly moral court of her father and grandmother had made her prudish. She shouldn't take his gallantries seriously. He was amusing and would make her sojourn in France — however long it turned out to be — seem shorter. He would help the days go by till she could be with her love once again. With these thoughts to encourage her, it wasn't long before she forgot her qualms and he had her laughing again.

About half-a-mile outside Abbeville the procession was again halted as the chief men of the town, followed by a great crowd of other citizens, archers, musketeers and the captain of the town with about thirty liveried men, came out to greet her. Mary, her confidence growing, greeted them graciously and was pleased to see their approval. They fell in at the head of the now considerably swollen procession and escorted her the rest of the way.

At last, they came to the walls of Abbeville, where again the train was halted so that Mary could prepare for her entry. She had dismounted to enter Notre Dame de la Chapelle to greet the waiting clergy when the heavens opened. Fran-

cis, blasphemous as before, whispered in her ear as he rushed
her to shelter that the priests' fine garments must have displeased the Almighty.

Mary stifled an unseemly desire to giggle. For the sudden
downpour that made the magnificently-clad clergy so bedraggled certainly signaled omniscient disapproval of their
failure to wholeheartedly embrace poverty. Fearing she
would breach etiquette and scandalize the citizens of the
town, Mary begged him to be silent. But Lady Guildford almost proved her undoing. For her Mother hadn't been quick
enough to dismount and seek shelter. Drenched and fuming,
she scowled as her limp, wet hat feathers drooped forlornly
over one eye. Francis' conspiratorial wink at Mary forced her
to bite down hard on her lip. When she was able, she quietly
reproved him. 'It isn't seemly to laugh so at my Mother
Guildford, Francis. She must be very vexed.'

'The trick with wearing such fine feathers, pretty Mary,
is to have a fleet turn of foot,' he told her. 'That way, the
weather can't make a fool of you.' Needless to say, Francis
had ensured his own, and Mary's, fine feathers remained intact.

'Poor Mother. Could you not have assisted her, Francis?
She's no longer young.'

'But I have devoted myself to you, ma Mère,' he protested.
'That way, when you need me, I shall be available. How can I
spare aught of my help for others?'

'So you would leave my Mother Guildford to slip in the
mud? For shame, Francis. Your gallantry is very selective, I
fear.'

'Tis true. I confess it. Would you have me a faithless churl so soon to abandon you to the tender mercies of other men? Nay, I'll not do it. Let your haughty Duke of Norfolk see to her.' Francis gave a graceful bow. 'You are now my Queen and I must look after you.'

The rain was still falling when the party emerged from the church. The horses' hooves had churned up the mud into a quagmire. For her entry into Abbeville, Mary had changed her garments yet again and was now dressed in gold brocade with a white gown made in the English fashion, with tight sleeves, decorated with jewels and more heavy goldsmith's work — 'tout or et diamants —all gold and diamonds as Francis admiringly commented. Surrounded by her running footmen and the Scots Guards, Mary rode under a canopy of white satin embroidered by roses which the clergy had prepared for her. Borne by the officers of the town, it helped to protect her from the rain. By now it was around four o'clock in the afternoon and Mary was tired after being the centre of so much formal ceremonial. But, well-schooled in what to expect, she knew it would be some time before she could retire for an hour, climb out of her weighty clothing and relax.

As the procession entered the town, Mary was welcomed with bells, trumpets and artillery, all vying together to give her the greatest welcome. The noise was tremendous and made her ears ring. It didn't seem to disconcert the townspeople who stood in the rain paying it no heed at all in their eagerness to see and greet their new Queen. Their exuberant cries of 'Vive la Reine' added to the cacophony, but their obvious delight warmed Mary's heart. Still a little pale, being but recently plucked from the ocean's icy clutches, she smiled and waved all the while and was outwardly as enthusiastic as any. The fleeting thought that her brother — who had always known how to appeal to a crowd — would be proud of her made her smile even more. Now Mary, too, was learning that she had the gift of pleasing the people. It was a heady gift.

Surrounded by her jostling new subjects, she rode through the Porte Marcade and down the Chausée. Francis told her the name of each location and pointed out the tapestries which hung down from every available pole and window, billowing in the breeze. He explained the intricacies of the mystery plays that were enacted on every corner, leaning close beside her so she could hear above the noise.

They arrived at the Church of St Wolfran, the patron saint of the town and Mary dismounted to give thanks. She went once more through the noisily shouting populace and she and her ladies were at last conducted to their lodgings, where Mary met the fifteen-year-old Madam Claude, Francis' wife and King Louis' eldest daughter. With difficulty, Claude, who was very fat, sank into a deep courtesy. Claude's pallor reminded Mary that she had but recently risen from her sick-bed and she bade her rise and commiserated with her over the recent loss of her mother. Gently, she chided the wan face before her. 'You should really have remained in bed. We could have greeted one another just the same.' Mary studied the girl's white face with concern. 'Are you sure you're feeling quite well?.'

Francis interposed. 'She could not remain in bed whilst your Majesty attended on her. It wouldn't be right.'

Mary was saddened to note that Francis' young wife received none of the gallantry he had shown her. Clearly, this was no love match, at least not on Francis' side, though poor Claude's sad gaze seemed to follow her husband about with mute adoration. But Mary couldn't expect the tall, elegant and witty Francis to adore his frumpy little wife even though she would, in time, bring him great riches.

As though he sensed Mary's thoughts and wanted her to think well of him, with every appearance of husbandly solicitude, Francis enquired of Claude, 'You're well enough now, Claude, are you not?'

'Yes, my lord. Francis is right, Your Grace,' she told Mary. 'It would not be seemly for me to abide in bed for your greeting. My father would be most displeased.'

However strongly-felt was her desire to please her father, her desire to please Francis was clearly even stronger. Mary wondered what heartbreak lay in store for the crippled and vulnerable Claude. 'Even so, she said gently, 'you must take care of your health. You do not want to be unwell for the ceremonies.' These would be an ordeal and would tax the resources of the strongest, Mary knew. She turned back to Francis and asked, 'Do we bide here for a while, my lord?'

Thankfully, Francis confirmed it. 'Yes, you may rest for a few hours,' he told her. 'You must be fresh for the night's dancing. I intend to claim a lot of dances.'

Mary laughed and turned to Claude, 'Your husband is very gallant, is he not, Claude?' She called to mind her own gouty and black-toothed husband, and added enviously, 'You are fortunate to have such an entertaining husband.'

'Yes, Madam,' Claude answered uncertainly.

'Oh Claude doesn't find me amusing at all,' Francis told Mary. 'She thinks I am wicked and blasphemous. Claude is very religious,' he explained to Mary, 'and spends a lot of time on her knees—doubtless praying for me.'

Mary smiled. Francis certainly offered light relief after thoughts of Louis. She had but a few days before she must endure more than sickening kisses from her husband. Her sad thoughts must have shown on her face, for Francis was instantly attentive.

'Such sad looks, my pretty Mother. Why so?'

Unable to explain they were caused by distaste for her husband, Mary merely smiled. But even the demands of diplomacy allowed a young girl a few pangs of homesickness and she was able to excuse her sad looks by expressing wonder as to whether she would ever see England again.

'We must make her forget that damp country, Claude,' Francis instructed, mock-sternly. 'I will consider it my duty to help you achieve the necessary amnesia, Mary, if thoughts of England make you sad. France is your home now,' he reminded her, 'and we your family.' He drew her to him and kissed both her cheeks, then insisted his young wife do the same. 'Now it is my turn to look sad,' he said, 'for I must leave you to rest. Till this evening, my Mother. Claude.' Francis swept low and backed out of the room.

Mary, not sure whether to be pleased or sorry at his departure, smiled at her daughter-in-law in and said, 'Come along, Claude, ladies. Let us relax for a while. I shall want plenty of energy for the ball tonight.'

Once in the bedchamber, Claude, Mary and their ladies quickly undressed one another and spread themselves around the room to rest. The streets were still noisy from the shouts of the excited populace, however, and sleep was impossible. They chatted desultorily, Mary taking the time to learn more of her new family. The young Madame Claude was rather shy and Mary worked at drawing her out. Claude still looked far from well and Mary asked her, 'What ails you, Madame?'

'I get pains in my stomach and legs that make me feel sick, Your Grace,' Claude explained. 'The physicians are reluctant to put a name to this illness.'

Lady Guildford snorted at this. 'They usually are,' she commented dryly. 'When I was last ill, they clucked around me like a bunch of old hens. They bled me here and bled me there, till they thought me sufficiently weakened to put up with more of their torture. But I rallied despite them and cleared them all out and cured myself with herbal concoctions. I've not been ill since,' she added with satisfaction.

'Tis a pity we do not all have your constitution, Mother,' said Mary, with a wry smile at Claude. 'Perhaps you could make up a potion to help Madame Claude.'

Lady Guildford glanced at this young lady's overweight body and pale face and said forthrightly, 'What Madame Claude needs is fresh air, exercise and some good, plain food. Rich cooking is not good for young people.' Having given her opinion, Lady Guildford leaned complacently back against her pillows.

'Take no notice, Claude, 'Mary whispered to the embarrassed-looking Claude. 'My Mother Guildford is not nearly as fierce as she sounds.'

Claude smiled uncertainly at this and ventured a comment. 'My father must be very happy in his choice of bride, Your Grace. You're very beautiful.'

Mary was touched. She felt honour-bound to find a compliment in return. 'You're very kind. The King, your father, was most gracious when we met on the road and gave me a hearty greeting.' Mary's lips curled at the memory, but she forced herself on. 'You give me courage for all the ceremonies that lie ahead. I fear they will be an ordeal, especially as my French is not as practised as I could wish.'

'You shouldn't worry, Your Grace,' Claude told her. 'You can't fail to please the court and the people. I'm sure you already please my father. You will find him a kind and generous husband, I'm sure. He and my mother were very happy together.' Claude's voice trembled, though whether this was caused by the loss of her mother or her anxieties about her own marriage, Mary couldn't tell.

She assumed the former and tried to comfort her. 'I, too, lost my mother young. I wasn't quite seven, but I can still just remember her gentleness. We can be as sisters,' Mary told her. 'There are only a few years between us, after all.' Mary's curiosity got the better of her and she tried to draw Claude out further. 'Have you been married long, Claude? You are still very young.'

'Oh, no, Madame. Francis and I were married in May, though we were betrothed at my father's wish, long ago, when I was seven and he twelve.'

'Don't you think it strange, Claude—here we are, both new brides, made kin by my marriage to your father, and yet we were both, in turn, promised to the young Prince of Castile? Indeed, I was to have been finally married to him this year.'

'Yes, Madame. It was my mother's desire that I should marry Castile's prince, but as my parents had no son the people were against it. They didn't wish their princess to be married out of the realm. So when my mother died, my father pushed through the marriage to Francis.'

Their dishabille and enforced intimacy had loosened the bounds of formality and Mary found herself asking, 'Are you happy with Francis? Is he a kind husband?'

Claude's reply was sadly revealing and uncharacteristically worldly. 'He is as kind as most husbands, Madame. I've become very fond of him, though with his charm he could have married any. I was fortunate he wasn't a stranger. If God had granted my father sons, I would have been married far from my home.'

'Like me.' Mary wasn't aware she had uttered her sad thought aloud, till Claude moved closer, took her hand and smiled sympathetically. 'Don't be sad, Your Grace. I know my father is very aged, but I promise you he will love you. Indeed, I'm sure he must be delighted with you and eager for the nuptials.'

Mary wished she were half as eager as her bridegroom. But she forced the thought down and said with as much cheerfulness as she could muster, 'I'm sure we can get to love one another as husband and wife should.' She told Claude about the cumbersome gown etiquette demanded and how sympathetic Louis had been. 'I was grateful for his kindness. It is a marvellous thing in a husband.'

Claude nodded as though Mary had revealed a great truth. They fell silent after that. Outside, the noise seemed to have dimmed. Perhaps the citizens had shouted themselves hoarse. Now Lady Guildford's gentle snores could be heard. The two girls looked at one another and giggled.

After a while, Claude excused herself. She was the hostess, as she explained, and had to go and oversee the preparations for the ball.

A little later, Mary and her ladies bestirred themselves in turn. After being served a light meal, they called for water and scented linen and started to prepare themselves for the evening's festivities. The indefatigable Lady Guildford bustled about in her usual efficient manner, chastising the servants and bossing the Maids of Honour, until all was done to her satisfaction. Mary knew she was determined to ensure her entrance to the ball gave the French nothing to criticise.

Although her mirror told her she was still a little pale, Mary felt more relaxed than she had for days and bore her ladies' ministrations with patience. At last, dressed in a magnificent gown of white cloth of gold with matching head-dress, she slipped a simple necklet of beaten gold about her throat and gazed in the glass at Lady Guildford. 'Will I please the King and his court, think you, Mother?' she asked, anxious now that the moment of her presentation was at hand.

'The more fool them if you don't,' Mother Guildford retorted. 'Though your jewellery is too plain. We would not wish the French to think us paupers.' She picked up a magnificent diamond and emerald necklace from the jewel casket and replaced the simple necklet. 'Your flaxen beauty will outshine all the cloth of gold in the place, child.' Lady Guildford's face shone with proprietary pride as she studied Mary. 'Are you ready, Your Grace?'

Mary straightened. She held her head high and nodded.

The ball was a glittering affair. The nobles of France had turned out in force to see her. And as Francis escorted her up and down the lines of nobles waiting to greet her, she was vain enough to be pleased at their response. Each glance told Mary she looked beautiful. The knowledge put a becoming colour in her cheeks and a new-found confidence in her step.

The courtiers, elegant in their brocades, silks and cloth of gold, made a shimmering spectacle in the candlelight. And as the flames flickered over the fire and ice of rubies and diamonds Mary was glad Lady Guildford had made her replace the simple necklet. The scene brought a poignant reminder to Mary of her last nights in England, but she forced such thoughts aside. She couldn't lose herself in memories tonight. She came to herself just as Francis led her up to yet another dazzling courtier. She smiled as she recognised San Severino who had accompanied Francis when he had met her on the road. San Severino's costume of cloth of gold lined with superb sables outshone everyone in the room. He told her of the difficulties such elegance had put him through. The material had only arrived from Florence the day before, he explained. The tailors had had to toil all night to finish, but he had been so determined to impress her that he had begged, pleaded and finally bullied the tailors till it was ready.

Mary laughed at his delight and knew she had gained another admirer. She finally came to the end of the long line of courtiers. Francis led her to the top of the hall to the king. Seated on a great chair of state, he greeted Mary warmly before signalling for the musicians to strike up. The crowd moved to the edges of the room as Francis led Mary on to the floor to start the ball. Louis led Claude and soon the room was filled with colourful dancing figures.

Francis, as Mary had expected, danced with ease and grace. She couldn't help but compare him with Louis, whose dancing days were over, even though he stepped out bravely enough with his daughter, as eager to shine in her eyes as any even though his gouty limbs made him ill-equipped for the task. Bravely, masking whatever pain he felt, he took to the floor twice with Mary. But it was quickly apparent what this exercise cost him. She was thankful, for his sake, when with a pretended unwillingness, he gave leave to his young nobles to claim her hand so that he could retire to his chair to rest.

Mary had felt it kinder to dance very sedately with Louis out of consideration for his gouty limbs. But she loved to dance and once her hand was claimed by one after another of Louis' young nobles, she began to enjoy herself. Francis claimed many dances, whispering compliments all the while. The hall was hot and Mary had drunk more wine than usual in an attempt to drown the thought that on the morrow she would be wedded and bedded with Louis. The hateful thought made her reckless. She smiled at Francis' compliments, laughed gaily at his risqué sallies and danced more dances with him than a modest bride should. But tonight, she didn't care. She ignored her Mother Guildford's admonishing eye. Determined to forget what awaited her, if only for one night, she responded flirtatiously to Francis' blandishments.

Encouraged by Mary's wine-heady gaiety, Francis became bolder, touching her whenever he had occasion during the dance, searing her with heated glances from his glittering dark eyes all the while. Mary, her head turned by all the admiration she had received, far from home and separated from the man she loved, was filled with an even greater recklessness and encouraged Francis' attentions all the more. Why shouldn't she enjoy herself before Louis claimed her for himself? she thought. Francis was young, like her, outrageous and amusing. He took her mind off the many things she did not wish to think about. She felt drunk not only with the wine, but also with the many conquests she knew she had made that night.

She was conscious of her aged bridegroom; his dull, yellowed eyes watched her all the while. She shivered and flung herself with even more abandon into dancing and enjoying herself, ignoring the tiny voice of caution that warned she might pay for her recklessness. Tonight she didn't care. She didn't care, either, to remember Lady Guildford's advice that she should be careful of Francis. He might be only twenty, she had said, but he was already an accomplished seducer.

Mary had scoffed at this, saying that Francis wouldn't dare to try to seduce her. Was she not the Queen of France and his mother-in-law?

Lady Guildford had replied that Francis was a young man who would dare much, especially for such a conquest as Mary. That she was his Queen and married to King Louis would be more likely to spur him on than otherwise.

Mary forgot Lady Guildford's counsel and the eyes full of reproof each time she danced past. She had been forced to sacrifice the love of her life, so why shouldn't she console herself in pleasurable dancing? The admiration she had received had gone a long way to bolstering her confidence and had resigned her a little more to the French marriage. She let herself hope that a Louis so easily tired by a few dances would be happy just to have her as a companion. He might even be relieved that his young bride expected nothing more from him. The sight of him looking so old and worn encouraged this hope.

The evening's gaiety continued far into the night, lit by the flames from the candles and the fire they sparked from Francis' eyes.

Across the river, in the poorer quarters of the town, other flames were flickering, concealed from the court by the thickly curtained windows. A small fire had started in one of the many wooden hovels. Increasingly high winds fanned the flames till they had consumed a large part of the district. The flames spread with terrifying speed and the people ran about hysterically hither and thither in their panic to escape the all-devouring flames. Their homes destroyed, many were lucky to escape with their lives and the rags on their backs.

Others weren't so fortunate. Their cries for help went unheard. The King's pleasures were not to be disturbed, so the tocsins were forbidden to ring to summon the desperately-needed help. Mary danced on, happily unaware of this latest tragedy her arrival in France had brought.

CHAPTER FIVE

Mary opened her eyes to greet her wedding day. The ball and its pleasures forgotten, she remembered only the importance of her new role. As her brother and Wolsey had impressed on her, not only was she now Queen of France, she was the first English princess to carry the title since the Norman Conquest over four hundred years before. That she was to be married on the day of St Denis, France's patron saint, imbued the day not only with an historical significance, but a saintly one, also, and added to the weight of expectations of her.

Nervously conscious of what would be expected of her, her anxieties weren't helped by the fact that her limbs felt heavy and reluctant and that her head swam from the quantity of wine she had unwisely drunk the night before. Mary consoled herself with the thought that she was unlikely to be the first Queen of France to greet her formal wedding day suffering from a *gueule de bois* after drinking too much wine.

There was no escaping it now. The day had already begun. Mary forced herself from the bed as she heard muffled whisperings beyond the bed-curtains. It was still early, but the day was bright and made her blink. Now, with the reali-

sation of the onerous ceremonies the day would bring, and
the reckoning for the previous night's pleasures called in,
she wished her dancing had been a little less abandoned, her
drinking more abstemious. But the ball had gone on till late
and yesterday, she had been only too willing to give herself
to its pleasures. No doubt Lady Guildford would tell her such
regrets were the result of foolish self-indulgence and that if
she had paid heed to her wise words yesterday she would
have retired earlier to be fresh for today. It didn't help that
the lady would have the right of it.

Mary and her party had been lodged on the corner of the
street leading from the Castle of Ponthieu to the Rue St
Giles. A temporary gallery had been made to connect it to
the Hotel Gruthuse, the king's quarters. But as Mary glanced
out of the window, she saw that a pall of dark smoke hung in
the sky across the river. On questioning her ladies, she was
appalled to learn that a small fire started during the previous
night's ball had spread rapidly, fanned by strong winds. And
when she asked why she had heard no warning tocsins, she
learned that the king had given orders that nothing was to
disturb the ball in her honour. This second bad omen cast an
even darker pall over her wedding day than had the smoke
from the fire. Mary gazed at the blackened and gutted buildings, whose skeletal fingers seemed to point accusingly at
her. 'You mean I danced whilst others were dying?' Like Ne-
ro and his fiddle, she thought. Twice now, people had died
because of this marriage; once by water in the shipwreck of
The 'Great Elizabeth' and this time by fire. Mary wondered,
if a third tragedy occurred, what force of nature would bring

it about? Should she expect an earthquake next? Some dreadful disease? Fearing the answers should she pose these questions, she forced herself to ask another. 'How many were killed in the fire?'

'Not many. Most escaped,' Lady Guildford assured her, before she added, less reassuringly, 'but a few unfortunate babes and children lost their lives.'

Mary was beginning to think her marriage to Louis was truly cursed. How could it be otherwise? she reasoned, when her arrival in France for the ceremony had brought about the loss of so much life? She repeated her previous thought aloud. 'It is a bad omen. Another one.'

'Nay, put such notions from your mind,' Lady Guildford told her firmly. 'It is no omen, merely an unfortunate accident waiting to happen with so many wooden buildings packed so tightly together.'

'What of the dead babes' parents and the other poor people? To be homeless with the worst of winter coming on, what will become of them?' For the moment, Mary forgot her own troubles and said, 'We must send them some aid and—'

'Calm yourself, Mary. You must try to curb this tendency to be over-emotional and dramatic. You will not find such inclinations a help in your new role. If you follow the example of Queen Catherine you will take no wrong steps.'

Catherine, serious-minded and as pious as her Mother Guildford, was known for her generous alms-giving and much respected for it. She was never frivolous as Mary had been the previous night. Mary was in no mood to listen to further chastisement as to her shortcomings, but thankfully,

Lady Guildford said no more about that. Instead, she told her, 'The King has sent men over to help. No doubt there'll be food provided from the kitchens. Such flimsy structures will be built up again in a few short days, you'll see, and you'd scarce think aught had happened.'

'The parents of the dead babes and children will not think that, Mother, I'm sure,' Mary gently chided. 'When I think of the enthusiasm with which the people greeted me for all that I'm a stranger... They cheered me and gave me courage.'

'Aye, well, mayhap their enthusiasm was their undoing. It seems likely all the drunkenness brought the fire in its wake.'

'Still, it would never have happened but for my arrival.'

'Now, my lady, we want no more foolish talk. This could have happened at any time. As I said, it is just an unfortunate coincidence, nothing more. Forget about omens and portents and other such superstitious nonsense. I will not have you feel responsible for a drunkard's carelessness. I was talking to one of the French ladies earlier. It seems there are often fires across the river. These people build too close together and of the cheapest materials. It was only the high wind which made it especially bad this time.'

'Perhaps they can afford no other material, Mother.'

'Maybe. But if they didn't spend their earnings on drink they would be able to afford more respectable housing.' The abstemious and sternly-religious Lady dismissed the weak self-indulgence of the poor with the admonition that Mary should not waste her pity on them. 'They are undeserving. I won't have them spoil your wedding day. Come away from the window. We must get you prepared.'

The authority in Lady Guildford's voice was, as usual, compelling and Mary turned sadly away. But whatever Lady Guildford might say, Mary felt in her heart it was an inauspicious start to her marriage. Long-dreaded and finally here, it had all seemed rather unreal till now. But reality was her standing here shivering in the cold light of early morning, waiting to be bathed and dressed and joined to the sickly Louis for life. Reality was grim compared to the hazy dream through which she had previously peered at her future.

Mary stiffened her spine as she gave herself up to her ladies' ministrations. She had agreed to the match whether reluctantly or no and must now try to make the best of it. After all, she reminded herself yet again, this 'marriage for life' would only last as long as the term of years granted to the first of them to die, which might not be long at all. This last was becoming a daily litany. She had now seen the king for herself and it was true that his bones didn't look likely to get a lot older. Mary shivered again as her night shift was stripped from her body. And as she stepped into the tub of hot water she asked God's pardon for her wickedness, on her wedding day, in hoping for the demise of her bridegroom. What a sad reflection on the realities of marriage for such as herself.

It was some little time later that Mary, bathed and with her hair brushed till it gleamed, was assisted into yet another magnificent gown. The robe was of stiff, golden brocade, trimmed and lined with ermine. It matched her English hood, which fell in folds below her neck. Her jewellery for the occasion was equally as magnificent and very costly. But despite the beauty of her garments and jewels, Mary was conscious that she was not looking her best for the occasion. Her stomach felt queasy, whether from nerves, the excess of alcohol or a witch's brew of the two, Mary knew not. Subdued, she allowed Lady Guildford to lead her from the chamber. She waited quietly while her lords and ladies and the rest of the wedding party, all in golden garments as wondrous as her own, formed up behind her in the gardens. As they moved off through the gate and made for the hall where the ceremony was to take place, Mary noticed that the pall of smoke still lingering from the fire formed a dark back-cloth to their golden ranks. The contrast made the figures in the procession glitter all the more.

The crush was great as they entered the hall, but Mary and her train were assisted by the guards who lined the route. And as Mary made her way to the altar, she saw by the dim light thrown by the windows decorated to show the deeds of St Wolfran, that the king awaited her. He was clothed, like Mary, in cloth of gold and was seated on a chair. At her appearance, Louis doffed his cap. Mary sank into a deep curtsey and, as she rose, Louis gave her a warm embrace. He seated her on a chair by his side, over which the high nobles of France held a canopy.

Robertet, the treasurer approached the king and handed him a necklace set with a great pointed diamond and a matchless ruby. Mary was unable to conceal yet another shiver as Louis' clammy hands fastened this costly bridal gift around her neck, while his none-too-sweet breath fanned her cheek.

The marriage ceremony she had tried so hard to avoid began, conducted by the Cardinal of Bayeux. He sang the Mass, illuminated by the candles held by the Princes of the Blood. Mary kept her hands tightly clasped to still their nervous tremor till the Cardinal handed her and Louis half of a wafer each. Louis, after he had kissed and received his, turned and kissed the trembling Mary.

The ceremony was the long one she had been warned to expect. Weary, and emotionally drained long before its end, it was finally over and Mary was free to leave. She swept to the floor in another deep curtsey and departed to her State Apartments to dine privately with the French royal ladies as she had been told was the custom. Given the presence of Louise of Savoy, Francis' ambitious and, for the moment, at least, thwarted mother, Mary was glad of the sympathetic Claude's more friendly company as her own ladies were to dine separately in the great hall.

Anticipating some critical conversational barbs during the meal, and still feeling queasy, Mary could hardly eat a bite of all the rich food that was served to her by the Duke of Albany and the French officers. But then the appraising expressions of the royal French ladies did little enough to encourage an appetite. But at least it seemed they all admired one thing about her—her brother Henry. They had heard tell of his handsome looks and his intellectual pursuits and were eager to learn more of him. And although it had been her kingly brother who had forced this match on her, Mary was still proud of him and was glad to have the opportunity to praise him to the arrogant French ladies.

After she had satisfied their curiosity about Henry the talk moved to other things. Mary felt excluded from the conversation, an intruder at her own table, as her French wasn't quick enough to grasp the fast flow of the conversation. She wondered if this speedy speech was a deliberate attempt to snub Louis' English bride. She grew pensive, but came out of her reverie at the sound of muffled giggles. She could only guess these were at her expense as she intercepted several sly glances in her direction. Mary felt her skin flush. It betrayed the fact that her knowledge of French was rather better than her companions had been led to expect and a few of them had the grace to look as if they shared her embarrassment.

Had she last night encouraged Francis a little more than was seemly? The French ladies certainly seemed to think so, judging from the few of their critical comments that she *had* caught. Forced to remember Francis' attentions and her not-unwilling reception of them, Mary squirmed in mortification at her remembered behaviour. Wine and the daunting prospect awaiting her had made her behave foolishly, she knew. She hoped her behaviour didn't serve as a spur to Francis to increase his attentions. Embarrassed to recall how her behaviour had become more and more flirtatious as the evening had worn on, Mary forced her expression to remain calm. She would not give the French ladies the satisfaction of knowing her mortification. Instead, she held her head high and spoke proudly. 'I am a stranger, in a strange land,' she told them. 'The Duc de Valois was merely being kind to a sad and lonely woman. He is my son-in-law. What you suggest is unseemly.'

When her words earned her only a few more muffled giggles, Mary wished it had appeared unseemly to her the previous evening, especially as she had to make her little speech under the gaze of the vulnerable Claude, Francis' young wife, whom her behaviour must have wounded.

Anne of France, who had already shown herself to be a domineering woman, was one of those present at this not-so-festive banquet. This daughter of the Spider King, Louis XI, sat stiff and unbending and looked every inch the true daughter of that wily monarch. Anne of France examined Mary's now rosy face without a flicker of emotion. Suddenly, her commanding voice filled the hall, making Mary jump.

'Perhaps they suggest your behaviour was unseemly, Madam, because it was. You are Queen of France and are expected to behave as such. You drank too much, danced too much and laughed too much. Your youth does not excuse your lack of dignity. Nor does it excuse your wanton's behaviour with the Due de Valois.'

Flame-face, Mary sat and said nothing as the old lady continued her harangue. 'King Louis wants a son,' she now told Mary. 'Did you know?'

Mary's gasp of dismay at this unwelcome news provided the answer.

'I see you didn't,' Anne of France told her with a hint of spite. 'It's to be hoped you have better luck in that direction than my sister, Jeanne.'

Through her jumbled mass of feelings, Mary remembered that Jeanne of France had been Louis' first wife, discarded, so it was said, for her ugliness.

Anne of France went remorselessly on. 'Louis divorced her. Couldn't bear children, so he said. Who's to know?' she now demanded of Mary and the assembled company. 'She wasn't given the chance to try.' Her gaze settled sternly on Mary, whom she had termed 'a wanton'. 'The king wants a son, madam,' she told Mary again. 'Think you he'll get one on you?'

Mary felt the flush deepen at this coarse question. Old ladies were often-plain-speaking, she knew, but this imperious lady went beyond the limits. As the lady had said, she was now Queen of France and there was no reason why she should have to tolerate such lèse-majesté. Mary, considered how her brother Harry would react to such dismissal and was emboldened to defend herself. But before she could summon words sufficiently imperious to put the lady in her place, Anne of France went on, with words that Mary found comforting, although comforting her was, she suspected, far from that lady's mind.

'He can't get sons. Never managed it when he was younger, he'll not manage it now, for all your youth and beauty.'

Mary found her next words less comforting.

'Nevertheless, Madam,' Anne of France told her tartly, 'he intends to try. If you do become *enceinte*, just be certain the babe is the King's and not the Duc de Valois'!' This insult brought a gasp from the ladies assembled at the table. 'We want no bastard sprigs inheriting the throne of France.'

Mary gathered her so recently-acquired queenly dignity round her like a shield. It was vital that she defend herself, she knew. Her behaviour the previous evening might have been foolish, but it didn't warrant such ugly insults. 'What you suggest is a wicked slander, Madam,' she told Anne of France icily. 'And it's best, for your sake, that I pretend I didn't hear it. As for bearing the king a son,' Mary forced the words through unwilling lips, 'I shall do my duty as shall my husband, God willing. Neither of us can do more.'

Mary wished only to avoid any further insults from the foul-tongued old harridan. She turned to Claude, who indicated that Mary had only to rise and they would all be forced to do the same. Mary had forgotten in the heat of her shame, that she had such a power. Doubtless, next the ladies of the French court would be gossiping that she had soon forgotten that she was Queen of France and make a *double-entendre* of the fact. Upset at being caught out and so soon, Mary upbraided herself for her naivety and lack of queenly authority. She must never again forget that she was a Queen now; she must behave like one. Though, in spite of her brave words to Anne of France, she felt only young and inexperienced and far from regal.

She followed the kind Claude's advice and after joining the rest of the company in the hall for dancing, she soon retired to her bedchamber to rest and prepare for that evening's ball, relieved to get away from so many hostile, watching eyes. The unexpectedness of the attack from Anne of France had shocked her, though she recalled that Wolsey had warned her she might encounter envy and antagonism.

Courts were ever thus, he had counselled. But even Wolsey would have been shocked that the antagonism should have come so early and been so venomous. Mary was only surprised that Francis' mother, Louise of Savoy hadn't joined in.

Anne Boleyn, her youngest Maid of Honour, who had joined Mary's train from that of the Archduchess Margaret, waited in her chamber to attend her. As the youngest and least significant of her ladies, Anne would have been the one deputed to leave the celebrations in the great hall early. Mary was thankful not to have yet to face the expected barrage of questions from the more worldly-wise ladies in her train. And as the young girl helped her remove her gown and head-dress, Mary found herself envying the happily single Maid. Although Anne's only real beauty was her great, dark eyes, as these were mostly kept modestly lowered, they failed to reduce the plainness of the rest of her. Her hair was unfashionably dark, her thin, gawky body and sallow complexion made her something of an ugly duckling, while her youth and lack of consequence amongst the other high and noble ladies of Mary's train made her a natural outsider. No doubt she had been surprised to be chosen for the honour of attending Mary in France.

Anne looked tired, her olive skin even more sallow than usual. Lucky girl, Mary thought, you will never have to endure the unwanted lusts of a king. And tonight, you can eventually claim your solitary pallet bed. Unlike me.

Mary reflected on what had been said during dinner. Forced to admit, even if only to herself, that she had enjoyed Francis' amusing conversation, she wondered if her naive pleasure would be held against her and used to wound her during her entire sojourn at the French court. It was clear there were plenty eager to weave evil where nothing but a foolish, innocent amusement had existed. Mary knew she must be wary in future and deny herself even the small pleasure of enjoying Francis' amusing attentions. She had only recently met him. How could anyone truly believe she would let him into her bed after a few conversations and fewer dances?

As Anne turned down the bed linen and Mary climbed under the warmed sheets, she told herself that Anne of France's suggestions had been only the foul imaginings of an embittered old woman, resentful that her sister had not enjoyed Louis' favour, and not what the rest would necessarily think. And as she lay back, drained from the day's experiences, Mary resolved to put them from her mind.

Glad to find some peace and seeming solitude after such a hectic and upsetting day — the young Anne flitting discreetly about the chamber, tidying away her gown, seemed to sense her mistress's desire to be left undisturbed — Mary's eyelids began to droop, but as she remembered that in a few short hours Louis would be sharing a bed with her for their wedding night, they flew open again.

Even this quiet sojourn was destined to be short-lived, however. As she sat up, Mary heard the noisy clamor outside her bedchamber as her other Maids of Honour returned from dining in the hall. Their excited chatter, spurred on by the fine French wines, sounded louder than normal. And although Mary heard Lady Guildford trying to quieten them,

85

even this stern lady couldn't quell all their excitement on such a day. Resigned, Mary allowed her ladies to crowd round and exclaim with wonder at Louis' bridal gift. Mary was not as awed by the gift as her Maids. She had yet to earn it. Louis would expect his wife to show her gratitude for such a costly necklace. And now Mary was under no illusion what form that gratitude would take. Louis was still looking to get himself a son and fully intended to exert himself till he got one.

She had mistakenly assumed that Louis' desire for more children was long since over. Perhaps it had been wishful thinking on her part. Or perhaps Henry, Wolsey — even Lady Guildford — had between them conjured up this falsehood and put the idea in her head. She knew better now. Louis was a king, after all and kings all wanted sons.

Mary recalled her luckless sister-in-law, Catherine and her many disappointments. She remembered, too, how her brother, Henry's, merry and loving ways so often now turned to reproach and recrimination at Catherine's failure to provide him with a male heir. Perhaps, Louis, if he lived long enough, would also turn from his present kindliness towards her if she failed in her duty? Mary couldn't help but wish her predecessor in the royal marital bed had worked harder at doing *her* duty and relieved Mary of its burden. She gazed at the magnificent bridal gift with distaste and bade her Maids to put it away.

The 'delights' of the marital bed were now beckoning her, however, and only the evening's ball now lay between her and it. Mary had to be prinked and preened anew so

Louis could enjoy his purchase in prime condition, this time gowned in the French style as her husband had demanded.

Mary had a sense of *déjà-vu* as she entered the hall, for the same glittering throng who had graced the previous evening's ball were all present at the ball in honour of her wedding, some of them by now the worse for wear. Fine manners forgotten with the excess of good wine, Mary felt the men's eyes follow her as she walked to the dais, and was assisted to the chair by Louis' side.

Louis was very merry and attentive. He kissed and touched her till she felt clammy all over. Mary talked about she knew not what, though she seemed, later, to remember expressing a wish to visit Venice and Louis promising that they would go together.

The heat of the room with its crowds and banked mass of candles was almost unbearable, and Mary put aside her earlier resolution to drink little. Besides, she told her clamoring conscience as she drained another glass of the rich Gascon wine, coupling with Louis in the marriage bed was not something to be approached with sobriety.

Louis was trying hard to please her and insisted on helping her to each dish as it was placed before them, though Mary again ate little. Her wine glass, though, was no sooner empty that it was refilled. Tonight, Mary knew the wine would have little likelihood of making her behave foolishly. But she needed its help to dull her senses.

The evening passed all too swiftly. It was still early, no more than eight o'clock, when Mary felt a light touch on her shoulder and turned to see Claude beckoning her. It was time for the bedding ceremony. Mary's stomach lurched and threatened revolt. She swallowed hastily and tried to ignore the sly, knowing leers and the odd sympathetic glances from the courtiers.

Claude, her expression anxious and concerned, asked her if she was all right. Quickly, lest the unlooked for concern should reduce her still shaky queenly dignity, Mary assured her that she was fine and followed Claude to the bedchamber. Louis, she knew, was being escorted by the men of his household; Mary could hear their ribald comments echo up the corridor behind her.

Once again, Mary was undressed by her ladies. White-faced, she climbed into the big bed and waited for Louis. He entered the chamber ahead of his gentlemen, clearly keen to hasten matters along.

Louis, too, had been divested of his garments. The spindly legs that had chased Mary in her nightmare were visible beneath his night attire.

After much mirth and ribaldry, the chamber gradually emptied. Soon, only Lady Guildford lingered near the door. She spared Mary a compassionate glance and came back to give her a kiss and a few whispered words of encouragement along the lines of 'it'll soon be over.' Mary hoped she was right.

Still Lady Guildford lingered, as though reluctant to depart and allow the night's proceedings to commence. After Louis' pointed throat-clearings had no effect, he had eventually to order the lady from the room. Even then she looked likely to defy him. Mayhap, she too, whilst dining in the great hall, had been told of Louis' great desire that Mary provide him with a son.

Mary intervened. Now she only wanted the deed over and done with and she bid her Mother a firm goodnight. This shifted the lady and the door at last closed behind her. The soon-to-be-lovers were left alone in the now softly-lit bed-chamber.

Louis, all husbandly solicitude for his virgin bride, reached over to a side table and poured wine. He handed her a glass with the suggestion, 'Drink this, my lovely Mary. Wedding days can be traumatic, as I ought to know having now enjoyed three.'

Mary knew he was trying to be kind. She forced a tremulous smile. But his smile in return only served to repulse her as it revealed the blackened and decaying teeth she had till now forgotten about. She closed her eyes to blank them out.

Louis seemed to take this for his signal to begin, for Mary's eyes fluttered open as she felt the wine glass removed from the tight clasp of her fingers. She watched, mesmerised as Louis replaced it on the table, then quickly shut her eyes again before he turned back. Beside her, she sensed Louis' fumbling movements and guessed he was removing his nightshift. A brief glance from beneath lowered lashes had revealed a thin and wrinkled body. His manhood was limp. Perhaps, after all—

But before she could continue the thought, Louis climbed on top of her and set to with determination. As Mary squirmed in revulsion beneath him, he redoubled his efforts.

Mary couldn't help but wonder if he hoped will-power alone would stir his reluctant organ.

His hands, now clammier than ever, clutched at her legs, her breasts, her belly. He exclaimed at her beauty and rained kisses from her forehead to her feet Mary could only squirm still more while these indignities continued. Although Louis might be scrawny, his body pressed Mary down till she felt unable to breathe. She moved underneath him, wanting only to gasp some air that wasn't tainted with his foul breath. But Louis seemed to have mistaken her movement for the stirrings of desire, for now he strove even harder to excite his manhood.

Even Mary was moved to pity when Louis' disobedient manhood refused to do its duty. After what seemed an age, Louis finally groaned and rolled off her. Mary didn't dare to move in case he decided to try again to impress her with the ardor of French manhood of which Francis had so unwisely boasted.

But it seemed such a thought was far from his mind. It was clear his hateful fumblings had merely served to leave him feeling humiliated, too. He mumbled apologies to Mary for his failure and turned away.

Apart from that one brief glance, Mary's eyes had remained tight shut through Louis' exertions. She only opened them when she felt him roll away. She turned her head on the pillow and gazed at his naked back. It looked surprisingly vulnerable and she felt another stirring of pity for him. But he should never have sought to marry again. If he hadn't, they would both have been spared this miserable charade of wedded bliss. What had been the point after all? Louis must have realised when he had asked for her hand that he would never get sons from her or any other woman. His two daughters would have to suffice.

Mary, too, now turned over. She pulled the covers to her chin. Fat tears slid down her cheeks and dampened the pillow. She had lost her love, perhaps for ever, because her brother had insisted on marrying her to an old and impotent man. This night should have been shared with Charles, she thought, as more tears flowed, not with Louis and his shameful fumbling. Would she be expected to endure this night after night, she wondered, till, by some miracle, he managed to make her pregnant? The thought appalled her. It would surely be a lifetime's task.

Snores from beside her told Mary that, at last, Louis slept. But she lay awake far into the night, listening to the sounds of revelry from the hall, Louis' ever-increasing snorts and the plop of her tears on the pillow. Through the watery curtain of her tears, Mary stared into the room's shadows as if hoping to see revealed the glimmerings of a happier future. Sadly, none were revealed to her that night.

CHAPTER SIX

Despite her troubled night, Mary woke early. Beside her, Louis snored on. Sometime after she had fallen asleep, their bodies had come together and now Mary edged gingerly away. Although her movement was gentle it disturbed Louis. He opened his sleep-coated eyes and gazed at Mary in astonishment. Then he frowned, reached for the wine he had left on the side table and downed the glass in one.

Mary feared the wine would encourage him to test his manhood again. She breathed out on a sigh when he retrieved his abandoned nightgown and put it on. Confidence restored with the covering of his scrawny limbs, he turned to her and gave her a hearty kiss.

'What it is to have a young bride in my bed once again,' he said, a twinkle in his rheumy eyes. 'I feel rejuvenated, my dear. Better than I've felt in years.'

Mary, still anxious that Louis might yet find the strength to set about his husbandly duties, suggested they rise, a suggestion Louis agreed to with what might be construed an insulting alacrity. Worried, perhaps, in case she should demand her bridal dues from him, thought Mary, amused in spite of their tragic situation.

Louise called for breakfast. Lady Guildford followed the meal in, much to Louis' obvious annoyance, and began fussing round Mary, clucking at her dark-shadowed eyes till Louis told her to leave her fussing till he had gone. Lady Guildford cast him a look of dislike and left the room muttering.

Louis didn't linger long abed after that. Nor did Mary. She rose as Lady Guildford bustled in for a second time, this time with Mary's Maids of Honour trailing behind her, all eager to see Mary for themselves and learn how she had taken to being a wife. They peeked at the sheets, looking for the tell-tale red stains that would reveal Mary was no longer a virgin.

Hot colour flushed Mary's cheeks at the remembered indignities she had endured the night before. But the Maids didn't find the stains they were looking for. The sheets were still as pure and white as Mary's virginity. And after much eyebrow raising and furtive glances between themselves, the Maids gazed at Mary with a prurient curiosity until Lady Guildford intervened and sharply rebuked them.

'I'd like to bathe, Mother,' Mary told her quietly.

'Of course you would, child. A natural enough desire, I'll vow,' she remarked. While her meaning was clear enough, even Lady Guildford didn't quite dare to insult Louis to Mary's face, especially with the indiscreet Maids of Honour hovering.

At last, lying in the warm, scented water, Mary began to relax. She scrubbed vigorously, trying to wash away the imprint of her husband's clammy, clutching hands. Bathed and gowned, Mary and her ladies went down to the hall. There, to her embarrassment, Mary found Louis loudly boasting of his previous night's exploits with no trace of a blush for their falsehood. His companions' sly sniggers aroused Lady Guildford's ire.

She turned to Mary. 'Come, Your Grace,' she said. 'You should not stand here and listen to such talk. Is this how Queens are treated in France?'

Lady Guildford had a carrying voice. This time, as she had no doubt intended, it reach Louis. He scowled and came over to greet Mary. Ignoring Lady Guildford, he took Mary's arm and kissed her hand with genuine affection.

'Ma Cherie,' he told Mary. 'You look lovelier than ever this morning. Forgive us men our rude talk. I hope we didn't embarrass you.'

'A little, your Grace,' she admitted. 'But 'tis only that so many of the faces are strange to me. The men speak in like manner at my brother's court after all. It is common enough.'

Louis gave a rueful smile that he, an anointed king, should be found out coarsely boasting like some peasant bridegroom. Perhaps to make amends, he took from inside his doublet a marvellous table-cut diamond with a great, round pearl hanging from it. 'For my exquisite Mary, an exquisite jewel,' he said as he presented her with it, amidst gasps from her ladies. 'This, my dear, is our wondrous *Miroir de Naples*. Is it not fine?'

Mary could only nod as the diamond flashed white fire as it caught the light.

'It is the custom for each Queen of France to own the '*Miroir*' in turn,' Louis told her. 'So now, my Queen, the jewel is yours.'

Mary was touched. But then she reminded herself that Louis, as her purchaser, was only fulfilling his side of the bargain he had made with Henry. Still, she must say something. Louis would expect some return for his gift. Mary felt obliged to kiss him as a loving wife should before the assembled courtiers. She repressed an involuntary shudder as he began fondling her neck under its hood. His touch made her think of the night ahead and the night after that when the previous night's indignities would no doubt have to be endured again.

To her surprise, Louis took her arm and suggested they go into dinner. It was not much after eight in the morning. Mary knew that Louis generally kept early hours, but she had assumed that would only mean he retired early, after supper, not that the usual ten in the morning dinner would be taken the best part of two hours earlier. Seeing her expression, Louis confessed to his early habits. But then he added that she was making him feel young again and that he would perhaps start to take up a young man's customs. Mary hoped, if so, that it was only his customary meal time he altered.

The dishes were plentiful, though, following the custom of the king, most were on the plain side. Louis ate little, only some boiled fowl. He was equally abstemious with his wine, though he helped Mary with a generous hand to everything that was laid before her, chatting to her all the while, regaling her with tales of his court as though he wished to demonstrate that his son-in-law, Francis, wasn't the only one able to entertain her.

Later that day, Mary was sewing in her chamber, when Lady Guildford entered, her face a mask of anger, her lips thinned to a vexatious line.

Alarmed, Mary asked her what was the matter. 'Has the Duc de Valois been upsetting you again, Mother?' Francis seemed to have taken it as his chosen task in life to tease her at every opportunity. And as Lady Guildford's sense of humour was never her strong suit, he would have found it a satisfying task.

'Would that it were something so trivial, Madam. I wouldn't trouble you with it.'

Thoroughly unnerved now, Mary threw aside her sewing and stood up. 'What is it, then, Mother? What has happened?'

'Proud Norfolk, my lady, has just told me I'm to pack my bags and make ready to depart. It seems I'm not wanted here.'

'Surely not, Mother? King Louis rules here, not Norfolk.'

'Aye. That's been made right plain. It seems the king, your husband, did give the order. Norfolk was but his messenger. Still, he made it clear enough I wasn't wanted here and great delight he took in the telling. What King Henry will say about their treatment of us, my lady, the Lord alone knows. I nearly boxed Norfolk's ears, such a smirk he wore.'

'Where's Norfolk now, Mother?'

'Closeted with the king. Doubtless hatching more plans. King Louis' a sly one. It's my belief he doesn't want you subject to any wise and experienced English counsel. Norfolk said I wouldn't be the only member of your train dismissed.'

Mary clutched at Lady Guildford's arm. 'What do you mean?'

'It seems your husband has taken a fit of pique about the number of your English attendants. Norfolk told me that only those named on the marriage contract are to stay. The rest are to be dismissed and replaced with ladies of the French court. They've summoned a meeting of the Council to discuss it.'

Stunned, Mary wondered how it was that the husband who could act so loving in the morning could act with such unwarranted cruelty but a few hours later. He had said nothing of this to her at dinner. Mary was aware that Lady Guildford had annoyed him, but she had thought Louis had put his annoyance aside and forgotten it, regarding it as but a natural adjustment to his newly-married state as had Mary. Now she realised her mistake. 'How could he do such a thing?' she demanded as she touched the diamond and pearl jewel. 'He only gave me this wonderful gift this morning. He said nothing to me then to indicate what was on his mind. He was attentive all through dinner and couldn't do enough for me.' Mary frowned. She must have displeased him, she thought as she recalled their marriage night and Louis' failure. Was she being punished for witnessing his shame?

'Calm yourself, child. You must see the king and demand he changes his mind. You said yourself he wants to please you. You are his wife and his Queen, surely you have some rights? This is a fine way for him to start his marriage. You must make him understand how distressed you are. Shed a few tears. He will surely not be so adamant if, with a delicate sorrow, you make a pretty plea.'

Mary wasn't convinced that Louis would be so easily persuaded. He was a practised king, used to obstructing the desires of people far more skilled than she. Like her brother, he had also had years of practice of getting his own way. Hadn't he dismissed his first wife because she didn't please him? Dismissing Lady Guildford and the others in her train, would be small beer in comparison. Still, Mary knew she must try. She dismissed her doubts, assumed a confidence she was far from feeling, and said, 'You are right, Mother.' Mary turned to the Maids of Honour who had been sewing and gossiping before Lady Guildford brought her shocking news and said, 'Come, ladies. Help me look pleading pretty enough to persuade the king to change his mind. I've been told he be a kind-hearted man. Maybe he'll be of different mind when he realises how much it means to me.' Mary took comfort from this thought and once she had changed into her most becoming gown, she went in search of her husband. The Council meeting had just finished; its members bowed low in order to avoid her eye, then made themselves scarce.

Although Louis agreed readily enough when she asked for a private word, he wore a cornered look that told Mary plainer than words that she would be unsuccessful in her mission. 'Lady Guildford has it from my Duke of Norfolk that you have ordered her dismissal and that of most of my train. How can this be? I thought—' Mary faltered. She had thought Louis wanted to please her. His generous gifts of expensive jewellery, his attentive manner, had all told her this. Yet it was clear she must be wrong.

Louis tried to soothe her. He led her to a chair in the Council chamber and bade her sit down. 'I must confess it is true, though I had wished to tell you myself.'

'But why, Louis?' Mary thought again of their disastrous wedding night and forced herself to ask, 'Have I upset you in some way? Please tell me.'

Louis had the grace to look uncomfortable. But it was clear from the way he avoided her eyes and blustered his defence that he wasn't about to change his mind. 'You are very young and inexperienced, Mary,' he told her. 'You should be guided by me, your husband. You do not need all these people around you.' Louis waved his arms as though to describe vast hordes of English. 'I'm sure Lady Guildford is very dear to you, but you are a wife now.' With a furtive embarrassment, he added, 'And who knows but we may have children.'

It was clear his failure in their marital bed had rankled. But his reference to children indicated that Louis didn't intend to let one failure put him off.

'You are now Queen of France, my dear. Surely in such an exalted position you have no need of this 'Mother' Guildford?'

Mary thought she had more need of her now than ever. 'But my Mother Guildford has always been there for me,' she protested. 'I need her.' Mary's eyes filled with tears.

Her tears seemed to unman Louis even more than his failure to take her maidenhead. 'Come, my love, mine own little wife,' he pleaded. 'Dry your eyes. It is not such a terrible thing.' He put his arm about her. 'I'm paying you a great compliment, Mary, if you did but realise it.'

Mary failed to see how he could construe the dismissal of her attendants as a compliment. But Louis explained it to her.

'I will set no one over you, to order your days. I am making you your own woman, without guardians to interfere and run your life. Does that not please you?'

'Put in such a way, yes, of course it does. But—'

Louis broke in before she could voice her doubts. 'You don't realise as yet what you have gained. Look back on your life in England, little wife. Was there not always someone to tell you 'do this' or 'don't do that'?'

Reluctantly, Mary nodded.

'You were a child then, now you are a woman.'

The conversation was going Louis' way. Mary tried again. 'But Louis, we were only married yesterday. My life has altered so much in such a short time. I—I had expected to keep my ladies about me, some familiar faces at least for a time. To be separated from them so suddenly, 'tis a hard blow.' Mary became tearful again and was unable to go on. But she knew she had lost.

Louis seemed to sense her capitulation for he kissed her and said softly, 'I'm persuaded you will settle here more happily without all these familiar faces, my love. You are Queen of France and, as such, should have French lords and ladies about you. You will never be totally at ease with our language if you spend a great part of each day chatting with your English train. It is best for all the changes to come at one time than to have them spread over months. It would be very unsettling for you.'

Louis took Mary's small chin in his age-mottled hand and gazed at her tear-stained face. 'Please believe me, Mary, when I tell you I'm doing this for your own good. The Lord knows I hate to see you so distressed. It is for the best. In a few short weeks you will thank me for giving you such freedom.'

Freedom to be insulted by Anne of France with no one of her own to speak up for her? Freedom to have Francis continue his pursuit of her, with no one to help her keep him at arms' length? Such 'freedom' was more constraining than a dozen guardians. But, Louis wasn't about to change his mind. He had taken a dislike to Lady Guildford. Because of it, he felt obliged to dismiss all not on the marriage contract in order to conceal his desire to be rid of her.

Chastened, Mary returned to her apartments to reveal her failure. The news had spread and her ladies and gentlemen who crowded the chamber rushed towards her, all asking questions at once. The Duke of Norfolk wasn't amongst them, Mary noticed. She would speak to him later. She turned to find an expectant Lady Guildford at her elbow and rushed to break the news before hope took hold, 'The king is adamant. And although I pleaded with him he will not change his mind. Apart from a few of the younger Maids and others named on the marriage contract, you are all to go.'

Mary's eyes shadowed as she added quietly, for Lady Guild-ford's ears only, 'He means to have me to himself, I think.'

Uproar broke out. Mary understood their disappoint-ment. It was customary for those accompanying a royal bride to receive rich gifts as a reward for their service. Her women, especially, must be worried that they would return home un-dowered. It was yet another thing with which Mary must concern herself and she made a mental note to order costly gifts to soothe their disappointment But, for now, all she wanted to do was escape from their clamor and questioning.

She retired to her bedchamber. She did not wish to give way to tears in front of them all. Lady Guildford followed her and shut the door firmly behind her.

Mary turned to her. 'Mother, what shall I do? I'll be left with no one to advise me, but chits of girls no older than me.'

'We will write to your brother, child.' Lady Guildford tried her best to reassure her. 'King Henry and Wolsey will sort this out, you'll see.'

'Would that Wolsey were here now in place of the Duke of Norfolk,' said Mary. 'He would never have accepted this matter as easily as my lord Duke seems to have done. Surely Norfolk tried to remonstrate with Louis?'

'If he did, I doubt he tried very hard. He was over-pleased at the news and didn't attempt to hide it, knowing Wolsey would be annoyed. Norfolk was never in favour of this French alliance, anyway, especially since Wolsey arranged it.'

The proud and aristocratic Norfolk took the rise of Wol-sey, the low-born son of an Ipswich butcher, as an insult to himself and rarely troubled to hide his hatred. Mary could well believe that Norfolk had swiftly agreed to Louis' demands just to spite Wolsey with scarcely a thought given to her predicament. Norfolk had earned a right, royal tongue-lashing and he would have it as soon as he dared to show his face again. 'I will also write plainly to my brother of Norfolk's lack of zeal on my behalf. Let Norfolk make what excuses he can to the king.'

Lady Guildford nodded. 'A humble apology would do his soul good.'

Mary sat at the pretty little desk in front of the window and picked up a quill. 'I will write to England straight away. But should Louis dismiss you before we hear from Henry, don't cross to England, but wait at Boulogne. That way you will be close at hand when I am able to recall you. With luck, the separation should not be for long—Wolsey has a marvellous gift for persuasion. If anyone can change Louis' mind, it is him.'

'I trust you are right. I feel troubled at the thought of leaving you here amongst strangers, with an old and sickly husband. Should he manage to get you with child I should be here to tend you, not some over-perfumed Frenchwoman.'

Mary's heart gave a lurch at the thought. Unlikely as pregnancy might seem at the moment, who knew but that Louis would succeed in recovering his manhood?

The thought was repugnant and Mary refused to dwell on it. She must place her confidence in Wolsey. He would sort the matter out in a few weeks, she could depend on it. She must depend on it. But first, she must write the letters home.

Mary turned back to the desk and, with Lady Guildford at her elbow, suggesting a different word here and a different phrase there, the letters were written. But not before they received a fair sprinkling of her tears. Mary sat back. 'Now we wait.'

Someone knocked at the door. At Mary's response, the door opened and Francis came in. He must have learned of the threatened removal of Mary's English attendants, for when he saw Mary's tear-stained face, he was immediately all solicitude. He went down on his knee in front of her as if seeking her absolution. 'My beautiful Mary wears such a sorrowful face and I fear I am the bearer of more sad news.' He kissed Mary's hand. 'A messenger's duties are hard indeed.'

'What now, my lord?' Mary asked bitterly. 'Am I, too, to be dismissed?'

'The king wouldn't be so cruel, Mother. He knows how we love you. Indeed, how could he part with his delightful Tudor rose? He calls for you now, Mary. He is sickly again and wants you by his side. Only the sight of your lovely face, he says, can cure him of his pain.'

'What ails him, my lord?' Mary asked. 'He was hearty enough last ni—' Mary bit off the rest. Embarrassed, she gave a quick glance at Francis. His upturned lips and twinkling eyes told her he had understood her meaning only too well.

Mary lowered her gaze and asked again, 'What ails the king, my lord?'

'Tis his old trouble, the gout again. Only the presence of his beautiful bride, he feels, will tease away the pain. May I escort you to the king, Mother?'

After she caught sight of her tear-stained face in the glass, Mary bade him wait outside, while she quickly removed the marks of her sorrow.

Behind her, Lady Guildford muttered, 'So, after treating you so badly, he now expects you to nurse him. Mayhap your nursing of His Christian Majesty should not be too gentle,' she suggested tartly.

'Nay, Mother,' Mary chided. 'I will nurse him tenderly, as a wife should. He has already decreed that I am to be left practically alone here. Who knows what he might decide to do if I displease him?'

Louis looked dreadful. Suffering had made his homely face even plainer. His eyes were sunk back in his head and deeply shadowed, The lines of his cheeks seemed doubly-etched. Touched at the pitiful sight of him, even though he was the cause of her present distress, Mary excused him. No doubt he had been helped in his decision by self-interested courtiers. With her English ladies gone, there would be vacancies in plenty about her. Now they would be jostling for position and fighting for the right of their own wife or daughter to replace her English ladies. Each would be only too willing to spy on her and report her words and actions.

As she sat by the bed and took Louis' hand, Mary wondered if she was to have nothing left that was truly her own. Louis had the right to her body, and soon the ladies of his court would have the right to her mind and every thought that sprang from it. She forced back a sigh and said, 'The Duc de Valois tells me you suffer from the gout, Louis. Can nothing be done for you?'

'The physicians do all they can, my dear,' Louis told her. Ruefully, he added, 'sometimes, it seems they cause more pain than they cure.' He tried to smile at her, but the smile turned to a grimace as the pain caught him again and he lay quiet till it eased. 'I feel better for the sight of you, Mary. You are a greater tonic than any physician's foul remedy.' He glanced apologetically at her. 'I hope you can find it in your heart to forgive me for sending your ladies home. But, truly, they couldn't stay, Mary, you must realise that. The clamor for posts about a new Queen has ever caused problems. 'Tis better to sort the matter out swiftly than to let it fester on, causing resentment and bad feeling.'

It was as she had thought. But at least he no longer spouted about the 'freedom' she had gained. 'Let us not talk of such matters now. You should rest.'

Louis told her the pain gave him little peace for sleeping. Instead, he suggested she play him something soothing on her lute.

So she sat by him and played all the gentle airs she could remember; mostly those from her brother's court and one or two that she had picked up whilst in France. At the end, she was pleased to see that Louis had dozed off, his face relaxed as the pain loosened its grip. A fondling hand touched her shoulder and she jumped. She turned to see Francis standing close behind her.

'Has the king told you the good news, Mother?' he asked.

'What good news, Francis? I have had little good news today, as you know.'

'Some of us would think otherwise, ma Mère. Now you will be more in the company of French nobles like myself. A thoroughly delightful prospect for us all. And with no Lady Guildford's rebukes to warm my ears I feel doubly fortunate.' He stroked her neck, fingers lingering, caressing her nape.

She moved aside. 'Pray don't jest with me, Francis. I feel desolate enough. I don't know how I will bear to lose all my friends so quickly.'

'But you have many other friends, ma Mère,' Francis' caressing voice replaced the spurned caresses of his hand. 'And now they will be able to get to know you properly.'

Francis' honeyed words betrayed his intentions towards her. More than ever Mary regretted her foolish behaviour towards him on the night before her wedding. It seemed it was all the encouragement Francis needed, for he went on.

'Your Lady Guildford has tended to ward off friendly overtures with her over-protective ways. Even the king feels he must first ask her permission before he sees his own wife.'

'You exaggerate, Francis. You make her sound like some kind of ogre, which I can assure you, she is not.'

Francis conceded that he might have exaggerated slightly. 'But I promise you, he feels a certain awe of the lady. Anyway, enough of Lady Guildford. See, she dominates even when not in the room. The king earlier asked what he could do to cheer you. His remorse was quite touching. I confess, I felt tears start to my own eye at the sight of it. We French have very tender hearts.'

Mary glanced down at the bed where Louis was still sleeping peacefully, undisturbed by their whispered exchanges. 'And what did you suggest, Francis?'

'Something exciting, I thought. What better than a joust? Colour, crowds, spectacle. And not just an ordinary joust, ma Mère. We have instructed a herald to go across to England for the finest combatants to come to fight the best in France. You can look forward to seeing many of your old friends as well as many new ones. The king has instructed me to organise it in your honour. We do our best to make our Queen happy, you see.'

Mary felt a thrill course through her. Charles was a magnificent jouster and would surely come. She could scarcely believe she might soon see him again. Surely Henry, who loved to beat the French, whether at real wars as at Tournai or at the scarcely less violent play-acting of the jousts, wouldn't be able to resist sending him?

Francis begged her help with his costumes for the joust. 'I want to earn your admiration for my elegance as well as my valour,' he breathed in her ear. 'You will be proud of your son-in-law, ma Mère. I intend to be the victor.'

'You may find the English lords intend the same, Francis,' Mary told him lightly, adding, as she remembered Charles's skill in the lists. 'Perhaps you'll find the elegance easier to achieve.'

'I will take that as a compliment, Mary. I know you intended it as such. As yet, you have no knowledge of my prowess.' His tone of voice implied that the prowess to which he was referring was not the prowess of the lists, but another sort entirely, so his passionate promise of, 'that lack shall soon be remedied', filled her with foreboding.

But she kept her voice steady as Francis' hand again strayed to her neck and recommenced its fondling, and asked, 'When shall the joust be held?'

'In November. After you have made your entry into Paris. You will forget your sadness when you see me triumphant.'

Francis' confidence amused her. She asked him if he had not heard of the valour of the English lords.

'But you are French now, Mary You must cheer the French lords on to victory, not the English. This French lord, in particular, will be grateful for it. I hope you will honour me by giving me your sleeve to wear in the lists.'

Mary decided it would be wise to rebuff him. 'But I may favour another's victory and would perhaps prefer to promise my sleeve elsewhere.'

Francis drew back in mock astonishment at her rejection. 'Tell me who is this scoundrel who expects your favour?'

When Mary refused to tell him, he became thoughtful. 'Is it San Severino? I know his elegance must have impressed you. Or perhaps it is de Longueville? He was in England for many months.' Francis went down on his knees before her, apparently determined not to give up on his ardent wooing, in spite of Mary's equally determined rebuffs. 'Tell me it is not de Longueville, ma Mère, I beg you.'

'Please get off your knees, Francis. You will hole your elegant hose.'

Francis gave a Gallic shrug for his hose. 'If you don't tell me who will wear your favour, I will discover his name for myself, by whatever means necessary.'

His gallantries were becoming more impassioned and noisy and Mary told him to be quiet or he would waken the king.

Francis lowered his voice, but was no less importunate. 'Please, Mary. Tell me his name.'

Exasperated, Mary asked, 'Why should it mean so much to you, Francis? You have a wife, after all. Surely you should wear Claude's sleeve, not mine?'

Francis gave another shrug that said his marriage and his wife were no more important to him than his elegant hose. 'Naturally, I will wear my wife's sleeve. That is duty and is expected of me. But I may also wear your sleeve. That would not be a duty, but a delight.'

Mary reminded him she was now his mother. Did he not call her 'Ma Mère' in every other sentence? 'If you must wear another sleeve it should be that of a lady you admire, not your mother's,' she told him. From the gossip her ladies had recounted, Francis didn't lack for female company; his many amours were an open scandal at the French court. Mary, brought up, first in her father's chaste and serious court and then in her brother's, felt shocked at the number of liaisons that abounded. Now, it seemed Francis was eager to add her name to the list of his conquests.

He was persistent. 'There is no one here I admire more than you. For beside your golden beauty all other ladies look like dark crows. Promise me your favour, Madam,' he repeated. Still on his knees beside her, face inches from hers, he took her hands and kissed them fervently.

Mary rescued her hands from his kisses. She felt out of her depth and didn't know how best to rebuff him. She still refused to give him her favour and he had to be satisfied with her promise that she wouldn't give it to de Longueville, either.

Francis' dark countenance was hung with sorrow. But with a true gallant's grace, he smiled and kissed her hand again. His, 'Alors, Madam, I confess I will be satisfied with whatever you choose to give me,' should have reassured her. But the way his smouldering glances continued to devour her made a lie of his pretty speech.

To her relief, before Francis could attempt more gallantries, Louis woke up. Mary fetched the drink he asked for and held the goblet to his lips as he took a few mouthfuls. 'How are you feeling now?' she asked. 'Has the pain eased?'

Louis assured her that he was much improved. 'I told the physicians the sight of your face would make me better.'

Mary smiled. Louis was as keen on gallantries as his son-in-law. Somehow, she couldn't find it in her heart to hate him for his behaviour. His poor health would make him less able to stand out against the demands of his quarrelsome courtiers.

Behind her, Francis still hovered. And when Louis spoke to him he stepped out of the shadows.

'Your Grace. May I help you sit up?'

'No, no.' Francis was waved away. 'I want you to inform the court they must get ready for our departure. I feel well enough now to go on to St Denis.'

'Are you sure, Louis? So soon? Are you quite well enough yet?'

Mary's anxious, wifely questions seemed to startle Louis. But he immediately reassured her. 'But yes, ma Cherie. Thank you for your solicitude, but we must get you crowned, little wife, must we not, Francis?' Louis gave his son-in-law a sly look that indicated he was not unaware of Francis' gallantries towards Mary, but which said equally clearly that Louis and not he, was in possession.

Francis seemed to take no umbrage at Louis' sly look. Time was on his side, after all, not the king's. Lady Guildford had told Mary that his mother's spies had soon discovered Louis' lack as a husband, so he could afford to be patient.

'But of course, your Grace,' Francis said. 'It would be a shame to delay. The Queen's beauty will grace the crown. The Parisians will go wild when they see her.'

Louis looked satisfied and took Mary's hand. 'He is right, of course. They will think me a lucky dog.' He patted her hand. 'I have a present for you, Mary.'

'Another present, Louis? You will spoil me, I fear.'

'You should be spoiled and cherished and spoiled some more,' he told her gruffly. 'I know I'm a sick and gouty old man and people think us ill-matched, but you make me very happy, my dear.'

'I'm glad, Louis.' Mary squeezed his hand and was rather startled to find that she meant what she had said. Of course, she could never love him as she loved Charles, that would be impossible. But she was becoming fond of him. She would try to make him happy for the short time his poor health looked likely to leave him.

'Fetch me the box by the window, please, my dear. The silver one,' Louis instructed. When she had done so, he lifted the lid and removed a long rope of breath-taking pearls, lustrous and beautifully matched. Louis held them against Mary's skin and told her, 'Aye, they like you, ma Cherie. They glow more beautifully already. Pearls pine and lose their sheen if they are not worn by a young and beautiful woman.' He fastened them round Mary's neck, then looked at her expectantly. 'Do you like them, Mary?'

'How could I not, Louis?' she asked him. 'They are delightful. Thank you. I shall treasure them.' Gently, she kissed his leathery cheek. 'You are good to me.'

'How could I be otherwise?' He lowered his voice for her ears alone. 'I was denied beauty in a wife all my young years and now I have the beauty when I am too old to please her with my body. So I must please her in other ways. It is ironic, is it not? The good Lord must have his little joke, alas.' Louis chuckled ruefully, gave her cheek a fond pinch and asked her to play for him again.

Mary bowed her head, picked up her lute and began to play as Louis' gentlemen came in to light the candles. And whilst Mary's voice and music once more lulled her sickly husband into a restful sleep, she was tautly conscious of

Francis' close proximity, his ardent gaze and the way his hands stroked hers, as he pretended to help her pluck the new French tunes from her lute.

CHAPTER SEVEN

The horses stamped their feet in the chill morning air as the trunks and boxes of Mary's ladies and gentlemen were loaded on to the wagons. Louis had wasted no time in ordering their departure, thought Mary, though in spite of his demand that Francis organise the court's move to Paris it was still at Abbeville; Louis having to retire to his bed again after an over-hasty rising. Mary suspected his relapse was at least partly politic. He was scared her tears would weaken his resolve to be rid of Lady Guildford and the rest.

Louis wasn't alone in being hurt by his own orders. All the upset seemed to have aged her Mother Guildford also. She felt her dismissal keenly, regarding it as a disgrace. After her angry tirade against Louis had run its course she had taken to sitting quietly ruminating, no longer even rebuking the chattering young Maids in her previous imperious manner. Mary had never seen her so withdrawn. She had already said her goodbyes to the rest of her dismissed attendants and they had tactfully left the chamber, so Mary and Lady Guildford could make their goodbyes in private.

Mary gave her old guardian a loving hug and said as optimistically as she could manage, 'Cheer up, Mother. You may return to me yet. I'm still working on Louis and we have yet to hear from my brother and Wolsey.'

'Nay, child. King Louis will not change his mind. He has taken a dislike to me.' With a brief spark of her previous spirit, she added, 'but not nearly as great as the dislike I've taken to him, for the gouty old fool that he is—king or no king.'

Mary, glad to see a little of her Mother's verve return, but anxious that Lady Guildford's comments were not reported back to Louis, warned, 'Hush, now, Mother. You know royal palaces have ears.'

'Bah, what does it matter now if he knows my mind? He's too fond of you, for all that he has dismissed me and the rest, to wish to cause you more hurt and I'm returning to your brother's dominions, out of reach of any punishment. It's King Henry's wrath I fear, not the French King's.'

Astonished to discover this previously concealed worry, Mary said, 'Henry wouldn't do anything to harm you, Mother. He knows how close I am to you. Anyway, if he's received my letter he should be in no doubt as to where to lay the blame and it will not be on your head. Will you believe me on this?'

Lady Guildford nodded. 'Aye, child, I'll believe you, but mayhap you ought to write another letter lest the first needs a friend to support it.' Lady Guildford's eyes managed a little twinkle of mischief and although they laughed the laughter of both was very close to tears and they were soon serious once more.

'Tis a shame you won't be here for my coronation, Mother and the joust which the Duc de Valois is arranging. He told me there are likely to be many English arriving shortly.'

'Then it's to be hoped that popinjay, de Valois gets a sound thrashing from our lords. His opinion of himself is a deal too high for me.'

Mary, whose relationship with Francis involved a fine balancing act of, on the one hand, needing to retain his much-needed friendship at a hostile court and on the other, rebuffing his continued attempts to seduce her, felt compelled to defend him. 'He has been very kind to me, wondrously kind when you consider that he could with justification consider me the enemy. With Louis always so sick the court would be dull indeed if Francis wasn't here.'

'All the same, my lady, you want to be careful of that young man. If Louis succeeds in his duty and gets a son from you, the child would stand between Francis and the throne. A dangerous position for a vulnerable infant—and his mother.'

Shocked, Mary said, 'Francis would be incapable of doing me or any babe I might have any hurt.'

'Maybe. But his mother would not be. Louise of Savoy would let nothing come between her only son and the throne of France. Just be on your guard, child.'

The warning sent a shiver down Mary's spine, but she managed to shake it off. After all, as she told her Mother, she was unlikely to get any sons from Louis. Since his exertions on their wedding night he had been too sickly to attempt anything. 'I've had my flux since so I'm doubly sure I've no heir in my belly.'

'Just as well then, for I fear Louis would be unable to protect you. Francis seems to rule here now. The court looks to be just waiting for Louis to die in fact.

'He's already all but dead in reality. He looks a little sicker each day. I've said it to you before, lady, now I say it again—get yourself crowned as quickly as possible. Then, if Louis dies you won't be dependent on your brother. As a crowned Dowager-Queen, you'll have a large enough income to be independent of him.'

Lady Guildford was full of doom-laden warnings and Mary told her so. 'It's sad enough that you are all going home to England and leaving me here. Don't, I pray you, leave me with fears and suspicions for company instead.'

'I was but warning you, child. You are a deal too trusting. But you are right to chastise me. Come, give me a kiss before I go.'

After their embrace, she rose straight-backed from her seat and strode to the window. 'We should have got moving long before this. Half the day's gone already.'

In spite of her imminent departure, Mary was pleased to note that Lady Guildford retained enough vigor to criticise French incompetence. But it was a half-hearted criticism, voiced, Mary suspected, only to conceal other emotions. Mary's emotions were not so easily concealed and now the time for parting had finally arrived, she was overcome with a sense of loss. She flung herself into Lady Guildford's arms and gave herself up to a storm of weeping. Her Mother's warnings had brought home to her how vulnerable she would be. Strangely, she hasn't realised quite how much she had depended upon Lady Guildford's calm, authoritative presence till she was about to lose it.

Lady Guildford made her dry her tears. 'You don't want all the court to see you in such a taking. As your gouty husband says, you're a woman now and a Queen and must behave as such. Always remember the duty due to your rank. The less emotion you show the world the stronger you will appear.' Lady Guildford tutted, 'but there, you were always a headstrong, emotional child. Promise me, Mary, you'll restrain any impetuous actions should aught befall Louis.'

Her Mother's concern brought a fresh flow of tears from Mary. She clung to Lady Guildford as if she would never let her go.

But Lady Guildford was made of sterner stuff. She pushed Mary from her, gathered the last of her possessions and walked to the door. When Mary made to follow her, she stopped her. 'We've said our goodbyes, my lady. You don't want the entire court to see your red eyes. You can watch our departing from the window.' Lady Guildford paused at the door to add a blessing, 'May God watch over you. Goodbye, child,' before she went out, closing the door firmly behind her.

Bereft, Mary remained where she stood. She felt the urge to run after her, but knew Lady Guildford was right. The court knew how distressed she was at this parting, why display first-hand evidence of it? Instead, Mary raced to the window and was just in time to see Lady Guildford climb into her litter. Mary waved frantically. She felt desolate and terribly alone as the head of the train moved off, the rest slowly following in its wake. All too soon, the last wagon disappeared from sight. Her Mother Guildford was gone. Apart from the youngest Maids of Honour and the few English diplomats she was now all but alone in France.

Mary never knew how she got through the next few days. They passed in a misty blur. But then, emotionally exhausted, she finally slept soundly and when she woke on the third morning she felt calmer, determined to behave with dignity as her Mother had bade her. She called her remaining ladies to her and spoke to them. She had only young girls left to her out of the large retinue of titled ladies who had accompanied her to France. Not one of them was old enough to have acquired Lady Guildford's wisdom and Mary surveyed them sadly; the ladies Mary and Anne Boleyn, the latter having joined her from Margaret of Austria's court, Anne Grey and Elizabeth Grey, Mary Fenes and Mistress Anne Jerningham, her Femme de Chambre and Jean Barnes her Chamberiere. Few enough indeed, and lacking experience, but they were all she had so she must make the best of them.

Falteringly, Mary began to address them. 'Ladies, we are now on our own. 'It's sad, but it would have happened some time, so we must all learn self-reliance.'

'Will Lady Guildford not be returning, then, your Grace?' asked Mary Boleyn, the bolder of the two Boleyn sisters. 'I thought—'

'Tis unlikely,' Mary replied. 'So we must all help and support each other. You older girls must look to the younger and restrain any foolishness. The court will be watching us to see how we conduct ourselves.' Mary smiled at Anne Boleyn, the baby of the group. She was young to be away from home, but Anne's father was over-ambitious for his children and at an age when she should still have been with her family, he had despatched her to foreign courts to learn some polish and make her more marriageable. In this, Mary thought Anne would need all the help she could get. As thin as a stick and with unfashionable dark looks, Anne's chances of finding a husband weren't great and were not improved by her shabby gown. Gently, Mary upbraided her. 'Anne, your gown looks too short for you. You must change it before we dine.'

Anne's sallow skin blushed unbecomingly and the other Maids giggled.

Mary Fenes explained the girl's discomfiture. 'Please Madam,' she said. 'All Anne's other gowns are the same. She has grown too fast for her them and is unlikely to get more.'

The other girls giggled again. The awkward and gangly Anne looked as if she wanted the floor to open and swallow her.

Mary felt guilty that, with her other concerns, she had failed to notice Anne's want of suitable gowns till now. She took pity on the girl. 'Never mind, Anne. I have a number of gowns of the plainer sort. Perhaps you can make some over to fit you. Come, let us see what there is.'

Without Lady Guildford to rebuke them, Mary's Maids turned out her trunks and boxes with a girlish enthusiasm and soon the floor and the bed were buried under a multi-coloured pile of silks, rich brocades and cloth of gold and silver as well as gowns made of other, less costly stuff. Finally, three of Mary's less grand gowns were found that, with some small alterations, would fit the girl reasonably well. Mary was pleased, though she noticed that Anne, although she accepted Mary's cast-offs readily enough, was looking decidedly stiff-necked. Mary put it down to the unkind teasing of the other Maids and thought no more of it. Anne, she had noticed before, had a tendency to keep herself aloof, probably in humiliated reaction to the far from aloof behaviour of her elder sister. For all of Lady Guildford's rebukes, Mary Boleyn had already gained a wanton's reputation at the French court. The younger girl was shy, too, conscious of her immaturity and lack of the pink and white skin that commanded universal admiration. Still, Mary consoled herself, the gowns would look well on her and be a vast improvement on the chit's own clothes.

Mary left the Maids to tidy her gowns away and wandered to the window. As she gazed out on the bleak winter's day, she found herself again envying the Anne Boleyn whose only worry was the fit of her gowns. Mary had so many other things with which to concern herself. Louis' health had taken a turn for the worst since their marriage and she knew the courtiers blamed her for it. Had he not taken up a young man's customs as he had said he would? His previous early hours replaced by late ones in order to please her.

It was unfair that she should be blamed for this. Did they expect her to retire to bed at six of the evening as had previously been Louis' custom? Perhaps they did, for she had heard it whispered about the court that the King of England had sent his sister to the King of France the more speedily and gently to carry him to Heaven or Hell. It was a wicked slander and made her sound like some kind of angel of death.

She had been deprived of her love, deprived of the familiar faces of her older ladies and now blamed for Louis' weakened health. Had ever a young girl come more swiftly than she to a realisation of the cares of a queen? Francis was just one of these cares. He had become bolder since Lady Guildford's departure. Before, he had been satisfied with mildly amusing flirtation. But now, his gallantries were daily becoming more risqué and his fondling touch was less easily fended off. She had seen him and de Longueville whispering conspiratorially together, as though plotting some intrigue and from the glances they had directed at her as she had entered the room, she had felt convinced their plotting involved her. It made her uneasy. An uneasiness made worse by the behaviour of the rest of the courtiers who were prone to whispering together and casting speculative, side-long glances at her. It seemed only she and Louis were ignorant of what they discussed, though Mary thought she could guess well enough the subject of the conversations.

Had not Lady Guildford wisely bid her to behave with modesty at the French court? Mary wished she had followed this stricture when she had first arrived. For her innocent amusement at Francis' witty gallantries had only served to encourage him. Daily she endured the humiliating gossip concerning her and Francis. And daily, Francis compounded the gossip. Only this morning he had pursued her into the gardens where she had gone in desperation to gain some peace from all the gossiping lips and prying eyes. She had slipped out of a side door, unseen, she had thought, and found a bench in a quiet, deserted little arbor. It was quite sheltered. The relentless rain had stopped for several hours. The sun had even come out and warmed her face and she had leant back and closed her eyes. Only to have them fly open again seconds later, as, from above her, two muscular arms embraced her and lips swooped down hard and possessive on hers.

Even upside-down, Francis' saturnine face was unmistakable. He had her trapped. She couldn't move. She could only sit and struggle as his lips moved to her throat, to her bosom as it strained from her gown. She had told him to stop. Demanded he let her go. 'You must not—'

For a moment she had thought he was about to obey her, for he released her arms. But it was only so that he could embrace her closer still. He vaulted over the back of the bench and sat down beside her, pressing her against the wooden arm.

'Oh, but I must, ma Cherie. I surely must.' He kissed her again and buried his head in her bosom. His hand followed the trail of kisses. Soon, it was deep inside her bodice and beginning to explore.

Mary grabbed his wrist and tried to pull his hand away. To her surprise, she succeeded. But it was only because he had another target in mind. He dragged her skirts above her knees. She felt his hand slide along her thigh.

For a brief moment, she was free of his restraining arm. She took the opportunity to break away from him. She leapt from her seat, straightening her gown as she did so. She didn't linger to give him the chance to reach for her again, but picked up her skirts and ran as fast as she could for the safety of Louis' bed-chamber.

How strange it was, Mary thought later as she was dressing for supper, the sharp voices of her French ladies clucking, ignored around her. The one man she wanted to make passionate love to her did not dare. While Francis would dare anything, even the risk of fathering his own usurper. Of course, he was in his own country, which would probably, quite soon, literally *be* his own country. In truth, he dared little in his demanding clamour to possess her—only her shame and possibly war over her honour if Henry should hear of his doings. But then, as Francis seemed as lusty over the thought of war as he was over her, such a possibility was no deterrent.

A true innocent abroad, Mary had been astonished to find how full of intrigues and love affairs was the court of France. The younger courtiers followed Francis' lead and indulged in wild, passionate affairs right under Louis' nose. It was only Anne of France's vicious insults at the banquet that followed the French marriage ceremony that made Mary realise she was suspected of following their example with Francis, suspicions further encouraged by Francis' ungallant failure to deny they were having an affair.

With Louis so ill and retiring Francis had taken more to himself the mantle of kingship. His behaviour was making her increasingly nervous. What had begun light-heartedly enough for Mary, had, for Francis, turned into a deep and abiding passion which no words of hers had been able to cool. And although she tried to keep him at arm's length, Francis was unused to rejection and simply ignored her pleas that he stop.

He openly caressed her in public and was extremely blatant about his feelings for her, brushing aside her protests with the ease of long practise. His attitude made it clear that - with her protectors gone from the court and her elderly husband so sickly and retiring - he felt there were now none to say him nay. Wherever she went, he pursued her. He would back her against a wall, a pillar or a tree and force kisses on her, his hands fondling her all the while. In spite of his youth, his experienced love-making left her breathless. Mary knew he had mistresses and was determined not to become one of them. Thus far he had stopped short of forcing himself on her. Mary suspected this was simply because Francis' pride in his lover's skills would want her willing. But how long he would hold off before he had her, willing or no...

She was only saved from his ardent pursuit by Louis' desire that she spend much of her time at his side. He liked her to play the lute and sing for him. Mary was glad to do this. At least in Louis' presence she was safe from Francis' ardor.

She found herself often wishing that Louis' health would hurry up and improve, for on days when he felt well he would rise and sit late at the supper table to watch her dance with his nobles. He was doing this increasingly, whether he felt well or ill, which only increased the courtiers' hostility and Mary's guilt. But whatever she said, Louis was determined, with his later and later hours, to prove to himself, his courtiers and to Mary herself that he was worthy of her, even though he should really be taking it easy and convalescing after his latest attack of gout. She wondered if his determination was sparked by rumours of Francis' behaviour towards her?

Whether it was or not, at least it seemed unlikely that he believed the gossip circulating in the court concerning her morals, for he continued to shower her with jewels as though convinced they would make up to her for his lack as a husband. Rich rubies, diamonds, emeralds and sapphires went to join the pearls and the *Miroir* in her jewel-boxes. Never a day went by when he didn't give her several costly gifts. Mary accepted them in the spirit in which they were given. She felt they were her reward for what she had already lost and for what she was now forced to endure. For not only had she to suffer Francis' intolerable familiarity and the gossip of the rest of the court, she had also to be in constant attendance on her husband. It was her distasteful task to apply ointments of Deadly Nightshade or Hemlock to his limbs to try to reduce the inflammation. Louis would allow none but her to do this. He claimed no one was as gentle as she, so it became her regular task. He would lie quietly as she rubbed the foul stuff into his misshapen feet, doing her best to hide her revulsion. Louis at least, thought well of her. He was grateful for her ministrations and would frequently declare that no one had such a kind and loving wife as he.

At least no one could say she failed in this wifely duty. For at last, her care of him seemed to have the desired effect. Everything was finally set in motion for the court's removal to St Denis and her long-delayed coronation.

The courtly train moved slowly, in deference to Louis' recent travails. They eventually reached Beauvais on their way to St Denis, where they remained for several days for Louis to gather strength for the remainder of the journey. Mary was in attendance on him as usual, when he casually mentioned something that made her catch her breath.

'We are to have a visitor, my dear,' he told her. 'Someone from England. I am sure he will have much news for you from your brother's court. It will make a pleasant change for you from these onerous nursing duties I put on you.'

'What is the gentleman's name, Louis?' Mary asked. She was increasingly desperate for news from home. Louis told her. Mary's heart lurched. She couldn't believe it at first. But when Louis repeated the name, she realised there was no mistake. Charles, her lost love, was coming here. Her first instinct was to rejoice that he would save her from Francis' intolerable behaviour. But then, as reality hit, her rush of joy drained away. She could never let anyone suspect her feelings for Charles. How she would manage to conceal them from the sharp eyes of Louis' courtiers, she knew not. She would worry about that later. For now, all that mattered was that she would see him again. It might be her last chance.

CHAPTER EIGHT

Since learning that her brother was sending Charles to the French court to speak to Louis about her dismissed English train and other matters, Mary had become very emotional, prone to bursting into tears at the least thing. So as she watched the door open and Charles Brandon, Duke of Suffolk and the Marquis of Dorset enter Louis' bed-chamber, Mary was torn between bursting into tears or leaping for joy.

But she could afford neither emotion. She was able to gain some control as they walked to Louis and knelt to pay homage. Louis made much of them, warmly embracing them and bidding them a hearty welcome. She scarcely dared to look at Charles, much less catch his eye. All she could do was glance at him under her lashes, marvel anew at his height and breadth and compare him to the poor aged and gouty husband who had once again taken to his bed.

'How goes my brother, King Henry, my lord?' Louis asked Charles. 'He is well, I trust?'

'Aye, your Grace. The king is in robust health.'

Mary bit back a fond smile at Charles's less-than-diplomatic response to her ailing husband. But then he had never had Francis' smooth courtly skills. Mary thought the better of him for it.

Charles hastened to make good his error. 'King Henry sends his regards and his thanks for the love you show his sister.'

Even to hear his voice, so strong and manly was like a balm to the sore-pressed Mary. Charles's gaze had strayed in Mary's direction as he spoke of her and their eyes locked. Mary looked hastily away. Thankfully, Louis appeared to notice nothing amiss. His next words showed he was more interested in topping Henry's gracious good wishes than aught else.

'My Lord of Suffolk, I promise you that if there is any-thing I can do for my good brother's pleasure, I shall not spare myself till it is done. Has he not given me the greatest jewel in his kingdom? What more could one prince give an-other?'

When Louis bade his visitors rise from their knees and greet her Mary sat hardly daring to move a muscle in case it betrayed her. But as Charles repeated Henry's loving mes-sages, she felt herself blush. To hear words of love on Charles's lips, even if he was delivering them from another, was something she had feared she would never hear again. It was too much and she swallowed the sudden lump in her throat. Daring her emotions to do their worst, she extended her hand for a kiss. Heat raced up her arm as his firm lips brushed her hand.

'Are you to stay for the joust, my lords?' Mary asked. She had herself under control now and the tremor in her voice was barely noticeable. 'I believe it is to be a great spectacle, many of our countrymen are expected to attend.' Her glance up at Charles was her undoing. Her heart, its feelings concealed for so long, gave a lurch. How handsome he looked. As tall and broad as Henry himself, he towered above her. His manliness made her feel weak and it was as well she was seated or her knees might have buckled under the weight of her feelings.

Still apparently oblivious to the wild tumult of her emotions, Louis added his urgings to Mary's, before beckoning over a page and sending him off with a message for Francis.

Francis was at his most charming when he arrived and assured the English visitors he would be delighted to have them as his Aides for the joust. Ruefully, he said, 'Her Majesty has told me of the valour of her brother's nobles and their skill on the field. She thinks I am full of conceit of myself, is that no so ma Mère?' Francis raised a reproachful eyebrow at Mary.

She didn't rise to his bait. 'The joust will reveal the valour of French and English alike, my lord,' she told him, 'better than any protestations you or I can make. Let victory go to the man who has the strength to seize it.' She raised her chin and gazed challengingly at Francis. But after a few seconds of meeting his gaze, she couldn't prevent her own from sliding past him to gaze with adoring eyes on Charles. Francis - never slow in matters of the heart - intercepted her glance. His frown and quick assessment of Charles's face and figure indicated he had guessed where Mary, with that spe-

cial aura of a woman in love, intended to bestow her favour
for the forthcoming joust.

Worried what the jealous Francis' would do if he suspected the depth of her love for Charles, Mary watched anxiously
as Francis took Charles's arm in a seeming-friendly manner
and bore him and Dorset off to supper. Forced to remain and
play nursemaid to Louis, Mary could only wonder, as their
meal was served in Louis' chamber, what other discoveries
the wily Francis might be making. And although half of her
wished to be present to hear what was said, the other half
felt relieved to have a few quiet hours. She needed to adjust
her composure if she was to bear herself with dignity. At the
moment, she knew that concealing her feelings from the in-
trusive eyes of the entire court would prove impossible.

Mary was saved from possible self-betrayal because Charles
and the other English visitors only remained for the one day
at Beauvais with the court before Francis and the other
young courtiers persuaded them off on a hunting trip. She
wouldn't see Charles again till they met up with the court at
Paris. And, much as she longed to see more of her love, the
circumstances of the situation urged discretion. If Francis
hadn't already guessed the situation between her and
Charles, his inquisitive nature would not be long in coming
to the correct assessment if he saw the two of them together
more frequently.

It made her angry, bitter at the fates and her brother and
all that made such a mockery of their love that she must keep

it not only silent but secret, as if it were something shameful. When she longed to shout about it from the rooftops.

Fortunately, Mary hadn't time to dwell on such thoughts for Louis claimed her attention. He was excited about the joust and frequently cursed the gouty limbs that prevented him from taking part; Francis wasn't the only one who wished to shine in her eyes. Poor Louis, he had to rely on his gifts of costly jewels to do his shining for him.

As he told Mary, all his good fortunes seemed to come too late; his kingship when too old and his beautiful wife when too sick. He felt he had never been able to properly enjoy either. Mary knew how deeply he envied her brother who, although he as yet lacked a male heir, just like Louis, had not only time enough to get one, but also had handsome looks and the vigor to enjoy his good fortune to the full.

Beside her, Louis' sigh made Mary wonder uneasily if he was thinking of trying again to at least best Henry in one thing—the getting of a male heir. But she didn't dare to mention the issue in case Louis felt obliged to take up the challenge. His health was a safer topic, so Mary decided to interpret his sigh as pertaining to mere mundane physical matters and asked him if he was ailing again.

He denied it. 'I was just wishing I had my youth back again.' He gave Mary a rueful smile. 'I wish to impress you too, you see.'

Touched, she tried to console him with a gentle reminder. 'But if you had your youth back you wouldn't have me. So you wouldn't be able to impress me—which you do, anyway, with your many kindnesses.'

'Ah, the logic of youth. So direct and to the point. But you speak truth, ma belle. I must thank God for my many blessings, of which you are the greatest.'

For all his words about counting his blessings, Louis still sounded wistful and although Mary didn't love Louis she had come to like him well enough and she tried again to offer some consolation. 'Skill at the quintain and the butts aren't the only attributes to be valued in a man,' she told him. 'A warm heart also has value.'

Louis smiled tenderly at this. 'You speak kindly to an old man, little wife. But you are young and naturally admire the gifts of youth.'

Mary, thinking he, too, had correctly interpreted her glance at Charles, hurried to deny it. But Louis simply shook his head at her denials. ''Tis the way of the world, Mary. Youth is stirred by youth. 'Tis natural. I am not chastising you, my love. You are right to admire your friends from England. I want you to enjoy life to the full. I am an old man, I have had my life and my youth with all its joys. How could I deny you a little innocent amusement?' He chuckled. 'I enjoyed my youth to the full and my pleasures weren't always very innocent.'

Startled, Mary wondered whether he was subtly giving her permission to indulge her physical passion for Charles. She didn't know what to say, but thought it best to say nothing in case she had read his message wrongly.

'I know it must be difficult to believe, Mary, but I, too, had my share of amours, much as Francis does now, in his youth.' Louis gazed fondly at her. 'I hope he isn't too gallant with you, my dear. I've noticed him looking at you and have to admire his taste. My poor little daughter, Claude, has nothing to offer a man like Francis; only the wealth she shall inherit when I die. Unlucky girl, neither of her parents was blessed with beauty.'

'But Claude has many good qualities, Louis. She is kind and loving, like her father and she has the sweetest disposition.' Too sweet for her own good, Mary thought. Poor Claude, to be married to a man like Francis. And even though their marriage, like her own, had been made for reasons of state, poor fat, plain, deformed Claude loved her philandering husband deeply. It was too cruel. Claude had the man she loved but he didn't love her and Mary loved a man she couldn't have. Mary was only sorry that her own thoughtless behaviour and Francis' passion for her should cause Claude more heartache.

Since Louis had mentioned Francis' interest in her, Mary seized the opportunity to confide in him and get him to put a stop to it and thereby save both Claude and herself from further distress. But after a few faltering sentences, she realised that Louis hadn't intended to invite her confidences or complaints, much less put a stop to Francis' pursuit of her. It was clear he didn't really want to be bothered. His poor health gave him no energy for anger or jealous passion. Anyway, she knew that any emotional upset had a detrimental effect on his health. He had spoken earlier about getting up from his sick bed; she didn't want to be the cause of setting back his recovery. If she did it would mean she would once more be at Francis' mercy and be on the receiving end of more acid criticism from the courtiers.

As though to console her for failing to champion her, Louis reached for a box at his bedside and proceeded to shower her with yet more gifts. 'At least, in this, I can beat Francis,' he told her. 'He is not in a position to shower anyone with jewellery. His mother holds the purse strings. He has little money of his own; nor will he have till I oblige him by dying.'

But it seemed that, for the time being at least, Louis had put aside thoughts of death. He kissed and caressed her and took his pleasure on her as much as his ailing manhood would allow. Mary bore his roaming hands with as much stoicism as she could muster, shutting out Louis' face and replacing it with that of Charles. Though she couldn't help but wonder how much longer the situation would endure and whether one day soon Louis would regain his manhood and set seriously about getting himself a male heir. Or whether the demanding and increasingly reckless Francis would force himself on her and beat Louis to it, as his mother feared.

Travelling in easy stages, the court finally arrived at St Denis at the end of October. Louis recalled the English ambassadors and was closeted with them for hours.

Mary knew that Louis and Henry were planning a meeting and the details were still being haggled over. She was excluded from their meetings and had, instead, a far more daunting task; that of greeting Francis' mother, Louise of Savoy, who had returned to court to witness Mary's coronation. Francis had told her that his mother had retired from the court because in her ambitions for him she couldn't bear to watch the way he pursued Mary, thereby risking his own future as well as that of his family.

At thirty-eight, Louis of Savoy still retained her youthful good looks and the light auburn of her hair. Slim, in spite of her pregnancies, unlike Henry's poor Catherine, she carried herself proudly and wore an air of gravity, which Mary tried hard to emulate. Although she greeted Mary politely and made homage to her as queen, Mary was conscious of her slate-blue eyes as they rested on her belly and the snap of satisfaction they wore as she studied its flatness.

Louise of Savoy was gracious, but Mary sensed the undercurrents, knowing their cause only too well. How could Louise not feel antagonistic towards her when any pregnancy of Mary's could oust her beloved Francis from the succession? Her spies, too, would have informed her that Francis still continued his dangerous and foolhardy wooing. Mary could guess at what Louise would feel should Francis press his intentions to the ultimate and succeed only in costing himself the throne.

Mary hoped his mother's arrival would stem Francis's ardor. She knew they were a close family and ambitious for the throne. Between them, his sister, Marguerite, and his mother would surely manage to convince Francis of the dangers inherent in his behaviour.

While Louise of Savoy and Mary batted conversation back and forth, their real thoughts concealed beneath a veil of politeness, for a brief moment, Mary saw beyond the grave

slate blue gaze to the turbulent emotions that their determined gravity concealed. And as she caught a glimmer of
Louise's true feelings towards her she felt a tremor of fear.
This woman would do her harm if she could, she realised, if
she looked likely to threaten her high hopes for her son.

The thought unnerved Mary and made her even more
wary. Louis wouldn't save her. Kindly, but sometimes foolish, Louis would be no match for this determined woman and
the strength of her maternal ambition. It made Mary even
more thankful that her womb was empty. And as she remembered Lady Guildford's warning, before her departure,
of the dangers of her situation, she felt a shiver of dread. She
must pray that her womb remained empty. Because if it
didn't there was no knowing of what Louise of Savoy might
not be capable.

The day of Mary's coronation had arrived. Delayed by Louis'
poor health, it wasn't till the 5th of November, a Sunday,
that she was escorted to the Abbey Church of St Denis by
Francis and his fellow nobles. She walked slowly up to the
altar, doing her best to ignore Francis' amorous whispers;
his mother's arrival had, unfortunately, failed to stem his
ardor. She saw Charles, her love, standing in the choir stall
beside the altar. He gave her a reassuring smile. She didn't
dare to smile back. There were so many curious eyes on her
that she hardly dared look at him. Instead, she looked for
Louis and found him seated above Charles as a private spec-
tator, watching her and following the ceremony from his
closet window.

Mary knelt before the altar and after Cardinal De Pre had anointed her, he put the sceptre in her right hand and the verge of justice in her left. Then, he put a ring on her finger and the great crown of Jane of Navarre on her head.

Mary swayed under its weight, but quickly steadied. After her crowning, Francis led her up to a raised platform to a chair of state under the canopy of the throne, by the altar. Mary sat down cautiously, worried in case she dislodged the crown. Already her neck was aching from the weight of it. Her nerves had been stretched taut as bow strings lately and the near presence of Charles did little to relax her; an anxiety not helped by Francis' speculative glances from one to the other as though trying to gauge how far the love between them had advanced.

Matters weren't helped by the presence, amongst her few remaining English Maids of Honour, of Mary Boleyn. The elder Boleyn girl had proved appallingly flighty and as different from her virtuous younger sister as it was possible to be. She had already served her turn in Francis' bed and that of a number of the courtiers. Her reputation for promiscuity reflected back on Mary and her other English Maids of Honour and did little to incline Francis to believe in or respect her own virtue. She would have sent the girl back to England but for the fact that, if she did, Mary Boleyn would doubtless be replaced by another spying Frenchwoman.

But at least these ladies now saw how false was the gossip about Mary's virtue. Previously believed by them to be an immoral slut, they had performed a volte-face and their whispers, when they believed she could not overhear them, told her they now believed her to be a foolish virgin, too stupid to usurp Francis, the king-to-be, with his own bastard and so continue on the throne after Louis' death as Regent for her son. They marvelled at her failure to grasp her opportunity. Even Francis had told her she would profit from studying at the feet of Mary Boleyn. 'She has taken easily to our French ways,' he had told her. 'Sometimes, her behaviour even shocks me.' Though he had not been so shocked that he had neglected to take the wanton Boleyn girl to his bed.

She wondered what her immoral French ladies would say if they knew she would give it all up tomorrow for love of the low-born Charles Brandon? Had she not learned that, at the French court, lust was called love while the lust lasted and that constancy and true affection were faults to be sniggered at? She had learned that so base were the morals of the sophisticated French that no child could be certain who was his father.

As the lengthy ceremony continued Mary's thoughts moved on to the previous weeks' events. Her life had become even more difficult and complicated after the arrival at court of Charles and Louise of Savoy. The pleasure she got from just knowing Charles was close by was over-shadowed by the presence of Louise, whose eyes were as sharp as her son's and well able to ferret out their secret passion. Worse, being female, Louise of Savoy had even more opportunity than Francis for snooping. In her own way, she was as dangerous as her son. Mary knew that her every word, every look, smile and gesture were intercepted, speculated upon and squeezed dry for significance.

Francis' attentions, too, were becoming more and more pressing; even now, during the solemn coronation ceremony, he stood too close. The court was rife with gossip about his passion for her. Mary had heard rumours that he had even planned to invade her bed-chamber and seduce her. Fortunately for her peace of mind, it seemed a more cautious friend had persuaded him from it.

Thwarted in his desires, his jealousy of Charles only increased and he had caused Claude, his young wife, to be placed with Mary. She was rarely alone, even at night. And as she now seldom shared Louis' bed, Francis and his mother had arranged for one of Louise's ladies to sleep in her chamber. Each had their own motives, of course. Francis determined to ensure that Mary didn't give Charles the welcome he was denied; Louise anxious in case Francis tried an even more determined assault on Mary's virtue. She wasn't sure how much longer she could endure it. Some days, Mary felt her entire body was stiff as a corpse from the strain of it all.

She jumped, as Francis, standing behind her, ignored the formality of the occasion and tickled her neck. Mary quickly steadied the crown. Its weight was becoming unbearable and her head throbbed sickeningly. But, for once, French court etiquette came to her rescue and she was relieved of both the heavy crown and Francis' distracting attentions. As first prince of the blood royal it was his duty to take the weight of the crown if it proved too burdensome for his queen. Mercifully, his teasing hands were now fully occupied in holding the crown above her head.

The High Mass commenced, sung by the Cardinal. Over-awed by the solemnity of the occasion, weighed down with the many burdens that her role brought, Mary felt the ritual of her coronation served only to thrust Charles further away from her than ever. It confirmed her fears that the situation would go on and on for years, with her forced to endure the unwanted caresses of both Louis and Francis while the one man whose caresses she longed for tired of waiting and found himself another wife.

To Mary's relief, the long ceremony finally ended. Sagging with weariness, she was at last able to retire to rest. Louis went off with the English ambassadors and was closeted with them for the rest of the day. Relieved of the necessity to attend on him, Mary relaxed quietly in her chamber with her ladies and Claude.

But her quiet retreat was not to be long enjoyed. For, as had become his custom, Francis intruded on their peace. And in spite of the presence of Claude, his humiliated young wife, he began once more to court Mary. He paid no heed to her Maids, his wife or indeed, to Mary's protests. Forced to jump up to get away from him, he pursued her round the chamber till he had her trapped in a corner. Mary tried to fend him off, but he was strong and ignored her pushing hands. Claude had fled the room in tears, unable to endure yet more humiliation at her husband's hands. Mary's ladies didn't dare to intervene, though their cries of alarm brought an unlikely defender to Mary's rescue.

As Louise of Savoy entered the room and saw what was going on, she spoke sharply to Francis. To Mary's surprise, Francis turned bashful. Embarrassed to be caught and subjected to his mother's rebuke, he left the room without a murmur. He was followed by his mother, though not before Mary had intercepted a look of pure hatred in her eyes. Surely Louise didn't suspect her of trying to seduce her son in order to provide France with the heir that Louis was unable to get on her? Anyone with eyes not blinded by love must have seen who was the would-be seducer and who the seduced. But Louise, who had waited so long for what she regarded as her 'rights', would be suspicious of anyone who looked to threaten them, however innocent.

Badly shaken by the latest incident, Mary returned to her seat. How much longer could she ward Francis off? What if Louise of Savoy hadn't been conveniently close by to separate her son from his folly? There would be occasions when even her vigilance would fail. Francis' increasing obsession about possessing her increased by the day, by the hour, and with it increased Mary's fear. But what could she do? Who could she confide in? Louis had made clear he was not to be troubled. Her French Maids seemed to enjoy the piquancy of the situation for all they cried scandal like the rest of the court. Even Henry, far away in England, didn't seem to take her worries seriously. That left only Charles. Mary had hoped to avoid confiding her anxieties to him. There was no knowing what his reaction might be. His low birth had made him the more proud of any slight. He might even challenge Francis to combat. It wasn't that she truly feared that

Charles might be killed in such a fight. But Francis, while he might lack Charles's skill in arms, was his superior in guile and might injure her love through some trickery. And even if he didn't do so, what might be the fate of the Englishman who, even if in fair combat, slew the heir-presumptive of France?

Torn by indecision, she stared sightlessly down at the embroidery she had been working on before Francis' intrusion. If only he would leave her be. But she knew in her heart that he wouldn't, couldn't. He was a man obsessed and she was the unfortunate object of his obsession. Mary felt she had no choice but to speak to Charles. Even so, she thought it best to try to make light of Francis' behaviour. She daren't let Charles know the true extent of Francis' pursuit or Charles would likely feel honour-bound to demand satisfaction.

It wasn't till that evening that Mary had the opportunity to speak privately with Charles. After she had spoken to him and the other English ambassadors of various matters, Mary took Charles's arm and drew him to a corner away from the rest. His reaction to her confidences was even stronger than she had feared.

He was furious and demanded, 'By the Mass, how dare he? To think that King Henry's own sister should be so insulted.'

He looked as if he intended there and then to go in search of Francis and Mary did her best to soothe him. 'Pray, Charles, keep your voice down,' she entreated. 'Do you want the entire court to hear you?' Even more worried now, Mary tried to make light of what had been happening. 'Francis is young and trying his wings. He has truly done me no great harm.'

'No thanks to him that he hasn't,' Charles replied. 'I have seen him watching you and wondered at his looks. But then I thought if he was truly threatening your virtue you would have confided in me ere this.' Suddenly, his suspicions were directed at Mary herself. 'Why didn't you?'

'Pray don't look at me like that, Charles,' she begged. 'It was only that I feared your reaction.'

He stared broodingly at her, then demanded. 'What of Louis? Has he said nothing?'

'Little enough. I don't think he wishes to be troubled. And Francis, of course, stops his play when Louis is present. But few would make clear to the king what his son-in-law is up to. And even if they did, I'm sure Louis would simply ignore them. As long as he doesn't witness Francis' behaviour towards me for himself he won't do anything to put a stop to it. He even admitted that he had seen Francis watching me and all he said was that he admired his son-in-law's taste. I can expect no help from that quarter.'

Charles snorted. 'It is what I would expect of the French. They think all are as base as themselves.' His anger seemed to have abated a little with Mary's explanations and his own hearty contempt of his hosts. 'At least you have told me now. I will be able to do something about it.'

Nervously, Mary asked him what he intended to do. 'I don't want any harm to come to you over this.'

This only brought a laugh from Charles and the comment, 'Harm come from that strutting peacock? Now it is my turn to feel insulted. I see little in Francis to instil fear.'

Worried that his over-confidence would be his undoing, Mary reminded him that he was in a foreign land and that Francis had many friends at court. 'We don't know to what actions they might encourage each other if Francis came to any harm at your hands. Remember he is the heir-presumptive.'

'I'll remember that when he remembers that you are the Queen.' Charles retorted. 'But you are right. Anyway, there is little need, from what you have told me, to cause any damage to such a conceited young fool. It would seem he is his own worst enemy. He has no need of more. And now that his own mother has caught him in the act, as it were, I feel confident she will keep him in check. Nevertheless, I shall have a word with him.'

Seeing Mary's anxious look at this, he added, 'Don't worry. I said I wouldn't harm him and I won't. I shall only remind him of his position and that he will have me to deal with if he persists, heir or no heir. I'm sure he will pay heed to the warning.'

Relieved, Mary now wished she had spoken to him sooner. She might have saved herself a lot of anguish. But she had been right to minimise the extent of Francis' pursuit. Fortunately, Charles's French was far from fluent and he was unlikely to catch the more colourful, colloquial gossip doing the rounds of the court. She dreaded to think what might happen should someone trouble to enlighten him.

'Did you see my Mother Guildford when you arrived at Boulogne?' He nodded and Mary asked. 'How was she?'

'Chafing at the bit to return to you. King Henry and Wolsey have written to King Louis about it as you asked, so mayhap she will return to you ere long. She would soon put a stop to the Duc de Valois' gallop.'

The image this conjured up made them both laugh. It eased the tension between them and Charles added, 'She bade me give you her love.' He bowed slightly and added in a low voice, 'I lay mine beside it.'

His fond words loosened Mary's discretion. Her face radiant, she gazed up at him. 'Oh, Charles, 'tis so good to have you here. If only—' Mary was forced to break off as her throat thickened.

Her tears were the one thing likely to unman Charles and he pleaded with her, 'Please, Mary, no tears. I can't bear to see you upset again. Let's try to be happy for the short time I'll be here.'

Mary dabbed her damp eyes with a tiny scrap of gossamer. His reminder that he would soon be returning to England threatened to bring more tears. But she got herself under control and found a bright smile for him instead, all her love for him visible in her eyes. 'Tell me of home. How is my brother and Queen Catherine? Does all go well with her? She looked exceeding ill when I left.'

'The king is well. As for the queen, she is due to be brought to bed in February.' He frowned. 'We must pray that this one lives. 'Tis strange that such a strong and hearty man as King Henry should father such sickly babes. But, of course, it is well known the fault in such matters lies with the woman. King Henry gives Queen Catherine babe after babe, only to see her lose them.'

Fond of Catherine, Mary defended her. 'You make her sound careless, Charles, as if she had put them down for a moment and forgot where she left them.'

'You know I didn't mean it that way, sweetheart. Still, 'tis odd, as the queen not only has the fair colouring that indicates health and fecundity she also comes from a fruitful family. With such points in her favour, you would think she would be as fruitful as her mother and sisters.'

To Mary, it indicated that perhaps the fault for Henry's lack of an heir lay with Henry rather than Catherine, but she kept this opinion to herself.

Charles said, 'I'm sure the queen does her best. Perhaps this time she will bring forth a fine son, a healthy boy as a New Year's gift for the king.'

'Let us hope so. It is not always such a great thing to be a queen, far from one's family in a foreign land.' And as Mary recalled what she had learned of Catherine's suffering after the death of her first husband, Arthur, she couldn't help but wonder what might lie in store for her if - when - Louis died. Would she be haggled over by Henry and Francis as Catherine had earlier been haggled over by her father and father-in-law? Would she, too, be reduced to poverty and be forced to write pathetic begging letters to her brother? At least she was likely to be spared the torments that Catherine still endured as no one really expected her to give Louis a son. During her time at the French court she had come to have a much greater appreciation of Catherine's situation. Daily made to feel her failure, she was totally reliant on Henry for her position and happiness. If he should turn away from her her life would be cruel indeed.

'You seem pensive, Mary. Is there something else troubling you?'

Mary shook her head. What was the point in burdening Charles with such thoughts? ''Tis only being so far from home and everything that is familiar and being spied on all the time. I cannot move or change my gown without the whole court knowing of it.'

'That is the lot of queens, Mary, 'tis accepted.'

'Perhaps, but not by the queens who must suffer it.' It had been embarrassing enough when her English ladies had examined her sheets. It was intolerable that now it was done by the unfriendly French spies paid by Francis and his mother to confirm her maidenhead was still intact. Even her undergarments were taken and peered at, she was sure, when they were taken for washing. She would throw them in the fire each night and order new but for the speculation such an action would bring. She forced an ironic laugh. 'Did you know that Francis' poor little wife, Claude, is forced to remain with me all day, lest you succeed in seducing me where he has failed?'

Charles looked alarmed at this unlooked for confidence. 'He knows then, of our love? How can this be? I have done nor said anything to rouse his suspicions.'

Mary regretted her latest confidence. She hastened to put matters right. 'Don't worry, Charles. He knows nothing. He

153

suspects a great deal, Francis being Francis, but suspicions prove nothing. You will find that little escapes his notice and what he misses his mother or their spies catch between them. He has probably set a few spies on you, too. Have you noticed anyone?'

Charles shook his head, but it was clear the possibility alarmed him and he glanced over his shoulder.

Mary laughed. 'You are safe enough here,' she told him. 'Even Francis would be unable to conceal a spy here.'

Shamefaced, he cleared his throat and quickly changed the subject by enquiring after Louis. 'Does his health improve?'

'Nay. He weakens every day. The physicians cannot help him. What will become of me should Louis die, I daren't think.' Mary bit off any further words. She had forgotten, for Charles's benefit, that she had minimised Francis' pursuit of her.

Fortunately, Charles only looked puzzled by her words. 'What should become of you? You would merely remain in France a little longer before King Henry sent for you. He wouldn't leave you in France unless you wished it.'

'He may bring me home, but home for what purpose? Another foreign marriage for the sake of an alliance?'

'Tis not like you to be so suspicious,' Charles told her. 'You have his promise, Mary. Did you not tell me he had agreed to your choosing a second husband yourself should aught befall King Louis? Why should you doubt him now?'

Why indeed? thought Mary. But her time in France had educated her in unlooked for ways on the natures of kings and would-be kings. It seemed they all pursued their own desires. Why should Henry prove the exception? Mary gazed thoughtfully at Charles and asked, 'Has Henry said anything about it to you?'

Charles had the grace to look uncomfortable as he admitted, 'Well, he did speak to me privately 'ere I left England and asked me to promise that I would not seek to wed you should King Louis die while I was here. But that proves nothing.'

'You think not?' It was now Mary's turn to be alarmed. For Charles's revelation gave a clear indication that, in spite of his solemn promise, Henry had other plans for her. Why else would he extract such a vow?

'You're making too much of it. King Henry has much on his mind at the moment. He is anxious about the queen and her coming confinement. You know how he is when she is with child.'

'Perhaps.' But Mary wasn't convinced by Charles's argument. Why should she be when it was she, not Henry or Charles, who would be packed off to some other foreign court in another state marriage? And as they re-joined the other English ambassadors, Mary's troubled thoughts were on her future and what Henry might be planning for her.

CHAPTER NINE

A t nine the next morning, still troubled by what her brother might, even now, be organising for her future, Mary set off in her golden chaise for Paris, two hours later than Louis, to make her formal entry. She was accompanied by the usual procession. They made a merry throng. Some of the minstrels strummed their instruments as they rode along and a few voices joined in the melody. Mary's wasn't amongst them. She was worried by Charles's revelation that Henry had extracted a promise that he wouldn't marry her if she became free to wed again. If Henry meant to keep his promise to her, he wouldn't have extracted such an oath from Charles. Charles's attempts to smooth over this question was another anxiety. She had been ready to give up a grand marriage, a grand title, everything that the world regarded as important. Yet Charles would not even ask Henry to keep the promise he had made to her.

To her annoyance, Francis again attached himself to her side—in spite of the 'words' Charles had had with him and, in spite also of his mother's rebuke. His persistence made Mary wonder if they had made a mistake in all the ceremonies and it was Francis, not Louis, who had married her.

157

She tried to ignore the many speculative glances she and Francis attracted, but, though she pretended to ignore the watching eyes, it seemed that even her thoughts must be spied upon, for as the procession made its bumpy way over the treacherous wintry roads, Francis kept begging them from her, doubtless hoping he would be favourably mentioned in them. She couldn't escape him. It seemed nothing would deter him, not even the threat of what Charles would do to him if he didn't stop. Impervious to threats, insults, rejection, he carried on regardless. And although he attempted to hide his jealousy of Charles, it was clear from the way he kept asking about their friendship that this jealousy existed.

'I understand the Duke of Suffolk is great friends with King Henry,' he probed. 'Tis said they are more like brothers than king and subject.'

Mary nodded. She hoped such a friendship would protect Charles should Francis seek to injure him. 'Henry and he are bosom friends, my lord. He was brought up with my brothers when his father died in battle defending our father from Richard Crookback,' Mary told him. 'My family owe his family a lot.'

'Just so. But I thought we had settled on my name, Mary. Why am I suddenly 'my lord' this and 'my lord' that? 'Tis scarcely friendly.' Francis pulled a sad face and stroked Mary's arm through the curtain of the chaise.

Mary drew her arm back and attempted a rebuke. 'My lord, you must hear the shameful rumours circulating at the court concerning us. If they should come to the ears of my husband, the king, I know not what would be the outcome.'

This provoked laughter from Francis. 'King Louis has always had the ability not to hear that which he likes not,' he told her. 'You will learn that in time, Mary.'

'Surely, he must listen to that which concerns his honour and mine?'

Francis recommenced his arm-stroking. 'I do not wish to dishonour you, Mary. I love you too much for that. I would marry you if I could.'

Francis' easy protestations didn't impress Mary. 'But you cannot, Francis,' she reminded him. 'That is the dishonour. And what of Claude, your wife? Have you no love for her? She pines for want of your affection, my lord, did you not know?'

Francis' shoulders shrugged aside his pining wife. 'Claude and I understand each other. We married for reasons of state, not love. She has her religion to console her. I'm fond of her, she is a sweet-tempered child, but how could I love her with the passion I feel for you when she is as she is? You and I would make a perfect pair.'

'But we are not a pair. We are each part of separate pairs. Your pursuit dishonours me and reduces my standing at the court. What if Louis were to die? You would have my character so stained, I would never be able to marry again, even should I wish it. It is an odd way to show this love you claim to have for me.'

Mary's rebuke subdued the normally ebullient Francis. After giving her a solemn, mocking bow, he left her side and rode off to join the other courtiers.

Mary sat back against the cushions of the chaise and wrapped the fur coverlet closer against the winter's chill. Her upbringing had ill-prepared her for coping with someone like Francis or his unwelcome ardor. But then, who could have known that she would be placed in such a situation?

The long procession reached the gates of St Denis. Mary fixed on a bright smile and pretended a keen interest in everything. As the citizens praised her in song she leaned forward and listened with a show of attention:

> *"Wake, wake, ye hearts asleep!*
> *All ye allied to English Powers,*
> *Sing Ave Maria.*
> *The fleece of gold, the purple towers,*
>
> *The eagles, and the lily flowers,*
> *Rejoice in Dame Maria.*
> *Reveillez-vous!*
> *Joy to Lady Maria."*

Mary interpreted the allusions: the fleece of gold was Prince Charles, the heir to Burgundy and the low Countries; the purple towers referred to the arms of Castile; the eagles referred to the Emperor's German banner and the lily flowers were the emblem of Louis, her husband.

GERALDINE EVANS

She dutifully admired the many pageants as she had at
Abbeville. Twilight had fallen before she had viewed them all
and made her offering at the magnificent cathedral of Notre
Dame. By now thoroughly bone weary and chilled, with her
breath steaming around her on the November air, Mary
would gladly have retired to bed. Instead, she was led by
torchlight along the quays of the river to the palace of St
Louis. Even here, she knew she would have little respite. As
queen, she was as much an exhibit as the banners that welcomed her. Happy or sad, lively or weary, she must act the
part demanded of her. She was escorted to her chambers
where her ladies fussed around her, readying her for the
evening's banquet where she must sup in public at a great
marble table.

As she entered the hall – *the Grand Salle* – with its huge
double nave, reputed to be fully 70 metres long, Mary gazed
around her. She saw the many statues of previous kings of
France which stood on the eight central pillars and on the
responds on either side. Louis had told her of the tradition
that these statues of the kings were portrayed with their
hands held high if they had been considered kings of valour
and with their hands by their sides if their reigns had been
undistinguished. Ruefully, he had speculated as to how he
would be depicted.

Music from clarion and trumpet had sprung up at her entrance. She was led past the gilded figure of an immense stag
to the high table of black, Alsation marble at the west end of
the room. It was mounted on a dais of three steps and occu-

161

pied nearly the entire width of the hall. She was joined by Francis' mother and sister and the other noble ladies. Once again she was separated from the familiar faces of her now tiny English train. Mary hoped that Anne of France didn't intend to again publicly attack her as she had after her wedding ceremony and was relieved to discover that, on this occasion, she was saved from the woman's vitriol as Anne of France was seated too far from her to easily offer more insults.

Fatigued as she was, Mary didn't have to feign astonishment at the wonders of the cooks' labours. Course after course was brought to the table and presented to her; a phoenix battered its wings till consumed by fire; a cock and hen jousted and a St George on horseback led La Pucelle against the English. Around her, the French ladies made polite conversation. Louise of Savoy had regained her composure and displayed so little of what must be her true feelings that Mary wondered if she had imagined the look of hatred she had intercepted before. There was certainly no sign of it now as she chatted to Mary of Francis, her beloved son. It was clear his mother and sister were both proud of him; the conversation rarely strayed far from the subject of Francis; his height, his strength, his cultured taste, were all to be gone over and wondered at.

He sounded godlike indeed, Mary thought, to hear his family speak of him. She knew another Francis. And although his sister, Marguerite, naturally shared her mother's hopes for a still more glorious future for Francis, Mary felt a degree more affinity with her. For Marguerite, too, had lost the love of her life, the gallant young general, Gaston de Foix, who had died bravely at Navarra two years earlier. Marguerite was now unhappily married to the Due d'Alencon; for her there was no hope that she might rekindle her love at some future date. Surprised in view of such a tragic loss, that Marguerite had many amusing views on marriage and its woes, Mary warmed to her.

The interminable evening wore on, but finally, the ingenuity of the cooks ran its course and Mary was able to retire to her chamber. She slept soundly till morning much to her surprise as she was acutely conscious that not one of her difficulties had been resolved.

After Mass, Mary rode to the Hotel des Tournelles, where she was reunited with Louis. They spent the next week receiving the gifts of the guilds of the city of Paris; Mary, always emotional and now living very much on her nerves, struggled to conceal the woman beneath the public face of the queen.

Excitement at court mounted steadily during the following week as the long-awaited joust approached. Even Mary managed to thrust aside her troubles. She looked forward to watching Charles as he took on the pride of the French: Bourbon, Lorraine, St Pol, Aragon The Bastard, Lautrec, Bayard and the rest. Maybe he would be matched with Francis and give him the thrashing he thoroughly deserved.

She knew Charles was keen to meet him in the lists; he had no high opinion of Francis' abilities, thought him a conceited fool with an overly-indulgent mother.

Whether Charles was right about Francis' jousting abilities Mary had to concede that he had done a good job organising all the ceremonies, in spite of the appalling weather which threatened to make a damp squib of his efforts. Mary had never seen such a place for rain as Paris and hoped it wouldn't stop the spectacle. But Francis seemed determined that the weather was not going to wreck all his arrangements and he ordered the floor of the lists to be strewn with sand.

Gold and silver, flowing like a sparkling torrent, changed hands as fast as the rain came down. The armourers and tailors and other tradesmen could scarcely count their money it came in so fast. Each contestant was determined to outdo the rest and some were so determined on this they all but bankrupted themselves. Francis seemed more determined in this than any. Mary guessed he must be deeply in debt to the money-lenders - or his mother - as his garments were magnificent: cloth of gold covered with cloth of silver, with trappings of cloth of gold and crimson satin for his horses. Mary was upset to see that he flaunted the white and green Tudor colours, as though determined to further arm the scurrilous tongues of the gossips. Charles, at least, had shown discretion and like the other English jousters wore the red cross of St George over his armour.

Louis, although his health was poorer than ever, insisted on being carried out to watch the jousting, his expensive silks sagging on his bony frame and causing more hostile, accusing gazes to be directed Mary's way.

Beside Louis under the canopy as they waited for the jousting to begin, Mary bit back a sigh. What did people expect of her? Did they think she should adopt Louis's previous habit of early retirement? She was eighteen, not eighty, it was unreasonable to expect her to retire to bed at six of the evening. Besides, she needed to tire herself out in order to sleep, otherwise she would toss and turn half the night, weighed down by all her worries about what future her brother was planning for her. It wasn't even as if she had any say about the banqueting and festivities; the same demanding schedule of ceremonies would be required whatever the identity of the woman crowned Queen of France. Charles and the other ambassadors had comforted her with the reminder that time itself would call a halt to the late nights. Once the joust was over all the formal coronation ceremonies and celebrations would largely come to an end, life would become quieter and Louis could once again take to his bed at a reasonable hour.

Mary, too, would be glad of some quiet time. Perhaps when the joust ended she and Louis could retire to some peaceful chateau to rest and recover. The only drawback to such a plan from Mary's point of view was that the rest might strengthen Louis's body sufficiently to encourage him to seek her bed once more. Mary was dragged from this unappealing prospect by a fanfare of trumpets so loud it even drowned the noise of the partisan crowd as the joust competitors assembled.

The atmosphere was thick with antagonism between the French and English, an antagonism undiminished by the

165

supposedly friendly nature of the contest. Mary, as the new-ly-crowned Queen of France, knew her behaviour would be scrutinised even more – for partisanship now – as well as for all the other reasons. She was thankful that, even if his passion for her had in no way diminished, Francis's persistent attentions to her had ceased. And although he defiantly wore the Tudor colours, it seemed he had finally paid heed to the wise counsel of his mother, Charles and others, though it didn't prevent his jealous looks whenever she gazed at Charles in all the splendour of his manhood.

Francis' simmering antagonism brought a growing feeling of unease. Had he hatched some plot to injure Charles to punish him for the sin of having her love? Mary wanted to shout a warning to Charles, but she knew he would never hear her above all the tumult. She just had to sit and wait with the rest, tending patiently to the invalid Louis' demands for her attention, while worrying about what Francis might have planned.

Her tension increased as the noise from the crowd of on-lookers grew. Everyone, it seemed had their own favourite and shouted their preference at the top of their voice. Mary's head began to hammer. She began to feel a little sick. And as she took in the brightly-coloured banners, limp from the rain, her dread of the outcome tightened her throat till she could barely swallow.

No one else seemed concerned as to whether murder might be done. Even the wretched weather hadn't dampened the crowds' appetite for blood. Charles, of course, was in the thick of it. And as each day passed, Mary's pride in his feats of arms battled with her fear that some harm would come to him. Each time he entered the lists she feared it would be his last. Each time he acknowledged the cheers of the crowd as he gained yet another victory, Mary worried that his triumphs would only earn him more of Francis' enmity.

She remembered how she had boasted of the valour of her countrymen to Francis. Now she wished she had not. Because she had been thinking of Charles's valour. Francis would be in no doubt about that by now. What must he be thinking as, with each succeeding hour, each succeeding day, of the three-day contest, her countrymen proved their overwhelming superiority? The atmosphere had grown increasingly tense, the antagonism in the lists fiercer and more vicious as each participant remembered old scores to be settled for family, honour and country. One Frenchman had already been slain and countless horses. Another Frenchman had been mortally wounded and looked likely to die, though as he had near killed one of the English lords, Mary couldn't feel too distressed about it. She had forgotten her earlier determination to show no partisanship. Queen of France she might be, but her cheers now rung out loudly for her homeland and her love.

The weather hadn't improved. The rain made the ground dangerous to man and beast, notwithstanding the daily, generously-sprinkled sand. The cloying mud caused many a fall, but the contest continued unabated with more and more victories going to the English. In the royal stand, beside the supine Louis, Mary stood, clutching the rail, her cheeks flushed, her eyes fever-bright. The clash of lance on armour, sword on sword, reverberated around the arena. Mary cheered till she was hoarse as another Frenchman was knocked senseless. Even the French crowd, witnessing the undoubted superiority of Mary's countrymen, began to desert their favourites. Their cheers rang out for the English nobles, as time and again, French courtiers fell from their mounts to bury their dignity in the mud. Now their magnificent finery brought not admiration but shouted insults which implied that if they had paid more attention to the martial and less to the sartorial arts they might have put up a better showing.

Mary swelled with pride as she watched Charles, whose crest, rather aptly, was a bull's head, and her cousin, Dorset, hold the lists against all comers. The humiliation of the French was complete. In spite of her still-lingering fears for Charles's safety, Mary wanted Charles to know how proud she was of him. She forgot discretion and shouted his name for all to hear. The passions of the crowd had infected her, and made her reckless; as she shouted, her love for the tall and victorious Englishman was beyond concealment. Mary ignored the stares and the comments, amused or condemning of her behaviour, and shouted all the more. Her shame that, earlier, she had doubted the strength of Charles's love for her, made her shouts ring out the more defiantly, past caring if the entire world knew of her passion for him. Let them all know that the brave and handsome Duke of Suffolk was her love. And for all that people whispered about his lowly birth, with his fine physique, he stood head and shoulders above most of the French nobles. Mary felt that his was the true manliness. Not for him, the endless, meaningless gallantries of the French, with their excessive, promiscuous flirtations. Never had Mary felt her love for Charles so strongly. She would marry him somehow, sometime, on that she was determined. How could she bear to lose him again?

So strong was her pride and love that Mary didn't conceal her amusement when Francis retired from the lists with a slight injury to his hand, a mere nothing, which sent his mother into hysterics with fear. After what Francis had put her through, after his boasts of the valiant feats he would perform in the lists and after listening to his mother's boasts about how magnificent was her son, Mary was unable to suppress the glance of scorn she directed at Louise of Savoy. Francis had shown himself in his true colours, her glance said; he was very brave when relentlessly pursuing an unprotected woman, strange then, that this mighty warrior should be so quick to abandon the pursuit of battle when he merely grazed his hand. Mary felt she could be forgiven her thoughts. For once it was good to put aside her worries and give her feelings of love and pride full rein.

By now, there were many injured men. The surgeons were kept busy attending to them. Mary gazed at Charles's broad back as he temporarily retired from the lists. He had defeated all comers. There were no more noblemen left to be put against him, or, if there were, they had slunk out of sight lest they, too, shared the shaming of their fellows. Exhausted, Mary collapsed into her chair while she awaited Charles's return to the lists. Her throat was sore from shouting encouragement and she reached gratefully for the cooling wine that Louis handed her.

'Your countrymen are tremendous fighters, Mary,' he congratulated her. 'You must be proud of them.'

Mary held her head high. 'Yes, they're fine men,' she told Louis. Forgetting her queenliness, she demanded eagerly, 'Did you notice how even your subjects cheered them? But no one could blame them for their desertion of their own nobles.'

Louis pulled a rueful face. 'Alas, I fear you are right. My countrymen are more partial to the gallantries of the bedchamber than of the lists. Perhaps, after this debacle, they will put aside their swords of passion for those of steel.'

Mary was unable to prevent a comment about Francis' less than impressive showing. 'I was surprised to see Francis give up so easily. To retire from the lists with such a tiny scratch. After all his boasting, too.'

Louis gave a sad little nod. 'He was ever more keen on cutting a fine figure for the ladies than in the joust itself. It has now been brought home to him that clothes alone do not the man make. He and his friends have let your Englishmen bring shame on France.' To Mary's secret amusement, Louis' puny chest swelled and he boasted, 'They wouldn't have achieved such an easy victory in my young day. We Frenchmen knew how to fight then.'

Their conversation lapsed as the fighting began again. Mary stood up eagerly as Charles returned to the lists, this time to begin fighting on foot. Her knuckles clenched tightly on the rail as she realised that Francis had, indeed been plotting to harm Charles. Frustrated by Charles's overwhelming superiority Francis had apparently decided to cut him down to size by sending in an opponent so enormous he dwarfed even Charles's great height. Desperately afraid that Francis' guile would succeed in killing Charles where his feat of arms had failed, Mary beseeched Louis to stop the contest. But he would not. Mary could only stand, fearfully clutching the rail with white-knuckled hands as she awaited Charles's fall.

Charles seized the giant by the neck and gave him a hefty blow. Mary gasped as the giant retorted in kind with an even fiercer blow that sent Charles staggering backwards. Terrified that Charles had been seriously injured, Mary cried out, but Charles climbed to his feet and rushed so swiftly at the giant that his weight carried them both to the ground. Sensing what was behind this battle royal, the shouts of the crowd died away and were replaced by an eerie silence. Mary felt many searching glances in her direction at this reversal of Charles Brandon's fortune. Pale and trembling, she was beyond concealing her distress and could only watch as blow succeeded blow. Her heart rose in her breast till she thought it would choke her.

It was clear that both men were tiring. But fortunately, Charles found his second wind first and gave his opponent another mighty blow. It signalled the end. The now blood-soaked and battered giant beat a hasty retreat.

Mary collapsed in her seat as a great roar rose up from the crowded stands for the victorious Englishman. Mary, knowing that against such an opponent, her love wouldn't have got away unscathed, no longer felt like shouting. She wanted only to tend his wounds and check for herself that he wasn't grievously hurt. For a brief moment, she was tempted to flout convention and go to him. But then common sense prevailed. The courtiers would be outraged if she were to do so. What remained of her reputation would be destroyed by such a revealing action.

So she stayed by Louis' side, her pretended indifference to Charles's fate a thing of mere gossamer, as the many knowing glances made clear. Louis, at least, was kindly and magnanimous in defeat. He congratulated her again on the skill and valour of her countrymen. And as the rumours circulated that the giant was no French noble at all, but a German wearing disguise at Francis' bidding in order to humiliate Charles, he criticised Francis for his unsportsmanlike and cowardly behaviour.

Angered by Francis' low trickery, Mary resolved to have as little to do with him as possible. Had he not, by insinuating the common German giant into the nobles' lists, offended against all the laws of chivalry? Mary heard the muttered comments that Francis' actions had lost him much prestige and was glad. Louis agreed that Francis' behaviour had shamed all France. And coming from the heir-presumptive, who should guard his country's honour, made it even more shaming.

As they and the courtiers made their way back to the palace, it became clear the whole court shared their feelings. Even the supremely confident Francis was unable to ignore the murmurs and he slunk off to one of his mistresses to lick the wounds to his pride in private.

After the excitements of the joust, when it ended the court seemed slunk in torpor. And from the heady witnessing of Charles's triumph, Mary was brought down with a bump when Louis, in spite of entreaties from Henry and Wolsey, refused to countenance Lady Guildford's return to court. But, although disappointed, Mary was surprised to discover that Louis had been right when he had claimed that she would come to enjoy being her own governess. Perhaps she had grown up a little in the interval, for although she missed Lady Guildford's wise counsel, she missed her stern remonstrances not at all. Now that Francis had been persuaded not to persist in his pursuit of her, Mary found she was beginning to enjoy being her own woman, and the freedoms the situation brought.

Secretly a little ashamed that she was being disloyal, Mary was glad she had ordered such costly gifts of jewellery for her dismissed train. She had been forced to buy the jewellery on credit as her income from her demesne lands had not yet started to come in. It was partly to sort out these matters of her income that Charles and his fellow ambassadors had remained in France after their glorious showing at the joust. Mary thanked God for such problems; they meant her love remained close at hand.

Francis, after his ignominious showing at the joust, was consulted no more by Louis. Instead, it was Mary who sat beside him as he transacted business in his bedchamber. It gave her the opportunity to feast her eyes on Charles.

The court retired to St Germain-En-Laye. Here, Mary and Louis followed a quiet and domestic routine. But for Louis, this peace looked to have come too late. His health had deteriorated alarmingly after he had forced his body through the ceremonies and banquets following their wedding and Mary's coronation. Mary watched over him anxiously. Although she longed for her freedom so she could marry Charles, she feared what would become of her if—when Louis died. Would Francis, determined to enjoy his kingly power to the full, recommence his pursuit of her? And, with the crown safely on his head, how likely was it that he would be prepared to take no for an answer?

From the way Francis had taken to watching her, from the way he had set his spies over Louis' bedchamber in order to gain daily reports about his health, it was clear that Francis was convinced the final, ultimate victory would soon be his. Mary's only consolation was that Charles was still at court. She was pleased that Louis made much of him and insisted on his frequent attendance in the bedchamber. As Mary was also required to spend much of her time with Louis it enabled her to see more of Charles. It also meant that she avoided hearing much of the gossip that circulated about her behaviour at the joust. Now, in place of her name being joined with that of Francis, to her dishonour, it was Charles's name that was bandied about.

How could it be otherwise? She had been unable to conceal her obvious love for him during the days of the jousting. And while her love for Charles was clean, honest, true, the courtiers raked over it with a salaciousness that further dishonoured her. It pained her that she should be spoken of in the same breath as the wanton Mary Boleyn. The situation did nothing to ease her position or her worries and she feared that now her love for Charles was out in the open some vindictive person would find a way of damaging it beyond repair. That was why, even though she would miss him sorely, Mary felt not a little relief when Charles at last departed for England, even though he carried with him the news of Louis' still-declining health, which - assuming he hadn't done so already - seemed likely to prompt Henry to make plans for her future that she would find extremely unwelcome.

Mary found herself watching Louis nervously. He was now her only stay in this foreign land of meaningless gallantry and only too meaningful spite. She had begun to dread his dying, even though she would be free. Free for what? was the question with which she frequently tormented herself. Her position in the immediate aftermath of such an event would be intolerable. With Francis in power and herself at his mercy, protected only by the self-interested protectiveness of his not over-friendly mother, Mary felt like a wounded doe, running from a hunter. In such a situation there could only be one ending.

December wore on, with Christmas being celebrated very quietly. Louis was sinking fast. Mary did her best to comfort him. Somehow he found the strength to jokingly console her that he was about to give her the best present yet—his death.

Exhausted by nervous strain and her almost constant attendance at Louis' sick-bed, Mary retired to bed on New

Year's Eve. But she was unable to sleep. Full of dark fore-bodings, she lay listening to the gathering storm and the wind that seemed to howl with a banshee wail through the very rafters of the palace. Finally, towards morning, she fell into an uneasy doze only to waken and sit up in sudden fright when a loud banging resounded on the door of her bedcham-ber. Francis' voice called out to her, entreating her to let him enter.

Panicking, believing that her worst nightmare was about to be realised, Mary screamed and leapt from her bed, con-vinced Francis had come to seduce her at last.

CHAPTER TEN

Common sense quickly asserted itself. Surely even Francis wouldn't attempt to ravish her in the presence of her Maids of Honour? Gathering her addled wits, Mary fastened a robe about her and bid her ladies open the door.

Of course, Francis hadn't come to seduce her. He had come – as Mary would have realised if her nerves and wits hadn't been in shreds – to tell her that her husband was dead and that he, Francis, was now King of France. And although their roles were now reversed Francis went down on his knees to give her queen-ship one last benediction. When he rose to his full height, he looked a king in truth. Strength and power seemed to radiate from him and in a matter of hours he had grown into the role. Mary could see no trace of that meanness of spirit that had led him to attempt to do Charles an injury.

The years of waiting were over for Francis. Now he could afford to be magnanimous. He consoled Mary on her loss as though he meant every word. 'It was a happy release for him, Mary,' he told her. 'Louis had suffered much. It's a marvel he lasted so long. You must have put new zest into him, for last

January, after Queen Anne died, he looked to have little life left in him.'

'When did he die, my lord?' Mary, nervous of the swift change in Francis and uncertain how to react to it, kept her distance. Now Francis was king she felt the need for such caution had doubled. And although Louis had done his best to claim it, Mary still retained her virginity—a rare and precious commodity at the promiscuous French court. Now she clung to it as to a talisman, determined that having retained it for so long it should be Charles's prize and none other's.

'He died in the early hours of this morning. One moment he was here, though drifting, the next he was gone.'

'Why was I not called to attend him, my lord? My duties as his wife—'

Mary had forgotten to call him by his new rank, but Francis made no comment on that. Instead, he smoothly interrupted her. 'There was no time for it. He passed away so quickly.' Francis shrugged and told her softly, 'He hadn't looked any worse than before, there seemed no need to disturb you.'

His soft tone increased Mary's wariness. For Francis must now be feeling his power. He was a young man in his prime, the glories of kingship were only just beginning for him. Mary was convinced such an intoxicating elevation would surely go straight to his head—via his loins. She had never felt so alone. Sudden anguish caused her to cry out. 'What am I to do? Please advise me, my lord, for I know not what is required of me.' To her surprise, Francis restrained any temptation to lover-like impulses and behaved almost fatherly towards her.

'Calm yourself, my little Mother,' he told her. 'You need do nothing. As your widowhood has commenced you will be required to confine yourself to a darkened room, that is all.'

Mary misunderstood him. 'You mean to shut me away?' Alone in a darkened room, she knew she would be truly at his mercy. 'Have I not withstood enough?' Mary could hear the hysterical note in her voice, but felt unable to calm herself. The few remaining English Maids in her train tried to soothe her, but they were as young and frightened as she and infected by her hysteria. Never was the wisdom and experience of Lady Guildford more needed.

Francis broke through the anxious voices of her ladies. 'It is nothing to fret about, Mary. It is merely a custom of France and will be only for a short time. It is simply that, once before, a Dowager-Queen gave birth after the death of her husband, so, ever since, to be certain such an eventuality hasn't occurred, a newly-widowed queen is required to retire for six weeks till it is clear she is not with child. It's a safeguard, nothing more. You will enjoy the peace and quiet of seclusion after so many excitements. You will not be alone. My mother will be with you.'

The prospect of the antagonistic Louise of Savoy sharing her secluded sojourn did little to comfort Mary. Nor did Francis' next words.

'And I will take the time to visit you and try to cheer you.'

Mary shrank at that. She felt she could guess what form his cheering would take. The thought of such seclusion with

179

only his mother for company and the unwelcome visits of Francis to break the monotony was likely to send her mad. She longed for home, but that, too, had its perils. For all that he loved her, Mary knew her brother was more than capable of forgetting his ready promise if it suited him.

Indeed, she feared he had already done so and that once her six weeks' retirement was over and she had returned home he would swiftly pack her back across the Channel to some other royal marriage and she would suffer the same misery all over again.

Mary was determined she would not endure such a marriage a second time. Then she remembered the rumours doing the rounds about her elder sister, Margaret. The rumours said that Margaret had secretly married the Earl of Angus. Mary believed them, for although she barely knew her only sister, she remembered enough to know she had earned her reputation for being headstrong and wilful. If Margaret could choose her second husband herself, Mary thought, why shouldn't I? The thought gave her courage. Come what may, she resolved that Henry would keep his promise, whether he meant to or no. He and Margaret were not the only ones with lusty Tudor blood in their veins.

Mary lay back in the canopied bed. The dark circles under her eyes caused by sleepless nights were enhanced by a few candles. Otherwise, the room was gloomy, for her widowed seclusion had begun and, although it was still daytime, the windows of the Hotel de Cluny to where she had been removed, were covered.

The dark circles camouflaged her silent determination that she would, somehow, defy Henry and choose her own second husband. Her courage wavered a little as she remembered that Francis had said she must endure six weeks of this imprisonment. How could it not, when she must lie in a darkened room, secluded from reality and with Francis' hostile mother as her gaoler?

Her imprisonment was made all the more wretched, as daily, she waited for Francis' next promised visit. Her anxiety had invaded the nerves of her teeth and the pain she suffered made her even more wretched as her mind and body united to torment her. She tensed as a knock came at the door. It was a knock she had become increasingly familiar with. She sat up in the bed as Francis entered, his mother, the newly-created Duchess of Angouleme and Anjou following on his heels.

He approached the bed and sat down on the edge. He took Mary's reluctant hand in his and kissed it, lover-like. Snatching her hand back, Mary hid both hands under the bedcovers. She flinched as Francis traced the tracks of tears on her cheeks with his long, slender fingers.

'So many tears, Mary? Why so?' he asked her softly. 'I know Louis was kindly, but he was scarcely a true husband for you to grieve so strongly.'

Mary lay silent. Out of sight, her hands clutched each other. Why would they not go away and leave her be?

But Francis had no intention of leaving it seemed. 'Perhaps it is not Louis' departure you grieve over, hmm?' Francis' dark eyes stared hypnotically into hers, as though he would gain the answers he sought by sheer force of personality. 'Could it be that you grieve for another's leaving you?'

He stroked her arm through her thin, white gown and Mary shivered, conscious that his eyes never left her face. A sudden spurt of pain shot through Mary's clenched jaw and she groaned, dragged her hand from under the covers and clutched at her face while fresh tears flowed.

Suddenly, Francis was all sympathy. He wiped her tears away with his fingers and asked her, 'What ails you, Mary? You are as white as your gown.'

His sympathetic tone brought from her a fresh storm of weeping. She hugged her hand to her throbbing cheek and groaned as the pain took hold.

Louise came over towards the bed. 'She has the toothache, my son,' she told Francis. Her next words made clear she had extended no sympathy to Mary. 'It is nothing of much consequence. I know not why she makes such a fuss.'

Francis was immediately all solicitude. 'Toothache can be very painful, ma Mère. Has Mary seen a physician? Poor lady, to be reduced to such a state.'

Louise unbent enough to say, 'A physician has arrived from England, from King Henry's court. I suppose he could see her. She'll see no one I recommend.'

Francis made no comment as his mother's words revealed how matters stood between the two women. But his gaze was thoughtful as he turned back to Mary, took her hand again and asked, 'Do you hear, Mary? A physician from your homeland has arrived, from your brother's court. Will you see him?'

Although every movement brought fresh agony, Mary nodded. She felt grateful for his kindness, grateful for any kindness after his mother's cold indifference. She thanked him with a tremulous smile.

His manner now hearty, Francis said, 'Brave girl. I'm sure he'll have something to soothe you. I'll get one of your ladies to fetch him to you.' After patting her hand with a return to the fatherly affection he had shown her immediately after her widowhood began, Francis left the chamber.

After Francis had departed, Louise came over and stood looking down at Mary. Her expression as cold as her voice, she said curtly, 'Such a great fuss over so little, Madam. Think you my son hasn't enough to do now he's king, without dancing attendance on you and your little ailments?'

Angered by Louise's unfairness, Mary forgot her toothache sufficiently to retort, 'I did not ask the king to come to see me. I have never asked for his attentions, whatever you may think. Indeed, I'd rather he didn't visit me. It is not seemly, with us both of an age and I so recently widowed. Perhaps you should use your much-renowned influence to persuade him not to come here again. I have no desire to take him from his duties.'

Louise flashed a look of hatred at this. 'I am only his mother. How could I stop him when you flash your wanton's eyes at him? You are the scandal of the court, leading him on the way you do.' Louise's gaze narrowed. 'Think you I don't realise your intentions? You'll not regain your queenship by enticing my son into your bed. We want none of your bastards here, Madam.'

Mary gasped at this, then her anger flared. 'You are impertinent, Madam. It is your son who has done the pursuing, which you would realise if you weren't wilfully blind.' Now it was Mary's turn to make accusations. 'Which do you love more, I wonder? Power? Or Francis? How fortunate that you gain the first through the second. Would you claim such fondness for him if he had no title to kingship?'

Mary's words had penetrated Louise's strongly-erected defences. For a moment she feared the woman would strike her. But then, Louise gathered herself together and without another word, stalked from the chamber.

Mary sank back against the pillows. During the confrontation with Louise, anger had deadened the pain in her jaw. But now the pain returned in all its jaw-clenching misery. She prayed the physician would hurry and that he knew what he was about when he arrived.

Thankfully, the physician was skilled at his craft. Soon after he had left with his bagful of concoctions, the pain began to ease. Mary felt weak with relief and was grateful to Francis, so, it was that when he returned to see how she was, he entered to a smile of welcome rather than a frown.

It was all the encouragement Francis needed—not that he had ever needed any, of course. As she looked at him, she could almost see when his sympathy turned to an altogether warmer emotion. His smile had something of calculation in it as he stared at her. Too late, Mary realised that her hair had partially escaped its concealing covering and gleamed with the soft sheen of gold in the candlelight. She wondered that

Louise, her determined guardian, should have so neglected her guard duty as to risk her son's solitary visit.

Francis again sat on the edge of the bed. When she tried to tuck her hair away out of sight, he stopped her, telling her to leave it, before playfully pulling more and more of her shining fair hair from its bounds till it lay shimmering about her. Then, he pulled her nightcap away, too.

Mary saw her gold and white reflection in his eyes. Mesmerised, she could only stare as those self-same eyes, dark with passion, seemed about to devour her. She blinked and the spell was broken. She edged away from him. 'Pray, do not look at me like that, Francis,' she said.

'How can I help it?' Francis demanded. 'Your beauty torments me.'

Indeed, he did look tormented. Mary wondered that she, who had no such desire, should have such power over him.

He snatched her hand and held it to his brow. 'Feel my brow, it is on fire.' After forcing her hand against his forehead he brought it to his lips and kissed her palm, her wrist, each finger, one by one.

Mary's heart leapt in her breast. There was something strangely intoxicating in the situation, something strangely erotic. For all her innocence, Mary was enough of a woman for the power of Francis' passion to touch her also. He looked darkly-handsome in the candlelight with the candles matching the fiery heat in his gaze. Almost, Mary felt herself carried away, before she brought herself back to reality with a jolt and demanded. 'Where has your mother gone?'

'She is lying down. Something upset her. She wouldn't tell me what.'

Mary knew what - or rather who – had upset Louise. It had been Mary herself. Her successful penetration of Louise's steely defences had succeeded only in removing the guard between herself and Francis' passion. A pyrrhic victory indeed.

'Still,' Francis went on, 'I am here to tend you, Mary. We can let my mother rest.' His gaze traced the length of her slender body through the bedclothes. Mary shrank back against the pillows and brought her hands up in an involuntary attempt to restrain him. Unfortunately, Francis seemed to find such maidenly defences exciting, for he grasped her wrists and rained hot kisses on her throat and bosom. Mary tried desperately to push him away, but all self-control had deserted him. The weight of his body pressed her down on the bed and his lips kissed hers bruisingly.

Suddenly, he stood up. Mary thought for a moment he must have come to his senses and realised what he was risking. But instead of muttering apologies and fleeing from temptation, he bent and with one hand, wrenched back the bedclothes.

Too shocked to move, Mary froze, even though, as she unlocked her gaze from his, she saw that her gown had rucked up and revealed her legs to the thigh.

For a few seconds, the air was thick with tension, as Francis stood, drinking her in. Then he returned to the bed. Pressing her down once again, he opened her thin gown, pulling it from her shoulders. Her breasts tumbled from their confinement, their white softness gleaming in the flickering flames of the candles and Francis reached for them. His fondling hands moved down to stroke her from ankle to rounded buttock, whilst his lips began to explore her throat, her mouth, her breasts. As he drew her nipple into his mouth and sucked it with a devouring hunger, Mary felt a matching heat course through her. She fought it, tried to voice a protest and though pinned down by his weight, she began to struggle.

But her struggles served only to inflame him further. He stopped her mouth with his tongue while his hands explored some more.

Unwillingly, Mary felt her own passions begin to stir again. Although he was only two years her senior, Francis had, she knew, been in many beds and well knew how to give a woman pleasure. She heard a moan escape her lips as her body flooded with heat at his caresses. All at once, Mary no longer cared that her gown had rucked up even higher. She was now fully exposed to his gaze, his lips, his tongue. She felt a shudder course through him. He lowered his head, his mouth seeking to increase the pleasure she could no longer hide.

But once his hypnotic gaze no longer enthralled her, the face of Charles, her real love, floated in front of her and she froze. What was she doing? How could she play the wanton for Francis when Charles was her only, her true love? The thought gave Mary a strength she hadn't known she possessed. She managed to wrench herself from Francis' embrace and leap from the tangled bedclothes.

Francis looked stunned. For once, he was lost for words and could only stare unbelievingly at her as Mary adjusted her dress. Used to easy conquests, it was clear that Francis was at a loss in the face of her rejection. He had pursued her for months, flirting with her, caressing her, never could he have felt the need for such a long wooing as she had received. She wondered what he would do now and glanced anxiously at the closed door, thinking to make a bolt for it. But the anguish in Francis' voice when he finally found his tongue, kept her rooted to the spot.

'Do not stop me, Mary,' he pleaded. 'You know I love you, desire you, more than I have ever desired any woman. Have you no pity? 'Tis unfair that such warm beauty should have such a cold, unfeeling heart. You know you want me as I want you. I could sense your passion stirring under me, so why did you stop me?'

He rose from the bed and came towards her. He stood in front of her, dwarfing her with his great height and reached for the bodice of her gown. For the second time he freed her breasts. Cupping her bosom and kneading her soft flesh, he whispered in her ear, 'I can feel the wild beating of your heart, Mary. You cage it, yet it wants to be free.'

He bent his head to kiss her again, but Mary spoke sharply to him, as afraid of her own passion as she was of his. 'Leave me be, Francis. Stop this love-making or I'll call your mother. She'll stop you, for all she accuses me of leading you on.'

The determination in her voice stayed him and he looked sorrowfully at her. 'It is cruel of you, Mary. I may now be a king, but I am a man as well, as weak and human as any, for all the kingly anointing I shall soon receive.' His voice sounded ragged as did his breathing. 'You leave me wretched. I ask little of you, only your love. Is it so much to give?'

Hastily, Mary pulled her gown closed. 'You ask for my honour, also, sir,' she reminded him softly. 'I am Dowager-Queen of France, not a camp-follower and would be treated as such.'

A dangerous humour now glinted in Francis' eye. 'I can treat you right royally, ma Cherie,' he assured her. 'Louis isn't the only one able to shower you with jewels. Just let this secluded widowhood of yours end and I can arrange matters.'

Mary didn't doubt it. She did her best to quash the lingering hope she heard in his voice. 'We can end my seclusion now, this minute,' she told him. 'Its purpose is served. I carry no heir for Louis, as you surely know. I've had so many spies about me from the day I was wed. You can proclaim yourself king in deed. You shall have no challenge to the throne from me. But nor will you have anything else.'

It was clear that she meant what she said. Francis had finally got his passion under control. He even managed a mocking smile. 'I am grateful to you, Mary, for that at least. My poor mother had such fears when you arrived, young and beautiful as you are. You put such life into the old king, even I began to have my doubts. Now we need worry no more.' He kissed her hand in a brotherly fashion. 'I'm sorry, ma Cherie. If I could free you from your seclusion, I would.' He shrugged again. The action was very French, very Francis, who was inclined to shrug a shoulder at the entire world. 'It is the custom. Even a king dare not challenge the practice.' He smiled as he added, 'especially this king, who might be thought by the world to have something to hide.'

He bowed to her then. 'I will leave you, my pretty, virginal Mary. But I leave you my heart. Pray guard it well, for it is in torment.'

Briefly, Mary closed her eyes. When she opened them again, he had gone.

CHAPTER ELEVEN

Mary's toothache had returned. But now, all the efforts of Master John, her brother's physician, did little to relieve the pain which would retreat for a while before returning with increased ferocity. Mary's nerves were in shreds; daily, she expected another visit from a Francis more forceful, more determined.

Francis' mother was another torment. With Francis king, Louise was feeling her power, her hatred of Mary no longer concealed. Feeling increasingly trapped, caught between the spiteful, hating mother and the passionate, loving son, Mary's only hope of escape was a return to England, her brother and whatever schemes he might have for her future. Her worries on this score increased with the visit of two friars from England. At first, she had been glad to see chaste, holy men after Francis' unholy passion. They had been friendly enough at first, but when, unwisely, Mary revealed her fears about what might await her in England, their attitude changed. They became impatient and brusquely informed her that she was to be married into Flanders, into another loveless state marriage with a stranger. Their stern rebukes at her protests angered her and she stormed at them.

'No,' she insisted. 'I'll not do it again, not to please my brother the king, or anyone else. He cannot ask it of me, it is unfair.' How dare Henry think he could do this to her a second time?

Father Langley gazed frigidly at her. 'Is this how a dutiful sister behaves towards her king? For shame, Madam, your brother has been too lenient with you. He should have you whipped for such disobedience.'

'How dare you speak to me thus? By what right? I have my brother's promise that I may marry the next time where I wish, not from any demands of state. Who are you to tell me of my duty?'

'I come from the King's Council, Madam, and am a man of God. As such I cannot lie.' Father Langley's face became even more austere and self-righteous. 'You think to marry that upstart, Suffolk, do you not?'

Dismayed, Mary stared at him. How did this hateful creature know what was in her heart? Unless Henry...? But she didn't have time to pursue this line of thought, as Father Langley told her scornfully.

'You needn't look so startled. Your folly is the gossip of the court at home. I tell you plain, Madam, for the sister of King Harry to marry someone so low-born, even if he is now raised to a dukedom, would not be tolerated. The Duke of Suffolk is coming to France,' he told her. 'But not to marry you. He will, if necessary with soft words and endearments, escort you out of this realm. But it will not be to England that he will take you, but to Flanders, to marry the young Prince Charles.'

'You lie.' Mary shouted back. 'Prince Charles doesn't want me. We were betrothed once and he spurned me, so it cannot be true.'

Father Langley's lips compressed at this naive foolishness. Mary recognised her error. As, loftily, Father Langley now told her, matters of state could change in a trice. She, of all people, should recognise the truth of that.

'It seems the Prince's grandsire wishes for the match. His grandson won't go against him. The marriage will go through whether you wish it or no, you need have no doubt of that. You should remember the path of duty, Madam and set your feet upon it. It would seem King Louis was as indulgent as your brother. 'Tis soft-hearted foolishness so to treat a princess.' He came closer as though the better to impress her duty on her. 'You are a tool, Madam, nothing more. And if you are needed to repair an alliance, you will be so used.'

'Never. Not again.' Mary had had enough of these men and their cold talk of duty. 'I'll not listen to any more of this. Get you gone, get you gone, you and your evil tales.' Taken-aback by her vehemence they retreated to the door. Mary pursued them. 'Get out. Get out. I want no more of you.'

They left, muttering together at her wilfulness. Barely had the door shut behind them than Mary collapsed. It was as she had feared. Henry had betrayed her and broken his promise. Was there no one she could trust any more?

Each evening now, Francis visited her and resumed his love-making, Mary felt so cornered that she even considered giving into his demands. Perhaps if she did so, she might lose her attractions for him. After learning that Louis's end was near, Wolsey had written to her, advising her to give no hearing to any ideas of marriage that others might put to her. Mary had laughed bitterly at this. Was my Lord Archbishop mad? To advise her against a second foreign marriage when he knew she never wanted the first.

Henry, too, had written to her. His letters had been very loving and Mary had allowed tremulous hope to rise. Maybe, in spite of her fears and suspicions, her dreams would be answered. Henry had promised, after all, never mind that the two stern-faced friars had contradicted Henry's solemn vow to her. But whatever she might feel about the odious Father Langley, he had been right when he had told her she was a tool. She was indeed a tool, a sorely abused one. Never had she felt more abandoned. Even Lady Guildford had left Boulogne for England. And although Charles would be returning to the French court Mary knew he wouldn't come till after Francis' coronation. With Louis' death the difficulty of her situation had increased rather than diminished. Perhaps, if she were kindly treated she wouldn't feel so desperate, so very much at the mercy of Francis, his mother, Henry and the gossiping courtiers of both countries. But all she longed for were far away in England, too far to offer any comfort or ease of mind.

Mary tossed and turned in a light, troubled sleep, only to be woken by a kiss. She opened her eyes to find Francis' face inches from hers. His lips descended again and Mary cried out in alarm. Dear God, not again.

He stroked her cheek and asked, 'How are you this evening, little nymph?' He kissed her hand and she struggled to sit up. Her toothache had eased for now. 'You are quiet today, Mary. Of what do you think? Is it that you come round to my thoughts at last?' Francis' eyes searched hers. Not finding what he sought, he resumed his stroking, his long fingers working to unlock the key to her heart.

Mary protested. His lips cut her protest short. He was strong from many years of jousting and sports. Her struggles ceased and she lay supine under his caresses, hoping that if she made no response at all he would be disconcerted and stop.

It seemed to work. For he raised his lips from hers and although his gaze seared her and told her how much he wanted her, his expression was puzzled and revealed that he still wanted her willing, even eager. He reminded her of her likely fate. 'Why do you spurn me, Mary? I would help you if you would only be kind to me. You know if you return to your brother he will pack you off to Flanders and young Prince Charles.' He spoke condescendingly of his young rival.

His words revealed his hope that fear would instil desire where his passion had failed. Vehemently, Mary told him that she would rather enter a convent than entertain such a marriage a second time.

Francis soothed her. 'Why return to England at all? You could stay in France. You have seen but little of it yet. I could arrange a suitable match for you.' Although Mary shook her head at this, he pressed her. 'Why not? There is

nothing in England for you, you know it well. The Duke of
Savoy is looking for a wife. If you married him we could remain friends, perhaps deepen our relationship.'

And join a cast of hundreds of discarded mistresses,
thought Mary. Such a fate held no more appeal than the one
the friars had told her about. Besides, if she did as he suggested, her income as Dowager-Queen would go straight to
his mother's family. Mary saw no reason to enrich the coffers
of Louise of Savoy—or Angouleme as she now was. She refused to entertain the idea.

Francis suggested other possible suitors. Mary, with her
heart set on Charles Brandon far away in England, refused
all of them. But Francis hadn't yet exhausted his ideas' fund.
'Marry me, then Mary.'

She stared at him. How could she marry him? 'But you
have a wife, Francis,' she reminded him. 'Even a king may
not have two at the same time.'

'That could soon be remedied. Louis is not the only one
able to obtain a divorce from a malformed and ugly wife.' He
smiled, delighted with his idea. It was as if he believed there
was no way she could refuse such an offer. 'I will make you
Queen of France once again, Mary. Does the thought not
please you?'

Mary stared at him, mesmerised. How could she reject his
proposal without angering him? She could give Francis no
reasonable reason for refusing his offer. Nothing that would
satisfy him—if indeed, there was any explanation that was
capable of satisfying her rejection of him. The only thing
that might do it was if she were to reveal the secret of her

heart to him. But perhaps that would leave her even more at his mercy. He was staring at her, eagerly awaiting her response and seemingly in no doubt as to what her response would be.

Mary knew she must say something. Better to just blurt out her refusal than have his hopes grow with each second she remained silent. 'I cannot marry you, Francis,' she told him. 'It would be unfair to young Claude. She loves you dearly.'

Francis' lips pursed at what he must regard as her perversity. That his wife loved him was, for Francis, clearly no reason at all for Mary's refusal. But before he could speak, Mary made up her mind that she must confide her secret love to him. Maybe such a confidence would convince him that he would never win her love and he would then leave her in peace.

'I beg of you Francis, speak no more of this matter, for I can never marry you. But if you will promise me, on your honour as a king, to keep my counsel, I will tell you truly why I must refuse you.'

Although sulky, Francis placed his hand over his heart and promised.

Tremulously at first, nervous of rousing his anger and not totally convinced of the wisdom of placing her trust in him, Mary told him, 'This long time now, my heart has not been free for any man to capture, no matter how ardent his wooing.' She gave him the consolation of her smile. 'I am honoured that you should wish to marry me, Francis, but you are too late. I love another.'

'Suffolk.'

Mary nodded. 'Yes. The Duke of Suffolk is the man I would marry. My brother gave me his promise on it before ever I left England.' She sighed. 'But there are so many obstacles in the way that I sometimes fear it will never be. So you see, Francis, it is not your wooing that lacked ardor. That was persuasive enough for any,' she now admitted. 'Who knows, but if my heart had been free I might have given in ere this.' Mary hoped this last admission, revealing as it was, would soften his heart. No man likes to be spurned, least of all a king. She hoped that her cautious flattery would cushion his hurt pride and make him kind.

She waited for his reaction. But for some seconds, he said nothing and Mary, fearing her future hovered on the brink of disaster, hurriedly appealed to his chivalry. 'Please, Francis, I beg of you, help us. I'm sure my brother will honour his promise if you only ally your persuasion to mine. Henry has long known of the love Charles and I share. His heart can sometimes be tender with lovers.'

Mary gave a sad smile as she spoke of her love for Charles. She would have preferred to hug such thoughts to herself, but it was essential to have Francis on her side. He could make all the difference when it came to getting Henry to keep his promise. She must hold nothing back if she wished for his help. 'We had a language of love, Charles and I. Secret words known only to we two.' Mary's whisper confided the words she and Charles had used to signal their love. She watched as Francis' jealousy of his rival battled with his honour as a king. Watched as he began to accept that she would never be his and started to look for compensations.

Francis' lashes lowered concealingly. Mary guessed he was weighing the benefits to France should she be unavailable for use in the marriage market. With her sister, Margaret's secret marriage to the Earl of Angus, if Mary, too, was unavailable the childless Henry's alliance box would be empty of marital tools, which would weaken his bargaining position to Francis' advantage. But Mary, having been used once as one of her brother's tools, didn't care. If Henry was unable to make an alliance with Flanders by marrying her to Prince Charles, he would make another.

Francis' satisfied smile confirmed her guess as to his thinking had been correct. His words confirmed it. 'Of course I will help you, little Mother. How could I refuse? You have moved me with your pretty pleading. You will find me a strong champion,' he boasted. 'I, too, you see, have a tender heart for lovers.'

He kissed her hand with a flourish and bowed himself out of the room, leaving Mary to stare after him. In the midst of the preparations for his coronation Francis had given her his solemn promise to help. She could only hope and pray that his promise proved of sturdier mettle than her brother's.

In the trail of all the joyous Coronation celebrations, Charles Brandon returned to France.

Francis gave no hint that Mary had revealed their secrets to him. He greeted Brandon with a show of affection at the public audience, amused to see that Brandon was taken-aback at his loving greeting when, at the joust but a short time before, Francis had done his best to injure him. The man was no dissembler, it was clear.

After a few moments' silence, Brandon managed to convey his sovereign's congratulations to his brother king and his thanks for the comfort he had given Mary in her bereavement.

Francis, never one to resist temptation, gave in to the desire to tease his rival. Straight faced, he told Mary's would-be lover, 'I am sure the Dowager-Queen will tell you how lovingly I have conducted myself to her.'

It was obvious, from the way Brandon's gaze narrowed at this artful shot, that Mary had already done just that. Francis saw a shaft of pure venom beam from Brandon's eye. For a brief, delicious second, Francis thought Brandon would commit an act of lése-majesty. But Brandon, though his lips tightened at the taunt, and his clenched fists whitened, had the sense to say or do nothing.

Francis smiled to himself, aware of Brandon's fury that he was in no position to remonstrate with him on his 'loving' behaviour to Mary. Brandon's open countenance, ill-made for concealment of the emotions, revealed clearly that he desired nothing as much as to punch away Francis' complacent smile.

Later that day, the king saw Brandon in his bedchamber and decided to continue his teasing with the mock-stern accusation, 'You are come to marry the Queen, your master's sister.'

Taken aback Brandon could only bluster. 'I assure you, your Grace, I would not be so daring. Such a thing would be folly. I—'

Francis cut his protestations short. He wanted to see Brandon squirm. 'As you will not be plain with me, my lord, I shall be plain with you. Have you heard this word before?' Francis stepped forward, and into Brandon's ear he whispered a word from the lovers' secret language. He felt Brandon's body tense in recognition. When Francis stood back, Brandon's face was crimson, in his eyes there flickered fear that Francis' retribution for a man of low birth who dared to seek the hand of a queen would be swift and brutal. Brandon looked all but ready to flee.

But Brandon made poor sport and Francis tired of the game. Where was the fun when the prey was so lacking in defences? Now Francis held out a friendly hand to the disconcerted Brandon and told him, 'I give you my word as a king that I shall try to help in this matter between you and the Dowager Queen.' It was clear at first that Brandon didn't believe him. But gradually, Francis got under Brandon's weak armour of bluff denial and teased the admission from him that he feared King Henry might not prove quite so understanding.

Guilt and fear were sharply etched as he blurted his worries to Francis. 'If this matter comes to the ear of my master, I am likely to be undone. I swore a solemn oath to King Henry not to pursue my love for the queen.'

With a wave of his arm, Francis swept Brandon's anxieties aside. 'Leave King Henry to me. Queen Claude and I shall both write letters to your master, in the best manner that can be devised. I feel sure we can sway him in your favour.'

Looking scarce able to believe his ears—and who could blame him for that? Brandon stammered out his thanks and bent to kiss Francis' hand.

Francis, enjoying his magnanimity, basked in the warm glow of his good deed. But beneath the surface show, he admired his own cleverness. Mary would perhaps, with his help, gain a low-born husband, if such was truly her desire. But France would gain so much more if he managed to bring this marriage off. With the beautiful Mary removed from the marriage market it would be difficult for Henry to make a swift Flemish alliance. And should Henry decide to break with France, Mary's revenues as Dowager-Queen could be suspended. Quite a coup for a newly-anointed king, Francis told himself in self-admiration. He could scarcely wait to confide his achievement to his mother.

Charles Brandon entered the Hotel de Cluny and was ushered into Mary's darkened chamber by one of her ladies. He hadn't expected to gain admission so easily, but Francis must have cleared the lovers' way by telling his mother of the recent turn of events. She, in turn, made no difficulty and seemed only too happy to smooth their path.

Still bemused, but grateful not to have been clapped in a French dungeon, Brandon groped his way in the unaccustomed gloom of Mary's chamber and reached her bed. He frowned when he saw that for some reason, Mary's eyes were tight shut.

Mary's eyes flew open as he uttered her name. 'I thought you were Madam Louise come to torment me again,' she told him as she stretched out her hand in delight, drew him down on to the bed and embraced him. 'How is my brother? Has he said anything about our marriage? When can I go home?' Anxiously, the questions tumbled from her lips as she searched his face for answers. When he failed to answer her barrage of questions quickly enough, Mary frowned and asked. 'You are come to take me home, Charles, are you not?'

Charles's response came more swiftly this time, but it wasn't swift enough to reassure her. Dolefully, she told him, 'I have been told I am destined for Flanders. Father Langley and another visited me here and told me it was so. They seemed so sure of their facts. They told me you were part of a plot with my brother to entice me into Flanders for marriage with their Prince.' She stared searchingly at him and beseeched, 'Tell me it is not true Charles. Pray you tell me plain.'

His faltering reply that she was to return to England and her brother was scarcely reassuring. All her suspicions gushed like a river in flood, and she turned on him. 'Yes, but for how long? One month? Two? How long before my brother fixes another alliance?' Fear turned to anger at his betrayal of their love and she shouted at him, 'Are you not supposed to utter soft and loving words to me, my lord? That is what the friars told me. Come, soothe my foolish fears with some honeyed words. Make a few careless promises, Charles, as did my brother. You follow him in all else, why balk at this?' Tears welled in her eyes and she stormed at him, 'Marry me now, Charles, or if I come into England, you'll never have me.'

'You say that but to prove me withal. You cannot mean to marry me here.'

But Mary had decided on her course and would not be swayed by Charles's insulting lack of lover-like ardor. Stubbornly, she told him, 'Mean it I do. King Francis has also been with me here. He told me what I might expect. He said I am destined for Flanders. Why should he and the two friars have the same tale if it's not true?' Mary raised her fists and beat him on the manly chest she had so admired and told him, 'I'll not go. I'd rather be torn in pieces.' She began to weep in earnest.

Through her tears, she watched Charles wring his hands, before it finally occurred to him that he could make better use of them. He put them round her and tried to comfort her. 'Sweetheart, calm yourself. You'll make yourself ill with such passion. It is not true, my love, you are not for Flanders. Please believe me. I have it from King Henry himself.'

Mary didn't believe him. She continued to sob and ignored Charles's pleas that she stop weeping. But tears were the only weapon at her command.

'What can I do?' he asked her, helplessly. 'What can I say? How can I marry you now? You know I promised the king, your brother, not to further aught between us till we were both home.' Mary only shook her head and wept some more. 'Write to the king,' Charles pleaded. 'Obtain his good will and I'll wed you, right gladly.'

Only too aware that if she did not sway him now there would be no future for them, Mary was determined not to be so lightly fobbed off. Between sobs, she reminded him, 'My brother has consented to our marriage. Have I not his promise? He gave me his word before ever I left England that I could choose my next husband when Louis died. You know this well. King Louis is dead. I choose you. The King of France is happy to give his consent, why should we wait? Why should my brother want us to wait unless he means to betray my trust?'

Bitter at his lack of lover-like resolve, she demanded 'Is the agreement of two kings not enough for you? Perhaps Francis and the friars spoke truth after all. Confess it,' she screamed at him. 'You are here for one reason only, to entice me into Flanders. I'll never go should I die for it and so I told the French King before you came.' She glowered at him, in her passion, she wrenched off the cap covering her hair and threw it at him. 'If you will not marry me now as I ask, never look to have the proffer again.' She turned away from his pleading and his outstretched hand and refused to listen to any more of his denials.

But her tears had done their work. He grabbed her and folded her in a great bear hug as he muttered against her hair, 'For the love of God, Mary, all right, I'll marry you. Only I beseech you, stop this weeping. You tear me apart.'

Mary's smile pressed unseen against his neck. As if by magic, her tears dried. Now her eyes shone bright with love alone. She had got her heart's desire at last. It was a heady feeling. One she was determined would linger longer than this brief interlude. Worried that once he left her chamber and her tears behind, Charles might begin to fret in fear of what her brother might do, and renege on his agreement to marry her, Mary meant to make sure she held him fast. Her body would give him the courage of her convictions, she vowed, as she kissed him with the passion Francis had been denied.

It took just a few moments for Charles's passion to swell to match her own. Soon, the chamber echoed and re-echoed to the sounds of their mutual delight.

Caught up in the tumult of rapture, Mary's senses were oblivious to the sound of the door opening or the faint waft of the perfume Louise favoured.

But the lovers sprang apart at the harsh accusation when they heard Louise demand, 'What is the meaning of this?'

They stared fearfully at Louise as she walked towards them. Her voice scornful, she asked Mary, 'How can you behave in such a shameless fashion, Madam? How many men do you draw into your web? First my son and now my Lord of Suffolk. 'Tis no way for a queen to behave, I'll swear. And you sir.' Now the scorn was aimed at Charles. 'Is this how you behave to your master's sister, queen as she is though she be unfit for the role? You had better make good your promise and wed the lady here and now, before she causes more scandal.'

Mary turned hesitantly to Charles. Much as she wanted to marry him, it was demeaning to be caught like this and by

Louise of all people. Especially as, ill-concealed behind the scorn, Mary could detect the woman's triumph that, having caught them in each other's arms, her lustful son could be saved from the folly of his pursuit of Mary. Finding them like this must have been exactly what Louise had hoped for when she had set her spies. How richly she had been rewarded.

'Why do you hesitate?' Louise now demanded, as Mary and Charles both remained silent. 'You made the lady a promise, my lord. I presume you would honour it?'

It was a humiliating few moments for Mary before Charles said he would.

Once Louise had obtained Charles's agreement, she turned back to Mary. 'And you, Madam? You pushed him hard enough to wed you, I vow. I could hear your tantrums from the garden. Have you changed your mind so soon?'

Mary shook her head.

'Very well then. Adjust your disordered clothing and come with me.'

A few minutes' later, they followed bemusedly behind Louise as she strode briskly through the door to the exquisite little chapel that was along the passage from Mary's bedchamber. They barely had a chance to exchange a look or a word before a hastily summoned priest led them through their falteringly exchanged vows as they stood before the altar under the determined eye of Francis' mother. When the priest asked for the ring, Louise pulled one from her finger and handed it to Brandon. Mary could feel his hand tremble as he slipped it on her finger.

And so they were wed. But it didn't feel real to Mary. She only woke to reality when they were bid to kiss. The physical embrace broke the spell and Mary gazed at Charles in sudden fear as she realised the enormity of what they had done. But the matching fear she saw in her new husband's eyes brought back a measure of courage and defiance to Mary. This, however, didn't last any longer than the time it took them to retrace their steps back up the aisle.

What would Henry say? Mary asked herself as her heart thundered in her breast. Worse—what would he do? By now, fear had them both in its grip. Mary told herself that she now had her heart's desire. But only time would tell what it would cost them.

Again defiance crept into her mind. Let Henry do what he would. She was now Charles's wife. And, after all, she had Henry's promise—didn't she? Mary clung to this thought with the tenacity brought of desperation.

CHAPTER TWELVE

Alone again in Mary's bed-chamber, she and Charles gazed fearfully at one another. The spectre of Henry's wrath hung over them both. Mary, worried that Charles's dread of Henry's reaction to their marriage would encourage resentment that her love had put his very life in danger, flung herself into his arms. She was relieved when he clung to her instead of pushing her away as she had half feared. But it could not be long before he realised it would be *him* who would bear the brunt of Henry's anger. How could he not then blame her for it?

But, at least for now, Charles seemed set on quietening Mary's anxieties. He poured a glass of wine for her, then another. When she had quietened, he removed the glass from her trembling fingers. He stroked her hair and gently, at first, kissed the rest of her tears away.

Mary, her senses heightened by their plight, felt the last tremors of fear turn to passion. As their kisses grew more urgent, fear was thrust aside before an even stronger emotion. Charles undressed her, kissed her arms, her breasts, her belly, as each part of her clothing fell away. Hastily, he stripped off his own garments. Lifting her into his arms he lay her down on the tumbled covers of the bed.

Mary, eager to forget their plight, yielded with delight to his demanding hands. This was what she had yearned for for so long. After poor Louis, the experienced Francis had made her senses churn and reminded her of the feelings Charles had brought her to in England. Now, she was free to indulge such feelings. And indulge them she did. Her hands caressed Charles's muscular back as he rested on his elbows above her. She kissed his face, his chest, his lips.

She realised her inexperience only tormented him when he grabbed her hands and held them above her head so he could take charge. Masterfully, he did so, kissing and fondling every inch of her till she twisted and turned like a wanton. Finally, driven mad with desire, eager for the consummation, she arched herself to him and begged. She didn't have to beg for long.

Passion spent, they lay still. With the passing of passion, their fears had leisure to return.

Mary, used to strong guidance all her life, now sought the guidance of her new husband. But when she asked him what they should do it was clear that her earlier fears had been prescient. For Charles had no more words of comfort to offer her. He lay staring at the painted ceiling, as rigid as if he saw depicted there all the hellish sufferings a mere mortal must endure after defying the gods.

Certainly, the wrath of a Tudor could be every bit as awesome and Henry was Tudor to his very core. What might he not do to the man who had secretly married his sister and who had then compounded his folly by laying with her? Mary trembled as it dawned on her that Charles could lose his head over this.

It seemed Charles shared her worry, for he fingered his neck as if to check his head still remained attached to it. His breath became ragged. Did he, too, hear the voices of Henry's Council as they demanded death for his treachery, Norfolk's voice above all, baying for blood? As she watched, beads of sweat broke out on his forehead. She reached for him to offer what comfort she could, but he leapt from the bed, evaded her clutching hands, and began to throw his clothes on. He paused in his dressing for long enough to reply to Mary's earlier, unanswered question.

'We don't tell him. We won't tell Henry that we are wed and have lain together. You must write to him, Mary, ask his permission as though we had never exchanged our vows.'

But they had and they meant the world to her. Mary stared at him in dismay. Charles didn't notice, she saw. He was too keen to line up his defences.

'Write tenderly to him, Mary. Remind him of his promise. He'll relent and release me from my oath and we can be married again as though the first had never been. Your brother need never know of our folly. It is the only way.'

Mary scrambled from the bed. She put a robe around her nakedness, crossed the room and took his hand. It was her fault that her magnificent warrior of only a few weeks' past had turned into this fear-filled creature. She must do what she could to assuage his fears and reassure him. But to do that he must first face facts. 'You forget there were witnesses, Charles. Do you think Madam Louise will keep our se-

211

cret? She has no great love for me. She has long looked to do me some harm and she now has her weapon. We cannot conceal our marriage as easily as you say.'

He frowned as she forced him to face the truth. But if they were to come out of this with as little damage as possible, they needed to think clearly and make plans based on reality. Mary's next words damaged his hope even more. 'Besides, what if Henry refuses to be as accommodating as you hope? What if he insists on the Flanders match for me? Unless he knew of our marriage and its consummation he might push for the match only to have the embarrassment of extricating himself when he knew the truth. He would look a fool, ignorant of the doings of his own kin. It would not increase his kindness towards us.' Mary, anxious not to add to his worries, forbore to mention the possibility of their lovemaking bearing fruit.

As Charles was still reluctant to tell Henry the truth, they searched desperately for a solution to their dilemma. Possibility after possibility was considered and as quickly discarded till they ran out of ideas. They had been wed but a few short hours and already worry had tarnished Mary's bright happiness. Charles had retreated into a heavy brooding that was a silent reproach. Would he have married her at all without the forceful persuasion of Louise? For all his height and manly strength, Mary knew he was more frightened of the future than she—and had every right to be. Guilt gnawed at her as she accepted that her tearful recriminations and Madam Louise's scorn had combined to put him in jeopardy. Now, not only his worldly ambition, but his very life was threatened. And it was her fault.

Charles broke his brooding to ask, 'Why did we let that woman push us into such a hasty marriage? We could now be on our way home to England.' He put his head in his hands. 'What have your tears brought us to?'

Mary flinched as he put her fears into words. She tried to stay calm, for both their sakes. She pleaded with Charles to remain calm also. 'Anger will not solve our problems,' she told him gently. 'It may increase them by clouding our judgement.'

'Calm you say? How can I be calm when the Council are likely to be soon demanding my destruction? Is it your head that the axe hovers over? Nay. 'Tis my head they'll seek, not yours. You are safe enough.'

Mary threw herself on her knees before him. 'Don't, Charles,' she begged, as fresh tears washed her eyes. 'Please do not speak so.'

But her tears only served to madden him the more. 'Not more weeping? It was your tears that forced me to this. Why couldn't you have waited as I asked?' He wrenched himself away from her clinging hands and strode to the window to stare out at a wintry night bright with stars. 'Curse this day and your lovesick weeping.'

Mary staggered to her feet on trembling limbs. Was ever happiness so short-lived? In a small voice, she asked him, 'Do you no longer love me then, Charles, to curse me so?

He tore himself away from his angry contemplation of the stars and turned back to her. 'You know full well I do, Mary.

Has my folly not proved it?' He began to pace the room as if unable to keep still. 'Look at us.' He waved his arm at the ornate wooden doors. 'Skulking behind closed doors, scared of our own shadows. Do you expect love to blossom under such constraints?' Dumbly, Mary shook her head. He stopped his pacing and regarded her thoughtfully. 'What do you think your brother will do? Will he be swayed by the Council?'

Anxious to convince him as well as herself, Mary's answer came quickly. 'Nay, I'm convinced he won't. We must believe in Henry's intention to honour his promise. He loves us both well,' she reminded him.

'Enough to withstand the Council? Enough to forgive this?' As his hand described the disordered room, the rumpled bed, and the scattered, hastily discarded clothing, the enormity of the hoped-for forgiveness seemed to hit him again and he slumped in a chair as though exhausted.

Mary was desperate to comfort him. But how could she? She was the cause of his present misery. Any comfort she attempted to give him was more likely to rekindle his anger than douse it. Because he was right. Her tears had brought him to this. Who knew to what they would now lead him? She had scarce had a thought beyond her own needs and desires. Wishful thinking had made Henry's acceptance a thing easily imagined. Did she not have his promise? Blinded by the rosy hues of love she had been unable to see beyond to the consequences of her reckless actions. Now, as she watched Charles and his growing terror of retribution, she had all the time in the world to dwell on such matters.

Exhausted suddenly, she sank on to the bed. So much depended on her brother and how seriously he viewed his promise. And how much he truly loved her and her husband, the man he had often called his 'great friend' Maybe their one friend in all this might be Henry's over-worked conscience. Perhaps she should try pricking this delicate part of her brother to see if she could sting him into forgiveness. Mary knew how much Henry hated being made to feel in the wrong. He had often proved vulnerable in his attempts to escape such an unwelcome sensation.

Her gaze hovered over her new husband. She had cause to know how weak, how tender these big men could be. A few words might be enough, if coupled prettily with tears. She would have to be careful though, lest she pressed too hard. It would be better to let Henry's conscience provide most of the persuading. Henry's delicate conscience could be unpredictable if cornered and would be likely to turn on whoever caused it grief.

If only Wolsey could be persuaded to help them. He was a man of much ability and, in spite of his rather gross exterior, he could be surprisingly subtle. Often, he had caused a complete turn-around in Henry's thinking, with Henry believing it was his own mind which had wrought the change. She knew Henry depended on Wolsey for many things and was greatly influenced by him. If only, Mary thought, if only she could persuade him to raise his voice in their defence.

She left Charles to his brooding, crossed to her bureau. and picked up her pen. But words didn't come easily. Her gaze, wandering round the chamber, rested on one of her jewel boxes. It contained some of the countless valuable jewels that Louis had given her. Much help all the riches they contained were to her now.

She stilled, even as the thought entered her head. Unbidden, came a picture of her brother as he had looked at the waterside at Dover when he had confirmed his solemn promise. He had looked big, confident and decked out in expensive jewels. But surely none were more expensive than her pilfered dowry jewel with its glittering diamonds.

Mary stared pensively at her jewel boxes as a faint hope entered her heart and trembled on her lips. Unwilling to give Charles false hope, she turned the idea round in her mind for a while. She could find nothing wrong with it. Charles looked so forlorn that she knew she must seize on any chance to encourage hope in his breast.

He raised his head as she said his name and gazed at her with dull eyes.

'What does my brother love above all else?' she asked. 'Above his queen, his mistresses, his friends?'

Charles frowned as he pondered this. Then he shrugged. 'He has a great fondness for wealth, I suppose.'

Mary nodded. 'Aye. Wealth and jewels, of which I have an abundance. Do you think they might be sufficient to buy Henry's forgiveness?'

Relieved to see some of Charles's melancholy lift, Mary realised she might well have hit on the way to escape Henry's anger. Louis' generous gifts of jewellery would provide it, she was sure. But first, she must offer Henry the bait. Feverishly now, Mary took up her pen again. 'We must find out his feelings before we dare tell him of what we have done. I'll make him a deed of gift. Louis gave me many, many costly jewels. Worcester told me he had seven coffers filled with them. He's showered most of them on me.' Mary's voice sounded lighter now, as some of its heavy burdens eased. 'If need be, Henry can have them all. They are worth a king's ransom.' She gave a shaky laugh. 'Surely they will be enough to ransom a mere Dowager-Queen and her low-born husband? I won't send the deed yet, though. First, we'll see how the land lies. It may not be necessary to relinquish them at all.'

Mary's quill flew swiftly across the page, words coming easily to her now. Finally, she sat back. The atmosphere in the room was subtly different. Hope had slithered under the door. She could feel it.

While Mary and Charles awaited the response to the letters, her time in widowed seclusion came to an end and she was thrust from her quiet, if troubled retreat, back to the life of the court. But at least it gave them something else to think about than what reply the letters would receive.

She and Charles took part in Francis' joyous entry into Paris. They both felt they must be the censure of all eyes and checked furtively for sly looks and hidden laughter. Mary was surprised when they saw none as she had fully expected their secret marriage to have leaked out and be the talk of the court. But no one gave them more than a second's glance amidst the excitements the celebrations of Francis' coronation brought. And no wonder, thought Mary. The procession that entered Paris this February day was said to be the most gorgeous ever seen. In the midst of it rode Francis, on a magnificent white Arab stallion. With all the easy charm at his command, he graciously acknowledged the cheers while encouraging his heralds to throw even more gold and silver coins to the crowd.

Francis caught Mary's gaze on him and blew her a kiss. She quickly lowered her eyes lest he see their turmoil. For some reason best known to herself, Louise had kept the secret of their marriage to herself. She must have done, Mary reasoned, otherwise, even amidst all the ceremonies, Francis would have sought her out and cross-questioned her relentlessly. But he was ever one for prying and she couldn't afford to give him an opportunity to part her from this secret. Although it was true he had given their theoretical marriage his blessing, he might feel differently were he to know it was actually accomplished and consumated. Mary knew she couldn't afford to rekindle his jealousy. Who knew what might be the result? To cause the anger of one king was bad enough, but to anger two would be utter folly.

The days passed, uncertainty a continual torment as they waited for a message from Henry. Mary's monthly flux was late and this brought new fears. Let her not be pregnant, not here, not now. She needed all her strength to fight the terrors that came in the night. Such dreams she had, blood red and filled with gore as she watched Charles's handsome head struck from his neck. Night after night she woke, crying out, her body bathed in sweat and her hair clinging damply to her neck.

Daily, their worries compounded. Henry had, the previous year, gained the town of Tournai in battle. His new possession was a source of great pride to him, representing as it did his dreams of emulating previous victorious warrior kings. Francis, naturally, had an equally great desire to get it back.

As well as offering Henry's congratulations to his new brother sovereign, Charles's diplomatic mission to the French court included instructions to negotiate on the matter of Tournai. Mary's tears had come between him and his duty. But now he told Mary that he was commissioned to extract every last farthing of her marriage portion from the French king as well as negotiate on the question of Tournai. But how could he bring this off when he was under an obligation to Francis who had been so understanding of his and Mary's confidences?

Mary had no answer for him. Charles had told her also that, every day now, Francis called on him at his lodging to know what was happening on the matter of Tournai, reminding Charles how much of an obligation to him he was under. Mary, wracked with guilt, could only watch as Charles squirmed, caught as he was between the opposing demands of two mighty sovereigns.

This difficult situation was still unresolved when a messenger arrived from England. Mary and Charles snatched eagerly at the letters he brought, relieved that both Henry and Wolsey's letters to them were kindly. They both felt cheered that Henry had written to tell them how great was his love for them both and that he desired to see them happy. However, Henry's next words took the edge off their cheer. He told them there had been jealous murmurings in the Council against the match. Charles and Mary looked uneasily at one another as Henry confirmed what they had suspected would happen.

The long-awaited letters had resolved nothing. Their only comfort was that Henry had repeated his good intentions towards them. It would have to be enough because Mary, convinced she was pregnant and that concealment of this condition would soon be impossible in any case, felt they had no choice but to live openly in Paris as man and wife, something they hadn't dared to do before. But in spite of the ominous mention of the Council in Henry's letter, his own loving words gave them courage.

It was a courage they were soon to need because it wasn't long before rumours of their presumption reached England. The shock waves brought by this revelation travelled even more swiftly than had the previous rumours. Mary and Charles, cowering in their honeymoon chamber, were horrified that Henry, faced with the angry and bitter voices raised against Charles in Council, had back-tracked and was now strongly denying he had ever given them any encouragement.

They could only cling to one another, aware if they lost Henry as their champion, Charles was indeed doomed. It could be that Henry's display of anger at their actions had only been put on for his Council's benefit, Mary told him.

But Charles wasn't to be comforted so easily. 'What if your brother's anger is real?' he demanded. 'I have defied the solemn vow I gave to him. He would be justified in having me put to death for marrying you.'

Mary, feeling he would be better occupied doing something instead of brooding on such terrors, set him to write a contrite and humble letter to Wolsey, confessing their marriage and the probability that Mary was already pregnant with his child. Fear made Charles eloquent, Mary saw as, over his shoulder she read the words that flowed from his pen in which he begged Wolsey's help to conceal the truth of their actions from Henry. Hard on the heels of this letter, they sent the great jewel, the *Miroir de Naples* that Louis had given Mary, hoping its beauty would prove more persuasive than words alone.

Again they waited, hoping the clever Wolsey would be able to find a solution to their predicament. But Wolsey's reply when it finally arrived only served to confirm that they had good reason for their terror. For although the author was Wolsey, the anger of Mary's brother, the king, was writ large on every page. Wolsey had ignored their plea for secrecy: Henry knew all.

Mary and Charles read doom in every line of Wolsey's letter, filled as it was with bitter accusations. It made clear that Henry felt affronted, deceived and betrayed. And though the letter was ostensibly from Wolsey, it was surely Henry who had demanded that Wolsey write to remind Charles of his lowly birth and how it had been Henry who had raised him to his present lordly status. Wolsey's words made clear that Henry felt his generosity had been but poorly rewarded.

They stiffened as they read the line they had most feared to read. For in ink that looked somehow even more dark and threatening than the rest, Wolsey told them that the king was so angry that Charles looked certain to lose his head.

Near swooning, Mary reached for a chair and shakily sat down. Her first thought was to deny the fear that Wolsey's words had instilled in them. 'He doesn't mean it,' she insisted. 'He but plays with us, you'll see.'

Charles shook his head. 'He does right to threaten me. I feel ashamed. King Henry has ever been a benign sovereign to me and I have thrown it in his face.' He sat down on the bed, and stared down at the letter clutched in his hand with such an over-riding gloom that it might indeed be his death warrant. 'I can't expect the king to forgive this. Truly, I have earned his harshest revenge.'

Alarmed that Charles seemed so accepting of the death he felt he richly deserved, Mary cried, 'Don't say that. I don't want a dead martyr for a husband. Just let his anger cool and he'll be loving again, I know it.'

But Charles wasn't to be comforted. It was apparent that Wolsey's letter had made him so appreciate the depth of his betrayal that he believed he deserved to receive the ultimate punishment. Mary could only watch as he rose from the bed like one with the ague and stood gazing out of the window at the never-ending rain.

And no matter what she did, she was unable to persuade him from his melancholy. With a sigh, she picked up the letter and read it again, searching for some glimmer of hope. They had reached no further than the threat before and now, as she quickly scanned the rest of the letter, her heart gave a leap. Was Wolsey giving her a hint, a way out of their dilemma when he mentioned her jewels?

Whether it was a hint or merely wishful thinking, Mary snatched at it. How likely was it that a man with Wolsey's subtle brain would torment them with false hope? He had mentioned her jewels for a reason, she was sure. Wolsey would not have mentioned what might yet be their salvation if he had not gauged Henry's feelings on the matter.

Part of her was fearful of clutching too eagerly at this tiny thread of hope, lest it break. But it was all they had. She now pulled Charles from his gloomy study of the rain and forced him to read the rest of the letter. 'See, I told you,' she said, when he had done so. 'I told you Henry's temper would cool. Is it not clear to you now that between Wolsey starting the letter and finishing it, Henry's mind was altered by the reminder of my 'winnings' here?' And how he might wrest them from her, Mary added silently to herself. After Henry had helped himself to her Castilian dowry jewel Mary had no illusions about the strength of her brother's love for shiny and expensive baubles. It was something for which she now thanked God.

Mary took up her pen and urged Charles to do the same. Soon, more contrite letters were despatched across the Channel. Mary insisted on taking all the blame. She revealed the predicament in which her tearful demands had placed her lover who had felt unable to withstand such a torrent.

Again they must wait, tormented by growing doubts that Mary's eager interpretation of Wolsey's words had been mistaken. Caught in the eye of the storm, their lives stood still while the frenetic life of the court carried on around them. Veering from optimism to darkest terror, they could only await the arrival of yet more messengers and whatever news they would bring.

Mary tried to calm her mind with prayers. But Charles, like Henry, a man of huge physical energy, found the waiting intolerable. And although Mary tried to dissuade him from it, to her dismay, without waiting for a reply from Wolsey, Charles insisted on publishing the news of their marriage to all France. But first, he took the alarming step of telling Francis what they had done.

As Mary had feared, Francis' jealousy now returned in full measure, his rage fuelled by the lust she knew he still felt for her. How could he not feel doubly insulted, in his kingship and in his manhood also? Had he not wooed her determinedly for weeks, to no avail? Yet here was this low-born Englishman who need do nothing but deny her to gain her bed.

Mary's knowledge of Francis gave her even more reason to fear for Charles's life. Only this time the threatening monarch wasn't miles away across the sea, but here, close at hand and well able to extract swift retribution.

CHAPTER THIRTEEN

Fortunately, Francis, to conceal his dented pride, chose to pretend that by lustfully debasing her honour, Mary had killed his desire for her and he washed his hands of them both. But this didn't prevent him from coolly telling them that Charles would be held fast till he knew what Henry would have him do with them.

Mary breathed again when she learned Francis' intentions. They were in no worse case than before, apart from Charles's detention. Truly, Francis' rage had frightened her and its cooling was greatly welcome. However, his rage roared again a few days later when he discovered the magnificent *Miroir of Naples* had vanished across the sea into Henry's coffers. Furiously, he demanded its return. It belonged to each succeeding Queen of France in turn, he told her, and was not hers to dispose of as she wished.

While Francis continued to rage about the palace, Charles wrote urgently to England. But in their hearts Mary and he suspected these urgent pleadings would fall on deaf ears. Claude, Francis' wife, had little chance of ever seeing the return of such a fabulous jewel, as Henry's grasp on such baubles was as tenacious as ever. Anxiety filled their days

and nights as they waited to see what would be Francis' reaction when the truth finally dawned on him.

Francis ranted and raved at Charles as he tried to excuse his
actions. 'I had but thought to appease King Henry,' he told
the furious French king. 'I understood the *Miroir* belonged
to Mary.'

'Of course it didn't belong to Mary,' Francis roared at
him. 'She knew that full well.' Francis' gaze narrowed dan-
gerously. 'You try my patience, Englishman. First you seduce my widowed mother-in-law, then you steal my jewels.
What will you do next? Rape my sister, perhaps? Steal my
crown and prise out its jewels to pawn? Why should I not
part you from your head?'

Charles felt the colour leave his face at Francis' threat.
He swayed slightly and recoiled as Francis stood eyeball to
eyeball with him.

'Why should such a pleasure be saved for King Henry?'
he demanded. 'Mary is my subject, made French by her first
marriage. You think you have betrayed your master?' Francis' voice lowered, but if anything, its softer tones seemed
even more dangerous than the previous ranting. 'I tell you, I
am the more injured. Don't, I pray you, give me any more
cause for anger. You have already tempted me sorely.'

His uncompromising warning delivered, Francis turned
on his heel and strode off. Alarmed and humiliated, Charles
did his best to ignore the sniggers of the courtiers as he
made his way to Mary's chamber.

Mary rushed to Charles's side as soon as he entered the room and clutched at him in desperation to learn the worst. 'Was Francis very angry?'

Charles nodded. 'He threatened to save King Henry the trouble of cutting my head off. He said he would gladly do it for him.'

Mary gasped. Her hand flew to her mouth as Charles, denied an outlet for his feelings in the French king's presence, began to vent his spleen on her.

'I should never have sent that jewel to England. Compared to his present rage, Francis was before all sweet reason.' He scowled at the window. 'I can't take much more of this stinking prison. Will this accursed rain never end? Everywhere is mud, mud and more mud. God, but I'm sick of it all, sick unto death.'

To Mary's distress, he flung out of the chamber, his demeanour left her in no doubt that he intended to get blind drunk and that right soon. Mary couldn't blame him. But his anger made her feel even more wretched. How much longer could they endure this tension, which only seemed to increase as each day passed? She sank down on the bed. She doubted their love would recover from so many mortal blows. How could it? Was there a man alive who would continue to love a woman whose demands had brought him so close to death?

Mary remained dry-eyed at this latest worry. It seemed she had no more tears left to shed. Instead, she clutched at her belly. Within it lay the creature who could tip the balance between Charles's life and his death. But would the child save him or condemn him? She knew not. She was worn out with thinking. To add to her woes, her body betrayed her again and her agonising toothache returned in full measure.

They had heard nothing from England, not a word came from Henry or Wolsey. Mary became convinced now that she had wilfully mistaken Wolsey when he had mentioned the jewels in his last letter. Had she simply been clutching at a straw that had no existence other than in her own increasingly desperate mind?

Mary took up her pen yet again and wrote forlorn little letters to her brother, the tears she had thought all dried up scattered freely amongst the pages as she pleaded brokenly for his forgiveness. She begged him to allow them to return home or at least to have an open ceremony of marriage in France. She clutched her belly again, grimly aware that their secret marriage could yet be quashed and the child of their illicit union tainted with bastardy. What would become of them then?

All around them they felt the hostility of the court as the French, to a man, to a woman, sided with Francis. The courtiers felt as aggrieved as their king at the loss of the *Miroir*. Worse, they left Mary in no doubt that they felt she had dishonoured the title of Queen by taking Charles as her husband.

Mary and Charles could only wait, their sense of isolation increasing, as still no word came from England. Each day, they looked for a messenger so they would know their fate and each day they were disappointed.

Would Wolsey never write? He was their only hope, their only anchor in the angry seas that surrounded them. If he should desert them there would be no one to speak for them. No one to protect them.

Nerves stretched taut, Mary's head developed a nervous tremor and nodded on her slim neck like a flower on its stalk. Every noise, every arrival, set her whole body quivering in harmony with her head, such was her agitation. All her life she had been pampered and cossetted. The baby of the family, the prettiest daughter, she had scarcely known trouble. Always, there had been someone to lift her worries from her shoulders. Nothing in her short life had prepared Mary for the travails she now suffered. She could not even look to Charles for comfort as he was in a worse state than she. He had taken to regularly rubbing his hand over his neck as if to reassure himself that it had not been severed by the headsman's axe. As he had said, he had more cause to fear retribution than she. Which was the worse, she wondered? To suffer the penalty yourself or to watch the one you loved suffer it, knowing you had brought the suffering upon them?

But even now, in her secret heart, she couldn't feel that what she had done was so wrong. All she had done was marry the man she loved. What price her high estate when even the simplest village maid could marry where she wished? More woman than queen, Mary had placed a higher value on love than great titles and it had brought her more trouble than six dukedoms.

The weather was still grey and wet. As she sat watching the steadily-falling rain and waiting for Charles to return to her after their latest disagreement, the thought crossed her mind that he might take his chance and flee, abandoning her to Francis' mercy. He had proved his mettle in battle and his sword would find welcome anywhere he chose to offer it. Mary felt she could scarce blame him if he threw in his lot with the German mercenaries and fought the wars of the highest bidder. Didn't the cynical French believe that in all love-matches there is one who kisses and one who is kissed? In her heart, Mary suspected that her love for Charles was greater than his for her. The thought did nothing to ease her mind.

She started up in alarm as she saw a messenger arrive. He was wearing Wolsey's livery. Her agitation at the sight caused the tremor of her head to increase alarmingly. She stumbled to the door, but once there, her fear of what any letter might contain stayed her. She jumped in terror as someone knocked on the door. Gathering her courage, Mary found her voice and bid her visitor enter.

It was the messenger. Mary stared at him. Was he the angel of doom? Or the angel of their salvation?

The messenger seemed disconcerted by her behaviour. Barely had he stumbled out his words of greeting, than Mary, unable to bear the suspense any longer, snatched the letter from his hand and tore it open. She scanned the contents of the letter quickly, desperate now to bring the long days of wretched uncertainty to an end, and to know their fate one way or the other.

As the meaning of Wolsey's words penetrated her fear, she closed her eyes. Relief flowed through her, leaving her body so limp she was barely able to keep her feet. Wolsey had saved them. She would have to sacrifice all her jewels and plate and a large part of her dowry to secure Henry's forgiveness. But what did she care for any of them? All that mattered was that Charles would live. Willingly would she give up all her newly-acquired riches to save her husband's life.

Mary sank down on the nearest stool as her legs weakened further and threatened to give way altogether. She bid the startled messenger wait whilst she scribbled a hasty reply agreeing to all her brother's greedy demands, then bade him go the the kitchens to refresh himself after his journey.

But still they must wait whilst the haggling over valuables raged. She and Charles were not yet free to leave Paris and its accursed mud and rain. Francis proved as obstinate as the weather and demanded that Mary must pay her late husband's debts before she could take their possessions out of his realm.

Letters flew back and forth across the Channel, but still the haggling continued. Mary's earlier relief turned to despair. Would it never end? Her health had become poor from so many anxieties. She longed only for peace in the English countryside with Charles. But the prospect seemed to get no nearer. The weeks turned to months, the spring buds were everywhere bursting forth and still they couldn't escape. Mary began to feel they were destined to spend the rest of their lives suspended in this tortuous Limbo while first

Francis, then Henry, played with their lives. She shed so many bitter tears that the skin around her eyes turned puffy and her eyes sank back in her head. Truly, she felt she would now certainly be safe from Francis should any of his lust for her linger.

As for Charles, he had discovered a new vigor. Determined to get Francis back on their side, he spent much time in his company, leaving Mary to her thoughts.

At last, it seemed that Charles's efforts had paid off and agreement was finally reached. Mary learned that she was to get half of the plate and the sum of 50,000 crowns, which was about half the value of the jewels. She would also receive about two-fifths of her jointure. The lion's share of all this would of course go to Henry and now, pacified by such wealth, he gave his consent. They could at last go home.

But before this much longed-for event could happen they were to renew their marriage vows before the French court. As it was Lent, they must secure the permission of the Bishop, but this was granted with no difficulty.

Mary dressed with care, conscious of the number of hostile eyes that would be watching. The French, with their worldly cynicism, thought she was a fool and worse, had let her emotions and her bodily desires overrule good sense. She could have taken Charles to her bed without an eyebrow being raised, but to marry him damned her in their eyes. Charles, though, they admired for acquiring such a highborn wife. Not a few of the ladies of the court eyed him with interest, clearly wondering what erotic delights lay beneath the bluff exterior. With sly looks had they watched Francis' pursuit of Mary, then along had come the tall Englishman who had whisked Mary from under the king's nose. Clearly, the court found it most amusing.

In spite of the care Mary took for the occasion, she could do little to improve her looks. Her eyes were still shadowed and puffy from all her weeping, her golden hair had lost its sheen and hung about her shoulders fighting her eyes for dullness. The weeks of fearful strain had inevitably taken their toll on her golden beauty and now, when she was had most need of the assurance it provided, it had deserted her.

She gritted her teeth. So be it. She would have to face the stares as best she could. At least Claude had been kind and had wished her well. Luckily, Claude was unaware of how ready Francis had been to cast her off for Mary or she mightn't have had even her friendly face.

Mary took a deep breath, stole one last glance at her pale reflection and turned away. She was ready. This was yet another ordeal to be gone through, albeit one that would see her truly married to Charles with no risk of the marriage being put asunder. She walked to the door and as she recalled Lady Guildford's advice, she held her head high. She felt she had truly grown up at last.

Mary stood proudly at Charles's side and made her vows, ignoring the sly whispers. It mattered not that it was scarcely any more joyous an occasion than their secret marriage had been. All that mattered what that, in the eyes of the world, it was legal and they were truly man and wife. Mary closed her eyes and took a deep breath. Beside her, she felt Charles's body sag with relief.

They were finally free to set out, first to Calais and then home to England. The relief was tremendous. When she thought how it might have turned out... But Mary wouldn't allow herself to dwell on the thought. For all the past, nerve-wracking weeks, she had been convinced she must be pregnant, but now, with the ending of her fears and the relaxation of tension, her monthly flow returned. She cursed her traitorous body for giving them an additional, unnecessary anxiety to add to all the rest they had endured. But at least her false pregnancy had helped them accomplish their marriage so it could not be despised. She wondered what Henry would say when he realised her body had deceived him also.

The weather brightened as though to match their mood. They rode at a goodly pace along the road to Calais, accompanied by many of the French nobles, half-fearful that even now Francis might change his mind and demand their return. Francis had seen them both before they left. Still vexed by the loss of the *Miroir*, he could barely be civil to Mary, blaming her for its being sent to England. His gallantry had vanished as surely as the jewel and there was little chance of either returning. Mary didn't care. She had what she wanted and would soon be gone out of his reach. She smiled ruefully as she opened the traditional gift for a widowed queen returning to her homeland. Francis had sent her several jewels of little value. His subtlety gone the way of his gallantry, his paltry gift revealed what he thought of her better than any words. But she was pleased that Francis had been pleasant to

Charles, glad for her husband's sake that Francis chose to be friendly towards him.

The road was dusty, but to Mary it was a glorious dust after Paris and its endless, enclosing prison of mud. She turned to Charles, caught his eye and they both laughed, albeit with a touch of hysteria. Everything delighted them. They were free, in love and married. Soon they would be home in England. They threw coins to the urchins who ran beside them when they passed through villages and laughed at the children's delight. They could ill-afford such generosity, but neither of them cared. It was now Henry's money. Recklessly, they threw some more. They would worry about their lack of funds when they reached England. For now, they simply wished to bask in the warm sunshine of freedom. Nothing could dismay them.

Henry's town of Calais rose up before them and they spurred their tired horses towards it.

Calais was quiet and offered them little welcome. Mary, upset by the sullen looks directed at them after all the hostility she had experienced in France, was doubly-wounded to be treated in like manner by her own people. Her previous high spirits lowered. Was this how they would be received in England itself?

As they arrived at their lodging and retired to the chamber allotted to them, the thought made her imagination lively with fresh anxieties. Had Henry only agreed to their homecoming to get his hands on her riches? Did he still intend to wreak his revenge on them?

The scowling faces of the townspeople of Calais filled them both with such unease that Charles sent for Sir Richard Wingfield, the Deputy of Calais and demanded to know why their welcome had been so poor.

Sir Richard explained he had forced certain of the people of Calais to delay a long-planned visit to England, thinking they should be here to greet the king's sister. But they had been expected weeks ago. The many delays had caused frustration.

Charles was irritated that Wingfield's actions should have caused them additional, needless distress. Curtly, he dismissed the man. But Mary was relieved that it was merely frustration and nothing more sinister that had caused the sullen looks. Even so, their lack of welcome had distressed her, bringing back as it had all her old fears in full measure. And by the next morning's dawning her anxieties had had time to gnaw away at her. She was filled with disquiet and suggested to Charles that it would be better if they proceeded slowly. 'Better, I think, for us to remain in Calais rather than cross to England just yet. It would be safer to bide here till we hear from Henry and can better judge his intentions.'

Charles was impatient with her. 'Your nerves but play you false, Mary. You heard Wingfield. It was he who caused the sullen looks, not anything we have done, nor any instruction from the king. Calm yourself.'

But Mary wasn't to be calmed. She felt uneasy. 'I don't care, Charles. I feel there is more to it than the townspeople's frustration at having their trip to England delayed. You said yourself you felt threatened when you ventured out of doors. Yet why should that be when it was my arrival for which they were forced to tarry?'

Her words failed to breed caution and she was forced to reveal what was troubling her. 'I fear we but get a taste of the welcome that awaits us in England.'

She took his hand in hers and pleaded with him. 'Please, my love, humour me. It would not be safe to cross to England just yet. We have waited so long, what difference can a few more days make? Better, too, I think, if we do not venture out while we are here.'

A look of exasperation marred her husband's handsome looks and Mary knew her entreaties had annoyed him. He did not take kindly to being cooped up. He had had enough of that in Paris. Her eyes filled with the tears that her recent travails had made too-ready. But at least, at sight of them, Charles's resolve weakened sufficiently for him to promise her that he wouldn't venture outdoors again.

Mary could only pray his confinement wasn't a lengthy one. To make it as short as possible, she wrote a hasty letter to her brother. Just in case he was planning an unpleasant surprise for them, and reminded him of his promise once more, hoping such a pin-prick would shame him from any such plan.

To their relief, within a few days they received such loving letters that even Mary's fears vanished. There would now be no need to retreat back into France to the uncertain sanctuary offered by Francis. They were safe to cross the sea.

Mary still felt some trepidation about their likely reception, but now she believed that Henry at least meant them no harm. They could brave the rest. She was glad to see that Charles had quickly thrown off his worries. After witnessing his vulnerability and all too human fears, she had become more tender towards him. She felt the need to make up to him for all the misery she had put him through.

Now they could begin to put the dreadful start to their marriage behind them. In future, Mary was determined she would be a loving wife to Charles instead of the tying problem she had been thus far.

RELUCTANT QUEEN

BOOK TWO

CHAPTER FOURTEEN

T he water of the Channel was gentle for this journey. Mary had feared the same fierce seas that had brought her to France, a weeping, reluctant bride, going to her aged husband. How well had the tempest-tossed sea suited her unhappy mood.

Now Fortune's Wheel had turned in her favour. For this journey she had a husband who was beloved by her side rather than an unloved one awaiting her at journey's end. It was an omen of the bright future that was to be theirs. She took Charles's hand as they stood at the ship's rail and waved goodbye to sullen Calais, mud-sodden Paris and all their woes.

Charles smiled down at her. 'Happy, sweetheart?'

Mary gazed up at him with shining eyes. 'I'm so happy I feel drunk with it.' She laughed and squeezed his hand. Nervously, given all that she had put him through, she asked, 'And you, Charles? I wanted to come to you a properly dowered bride. Instead, I'm a widow, almost a paupered one at that. Can you forgive me for all the trouble I've caused you?' Tremulously, she waited for his reply.

He silenced her with a kiss. 'I have a Queen. A beautiful Queen. 'Tis enough for me. You would be enough for any man, let alone one as low-born as I.'

Mary felt tears wash her cheeks at his words. But these were tears of joy and she was glad of them. Glad, too, to hear his reassurances. After all, Charles was a man of great ambition; it was one of the things she had admired about him. Yet he still loved and wanted her, with or without her dower. Everything had happened so fast that he hadn't had time to think about how their actions might yet affect him. She feared remorse might yet set in over his broken oath to Henry and possibly blighted future. She suspected also that he would be disappointed in his high hopes that Henry would give them back a large part of her wealth as a marriage gift. But for now, she put such thoughts to the back of her mind. They had waited long enough for this happy time to come and she intended to enjoy it to the full. She snuggled up to Charles and together they turned their faces to the receding shores of France. Soon, it was just a misty blur on the horizon. The sun was shimmering on the water as they went below, the promise of love in their eyes and in the lightness of their step.

The crossing was swift. The bright breeze filled the sails till they rounded like a full-bosomed matron and pushed them and all Mary's 'winnings' in France - the many riches the sickly Louis had showered on her - onward to Dover. The closer they came to home, the more Mary had to steel herself.

And, in spite of Charles's confident words, she suspected he, too, expected to receive a mixed reception.

All too quickly their loving solitude came to an end. Soon, they were able to pick out individual faces from those waiting to greet them. Mary scanned them anxiously. She couldn't see Henry or Wolsey. Where were they? Why had they not come? Was it a sinister portent that neither man had come to welcome them home? Mary, well aware that her brother preferred to leave any unpleasantness to others, felt a fresh rush of anxiety.

She saw Lady Guildford. Her old governess had managed to push her way to the front of the throng and Mary scanned her face for any hint that trouble loomed. But Lady Guildford's countenance, schooled to show no emotion, told Mary nothing and she had to wait till the ship had docked before she could pose any questions.

As soon as the gangplank was down, Mary flew across and threw herself into Lady Guildford's arms, glad to feel the familiar security fold itself around her. But even then, she had to wait to ask her questions. The proprieties still had to be observed. Her old governess expected nothing less.

After a swift hug, Lady Guildford held Mary away from her and exclaimed, 'What foolishness is this, my little Queen? As soon as my back is turned you throw discretion and sense to the winds it seems.'

'Ah, but Mother, I'm happy, so happy.'

Her obvious joy softened the stern old lady. Mary had expected a lecture, but instead all she received was the warning, 'Well, you're married to him now, my lady, for better or worse. Naught I can say will alter that, so I give you my blessing.'

Mary smiled, brought Charles forward and bade them kiss each other, which coaxed a couple of chilly pecks. Finally able to pose the troubling question, she was relieved to learn that the absence of Henry and Wolsey heralded nothing sinister and that they awaited her and Charles at Wolsey's manor at Barking. They set off eagerly. Mary gazed about her with delight to be back in England. How fresh and clean everything looked under the May sunshine. The trees seemed more green, the grass more lush, the countryside more rich than anything France could offer.

Wolsey met them along the road. Charles was inclined to be a little sheepish at first, but Wolsey, subtle politician that he was spoke to him in a friendly manner and soon put Charles at his ease. Mary chattered away happily, glad to be home and grateful to Wolsey for his kind greeting and for all his efforts on their behalf. They were nearly at Barking when they spotted the unmistakable figure of Henry riding towards them. Mary and Charles exchanged nervous glances. She saw him lick his lips as if they had suddenly become dry. Mary, too, felt a tremor course through her body as her brother approached. Henry looked as big and handsome as ever. He stopped his horse a few paces from them and regarded them solemnly.

A sudden hush descended at this silent regard. Mary glanced again at Charles and he at her. As their gazes returned slowly, reluctantly to the king, from the corner of her eye Mary saw Charles's hand steal to his neck, in a repetition of the nervous habit he had developed while in France.

The silence lengthened. Suddenly, Henry broke it with a great roar which made them jump. But their fear was soon allayed. Henry had been playing with them. He slapped his thigh and cried out in a hearty manner, 'Welcome. Welcome.'

Mary slumped in her saddle. For all that he was a grown man and a mighty king, her brother's sense of humour could be surprisingly childish. Childish, and with a hint of cruelty. Henry had just been reminding them of his power.

Henry leapt from his horse and strode towards them. Mary knew she was truly home when he swept her to the ground and enclosed her in a huge bear-hug

When Henry released her, she stood back and smiled up at him. 'You look well, Henry. Indeed, everything looks good here in England.' Mary heard the breathlessness in her voice and hoped Henry hadn't noticed it. She had been so determined to be calm and serene. 'How is Catherine?'

'Well enough, Mary. Well enough, though she lost the babe.' Henry's queen and her health were dismissed. He held Mary at arm's length and gazed at her. 'So, you're finally home. 'Tis good to see you, sweetheart. We've missed you.'

Mary bit back an ironic smile at this revelation of filial devotion. Who would have thought there had ever been any anger or disagreement between them? Or that Henry, through Wolsey, had haggled over her rich French 'winnings' till he had got his way? She could have been home weeks ago but for Henry. But with him ready to play the magnanimous brother now was not the time to remind him of this. Instead, Mary kissed him and allowed him to lead her over to her husband.

Charles had hung back. He attempted a smile for Henry, but it only betrayed his nerves. Mary felt a surge of compassion. Doubtless, he would tell her afterwards that his low birth had never prepared him for showing defiance to a king.

But Henry was set on playing the jovial prince. He slapped Charles on the back and bellowed, 'Well, brother-in-law, so you've brought our sister home to us. We are pleased.' With narrowed gaze he asked, 'You have her dower safe we trust?'

Mary bit her lip as Charles threw himself on his knees before Henry. He clutched Henry's hand and kissed it fervently. His lips moved, but it seemed his ability to speak had deserted him. Before Henry began to suspect they had lost her dower, Mary answered his question.

'Aye, brother. We have my dower. My lord Cardinal has it safe for you.'

Henry smiled. 'Good, good.' He gazed benevolently at his handsome friend, humbly kneeling in the dirt of the road. 'Get up, man, get up,' he told him. 'There's no need for you to kneel in the dust. We forgive you your presumption in marrying our sister. We gave her a promise and kings, my lord, do not forget their oaths.'

This was a taunt for the vow-breaking Charles. Mary felt the temptation to respond in like manner with the rejoinder - especially when they've been well bribed so to do - wisely, she remained silent. But for her rich dower their homecoming might have been very different. She must be grateful for that.

Henry made much of them both as they rode the short distance to Barking. He was boisterous and merry as he related to them all the doings of the court.

He could well afford to be merry, was Mary's thought. This day's dawning had brought him great riches and Henry's delight in them was evident. It soon became apparent that others were less delighted. Mary noted the many envious and grudging glances directed at her husband. She could read in their faces what they were thinking—that Charles was a low-born upstart who had wed a queen when he had naught but a king's stature and handsome looks to recommend him. Mary supposed it was natural that many were jealous of his altered circumstances. She was thankful the king was behind them. They could weather the jealousy of others.

Soon, they travelled on to Greenwich, their journey made doubly joyous by the brightness of the May sunshine and the anticipation of another celebration of their marriage. This one, the third, was all that Mary could have wished for. After so many betrothals and weddings, she felt fully able to do justice to the occasion. Her looks had recovered and her mirror told her she had never looked lovelier. At last, as she clung proudly to Charles's arm, she was truly a willing and beautiful bride.

Henry was still being magnanimous, but he was keen to cover up their previous marriages in France, the first and secret one and the second, more open ceremony. The first he could conceal, but the second was too widely known and its concealment proved impossible. Mary didn't greatly care. She and Charles threw themselves into the public celebrations of their marriage. They had been unhappy forever it seemed. Now they were free to enjoy life. Mary was determined to do so.

Henry held tournaments in honour of their nuptials at Greenwich Palace. Mary watched with bright eyes as her husband rode out, his relief and gratitude inscribed on his banner for all to see:

> *'Cloth of gold, do not despise,*
> *Though thou hast wedded cloth of frieze.*
> *Cloth of frieze, be not too bold,*
> *Though thou hast wedded cloth of gold.'*

This gesture of humility pleased Henry. Mary thought it might well have saved her husband from harm as the resentment of certain of Henry's Council still seethed. Norfolk still made loud calls for a bloody revenge for Charles's presumption. She discovered that he had been behind the plan to use her to cement an alliance with the Low Countries for the good of trade and to still any warmongering urges that King Frances might harbour. Thwarted in this by her marriage to Charles, Norfolk went about the court with his friends, all wearing long and scowling faces.

Mary wondered that they dared. She and Charles had Henry's backing and that was all that mattered. Let Norfolk scowl as he may, he couldn't harm them.

So Mary and Charles ignored the ill-feeling. Mary, especially, considered the world and Norfolk's friendship well
lost for love. She was home. Now their love could be freely
expressed and she thanked God for it. God and Henry.

Charles was full of plans, as happy as she'd ever known
him. Henry's name was mentioned in his every sentence. In-
wardly she would smile as she listened to him when he spoke
to his friends. It was all 'the king, my brother-in-law', or 'my
wife's brother, the king.' Mary couldn't resist teasing him
about it when they were alone.

'For such a reluctant bridegroom, Charles, you certainly
make a keen brother-in-law.' She saw by his frown that she
had touched a tender spot and instantly regretted her words.
'Nay, don't look at me like that Charles. I'm only teasing. But
did you not realise how often you mention your brother-in-
law, the king, in your conversations? I'm sure Henry would
be flattered if he realised.'

Charles pulled a face. 'What else can I call him, Mary? I
don't feel he would welcome the presumption of me calling
him Henry. I've presumed enough for one lifetime. I aim to
please the king now in all things. He'll find none as loyal to
his desires as me.'

Piqued and more than a little jealous, Mary asked with a
pout, 'Can you spare a little time to please the king's sister
also, Charles? It seems your thoughts are so much on the
king that I feel sore neglected.'

His scowl vanished at this. But he took the hint and
quickly covered the two paces that were between them. He
picked her up bodily and threw her on the bed.

Mary gave a mock cry of fear.

Charles told her, 'Now woman, I'm about to stop neglecting you. I'm sure my brother-in-law, the king, can spare me for long enough to pleasure his sister.'

Mary gave him a lazy smile. 'He'd better, Charles. I feel sure I'm going to require a lot of your attention. A wife surely has first call, ahead of a mere in-law on her husband's time.'

Charles bent over her, his body shutting out the light. 'You can be sure, sweetheart, that I'll always have my priorities well ordered. At worst a king can only kill you, but a frustrated wife can make of life a hell on earth, if she's a mind to.'

Mary gave a contented sigh. 'It's true. I hope you remember that, my love, should you be tempted to neglect me again. I'm sure my Mother Guildford could give me a few tips on how to correct errant husbands.'

He drew back in mock horror. 'No Mary, anything but that. I'm yours, now and forever. Please God don't learn any tricks from Lady Guildford. I'm sure she would teach you things that would make of me another Louis. From what I hear, she helped to unman the old king.'

Mary softened. She curved her body into his and gazed lovingly up at him. 'Don't worry, Charles. With you, I have no desire to learn such tricks.'

'I'm glad to hear it, sweetheart.'

Mary smiled and demanded, 'Is your pleasuring made up of words only, my lordly husband, or do deeds figure also?'

'You're lucky, sweeting. I was ever a man of few words and much action.'

To Mary's delight, he proceeded to demonstrate just how much of a man of action he was.

Daily now, Charles expected Henry's forgiveness to take a more tangible form. They had handed over the money that had ransomed his life and Charles had waited, confident Henry meant to make them a gift of much of it. Only slowly did it dawn on him that his optimism had played him false. For even though their expenses were mounting, still Henry made them no offer. Charles began to worry. He was head over heels in debt to the crown and to others, as the cost of his embassies, tournaments and marriage had been large. How casually he had incurred the debts. But then he had not expected to have to pay them. As it sunk in that his jovial brother-in-law had no intention of paying up, Charles became so hung with gloom that Mary asked him what had happened to so lower his spirits.

'It's what *hasn't* happened that worries me, Mary,' he told her.

'Were you expecting something to happen, then? What could it be? Is it a surprise?'

It was clear Mary thought he had planned some treat for her. He was quick to disabuse her of the idea. 'It's a surprise, all right. One I wasn't expecting.'

Her face fell. 'Can you not tell me plain, Charles? I'll not break, you know.'

'It is all these debts, Mary. How are we ever to pay them. They mount daily.'

To his consternation, Mary's pretty mouth puckered as she realised what he had been hoping for. 'Did you think Henry would settle the debts?' He nodded. 'But—but you said you didn't care about my dower money. You said you were satisfied with me and didn't want the money also.'

'That was before I realised the true extent of our debts. We can't pay them, Mary. We'll have to leave the court. Leave the king.'

'Is that all?' Mary smiled. 'Surely that wouldn't be so bad, my love? I could enjoy seclusion in the country with you.'

He scowled. 'You don't understand, Mary. I have no desire to leave the court.'

Charles was aware that his revelation that he had no desire for seclusion in the country with her had wounded Mary and he was sorry for it. But what did she expect? She had known when she had first married him that he was a man of ambition. How else was he to achieve those ambitions but by remaining close to the king? She was the daughter and sister of kings, had been wife to another. All her life everything she needed and more had been provided for her. Royalty didn't bother their heads about debts. He could see that she truly didn't understand why such matters should cause him to worry. But for all his high title, he was still of low birth. And men of low birth had no choice but to worry about debt. The world insisted on it.

The world, in the shape of Cardinal Wolsey, was quick to remind Charles how sharp was reality. Henry, his jovial brother-in-law, wanted his money. And as soon as it became widely known that Henry didn't intend to undertake the role of bearer of gifts to his new kin, the other creditors became even more pressing, their demands for payment louder and more persistent.

Desperate, as his high hopes dissolved around him, Charles allowed Mary to persuade him to see Wolsey and plead for his intercession with the king. If Henry was willing to drop his demands, she had suggested, maybe all the demands of the others would ease off. Charles didn't hold out much hope for this plan. And Wolsey, the true servant of his master, made the position even clearer.

'My lord Duke, he told Charles. 'Much as it grieves me, I am unable to help you. I have spoken to the king on this matter already and he is not without sympathy. But these debts must be paid. There is no getting out of them.'

For all Wolsey's smooth apology, he exuded a smug self-satisfaction that angered Charles. His promise to Mary that he would keep his temper only served to increase his anger. It was one thing to grovel to the king, but Wolsey was of even lower birth than himself. Damping down the slow burning rage that he should be forced to beg from a man who had been no more than a butcher's cur, he tried again. 'My lord, cannot the king and yourself appreciate our difficulties? You know how large our expenses have been of late, all these celebrations have consumed large amounts of money. I had thought that the king, now his sister and I have been publicly married, would be willing to forget these debts.' A note of desperation entered his voice as he admitted, 'I had depended upon it.'

At Wolsey's sympathetic nod of understanding Charles forgot his shame at begging from the butcher's cur. He could not afford to take a high and mighty attitude with Wolsey. Instead, he softened his tone and pleaded, 'You helped us in our troubles in France. Can you not help us now? You know you have our gratitude for all your exertions on our behalf. These new problems have greatly upset my wife, the Dowager-Queen. God knows we have both had anxieties enough of late; we had hoped they were at an end.'

Wolsey appeared unmoved by this tale of woe. He took the trouble to remind Charles that his present difficulties were entirely due to his own folly. 'No one but you brought your troubles about. We have all tried to aid you in your many difficulties, but this problem of debts you must resolve yourself. I cannot help you.'

Wolsey rose from his chair in a lordly manner to indicate that the interview was over and Charles's hackles rose. To be dismissed like an erring page by Wolsey of all people was more than he could bear 'I take it that that is your last word on the subject, my lord Cardinal?' he demanded icily.

Wolsey inclined his head. The movement made his fleshy jowls wobble. 'Unfortunately, yes. I can think of nothing else I can say that might help you.'

Wolsey reminded Charles of a big, over-fed tom cat who had eaten too much cream. His fat, self-satisfied face with its hint of amusement at his visitor's discomfiture infuriated him all over again. It was galling that he had lowered his pride and all for nothing. Who was this Cardinal, anyway, to regard him with such ill-concealed scorn? Wolsey came from the gutters of Ipswich, yet still he had the temerity to call *him* low-born.

Charles felt his face flame. He bunched his thick fists on the table between them and stared over its top at Wolsey while a red mist descended. Determined to salvage some of his pride, he demanded, 'You had no intention of helping us, did you? You prefer to see me beg.' For a penny he would punch Wolsey's fat face. It was only Mary's remembered words of caution that held him in check. He took a deep breath and the red mist began to clear. But he still felt the urge to remind Wolsey that he had played his part in so reducing their means.

'You were the one who encouraged Mary to sign all her riches over to the king so that we might secure his forgiveness. You were the one who did all the negotiating. How can we know whether it was necessary or not? King Henry has a great fondness for his sister and has always wished her well and happy. We have only your word that it was necessary for her to sign away all her pretty jewels. How much of her wealth found its way into your coffers, I wonder?'

'My lord, you go too far,' Wolsey protested.

But now that he had spoken of his resentments, Charles couldn't keep the rest back. 'You were the one with the ear of the king,' he said again. 'Who knows what you whispered into it? He would probably have allowed Mary to keep her 'winnings' if he hadn't been discouraged from it.'

'Such ingratitude, my lord. It is unworthy. What of the Council? Did I whisper in their ears also? But for me, your head would have parted company from your shoulders ere this.'

Charles drew back at this reminder. Somehow he had lost the initiative. He sought to regain it. 'I, too, have friends on the Council. They would never have agreed to that.'

'Such quiet friends, my lord,' Wolsey taunted. 'I wonder why I didn't hear them speaking for you? Perhaps they gave their support in letters? I'm sure you must have received words of comfort and support from them whilst you were in France.'

Wolsey's voice had turned cold, but Charles refused to take the warning. The Cardinal knew very well that his friends hadn't written one word. He was only too conscious of it. His humiliation complete, Charles stalked to the door and turned for a parting shot. 'I'll speak to the king and discuss the matter with him. He and I have always been like brothers. He'll not see me driven from the court by debt.'

Wolsey merely shrugged at this. 'You may try, of course, but I must warn you the king does not like being put in awkward situations. He likes those who force those situations on him even less. Take care, my lord, that you do not antagonise the king. I've told you his feelings on the matter, that should satisfy you.'

Charles thrust his head forward on his strong neck and retorted, 'I will have my answer from the king himself on this matter, not from his pork butcher. I trust that satisfies *you*, my lord Cardinal,' he retorted, before he yanked the

door open and stalked through it, slamming it violently behind him.

CHAPTER FIFTEEN

Whether by good luck or ill, the king wasn't to be found. So Charles took himself and his anger back to his apartments. Mary was there, sewing with her ladies. She looked up expectantly as he entered and dismissed her women. When they were alone, she asked him, 'How went it, Charles? Can Cardinal Wolsey help?'

'No. Can't help or won't.' He threw himself into a chair. 'He vexed me so much that I told him what I suspected of him concerning our affairs.' Charles saw her puzzled look and wished he had kept silent. He was reluctant to demean himself still further in her eyes after his unheroic showing in Paris, but of course she got it out of him in the end. ''Tis my belief he persuaded the king to take your pretty jewels, convinced Henry to withhold his forgiveness till they were promised to him.'

'And you told Wolsey this? You challenged him with such suspicions?' Charles nodded. 'Oh Charles, you fool. Surely you must realise how much influence Wolsey wields with my brother? So far he has used his influence in our favour, but if he should turn against us... He is a clever man and would be a dangerous enemy.'

He turned sulky at her words. He had already been made to feel a fool once this day. He didn't relish his own wife telling him he was one, nor at the same time praising another man's brains.

She came and sat beside him. He felt her soothing hand on his arm.

'I'm sure my lord Cardinal realised it was worry that made you say such things. He will forgive you and not think any more of it, I'm sure.'

Her words, instead of soothing him, merely angered him all over again. 'Forgive me?' he demanded. 'Who is he to forgive me?' Irritated, he stood up and turned away, shaking her hand from his arm and knocking over her tapestry frame as he did so. 'It is for me to forgive him, if, as I suspect, many of your jewels have landed in his coffers. I told him plain that I would deal with the king, not his pork butcher.' He tried to ignore her horrified expression.

'You didn't say that? To the Cardinal? Oh Charles. What did he say?'

Charles gave what he hoped was a nonchalant shrug. 'Some nonsense about the king not wishing to be troubled by our problems. That I shouldn't put the king in the awkward situation of being asked to help his own sister. I took little notice of that, you can be sure.' He flung himself down again then, on a chest this time and refused to speak further on the matter.

Charles had retreated to the brooding silence that Mary had come to know so well in France. He would speak no more about it for the present that much was evident. Upset, she settled back to her discarded needlework, hoping the repetitive work would soothe her mind. She felt hurt that Charles should put his ambition to rise in her brother's service higher than he put his wife. No doubt he would say she was being ridiculously romantic and perhaps he was right. But theirs had been a love match; surely it wasn't foolish of her to feel hurt that he hadn't put her first? But even if Charles did share others' feelings that romance was but a light game, his clear reluctance to share a married idyll with her in the country was another matter. His admission that he had thought greatly on her jewels was yet another stab in her heart. She had believed he had cared little for her jewels. Had he not said so?

But as, beneath her lashes, she studied his sullen expression, Mary wondered if she was not being too hard on him. It was reasonable that he should want her suitably dowered; other men expected as much. That she had been forced to barter most of her dower was now causing a strain between them and that was the last thing she wanted. She put down her sewing again and came to sit beside him. 'Will you listen to me, Charles, if not to the Cardinal?' She took his ungracious mutter for agreement. 'You may not like the Cardinal's manner of speech, my love, but I would caution you to pay heed to its content. I know my brother. Oh, I know he can be charming and boyish with his short-lived enthusiasms, but there's a darker side to him. You should take notice of Wolsey. The king likes not to be placed in difficult situations. Before you married me you were simply a courtier, one of many. Your only duty was to please the king. He likes you well, but if now, in your new position, you tried to make demands on him, do you think he would still favour you as much?'

He didn't answer, but Mary could see he was listening. Softly, she asked, 'You've not seen Henry, yet, I trust?'

Charles shook his head. 'I couldn't find him to ask him anything.'

Mary thanked God for that at least. 'Please Charles, do not make my brother feel guilty on our behalf. Guilt is not an emotion he enjoys. You can feel sure that if Wolsey is dealing with the matter it is only because my brother doesn't wish to. All you would do if you managed to speak to Henry would be to annoy him.'

Some of the sullenness left Charles's face and he admitted, 'Wolsey said the same. I thought he had some motive of his own for trying to keep me from the king.'

'Will you believe me? I am your wife and love you.' Mary gazed worriedly at her still-sullen husband. 'Promise me you'll not trouble the king with this matter.'

Charles heaved himself to his feet and made for the door. His voice sounded bitter. 'Very well. I'll not see him, but don't expect me to see Wolsey again either. I begged for his help and he refused me, told me our troubles were all of our own making. I'll not forgive him for this humiliation, so don't ask it of me.'

He went out then, clearly still angry. Mary was left alone with her unwelcome thoughts and the realisation that her dreams of married bliss were just that—dreams. She was now seeing another facet of her husband's character, one that worried her. She hadn't realised during the days of her girlish hero-worship that Charles Brandon's bluff exterior hid an unreasoning pride. She remembered a casual remark of Lady Guildford's—that the low-born who rose high were often more proud than those of inherited rank. Mary hadn't taken any notice then; she did now. Her head began to nod on her neck again, as it had done in France. What might Charles's pride bring him to?

When he had got over the worst of his temper, Charles allowed Mary to persuade him into the country; at least he would get away from his creditors for a while.

They had many estates from which to choose as the king had granted them property from the previous Dukes of Suffolk, the de la Poles. They had Donnington Castle and Letheringham Hall, Wingfield Castle and Westhorpe in Suffolk, as well as their London home, Suffolk House in Southwark. Mary's favourite was Westhorpe.

Six miles north of Stowmarket, the hamlet of Westhorpe had a beautiful little church, St Margaret's. With its floor of medieval tiles, bricks and ledger stones, it had a simple, unspoiled atmosphere, which appealed to Mary after the unhappiness she had experienced in the magnificent buildings of France. She enjoyed the country life, too. Charles did not. He longed to be back at court—if only his creditors would let him. He was afraid his enemies would pour poison in the king's ears if he was not there to provide the antidote. Mary tried to distract him with entertainments as lavish as their straitened circumstances allowed, but, even as he pretended pleasure for her sake, he was conscious that all her efforts succeeded only in getting them deeper in debt.

Although he had done his best to snap out of his sullen mood and had managed to convince Mary that he was happy and not so concerned with ambition, he still, more and more often, found his gaze straying to the road that led to the court. He had told her he had no interest in her money, that it was the king's money now. She wasn't sure if she had believed him. She suspected Charles wasn't sure if he believed it himself.

Desperately had Mary wanted to believe Charles when he had spoken of the money, but she felt he hadn't been honest with her and suspected he cared very much about it. The great differences in their backgrounds was creating a division between them, one likely to widen with the years especially if his ambitions continued unmet.

The thought saddened her anew. She, who had lately had more than her share of unhappiness and despair had hoped the Wheel of Fortune had turned sufficiently to allow that first, brief joy to continue. She could be content in the quiet of the country with Charles if he would only give over brooding about what could not be.

It was late summer. The countryside looked lush and ripe, the hedgerows garlanded with cow parsley and foxgloves, the fields full of swaying corn; a fitting time, Mary felt, for her body too, to ripen with the fruit of the womb. Although she had only missed one of her monthly courses and could not be certain she was pregnant, Mary still longed to share her hopes with Charles. But given his current preoccupation she wasn't sure how he would take the news. Maybe he would balk and complain at the likely cost of the ceremonies due to such a high-born infant.

Besides, at the moment, he spent so much time out on the estate or with their neighbours, seeking news of the court that he was scarcely at home. And when he did return he was so inclined to be morose she scarce knew how to broach the subject. So she nursed the secret to herself.

One day, gathering roses in the garden, her eyes misted over as she thought back to that other time in the garden, with Charles. How long ago that seemed. Their love had been so new then, so fresh. They should have seized their chance for happiness then. They would scarcely have endured more trouble if they had done so. She smiled through suddenly damp eyes as she remembered how he had plucked red and white roses for her, the white for York and the red for Lancashire and how their passion had scattered them on the ground. Her smile faded. Such bitter-sweet memories.

She glanced up. Charles was striding towards her. She smiled a welcome and quickly wiped any hint of tears from her lashes as she tried to gauge his mood. 'Hello, my love.' She pressed her nose against the flowers and breathed in their heady scent. 'I was just gathering some flowers for our bed-chamber. Do you remember when—?'

Brusquely, he waved away the fond memories she had wanted to share with him. 'You're lucky to find something to occupy you, Mary. I would that I could find pleasure in such trivial pursuits.'

Mary's smile faded as his words made plain he had little interest in recalling the early days of their love. But once, he had found joy in such simple pleasures, she reminded herself in an attempt to ease her hurt. Tentatively, she asked, 'Why are you so vexed, Charles? Has something happened to annoy you?'

He banged his hat against his thigh with such ferocity that he knocked it out of shape which only increased his ill-temper. 'Nothing but the same old annoyance. The same man who irks me. Stuck in this backwater for weeks is sufficient to make any man brood on the wrongs done to him. It's well enough for a woman, such a life. But a man, Mary, needs to be at the centre of things, to help run affairs, to have a voice on the Council. I cannot be satisfied with the life of a simple country squire.'

Such was his frustration that Mary decided to keep the news of her suspected pregnancy to herself for a while longer. It was clear he was not in the right mood to share her joy. Always emotional, pregnancy made her more so. She blinked away the threatening dampness from her eyes, only too conscious he had grown impatient with her tears. She didn't know whether to be pleased or sorry that he hadn't even noticed them, never mind enquired as to their cause. Instead, he turned remorselessly on to the subject he had ranted about these many weeks: Wolsey.

'He was the one who forced us from the court,' he complained. 'He fears my friendship with the king. He wants to be the only one able to influence his thoughts.'

Roughly, he pulled a rose from its bush and robbed it of its pretty petals. 'These accursed debts. They could be settled tomorrow if Wolsey desired it, I know. Damn the man for the butcher's cur he is.'

Mary stiffened behind the screening bouquet and pleaded, 'Please, Charles, do not speak so. Wolsey has been a good friend to us. He was the only one willing to help us in our troubles. But for him, Henry might have let the Council have their way,' she reminded him, hoping to recall to his mind the fear he had endured in Paris and thus kill his resentment before it grew dangerous. 'They would have had your head, my love, but for Wolsey. We both do know it.'

'How long am I expected to be grateful that he wrote a few letters and spoke a few soft words to the king? Simple enough deeds. Anyone could have done such.'

'But they didn't, Charles, did they?' Mary reminded him. 'Your friends at court were conspicuous by their silence.' She grasped his arm. 'We owe the Cardinal much, Charles. Pray don't make an enemy of him. He's a very clever man.'

Charles pulled his arm from her grasp. 'And I am not? Is that what you are saying?' He scowled 'Why should I fear the butcher's cur? What could he do to me that he hasn't already done?'

'I don't know, Charles,' Mary told him wearily. 'But I'd rather not find out. Leave him be, please. Don't vex him any more. My lord of Norfolk would be only too pleased if you made of the Cardinal a mortal enemy.'

As Mary looked at his bitter expression fear clutched at her heart. Why couldn't he be happy? There was such peace here in the country, such tranquillity. She couldn't understand how anyone could fail to find contentment in a home as beautiful as Westhorpe. But Charles wasn't happy and the realisation saddened her. His heart was with the court and its doings and not with her. Briefly, Mary thought of King Louis, her aged first husband, and how easily contented he had been. He had asked only for her company, music from her lute and a little fondling. She had made him happy. Why could it not be the same with this husband whom she so desperately wanted to please?

But nowadays it seemed nothing pleased him. Certainly, nothing she did seemed to do so. On a small, sad sigh, she left him to his brooding and turned away, heading for their bed-chamber, so she could arrange the pretty roses that had now, for her, lost their bloom.

After all Mary's misgivings, when she finally told Charles of her pregnancy, he was delighted. To her great joy he was very attentive during the long months of waiting. They were both pleased when they learned that Queen Catherine had, in February, the month before Mary's own babe was expected, finally produced a healthy babe herself. Although only a girl, it seemed likely to live, unlike the son she had been carrying at the time of Mary's departure for France. That infant, although full-term, had died shortly after his birth, during Mary's sojourn at the French court.

Mary's child arrived not many weeks after Catherine's daughter. Her labour was long and agonising, but, late in the March evening, she presented Charles with a son and heir.

The birth of the child seemed to help Charles regain his good humour. His attentiveness during the pregnancy happily continued after the birth. Mary was overjoyed at the way he kept popping into her chamber to check on her and his son, round-eyed with wonder that she had presented him with such a precious gift. Mary, full of the happiness of new motherhood, now understood how much sadness the loss of previous babies had brought to her brother and Catherine.

Charles wanted to name their son after the king. 'Who knows?' he said, 'but that it may persuade your brother to be kinder to our son's foolish father.'

Although his words revealed that Charles hadn't lost all his worldly ambition, Mary was glad to see that he could mock himself. She felt overcome with love for him and grasped his hand. She had had a long sleep after her ordeal and felt rested.

Susan, her maid, had freshened her and she was glowing with the radiance that new motherhood bestowed. Readily, she smiled her agreement. 'Henry, it shall be.'

She knew, from his pleased expression, that she had won her husband's heart all over again. But this time, Mary forbade herself from entertaining romantic girlish notions of love. She was a woman now and a mother. She accepted that although her love for Charles was strong, his for her was lighter and more easily borne. She believed he truly loved her, even so, as much as he was capable of loving any woman. It was simply that he lacked her ability for deep emotion; had he not always sought love where there would be other benefits also? It was the way of the world and he had his way to make in it, not being born to high estate. He had had dalliances in plenty, Mary didn't doubt it. He had even been married. Several times.

Mary, older and a little wiser, forced such unwelcome thoughts from her mind. Charles was hers now. He loved her. They had a son. And as he rightly said, this son she had given him might indeed bring her brother's favour.

King Henry, wistful as he was for a son of his own, made much of his young namesake. He even acted as his Godfather. After Henry's little daughter, the Princess Mary, he named his nephew by Mary and Charles as heir to the throne. Charles had been overwhelmed by this, especially as Henry had set aside the prior claim of his elder sister Margaret's sons in their favour. Mary's labour completed the trinity of royal lyings-in, for her sister, Margaret, had presented her second husband with a baby daughter, Margaret, the previous October.

Great state was held at little Harry's christening. The king and the Cardinal both acted as sponsors. Mary began to hope that this indicated a rapprochement between her brother, the Cardinal and her husband. Charles had, for some time, been barely tolerated, as he had opposed the league against France for which Wolsey had pushed. In consequence, they had been forced to spend most of their time banished to their estates, much to Charles's frustration.

Now, Henry made much of his young namesake. Mary would catch him gazing wistfully at her son. She knew how much he longed for a boy of his own. Daily, she prayed that

he and Catherine would be blessed with a son as had she and
Charles.

Quiet in the country after the birth celebrations, Mary followed with astonishment the adventures of her elder sister,
Margaret. After her secret marriage to Archibald Douglas,
the Council had transferred the regency of her two sons by
the king to her late husband's first cousin, John Stewart, the
Earl of Albany and next heir to the Scottish throne after
James IV's two sons by Margaret. Besieged, the pregnant
Margaret had been forced to flee the country, leaving her
boys and her regency in the power of Albany. She had given
birth to Archibald Douglas's child, Margaret, in Northum-
berland the previous October.

Now, Mary heard her sister was heading south and Mary
and Charles were amongst those summoned to court to welcome her.

They returned to court in May. Mary was excited. It was so
many years since she had seen her elder sister that she could
scarce remember her. Margaret had been married into Scotland, to King James IV, years before at the age of thirteen
when Mary had been a mere child of seven. Widowed just
before her twenty-fourth birthday, Margaret had secretly
married Archibald Douglas, the Earl of Angus.

Mary, her memories of her sister few and hazy, was convinced she and Margaret would have much in common; had
they not both dared to enter into secret marriages? Were

they not now both mothers? Excitedly, she looked forward to their reunion.

The court was at Greenwich and it was to Greenwich Palace, its gardens bursting forth with the buds of May, that Margaret came. To Mary's disappointment, though Margaret had her new daughter with her, she saw it was true that she had been forced to leave behind her two sons by the king.

Mary remembered her sister had been a pretty girl. But pregnancies and discontent had tarnished her looks. Only in her middle twenties, not only were her looks and figure more those of a middle-aged matron, her manner regally arrogant, she also spoke down to her younger sister, as if she were still truly a child to be dismissed.

Mary was disappointed to find the combination little to her liking. But this was her long-absent and only sister, she reminded herself. Margaret had had much with which to contend and she must not expect her to readily shed her troubles and indulge in sisterly confidences. After the many travails she had experienced in Scotland, Margaret's character would inevitably have formed into a tougher fabric. She must make allowances.

'Well, sister,' Mary said with a smile. 'It is good to see you. Let us hope our next meeting is not so long-awaited.' She made to kiss Margaret, but her sister's kiss in return, was perfunctory.

Instead of returning her friendly overture, Margaret ignored it and burst out instead in an angry tirade of grievances against the way the fates had treated her. 'I wouldn't have been here now, but for that foolish Council,' she told Mary, bitterly. 'They had the temerity to offer the regency to that French cur, Albany, instead of letting it remain in my hands. I am, after all, the mother of the king. That Frenchman, brought up in France as he was, can't even speak the language.'

Taken aback by her sister's anger, Mary tried to soothe her. 'He is the heir-presumptive, Margaret, cousin to the late King James. Surely it is his right? Scotland has need of a strong man to rule it. It has ever been a wild, ungovernable place. I'm sure the Council thought it would be too much for a woman.'

'What do you know of the matter, Mary?' Margaret demanded sharply. 'Sheltered by our brother till you were all of eighteen, how could you know aught of Scotland or her problems? You say they need a man to rule? They'll have a hard task finding one of those in Scotland.' The lords of the north were dismissed with a contemptuous wave of the hand. 'I'm more man than any of them, but they're too full of overbearing male arrogance to realise it.'

Dismayed, Mary stared at her sister and thought that maybe Margaret's own arrogance might have had something to do with her rejection by the Council. It was a thought she kept to herself. Instead, she asked, 'Where is your husband, Margaret? I had expected to see him also. Will he be coming to court?'

'Nay. He let the Council reject me for the regency. Let that fool Archibald Douglas stay in the north. What would I want with him here?'

From her sister's dismissive tone, Mary guessed that this second marriage had already soured. Mary was sorry for it. Hoping her assumption was in error, Mary said, 'Surely, sister, you wish the father of your new daughter to be with you?'

Margaret let out a harsh laugh and laid a hand on her belly. 'Douglas did his work,' she said. 'He was quite content for me to do the rest alone. As I said, Mary, let him stay in the north. He's not wanted here.'

Mary, optimistically still hoping for those exchanged girlish confidences, persisted. 'I had thought you and he were a love-match, Margaret, like Charles and I. Was he then not your choice? Do you not love him?'

'Love him?' Margaret echoed. For a moment she looked thoughtful and admitted, 'Perhaps I did once. It seems a long time ago now. Nowadays, lust is the nearest we come to love. It serves well enough. I had expected him to be a strong support in the north, but, just like the king, my first husband, he's turned out to be a sore disappointment to me.'

Mary knew not what to say to this embittered sister and a silence fell. She was thankful when Henry arrived and swept Margaret off to see Wolsey and confer on developments in Scotland. She had so hoped she and Margaret could become friends; the wide gap in their ages when they were children had done little to encourage friendship then, but she had thought it would be different now they were both women and both mothers.

But it was apparent that years were not the only thing which separated them. Their experiences had been so different. Mary had heard whispers of what Margaret had endured whilst married to James IV. As was King Francis now, James, too, had been a notorious womaniser, with many mistresses. It must have been difficult for a romantic, newly-wed girl of thirteen to accept such endlessly repeated humiliations. Little wonder her character had curdled.

Then there were her sister's more recent troubles over the regency, though Mary found it hard to understand why Margaret should so long for the role of regent with all its accompanying problems. She herself had been only too ready to leave France and return home, her French queenship well lost for love. Marriage and motherhood suited her in a way it clearly didn't suit Margaret. Margaret, it was apparent, wanted more.

Mary had greatly missed England, too, whereas Margaret seemed to lack the same strong love of her homeland. Of course her sons by the king were in Scotland. It made a difference. Now her ties were with that cold, wild country, rather than with England.

Completely different in temperament and personality though they were Mary admitted a certain admiration for Margaret's courage. Scotland had ever been a difficult land to rule, a fact successive kings had discovered to their cost. That unhappy country had had several child monarchs and as a consequence the lords had become over-strong. Many were all but kings in their own territories which would make the task of ruling far from easy.

Mary, back in their apartments, cast about for something to occupy her. She found the shirt she had been embroidering for her baby son and picked it up. Sewing was second nature and soon her thoughts returned to her sister and her adoptive country. Margaret's first husband, the late king, had, for all his womanising, been considered a strong monarch. At least he had managed to keep the lords in their place. But he had died at the rout that was Flodden, killed by the army of his brother-in-law, Henry of England. Many of his lords had died with him. Now his small son, James V, Mary's young nephew, was the monarch. That yet another child monarch occupied the Scottish throne had led to much faction as the lords jostled for power.

Mary thought sadly of the poor little nephew she had never seen and how worried her sister must be about her two boys. Mary could excuse her sister's overbearing manner on this alone and she resolved to make more of an effort to gain Margaret's confidence.

Mary's needle flew with her thoughts. When Margaret had decided to marry again, the Council had sent for Albany, he being, as they considered, the lesser of two evils. But Albany was more Frenchman than Scot, having been brought up in France and had, as Margaret had complained, no grasp of the language of the country he was expected to rule as regent. He had been urged to take on this thankless role by the King of France in order to the more easily use Scotland to further his own ambitions. The French had ever used Scotland as a stick with which to beat the English. An England tormented by Scots aggression would, so Henry had claimed was the French reasoning, be less able or willing to attack the French while that country's monarch was left free to engage in his Italian adventures.

Henry had hoped that Margaret and her second husband, the Earl of Angus, aided and financed by him, would be able to break the 'Auld Alliance' between Scotland and France. With Scotland a friend rather than a foe, Henry had hoped he would be stronger for any future attack on France. He had paid out large sums to the Scottish lords in order to win their allegiance in furtherance of this hope. Now, after the appointment of Albany as regent and with Margaret's disenchantment with her second husband, it seemed that Henry's hopes had gone awry.

Strangely he hadn't appeared too cast down by this. Mary presumed she could put her brother's good cheer down to the fact that Catherine had finally presented him with a healthy child, albeit a daughter only. Mary had been touched that Catherine and her brother had named the child Mary.

How proud Henry was of the child. Never had a child such as his daughter been born. He insisted that everyone must admire her. Even foreign ambassadors on important missions had to pause in their diplomacy in order to make the pilgrimage to her nursery and find appropriate adulatory responses.

The days flew by. Margaret, after several conferences with Henry about events in Scotland, would join her sister queens, Catherine and Mary and compare their babies' progress. Though Margaret, in emulation of her absent husband, was a disinterested parent and rather put out that she had borne a mere girl. It seemed her husband hadn't been greatly impressed that the first child Margaret had presented him with had been a daughter rather than the son he had wanted. Certainly, he still failed to put in an appearance at his wife's side.

Shades of our brother, thought Mary, pityingly. But at least Henry doted on his little daughter as much as Charles doted on his son. The contrast between these two new fathers and the third, Margaret's husband, was vivid and must, Mary felt, hurt her sister greatly, even though Margaret didn't betray her feelings on the matter.

Mary couldn't help but feel sympathy for her sister in her sad situation. And if the babe's father failed to proffer the expected words of praise, the child's aunt could manage a few. 'You've borne a fine babe, Margaret,' she told her on the next occasion they had had an opportunity for womanly conversation. 'She must be a comfort to you now that you're separated from your sons. It's a shame you were unable to bring them with you. I admit I feel curious about my little nephews and would have loved to see them. Do they resemble our brother at all?'

Margaret shrugged. 'I don't know who they resemble, truth to tell. I've not seen them these many months. Besides, when I was in Scotland, they were in the care of Lady Erskine. I had other things to attend to than playing the nursemaid.'

Deciding this brusque exterior but defended the wounded heart of a mother parted from her sons, Mary tried again. 'But you must have seen enough of them to notice any resemblance? Lady Guildford told me our brother was a bonny babe.'

'Tis a shame he's not so bonny now, then,' Margaret retorted, with a sly glance at Queen Catherine. 'You should have heard him rant at me about the state of my marriage. Why so curious, anyway, sister? You have a son of your own to coddle now, if coddle you must. Just don't expect me to do the same. I bore the pangs of childbirth; 'tis enough. Let someone else labour over them till they're full grown.'

Mary was surprised that Margaret should take so little interest in her own children when she could scarcely bear to be parted from her little Harry and left him to the care of nursemaids only with the greatest reluctance. 'I find babies delightful creatures,' she confessed a little shame-facedly to her hard-faced sister. 'Indeed, I prefer to tend my son myself whenever I can. It is a pleasure, not a chore.'

'I suppose the boy takes your mind off that great sulk of a husband you've managed to acquire. Brandon's glum looks must silence the brat, withal.'

Mary rose to his defence. 'He has a lot on his mind at this time, Margaret. He has reasons for looking troubled.' As Margaret broke in, Mary realised to her dismay that her sister was determined to pick a fight.

'All do know your husband's troubles. He's trying for friendship with France. You should warn him he's liable to get more trouble than joy from the wily French king. Brandon's not clever enough to outfox Francis. He surely learned that when he was in France cowering behind your skirts after your hole-in-the-corner marriage?'

Margaret's sharp tongue brought an angry colour to Mary's cheeks. Her sister, after all, had made her own 'hole-in-the-corner' marriage. 'He didn't 'cower behind my skirts' as you put it,' Mary retorted. 'It was I who urged our marriage, not Charles. So if you would reproach any it should be me.'

'How you defend him, Mary,' her sister mocked. 'The Lord knows his love-life and marital history do not give forth the most sweet of smells. Let's see if I can get it right. Wasn't he contracted to marry one lady who became pregnant as a result? Her he jilted so he could marry her aunt, twenty years the girl's senior, so he could lay claim to large inheritance. He then, as I understand it, had this marriage annulled on the grounds of the relationship between the aunt and niece, and while keeping the inheritance went back and married the first lady. A pretty tale indeed.'

The way her sister described it, it did sound a sordid tale. But Mary had known about his previous marriages. It was natural that Charles, some twelve years her senior, should have had other romances. Thus, had she excused him. But, although she had been willing to excuse his marital adventuring, how could she, on occasions, especially when there was trouble between them, not reflect on his past life? There had been other rumours too. It was said that, with Henry's connivance, Charles had proposed marriage to Archduchess Margaret after their success at Tournai. Charles's proposal had been graciously declined, though the Archduchess had been sufficiently taken with him to agree to his daughter by one of his earlier 'marriages' being educated at her court.

Charles had obtained a divorce from his first wife and had been forced to gain the approval of the Pope for his marriage to Mary.

It was a tangled enough tale and one that had kept the gossips busy, especially after Mary had married him. Her thoughts were interrupted by another unwelcome comment from her sister.

'We must hope he appreciates what a prize he gained when he so 'unwillingly' wed you. Still, he's handsome enough, I admit. It's a shame his brains aren't of the same quality as his looks.' Margaret's shrug dismissed the subject. 'Husbands,' she said, 'what good are they, anyway? The first ignored me till he wanted sons. He managed to spare the time from his mistresses to get heirs at least. And the second.' Margaret gave an unladylike snort. 'Brave Douglas, now there's a great man. I tell you sister, you were a fool to give up your gains in France to marry a fortune-hunter like Charles Brandon. When war comes with France, as it will, for our brother's determined on it, you and your handsome, low-born husband will lose the small French income our brother let you keep. I wonder will the great sulk be so fond when he shares you with poverty?'

Mary, who had hoped they could be friends and confidantes, was shocked to discover what a vicious tongue her sister had. But Margaret's tongue had touched unerringly on another particularly sensitive spot. For their debts had, indeed, made Charles less lover-like. At the unwelcome news that their income might be further reduced, Mary couldn't help but hit out at her sister. 'You're an unnatural woman,

Margaret. I begin to see why Douglas is reluctant to join you here.' The ready tears were close but Mary forced them back. She wouldn't cry in front of this hard-faced sister of hers. 'I'm only sorry you're here and that you're my sister.'

Mary leapt from her chair and with an apologetic glance towards the hitherto silent Catherine for her lack of courtly etiquette, she rushed from the room. She was followed by her sister's brittle, contemptuous laughter.

CHAPTER SIXTEEN

Mary, returning to her chamber in an unsettled frame of mind, found herself longing for the quiet of the countryside, far from the court where ambitious egos made life anything but simple. She wondered that her husband should so revel in the intrigues and gossip, especially after what thy had suffered from both during their time at the French court. Although Mary still enjoyed the masques and balls of the court she had learned the value of peace, both of mind and of place.

She had tried to get on with her sister, but Margaret had not only made all her efforts an uphill task, she had forced from Mary equal unkindnesses which she regretted. For Mary, the worst aspect of their spat had been the way Margaret forced her to look again at her husband. Mary thought she had succeeded in pushing the doubts to the back of her mind. But Margaret, bitter and spiteful after two unhappy marriages, clearly hated to see her younger sister happy in hers.

Mary wasn't altogether sorry when debts again forced a retrenchment into the country, even though Charles would rant and fume to be again away from the court. But Wolsey was once more pressing for payment, Henry firmly behind him, his delight in his new daughter and his sponsoring of his nephew in no way diminishing his love of gold's glitter.

What Margaret had prophesised came to pass in November when Henry and his Council agreed a defensive league against France with Flanders, Spain and the Swiss. All Charles's carefully nurtured friendship with King Francis availed them nothing and Mary's income was reduced still further. It did little for Charles's temper or their relationship. But at least Mary was thankful they were not forced to endure their reduced circumstances under her sister's mocking, 'I told you so' gaze.

'Wolsey's behind this,' Charles insisted, his bitterness at this ill-turn in their fortunes brought a fresh harping on this familiar theme. 'He guides the king in everything, the spiteful, grasping wretch that he is.'

Mary, convinced that Charles's growing enmity towards the Cardinal was making him wilfully blind, said, 'You wrong him. He has no more desire for war with France than do we. It is my brother who longs for war and glory. Wolsey has sought to restrain him in his ambitions. A wise man knows that wars are costly affairs both in money and men, but my brother is headstrong and will not be advised in this matter. You know how he longs to emulate his namesake, Henry V. How could cool wisdom ever, with him, compete with the heat of glory?'

'War would suit Wolsey's purpose, I tell you, Mary, so do not defend him to me. My friendship with King Francis is well-known. Wolsey knows what little use that friendship would be to me if war with France comes. Mayhap he thinks to persuade the king to throw me in the tower as a danger to the realm.'

Mary bit her lip to stop herself from again telling him he was being a fool. But truly, he was becoming obsessed with the Cardinal. She didn't know what to do about it. All she could do was to try to argue him from it. 'Think you he has naught to do but thwart you? I'm sure he hasn't the time to dwell on such matters.'

With a sweep of his hand Charles brushed her words aside. 'He knows the high favour I had from the king before I married you—' He broke off abruptly, but not quickly enough to avoid revealing his bitterness.

Mary swallowed down the sudden sick feeling as she remembered her sister's comments about his earlier, cavalier love-life. Was she just the latest in a line of women Charles had married for his own advantage? Would he discard her as he had the others when he had drained all the advantage he could from their marriage? It was a traitorous thought. She would not believe it of him. Still, she sought his reassurance. 'What are you saying, Charles? That you regret marrying me? Was I mistaken, like a simple maid, to think you loved me?'

He was taken-aback by her words. 'Mary, you know I didn't mean it. It is not that at all. It's Wolsey making me bitter, making me say things I don't intend.'

Even as his words of denial gushed over her, Mary was unable to entirely smother the thought that he couldn't afford to be alienated from both his wife and his mighty brother-in-law. But, whatever his feelings for her, Mary still loved him, so she allowed him to put his arm around her and comfort her.

'You surely know how strong my feelings are for you.'

'Perhaps you should tell me again. My sister—'

'I might have known your sister, embittered as she is against all men, would try to poison your mind against me. I suppose, determined to make you as unhappy as herself, she raked up my past and paraded it in front of your nose?'

Mary nodded.

'She must have put the worst possible construction on it, judging by how one unthinking comment from me should so upset you. Please Mary, forget my unhappy marital past and your sister's bitter words, neither of them matter. I love you, no other woman.' He raised her chin and gazed down at her. 'Say you forgive me if my thoughtless words caused you pain.'

Mary's thick throat made further speech impossible. She could only nod. When she could speak, she admitted, 'I know I've brought you problems, Charles. I wish it were otherwise. Alas, there is little I can do about it now. Give it time, my love,' she pleaded. 'Henry will come round.'

'Time only plays into Wolsey's hands. He's had plenty of it to sow seeds of mistrust in your brother's mind.' He dropped his arms from about her and gazed broodingly as if into a misty future. 'Time is my enemy, Mary not my friend.'

'If Wolsey were to hear of your ravings against him he would be your enemy in very truth. I beg of you, Charles, show some care or your lack of discretion will indeed invite the spite you insist he feels towards you and you will bring his vengeance down upon both our heads.'

As he bit back another angry retort, she could see he was chastened by her words. Would he learn the discretion he so desperately needed? Or would he continue to listen to the angry thoughts poisoning his mind?

Winter tightened its grip on the country. The weather became bitter, so cold that the travellers who managed to fight their way through snow and treacherous roads brought news that the River Thames had frozen over. Mary tried to imagine this thoroughfare, busy now with skaters and chestnut sellers rather than boats and barges. It must be a wondrous sight. But, snug in the country, Mary was content to miss this wonder. For time had proved a friend after all and Charles had indeed learned some discretion. His worst outbursts against Wolsey were curbed. Now Mary felt she could relax and enjoy her son and his amusing antics. Unable to ride out for the bitter cold, she sat for hours and played with little Harry, marvelling at his sturdy limbs and lively chatter. She suspected she was pregnant again. The thought delighted her. She was full of plans. The responsibility of parenthood suited her, she found, as it did Charles. And even though he was still inclined to be moody, he also found time to play with the boy. It pleased her to see him so proud of his little son. It pleased her even more to catch Charles gazing at her with love and the glint of possession in his eye. It was at such times that she was able to make him forget his grudges, his ill-temper and his thwarted ambition. They could yet be very happy.

Little Harry sneezed. Mary was immediately all motherly concern. 'Think you he has taken a chill, Charles? The weather is so bitter and he is so little.'

He took the child from her and raised him high in the air. Harry loved such rough romps and shouted his delight. 'Nay. Don't fret. He's much stronger now.' He lowered his son's little body and gazed into his face. 'My, but he's got a great look of you, Mary. You'll be a good-looking man, my son, if you take after your mother.'

Pleased, Mary gazed at her husband and son as they played together. Harry adored his large and bluff parent and squealed with delight whenever he saw him. Mary, enjoying the shared intimacy of simple family life, decided it was the right time to break the news that fatherhood might be about to claim him again. 'How would you like to be a father again, Charles?' she asked.

It took a few seconds for her meaning to penetrate, then he looked up and caught her expression. 'You don't mean...?'

Mary nodded.

Carefully, he rose from the floor, little Harry in his arms and came towards her. He gave her a great hug. Little Harry, between them, chuckled, and beat his father on the chest.

Mary's joy momentarily faltered as she saw him gazing at their son. Fleetingly, she wondered whether he was thinking that the new babe would be another nephew for the king to dote on. She forced the thought from her mind. It was simply a pregnant woman's fancies, she told herself. She must not let her mind dwell on such notions. She must not allow her sister's cruel comments to take hold of her mind. She would try to forget them as Charles had asked.

'When will the child be born?'

'In the summer. Late June or perhaps July. Are you truly pleased?' Mary could not shake off the anxiety that his pleasure rested more on what the arrival of another child would do for his position at court than aught else.

'I couldn't be more pleased, you foolish wench,' he told her. 'It'll be marvellous, won't it, young Harry, to have another playmate?'

Harry gave a solemn nod.

Charles laughed. 'There you are, you see. He wants a little brother and I'll be happy with whatever we get.'

Content now, Mary kissed him. Harry put his lips out in a pout, demanding a kiss, too. Mary was happy to oblige the child. She danced around the room with happiness. Charles bounced their little son on his knee in time to her dance and the lilting tune she sang to accompany her steps. At such times it was easy to forget her doubts and anxieties.

Mary bloomed as her pregnancy advanced. She felt curiously placid and was confident enough to persuade Charles to go to sound out Cardinal Wolsey again to see if their finances could in some way be eased out of their present tangle.

Charles travelled up to London, shivering through countryside draped in its winter wardrobe. It was a difficult journey as winter journeys invariably were, with icy roads a hazard to a careless horse or rider. And Charles had many thoughts to distract him. Now he was away from Mary, he wondered if he had been altogether wise to obey her entreaties. Oh, he knew it would be the wise thing to do to appease Wolsey. The trouble was, he wasn't sure he felt up to the task, the temptation to indulge in a second confrontation with the Cardinal might easily overcome such good intentions. Especially when he was sure, in spite of Mary's belief to the contrary, that Wolsey was the leading light in his current troubles.

Charles had convinced himself that if the Cardinal chose to advise the king to set aside the vast debts he owed the Crown, the king would be only too ready to agree, whatever the rest of his Council might say. But it was clear to Charles that Wolsey had made no such suggestion. Indeed, he had himself pushed and pushed for the debts to be settled. But instead of being settled they had grown, added to by the need to keep royal estate at court, expenses added to by the birth of their son, the king's nephew and the visit of Mary's sister, the Dowager-Queen of Scotland.

Charles could see no end to it. Yet if he only had the chance to regain the king's favour he was sure things could be settled satisfactorily. But Wolsey had the king's ear and his jealous guardianship of it showed how loth he was to share it. The war with France ensured the situation remained favourable to himself. It would cut off Mary's dower income and would limit even more their ability to make lengthy visits to court with all the expense such visits entailed.

Round and round his thoughts went, but no answers could he find. Charles Brandon knew that at heart he was a simple man, ill-equipped for courtly intrigues. Mostly, he found this difficult to admit, even to himself; how was a man of ambition such as he knew himself to be, to get on at court without indulging in a little intrigue? He longed to possess a mind as subtle as that of the Cardinal. But, for all his previous angry tirades against him, he knew in his heart that Thomas Wolsey was his intellectual superior and held his place from ability not favouritism. Perhaps that was partly why he hated him.

He shifted heavily in his saddle and gazed beyond his companions to stare at the bleak countryside. Neither man nor beast should be setting out on such a journey. Not if they had any sense. But it wasn't good sense that had set his horse's hooves on the road, but Mary's entreaties and his desire to please her. Truly, he thought, it wasn't always easy to please a Tudor. The thought did little to lighten his mood, nor did the realisation of the difficulties he would face at journey's end.

Strangely, it wasn't the difficulties he faced at the end of his outward journey that caused him most anguish, but those he encountered upon his return. He had made good speed so as to welcome Queen Catherine who was to rest at his manor of Castle Rising on her way to the shrine at Walsingham to pray for the still elusive son and heir for the king. He arrived to find the place in uproar, seemingly in the throes of wedding celebrations.

As soon as he had thrown his reins to a stable lad, Charles went in search of Mary, unwilling to believe the excited twitterings of the servants. Alas for his peace of mind, the servants' twitterings were true and the meddling Mistress Jerningham, one of Mary's ladies, had, in a fervor of matchmaking, presumably bored by the relentless winter, privately pushed the betrothal of the young Lady Grey to Lord Berkeley's son and heir.

Both the young married pair resided in his household and were in his keeping. The young groom was the king's ward. Suffolk trembled at the thought that, albeit unwittingly, he had again reason to fear the king's wrath. Who would believe that he had known nothing of the affair?

He found Mary in the solar with Mistress Jerningham. This lady's face fell when she saw him and took in his countenance. He spared her one furious glance that promised a reckoning, before he turned to Mary and demanded, 'What is this I hear, Mary? Can it be true? I can scarce believe you would permit such foolishness under my own roof.'

He saw Mary's face falter as she came forward to welcome him home, but she managed to put on a brave enough front as she told him to calm himself. 'It is but a little love-match, of no great concern to the rest of the world.'

Charles, never smooth of tongue, felt words desert him. Mary's gaze flickered for support to Mistress Jerningham, but one glance from him made this lady quail. Mary would receive no help from that quarter. It seemed she realised it, too, for she hurried into further explanations.

'Such a charming couple, Charles and so in love they put me in mind of us when we were first struck by Cupid's dart. They wanted to marry and fearing my brother's wrath they beseeched Mistress Jerningham's aid. Naturally, she came to me.' Beseechingly, she asked him, 'What could I do but help them, Charles? Poor, love-sick creatures. We brought the priest here and they were wed, so simply it was beautiful. It is a shame you were not here. You would have found it very touching.'

Charles found his tongue at last. 'Touching?' he bellowed. 'Oh yes, it touches me all right. For the love of God, Mary, why did you let this wretched woman persuade you to such a match? Couldn't you content yourselves with playing matchmakers to the likes of scullions and dairy maids? The king's ward of all people. It would seem your greatest desire in life is to raise the king's anger against me. Do you do it to have me eternally banished, woman, and by your side in the country?'

Mary paled and clutched at her belly. But he wasn't to be put off by such womanly tricks. 'You surely realised the trouble this will cause.' He turned and caught sight of Mistress Jerningham creeping quietly towards the door.

'Well might you creep out like a thief in the night, you meddlesome wretch. You're the cause of this, you stupid, misbegotten woman. Get you gone,' he shouted at her. 'I'll deal with you later.' His fury sent Mistress Jerningham scuttling out the door and he turned back to his now clearly apprehensive wife.

'Please Charles, don't be angry. They're so in love, it seemed a shame to keep them apart.' Her expression softened. 'They're so happy together. So young and tender. Who could deny them?'

Charles could scarcely believe his ears at such soft-hearted folly. It seemed that, whatever he did, no matter how often he was forced to abase himself, he would still end up in the wrong and in danger. Exasperated, he swore a mighty oath and begged the heavens to save him from love and its follies. 'It's to be hoped the king will be tender with me when he discovers this.' He scowled. 'You can be sure Wolsey will make the most of it.' Fear made his voice turn cold. 'It seems that once again you make me break the king's trust. Is it not enough that I'm forced from the court by debt? Do you wish me to be thrown into the Tower as well, Madam?' Furious, he banged the table. Mary jumped. 'What possessed you to do such a thing? You realise that once Wolsey knows of it the marriage won't be permitted to stand?'

He saw her face fall at this. For the first time he felt the twelve years difference in their ages. Mary, young and romantic, seemed still to believe that all the world loved a lover. Whereas he— He felt the hairs on the back of his neck rise up as if to meet the headsman's axe. Desperately, he searched for excuses that would prove pleasing to the king and found none. 'That woman must have bewitched you. Her and those silly soft-eyed lovers. I tell you again it won't be permitted to stand. They'll be separated, despite their great love and tender feelings.' In his fury he was pleased to see how his words had upset her. He strode to the window and turned his back on her. Outside, the day was as dark as the deepest dungeon. The thought made him shiver, made the hairs on the back of his neck rise again. He had hurried home, eager to see his wife and son, not even stopping for a meal. He was cold, wet, hungry and in need of comfort. Instead he found anything but comfort. What a homecoming this was turning out to be. He would have done better to remain at court and do a little advance cringing to the king and the Cardinal.

He turned back to the room with a scowl and went to warm himself at the log fire crackling in the hearth. Steam rose from his sodden garments. He wrenched his cloak from his shoulders and threw it on a coffer. 'Now, I suppose I'll have to write more begging letters to Wolsey, seeking his intercession. As if I've not written enough of those since our marriage.'

His words dismayed her, he could see. It was small enough recompense for this latest trouble in which she had embroiled him. He couldn't help but feel some satisfaction that during the next few days Mary would likely creep about the house like a disgraced housewife rather than a Dowager Queen. Charles, ever conscious of his lowly status, for the first time felt that he was truly master in his own home.

While they awaited the Cardinal's reply to their letters, Charles enjoyed a rise in status as Mary did all she could to please him; ordering his favourite meals and keeping the quarrelsome servants in order. Above all, she made sure to keep Mistress Jerningham from his sight—after his tongue-lashing, she crept about the place like a whipped pup, her matchmaking arrangements about to be put asunder.

It was a relieved Charles who learned the king had believed his protestations of innocence. But it was galling that the world must think he had little authority over his own wife and household. It would do nothing to raise his standing at court, nothing, either, to encourage the king to seek his counsel.

Mary had been much chastened by Charles's reaction to the marriage she and Mistress Jerningham had encouraged. She realised how foolish she had been to allow herself to be carried away by the romance of it all. As Charles had told her, her heart was too soft where young lovers were concerned. So she was glad for Charles's sake when, with the arrival of spring, Henry summoned them to court to join in the May-Day celebrations. It would be a chance to explain in person and to make sure any blame rested with her rather than her husband. She knew how much Charles chaffed at the bit to get back to court. Mary just hoped their many creditors didn't succeed in waylaying him when they got there.

But, as it turned out, even their creditors soon had their minds occupied by things other than money.

Mary, Charles and their household had barely had a chance to settle into the courtly round at Richmond before riots started up in the capital.

There had long been ill-feeling against all the foreigners in the country. The May revels had often in past years been the opportunity for mischief-makers to be about their work.

This year they excelled themselves. The London apprentices ran amok, rioting through the streets, attacking foreigners and sacking their houses, accusing them of greedily taking money from the people. The mob insulted the Spanish and Portuguese ambassadors and threatened death to the mayor and aldermen. They even had the temerity to threaten Wolsey in like manner and his London palace was swiftly fortified.

Tempers cooled with the evening's breezes. Miraculously, no one had been killed, though many were injured. The ringleaders were summarily executed, their quartered bodies displayed throughout the city. The rest languished in prison where they had leisure to repent their folly during what was termed 'Evil May-Day'.

Mary, like Catherine, so recently a mother, felt only compassion when they learned of the youth of the prisoners. They both felt sorry for their poor mothers, terrified about what would befall their sons for what had probably, for them, started as no more than boyish high spirits and love of mischief and they agreed to beseech the king to show mercy.

Henry, at first, would have none of it. But then Catherine dropped to her knees before him and begged him to spare their lives. 'They are young and foolish, your Grace, led astray by evil counsel. They've learned a harsh lesson and know your power. They'll not rise up in like manner again.'

Mary, watching her brother, saw he was enjoying himself. At almost twenty-six, he still had much of the boy in him. But now the boy, for all his still-indulged love of play-acting, had come to enjoy playing the tyrant more. He kept Catherine on her knees before him, while he played the role of all wise, all-forgiving monarch. It was a role Mary recognised. Hadn't she been on the receiving end of it while in France writing letters pleading for his forgiveness for her secret marriage? As on that occasion, her brother meant to extract as much as he could from the situation. Where now the elder brother from their nursery days? That Henry she had loved, adored even. But this one? This one she feared and feared for. Of what would he become capable as the flattery of courtiers encouraged his vanity and growing love of power? It saddened Mary to see how that power was beginning to corrupt him.

While Henry still continued to indulge his play-pondering, his head on his hand as he surveyed his queen, Mary grabbed her sister's hand and pulled her to the floor beside Catherine so the sister-queens could add their pleas to Catherine's. What matter, thought Mary, if the entire court had to grovel on their knees before him? She pictured again the terror and grief of the boys' mothers as they waited to learn what would be their sons' fate. The picture lent her eloquence.

'Come, brother,' she pleaded earnestly. 'I know how kind and forgiving your heart can be and how loving.' Feverishly, Mary searched her memory for the words that had proved most useful when she had sought his forgiveness herself. 'We know your power, but please, your Grace, show the world your wisdom so they can also appreciate your justice and mercy. They are but silly children, after all, as Queen Catherine said. For love of our long-dead mother, think of the mothers of these poor misguided wretches this day. News of the mercy of great King Henry will resound throughout the world. Come brother,' Mary softened her voice and held her hand to her now-swollen belly, 'Forgive your children and obtain their joyful thanks.'

Mary held her breath as her brother's mind turned over her words and those of his queen. She had been at pains to touch on all the things that would most appeal to him; she had extolled his wisdom, his justice and mercy, his power and how the news would be received abroad. She had also appealed to that streak of sentiment which had ever formed part of her brother's character. Would it be enough?

The entire court seemed to hold its breath. Then Henry, evidently believing he had extracted as much drama and praise as possible, told the hushed court that he was indeed pleased to spare the prisoners' lives. He did so at a splendid public ceremony at Westminster Hall. Handcuffed and chained by the neck, the prisoners were paraded past this modern-day Solomon, as Henry sat, looking suitably wise. He listened to their cries for mercy and graciously inclining his head, ordered their release, though not before even the powerful and corpulent Wolsey bent the knee to his sovereign lord on their behalf.

It seemed to Mary that summer as she awaited the birth of her second child that barely was one drama over than another must raise its head. The news that Cardinal Wolsey was sick unto death raced round the court. Mary begged Charles not to display too much glee at the news, at least in public.

Fortunately, given her condition, he was at pains not to upset her and Mary heard few reports of her husband proclaiming what joy the death of Wolsey would give him. But it didn't stop him dreaming, she knew; she often caught him in quiet moments, staring into space, a slight smile playing about his lips and needed few guesses as to its cause.

Others were not so discreet and little knots of excited courtiers would form in corners as they speculated on who would replace the great Cardinal. But Wolsey, with the strong constitution of his peasant forefathers, made a surprising recovery from his brush with death and, to the chagrin of Charles and not a few others, was soon again at the head of affairs.

It didn't take long, as Charles furiously asserted, for Wolsey to set about the business of ruining him once more.

Mary could only try to console him as his difficult position at court was again brought vividly home to him by the arrival of the ambassadors of the Emperor and the King of Spain for the formal signing of the defensive league against France which had been agreed the previous November.

Mary, feeling sick and cumbersome, could take no part in these formalities. Henry and Wolsey had expended a fortune to make the league possible. They expected the whole court to join in welcoming and entertaining the foreign guests. A costly business, requiring expensive gifts and much finery. Mary wondered how Charles would manage to conceal his anger and put a cheerful face on the proceedings when he was one of those expected to sign the formal documents which would most likely sign away Mary's dower income from France and with it any hope of avoiding an even more penurious future. It would be something else for Charles to hold against Wolsey. And not just Wolsey. Herself also, she feared. But Mary didn't blame the Cardinal. In her heart, she knew who was behind the desire for war. Who else but Henry? Where, but on the field of battle, could he find the glory and drama his ever-growing vanity demanded?

Her misgivings and worry about how her husband would comport himself, caused the pangs of labour to surprise her while travelling. Mortified that this baby, so keen to enter the world, might force her to give birth at the side of the road, Mary clutched her belly and struggled on towards Hatfield in the neighbourhood of St Albans.

CHAPTER SEVENTEEN

After the previous, bitingly cold winter the weather turned insufferably hot. Mary—still heavily pregnant for the pangs had been but a false alarm, felt the heat keenly. In the country she at least escaped the unhealthy stink that would hang over London, but it didn't ease her worry for Charles, Catherine, Henry and the rest of the court.

Her youth had been heavily influenced by Catherine's charitable instincts and she felt a keen concern for the capital's poorer citizens, who would find little respite in their windowless hovels. If the weather didn't break soon, the sweltering heat would bring its unwelcome companion, disease, to town.

And so it proved. Soon, inevitably, people fleeing the sickness that spread with such terrifying swiftness, brought news that had the servants hastily barring the doors from this enemy that could render a person who had been merry at dinner dead by suppertime. Restless, feeling powerless and sick unto death herself, Mary prayed that Charles had had the good sense to leave London, for this, it seemed, was a sickness that had no favourites. Bits of news filtered through to her in her bed-chamber where she had retired to await the birth of her child. As usual, the court had fled to the country at the first hint of disease, but with them they had brought that insidious companion, death. Many died along the road, the rich and powerful as well as the poor. Frantic, with worry for her husband and the rest of her family, Mary forced her bloated body to its knees. All she could do was pray and instruct her servants to leave food and drink by the roadside to succour any passing unfortunate victims.

As the days and the heat wore relentlessly on, Mary learned from news shouted from beyond the barricades her household staff had erected against this insidious death, that Henry and most of the court had fled to the country as she had expected. Next, she learned that some of his Council had fallen ill, that pages that had slept in Henry's bed-chamber had died. Well could she imagine her brother's fear that this contagion should have dared to touch him so close. Henry, her big and magnificently built brother, had a mortal fear of illness and disease. He would, she knew, keep on the move from manor to manor, attended only by a few trusted servants.

But where was Charles? Had Henry kept him with him? Or was he, even now, lying ill and abandoned at some roadside with none to aid him? Increasingly distressed as thought piled on horrifying thought, each more unbearable than the one before, Mary at last had news of her husband. He was safe and well, but feared to bring the sickness to her and the rest of the household. His message told her than London was as a dead city. The sick and dying lay in the streets, too feeble to drag themselves home, their cries for succour unheeded.

In her alarm, Mary was surprised to discover in her husband's message a note of unwilling admiration for Wolsey, who had, it seemed, bravely remained behind in the capital to keep a guiding hand on the affairs of the nation.

At last, Charles himself arrived. He had waited till he could be sure he and his companions had not caught the contagion, before he travelled by stages to Hatfield, keeping away from other wandering souls. Mary clung to him and when their first breathless relief was over, he told her the latest news.

Wolsey's household had not escaped. Many had already died, more looked likely to follow, including Wolsey himself, who had but recently risen from his sick-bed. Mary, just glad to have Charles safe, said nothing when she saw the thought that had stolen into his heart—let Wolsey not escape death this time.

But, for the second time, Charles's wish was not granted. Amazingly, if the limited news that filtered through to them was to be believed, Wolsey had survived no less than four onslaughts of the sickness in as many weeks. Even Charles had to admit that the Cardinal seemed to be truly under Divine protection. It didn't make him love the man the more. How could it, thought Mary, when the Cardinal had seemingly not only the favour of an earthly king, but of the heavenly one also.

The hot weather hadn't abated. Instead, it grew even hotter. Mary, trying for respite from the heat and finding none, turned restlessly on her bed. She felt beads of sweat break out on her forehead. Fear made her tremble. Had she caught the sickness? Was she to die as so many had died?

Terror caught and held her. She raised herself up in the big bed and called for Susan, her maid.

'Is it the sickness?' she asked when her maid arrived. 'Keep Charles and little Harry away from me, I beg you. I could not bear it if—'

'Hush, now Madam,' Susan soothed her. ''Tis surely only that your time is come. Calm yourself.'

The pain that followed Susan's words confirmed her maid's diagnosis. Another pang followed the first, then another. Soon, Mary was clutching her belly as waves of pain swept over her. It wasn't long before the oppressive heat and the pains between them had her entire body drenched in sweat. She could find no relief and as the hours wore on, she clutched harder and harder at Susan's hand while the midwives exhorted her to push.

The room grew hotter. It was airless in the closed chamber and Mary struggled to find sufficient air to give her the strength to deliver her burden. She called for Charles, but he didn't come. Finally, Susan admitted that he had yet to return from some business he had gone out to attend to that morning.

She became a little delirious, imagined she was Catherine and fear invaded her soul at the thought of all the lost babies as she cried out, 'How many more times, oh God? Let this one live, I beg you.'

Vaguely, she heard a familiar voice reassure her that all was well and that her ordeal would soon be over, felt a gentle hand wipe a cooling cloth over the sweat from her brow. The calm voice and cool water restored her and when the midwives exhorted her once more to push, she did so as though she were truly the unfortunate Catherine desperate to produce the son she longed for. A pewling, new-born cry echoed round the chamber. Exhausted, Mary lay back.

Susan brought the red and angry bundle to her. 'You have a daughter, Madam. A beautiful daughter. Lusty, too, from the sound of her.'

Relieved that her ordeal was over, Mary gazed down at the child in her arms. She felt a momentary fear that Charles would be angry with her that she hadn't given Henry another nephew to dote on. Was that how Catherine felt each time she failed? Poor lady, how hard she had struggled to do her duty by Henry. Time after time she had been through this ordeal, with only one daughter to show for all her agonies.

Mary sighed and asked what day it was. She felt she had been labouring for several and had lost all track of the passing hours.

'It is St Francis' Day' Susan told her. 'An auspicious day to be born.'

Mary nodded and gazed down at her red-faced daughter. In vain, she searched for any likeness to herself or Charles. Instead, in the pursed-up little mouth and pugnacious jut of the baby's jaw, Mary saw only her brother, Henry. Strange that a child so new to the world should show so much personality. A thought entered her head, one that Mary felt would appease Charles should he feel disappointed that she had given him a daughter. 'I think I fancy the name Frances for the little maid.' Perhaps the auspices of the saint's day naming would encourage the child's namesake, King Francis, to be kind to her mother and not steal away all her dower income if war came between England and France.

She remembered Francis' merry heart. It could be kind, too. He had helped her and Charles in their great trouble. She recalled some of the French king's other behaviour too, behaviour that had not been so kind, but time and the rosy gaze of new motherhood softened this view as the distance in time rendered memory hazy.

She nodded, her mind made up. 'The child is to be named Frances. It is a goodly name. Who knows but that it may bring some favour to her in the future.' And to her parents, she added softly to herself. How pleased Charles would be if this gesture should soften Francis' heart towards them.

Susan took the child from her. 'Let us get you presentable for when your lord returns. You would look your best for him. After that, you must rest and regain your strength.'

Mary nodded sleepily, content to let her maids have the ordering of her. She now had two fine children. They were a hard, painful struggle to bring into the world, but they surely brought their own reward.

Charles returned, dismayed and apologetic that he had been absent while she laboured. Mary brushed his apologies aside as he kissed her and asked anxiously how she did. After her reassurances, she watched the wonder on her husband's face as he cradled his little daughter who had been hastily fetched from her crib. Mary thanked God that she had some-how found the courage to defy her brother and marry against his wishes. Who knew, otherwise, to whom he might have married her and what might have become of her? She had failed to give King Louis a son, for all his fumblings. He had been an old man and had hope rather than great expec-tation of a son and heir from her. A younger man might not have been so forgiving of such failure. And as Charles kissed her and bid her sleep, into her mind came a vision of Henry, on his face a scowl, as he learned that his wife had once again failed in her duty. How cruel life could be.

As autumn brought cooler weather, the sickness that had so desolated the country at last departed. Gradually, the courti-ers crept back to the city. Cardinal Wolsey, for once, as Charles had it, following the dictates of the God represented by his Cardinal's hat, took himself off on a pilgrimage to Walsingham to give thanks for his life. Mary, too, felt cause to be grateful that autumn. She had for the second time come safely through the ordeal of childbed and her new daughter thrived and gave suck lustily. The plague had passed harmlessly over the house. And last, but not least, Charles had been very loving towards her since the birth. He was pleased with her fruitfulness and hoped for many more fine, royal children. Mary, too, her ordeal behind her and mercifully fading from memory, shared his hope.

She had been blessed. Her loved ones had been mercifully spared. And as she visited the nursery and gathered her chil-dren in her arms, she felt that life was good. Now, if only

Charles could continue to remain content in the country with her and the children, she would ask nothing more of life.

Strange it was, thought Mary, that now she asked nothing of the fates they should shower her with gifts, though they hadn't all dropped into her lap. It had taken interminable discussions with Cardinal Wolsey before it was at last conceded that if Henry's desire for war with France stopped the arrival of Mary's dower income, they wouldn't be pursued for the debts they owed to the crown. Even Henry couldn't extract that which was no longer there.

Added to this was Henry's repeated failure to push on with plans for war with France. And after Pope Leo had exhibited one of his occasional bursts of Papal piety, Henry had had to abandon his dreams of glory in France. For the Pope desired a crusade against Islam and had called for all Christian monarchs to be at peace with one another so as to present a united front against the infidel. Wolsey persuaded the various monarchs to join in a multi-national defensive league, whereby if one member country was invaded the other members would be obliged to declare war on the aggressor.

This put a curb on Henry. He had hoped to make use of the league, had striven for months to get his sluggish allies to move against the French in Italy. To this end, he had showered Emperor Maximilian with money to encourage him. Maximilian, however, had more interest in Henry's money than his empire-building ambitions. And after extracting as much money from the Tudor coffers as he could squeeze, solemnly swearing his loyalty to Henry's cause on the four Gospels, he promptly made terms with King Francis, managing to get himself betrothed to a rich French bride for good measure.

Henry's many plans against France had all fallen through one after the other. Perhaps the Pope's overture came as a welcome relief to him; he could, for the moment, give over his sabre-rattling with unreliable allies. A five-year truce was called and Francis promised that the dowry of his Belle-Mère would be paid. Mary and Charles relaxed a little, sure in the knowledge that Henry and Wolsey could be relied upon to swiftly exact fulfilment of this promise.

Easter found Henry still in the country, at Abingdon. He invited them to spend the holy season with him there. Charles, keen to clear his name of the accusation that he had colluded with the French, spent much time with Wolsey's secretary indignantly denying the charges. But as all knew of their money troubles and the need of French friendship that these troubles brought them, his denials weren't as readily believed as he had hoped.

Daily, Mary would await his return to her side so he could pour out his grievances and resentments; against Wolsey that he should be subjected to such cross-questioning, against the nobles of the court who resented his grand marriage. Underlying all was the unspoken resentment against Mary herself which always strained the atmosphere between them at times of difficulty. Although she still loved him deeply and felt certain that he returned her love, Mary was saddened to acknowledge that the endless disputes over money were changing her husband's previously optimistic disposition. He was often sullen nowadays. Such a short time ago she had been basking in the glow of his love after the birth of Frances, feeling positive about the future for the first time in weeks. Mary could only wonder where all their hoped-for happiness had gone.

She had thought that the peace brought by the truce and the promise of her dower would solve all these problems but it seemed there were always others to replace them. Even her health had become uncertain, the stress caused by her un-popular marriage and consequent lack of money had both taken their toll. She fell ill with an ague and took to her bed, which caused them to overstay her brother's invitation. With so many enemies dogging his heels Charles was anxious not to upset Henry and he urged her to leave her bed.

'We should be gone from here by now, Mary. The king will be displeased if we tarry longer. Come, surely, you can walk as far as the litter; I'll call your maid to get you ready.'

Mary watched with shadowed eyes as he hurried from the room, calling loudly for Susan. She hated to see her husband, the undoubted champion of the joust in France, reduced to such anxiety. Worse still was knowing she was the cause of it once again. Love and guilt forced her from her bed. Her legs trembled with weakness, the room spun and she hit the floor with a crash. Determined that, in this at least, she must not fail him, she tried to rise, but the remaining strength in her limbs dissolved and she was unable to drag herself to her feet and was forced to lie there till Charles returned with her maid.

Susan, ever careful of her mistress's wellbeing, shot Charles one quickly concealed look of reproach before she urged Mary back to bed. 'You're in no fit state to go anywhere, Madam,' she told her firmly.

'But my lord is—' Mary protested.

Susan was insistent. 'Never mind about that, my lady. The king will surely not force you on to the road, sick as you are. Whatever were you thinking of?' Although the question was to Mary, it was clear that it was really Charles to whom the question was addressed and it reduced him to a shamefaced but still-glowering resentment and he left her to her maid's ministrations.

Mary allowed Susan to settle her back in her bed. At least Henry, when he came to visit her to see how she did, was kindly and sympathetic. She found him to be in a sentimental mood and sat by her bed for several hours at a stretch, reminiscing about their childhood. Mary, although she would rather have rested, was eager to please her brother for Charles's sake.

Soon after, things started to improve for them. In July, part of Mary's promised French dower income arrived. Her health improved and daily they expected to be sent from Henry's side. However, Henry and Wolsey had other things to occupy their minds than guests who overstayed their invitation and they remained with her brother, enjoying the expensive and sophisticated entertainment with which he surrounded himself.

Autumn brought with it the arrival of a party of French nobles whose costumes competed with the showy colours of the season. They had come over for the signing of the peace; the price for this was the delivery of Henry's prized, but money-hungry Tournai and the betrothal of his only child, the now toddling Princess Mary, to the Dauphin of France. Arrangements were also set in hand for Henry to cross The Channel to visit Francis.

Mary had not seen her brother so happy in a long time. Not only was he rid of the financial burden of Tournai and had made a fine match for his little daughter, he could also enjoy planning a wardrobe for the upcoming French visit which even the elegant Francis couldn't match. But all of these, Mary knew, were as nothing compared to Henry's greatest pleasure. For at last, he had the son for whom he had longed for years.

True, the boy was illegitimate, but in providing him with a son, Henry's mistress, Bessie Blount, had proved Henry's manhood for him. Henry's lack of a son had long made him sensitive that such a lack indicated he was not as manly as other men, so Mary was happy for her brother's sake. She felt saddened for Catherine though, for the birth of this boy made her failure to do her duty even more evident.

Mary's sad-eyed sister-in-law moved around the court like a spectre at all the joyous festivities held to celebrate the boy's birth. Mary pitied the poor queen and guessed how wounded she must be by Henry's open pride in his son by Bessie Blount. But Mary was constrained for Charles's sake from showing Catherine her sympathy too openly.

But even though most of her sympathy lay with Catherine, Mary was able to understand something of her brother's feelings also. For Henry urgently felt the need of sons. Had not their father usurped the crown from the Yorkist King Richard III at Bosworth, thereafter marrying Elizabeth, Richard's eldest niece, the daughter of Richard's brother, Edward IV and thereby presenting a double-fronted edifice of his right to the crown? In spite of this, there were still some ready to whisper that the Tudors had no such right; so such a new dynasty had a desperate need of sons.

Conscious of the need to retain Henry's affection for her husband's sake, Mary daren't show her sympathy for Catherine's plight too openly. As Charles had reminded her, they had nothing to win and everything to lose if she showed that Catherine had the bulk of her sympathy. Besides, their financial wellbeing and with it their marital happiness, was too dependent on friendship with France; they must cleave to Henry and the match of his and Catherine's little daughter with Francis' eldest son.

Catherine, of course, favoured friendship with her nephew Charles who had recently inherited the title of Emperor from his grandsire, Maximilian. This was the self-same Charles whom Mary had expected to marry as a girl. Although aware that friendship with the Emperor was not something either she or Charles should encourage, Mary couldn't help but feel a certain curiosity for the man who could easily have been her husband.

Catherine encouraged Mary's curiosity. Catherine was greatly looking forward to the imminent visit of her nephew who was to come to England on his way to his crowning at Aix-la-Chapelle. She would expound on her mighty nephew by the hour till Mary was eager to see this paragon.

Mary had only recently given birth to her third child, another daughter whom she had named Eleanor. Her labour had brought another bout of ill-health and she had suffered the most dreadful pains in her side that had caused her to mope about her chamber feeling depressed and downhearted. Thankfully, the prospect of finally seeing her previous betrothed worked a cure and she was up and about again for the arrival of Charles V.

But, for all the competition between the three young monarchs; Henry, Francis and Charles, to the disappointment of Mary and Catherine, Mother Nature proved to be the strongest monarch of all, and Charles's planned visit of several weeks was by inclement weather reduced to only a few days. But at last the storms abated sufficiently for his ships to cross the Channel from his anchor at Corunna. Henry, Catherine, Mary and the rest of the court journeyed to Dover to greet him.

Mary's curiosity about the prince who had so nearly become her husband quickly died a natural death as she viewed the pale-faced, lantern-jawed and sombre twenty-year old Emperor, who, for all his claimed intelligence, seemed dour and entirely lacking in humour. He compared unfavourably to her own Charles. Even old Louis had proved a better bargain; he, at least, by his generous gifts, had enabled her to purchase approval of her second marriage.

Mary was at pains to conceal her lack of admiration for this hobbledehoy-appearing youth. But, as Charles had said to her only that morning, this young man – who was said to be wise beyond his years – and Catherine between them, might yet persuade Henry to change his allegiance from friendship with France to friendship with the empire. So she was relieved when, his visit curtailed, the solemn Charles departed.

It was time for the court to look forward to the real business of the year; Henry's long-planned meeting with the King of France. Mary was excited about the forthcoming visit, intrigued to discover if the intervening five years had wrought much change in the Mephistophelian looks of Francis, her previously oh-so- determined would-be lover. Court gossip about Francis and his amorous exploits were legion, the responsibilities of kingship had not lessened his energy, rather it increased his opportunities. It would be interesting to see him again now that she was a long-married matron of twenty-three and the mother of three growing children. Was Queen Claude still as fat and Madam Louise still convinced her son was some sort of Divine being?

Francis' pursuit of her had been common knowledge at the time and Mary knew the eyes of both French and English courtiers would be upon them both during the meeting of the two courts. She was determined to look her best so she would be able to outface all the watchful gazes, thankful that she was now an assured woman and not a frightened, lonely girl. This time, she could enjoy the French court and its intrigues on the arm of her husband. Her lips quirked upwards at the thought that she might even attempt a little harmless flirtation with Francis, but she immediately thought better of it. Flirtation with Francis could never be either little or harmless, she, of all people, should know that.

But at least the weather, which had curtailed the Emperor's visit, showed a kinder face to them. The wind was set fair as the many great ships of Henry's fleet crossed to France for the meeting between the two kings that Mary and Charles both hoped would secure their future financial probity.

CHAPTER EIGHTEEN

An ocean of canvas that formed the temporary, tented town, was spread as far as the eye could see. The incredible spectacle lay revealed as the English party approached the Valley D'or.

Wolsey had been in charge of the arrangements and with his usual skill he had overseen the transport of food, tents, horses and over five thousand nobles and their servants from England to Guisnes just outside Calais. No expense had been spared to give the rival monarchs a suitable setting for their egos. Mary could only stand and marvel, pleased she and Charles were back in Henry's good graces and could take their place on such an occasion.

They were lodged in a house specially built for the meeting, in the courtyard of the castle. The artists employed had excelled themselves and their efforts made a golden if temporary stage for England's nobles to strut. Windows glittered in golden mullions, walls were hung with golden tapestries and silk in the green and white Tudor colours. Tudor roses studded the ceilings. The chapel, its rich vestments borrowed from Westminster for the occasion, had a ceiling of blue and silver, but all other ornaments gleamed richly of gold. Jewels shone from every corner, from vestments, vessels, hangings. So many, that when the sun shone through the windows, it was almost like looking into the heart of that great, yellow orb.

A statue of Bacchus stood in the courtyard, dispensing a river of claret, hypocras and water, cups hanging by waiting for the thirsty. Sadly, the beauty of the scene was spoiled by the beggars and scoundrels who came from far and wide for the free drink. They lay about beside the statue of the god in drunken abandon, oblivious to their surroundings.

Mary, self-persuaded from the dangerous temptation of flirting with Francis, still experienced an occasional frisson at the thought of meeting him again. Although far from handsome, he had that certain devil-may-care air that was far more attractive than mere good looks—as, no doubt, his many and varied female conquests would agree. She hoped he retained sufficient gallantry not to speak of the many indignities she had endured at his hands or of how close she had come to succumbing to his demands.

But whether he did or no, Mary intended to hold her head high, concealing any nerves or anxieties beneath her expensive new gowns. As the recognised English beauty for this historic meeting, she knew she represented the pride of England. Henry was determined that she would outshine the French ladies. He wanted to make plain that the rose who had sadly wilted under French care could, under the benign English, bloomingly show her true beauty.

She smiled to herself. Henry could be fanciful. But he had made clear to her how important it was to him that he and his family should prove themselves, in everything, the superior of Francis and his family. It had been a costly business and her smile faded as she thought of the unnecessary extra burden of debt. But Charles, like Henry, had insisted that she must be dressed as befitted a Dowager-Queen. It was necessary that she not only look like a queen, but behave like one; any lack of decorum would, she knew, bring Henry's wrath down on her head. Another reason not to indulge in flirtatious behaviour. She would take her cue from Catherine, whose dignity, whatever the situation that confronted her, was innate.

Charles was, if anything, even more determined than Henry that she must shine. She sometimes caught her husband looking at her in her expensive queenly finery as though he found it difficult to believe that she was his wife and the mother of his children. She knew he was anxious about this meeting with Francis and what the French king might let slip in front of Henry and the court. He had denied it, of course, but she knew he had simply been putting on a brave face. Truth to tell, she suspected he was a little over-awed at the rich spectacle made by the two royal courts, for she had caught the occasional glimpse below the surface confidence to the man she knew lay beneath and was reminded that his father had been a lowly knight. Truly, in a single generation, Charles had made great strides up the ladder; no wonder he should sometimes catch his breath. No wonder, either, that like the even more lowly-born Wolsey, his ambitions should have climbed as high as himself. It was essential to his pride that this should be so, she knew. It was why he had raged against Wolsey when he had demanded the payment of the debts he owed to the crown which had forced them from the court and away from the ambition that could only be fulfilled there.

But now was not the time for thinking about such matters. As one of her ladies called her, Mary put her thoughts aside and prepared to assume the public role demanded of her.

After the first formalities were over, Henry and his companions rode off to visit Queen Claude and the other French ladies, leaving Mary, Catherine and the other ladies of the English court to entertain Francis.

Mary smoothed her gown, conscious that her hands had dampened with nerves, but the nerves didn't outlast the first appearance of Francis. She and the other ladies were hard pressed to hide their amusement when the still-elegant Francis rode up on a humble mule, his long legs trailing on the ground. This, thought Mary, was his way of outfacing Henry, who had ridden off on his visit to the French ladies seated on magnificent horseflesh, as usual. Her brother would be vexed when he learned of Francis' seeming humility.

The intervening five years hadn't been quite as kind to Francis as Mary knew they had been to her. She studied him from under discreetly veiled lashes and was shocked to see that, though he was only two years her senior, Francis' debauched way of life had started to take its toll. He wore a beard now, but it did little to conceal how fat his face had become. His great nose still dominated his face and looked to Mary's eyes to have grown even longer, if that was possible.

If it had, it would undoubtedly be from its owner's habit of poking it into the bed-chambers of other men's wives.

For whatever cause, a little of his lustre had slipped. Mary was sorry to see it; in his prime he had been something to see. However, to make up for any lack in other areas, he was more gallant than ever. His years of kingship had only added to his self-confidence and, as Mary watched, he kissed Queen Catherine's hand with all the old Francis-flourish.

Mary found herself stiffening just a little as he approached her, memories of their bedroom encounters sparkling in the mesmeric dark eyes that swept her figure in the old, familiar way. He looked delighted to find that he could still bring a blush to her cheeks. Happily, time and her situation had changed and now he could only look, not touch. Besides, Catherine stood stoutly beside her. Her pious presence would ensure that Francis behaved himself.

'Ah, ma Belle-Mère,' he greeted her, kissing her hand lingeringly as his eyes made clear he would still be delighted to again kiss the rest of her. 'I hope the Duke of Suffolk realises his great good fortune. Such loveliness is damaging to the eyes.' He held a hand over them for a few seconds as though to ward off such a danger.

'You look well, your Grace,' Mary lied, curtseying as she spoke. Surprisingly, given his debauched appearance and increased weight, he still, she now found, had the power to thrill the senses. He retained, too, whatever else the years might have tarnished, that aura of majesty and power that he had seemingly donned along with his kingship.

She was conscious of a faint tingle of regret, that was as quickly gone as good sense reasserted itself. As a lover, Francis might well provide a feast for the senses, but it took only the reminder that many others had shared in the feasting to curdle the appetite. Mary told herself there was no need of regrets; she was the wife of a fine man, a man who loved her and only her. How much better to be that than part of a crowd. As she collected herself, Mary heard Francis launch into fresh gallantries and realised he had not really changed at all.

'I have waited these many years to again hear my name on your pretty lips, Mary,' he told her. 'I beg of you to use it often. You'll not find it so difficult. I hear you have called one of your children after me.'

Mary nodded and recognised from the teasing twinkling in his eyes that he well knew the reason why. However, he made no comment on how much her and Charles's financial health rested on his friendship.

'I am truly honoured. I thought you might have forgotten me.' He tried to look suitably modest as if he genuinely believe this was a real possibility. Such modesty was, however, beyond him, in spite of his humble arrival on the mule. Francis considered himself utterly unforgettable, but he had the grace and humour to laugh at his vanity.

Catherine intervened to ask if he wished to dine now. It put an end to his gallantry. Francis inclined his head in agreement. He and Catherine led the way. Mary followed behind, schooling any show of amusement from her expression as she listened to Francis expend his gallantries on her brother's stout and pious queen.

Catherine didn't approve of Francis. Nor did she welcome amity between England and France. How could she, when such amity would damage her influence and that of her family? Naturally, she would prefer her kingly husband to be pushed into the arms of her nephew, the Emperor, than into those of the wily Francis. But Catherine rarely intervened in such policy-making and was making the best of what must be a disappointing situation for her.

Mary and Charles, of course, were desperately keen on this friendship and Mary set herself to charm the French king. It wasn't difficult. Catherine no longer danced, so Francis partnered Mary. Francis was still nimble on his feet and, after the banqueting tables were cleared for dancing, she found he still moved with an easy grace. As they moved around the floor, the memories of her time in France as a girl came flooding back to her. Conscious of his arm about her, she tried to recall how many times he had held her in that over-familiar fashion. Fleetingly, she wondered how her husband and brother were faring with the French ladies. She hoped Henry didn't embarrass shy Claude by being over-boisterous or heavily gallant.

Francis put his lips close to her ear. 'Of what are you thinking, Mary?' he breathed. 'You look far away.'

She gazed at Francis' penetrating dark eyes and as quickly looked away. She managed to keep her voice steady as she replied. 'Not so far, Francis. I was just remembering the balls that were held when I was Queen of France. It seems so long ago now.'

'You could still have been Queen,' he whispered. 'You know that you had only to say the word and I would have put Claude away. I would have given much to have you by my side.' His voice caressed her and a sigh escaped his lips as he continued. 'Alas, you preferred the commoner, Brandon, to the King of France. That was a sad day for me, ma Belle. How well I remember the pain you caused me.'

His long face was hung with sorrow which made it appear even longer. Mary was thankful to realise that the power he had once had to mesmerise her had vanished. It seemed he recognised this, for when she moved slightly away from him he didn't attempt to prevent her.

'Love cannot be commanded, Francis,' she told him lightly. 'It must be freely given and I loved Charles. I still love him. You have Claude. She has given you fine children, has she not?' she reminded him in gentle admonishment.

'Ah Claude. Sweet, gentle, loving Claude.' He smiled sadly down at her. 'Yes, I too, have much to be grateful for. But one can still yearn for what one has lost.'

Mary heard the note of regret and wondered if it was sincere. But who could be sure with Francis? His bedroom manners were as much part of him as his long, Valois nose and just as unalterable. Relieved that she had hit on the correct topic to make him put aside his gallantries, she listened as he spoke boastfully of his children. He was as proud a father as Charles or Henry and obviously convinced that no one had ever had such marvellous offspring. His eldest boy, the Dauphin, was of course now betrothed to Henry and Catherine's little daughter, Mary.

Francis waxed tender at the thought of the youthful pair. 'Who knows? Perhaps they will have the love together that you and I could only dream of, Mary.'

'Tis a pretty thought, Francis. Let us hope for their sakes that it comes true. I would welcome a lasting peace and friendship between our two countries.'

Francis gave a solemn nod. 'I, too. But peace is an elusive thing, is it not?'

The demands of the dance parted them for a short time and as their steps brought them back together, he commented teasingly, 'There are always aggressors who wish to take that which is not theirs. France must defend herself from such.' His thinly-veiled allusion to Henry and his French ambitions were a gentle reproach. 'I wish my son to inherit a strong kingdom and shall see that he does.' His expression was for a moment stern. But then he smiled, gallant once more. 'Enough of such talk. It is not fitting between you and I.'

They had come to a halt at the edge of the floor as the music stopped. But as it started up again he took her arm once more. 'Come, let us dance some more. A king, too, must have his dreams. Let me reawaken mine to warm my old age.' His strong hand in hers, Francis led her back on the floor.

But Mary's pleasure in the dance had gone with the talk of how fragile was the peace between their two countries. It had reminded her on what slender foundations her and Charles's happiness rested. One act of aggression from Henry could so easily cost her her dower revenues; they had only just started to flow again after his last attempt at war-mongering. Francis, too, had his ambitions and could be equally fickle. The truth of this realisation was quickly brought home to Mary as he made his excuses to her when he spotted a pretty new face amongst the ladies and went eager-ly off to flirt with the young woman.

Catherine had missed little of what had passed. When Mary re-joined her, she commented softly, 'These French—they lack seriousness, Mary, do they not?'

It was plain the thought pleased Mary's serious-minded sister-in-law. Mary sighed and thinking more of defending her future dower income than she was of Francis, she re-plied, 'But they can be amusing companions, none more so.'

'I'm sure that is so, as long as one doesn't expect more from them than amusement. I've heard how the French court is conducted. It is not necessary to breathe deeply to smell the sinful stench beneath the perfumes.'

Mary made no further comment. Instead, she and Catherine watched Francis as he flirted with her step-daughter, Anne Brown. Catherine murmured, 'The French have always had the tongue of quicksilver and the slippery body of an eel. It doesn't do to trust them overmuch. I think Henry will gain but little for all this expensive show. The money could have been put to better use in England.'

Mary was surprised to hear Catherine voice a rare criti-cism of Henry. It was a measure of the pain felt by the wom-an who lived and breathed beneath the courtly robes of a queen. Catherine had not only suffered the still-birth of the last child she had borne and, shortly after, witnessed the celebrations held in honour of the son Henry's mistress had born him, by a cruel twist of fate, Claude, Francis' twenty-one-year-old queen was heavily pregnant for the fifth time, having already presented Francis with a son and heir as well as a second son, born the previous June. Henry would be sure to rub salt in the wound of Catherine's misfortune by making some comment about how admirably Francis' queen did her duty in this regard.

Unusually, there was a trace of bitterness discernible beneath Catherine's surface calm. Normally, Catherine's face was wreathed in smiles. Whatever her private anguish, she could always find another smile with which to meet adversity. But today, the smiles were not so frequent. She showed signs of strain. Even so, conscious of how badly she had failed in one wifely duty, Catherine seemed to feel this imposed on her an obligation to excel in others. She set about excusing her husband's casual cruelties. 'He is still a boy in many ways, easily impressed by bright and shiny things and the French know how to glitter like no other.'

The ball came to an end and Francis, gracious as always, returned to where Mary and Catherine were seated. They had risen and were escorting him to the courtyard when, through a door left open in an attempt to cool the stifling air on this hot June day, he spied the other ladies of the English train dining and his gallantry was once again to the fore. He threw the door wide open, entered the room and insisted on kissing every lady present, amidst much coy squealing from the ladies.

Ruefully, Mary noted that none of the ladies appeared unwilling; far from it. And although many of the ladies' husbands were against an alliance with France, their wives, it was clear, thought France's king a far more attractive match than the one with the ungainly young Emperor Charles. They loved him, with his free and easy ways and lightly-worn regality. But even Francis, for all his gallantry, couldn't quite bring himself to kiss the old and ugly. He kissed the rest though, and there were around one hundred and thirty ladies present, the pretty ones being kissed so thoroughly as to give the impression that each one must surely be the love of his life. Mary and Catherine could only stand and wait whilst Francis amused himself. But he eventually ran out of ladies to kiss and he came back to them, his eyes shining with good humour.

Outside at last, back under the wilting heat of the blazing sun, he climbed back on to his humble mule and departed back to his canvas palace while his latest female conquests crowded round to wave him adieu.

The next day the competition in the lists began. Mary sat with her sister queens, Catherine and Claude, in the glazed gallery and watched their lords as they competed with gusting winds and each other. Like Mary, Queen Claude was now the mother of three surviving children. Claude was fatter than ever, her figure had not been improved by frequent pregnancies. She didn't look well. It seemed she had never really overcome the poor health of her girlhood and tired easily. Catherine and Mary both fussed over the heavily pregnant French queen. They placed cushions at her back and made sure she had a good view of her lordly husband as he strutted in the lists.

Although Claude's body was fat and unattractive, her face had acquired the look of a Madonna, doubtless, Mary thought, attributable to the many martyring humiliations her marriage to the womanising Francis would have brought her. She hoped no one had brought her tales of Francis' renewed attentions to herself; if they had, Claude gave no sign and was as sweet-natured as Mary remembered her.

It was pleasant in the gallery, out of the rough winds that buffeted their lords. 'Well done, Francis,' Claude called as he unseated a rival. She smiled apologetically. 'He likes me to applaud. Men need such admiration, I have found.'

'Men are much the same the world over,' was Catherine's quiet observation. 'They are welcome to their games. We're more comfortable here.'

'Francis seems as vigorous as ever, Claude,' said Mary. 'Does he still practise the manly arts with as much energy as in his youth?'

'Alas, his duties take up much time now. To his disgust, he has put on weight. Too many rich banquets, I fear. Do you remember how Lady Guildford warned me against eating too many rich foods, Mary?' Mary nodded. 'My pregnancies have completed the job the banquets began. As you see, I've become very stout. But my children are a great consolation. They have brought Francis and me closer together.' She turned to Catherine. 'Let us hope, your Grace, that our children will bring our two nations closer together. I was delighted at their betrothal, having got to know the little Princess Mary's Aunt Mary so well.'

A cheer rang out and saved Catherine the trouble of replying, which was as well, for Mary knew it was unlikely she would feel able to agree on the desirability of the match. It was now Henry's turn to strut as he acknowledged the applause of the crowd at his victory. Dutifully, Catherine applauded her husband. In an aside to Claude, she said dryly, 'It seems we are both married to champions, your Grace.'

The rivalry between the two kings was strongly evident. Both were tall, broad and much of an age. Mary glanced at Catherine and wondered if her sister-in-law was anticipating more reproaches from Henry at his lack of sons now that he had witnessed the fruitfulness of Francis' young queen at such close quarters. Catherine, well past her youth, looked and no doubt felt every one of her thirty-four years. Mary felt a twinge of pity for Catherine as she sat smiling down at the husband who chastised her for being all-but barren. She wondered if Catherine, in her present situation, didn't sometimes feel she would have been better left a poor, neglected widow and packed off back to Spain and the court of her father, Ferdinand.

Below, Henry acknowledged more cheers for his vigor. His horse didn't share the crowd's admiration; it collapsed, overcome by Henry's magnificence and died before them all, much to Henry's chagrin. It was his favourite horse, too.

Mary hoped the horse's death didn't put her brother in an ill-humour. For she had sometimes wondered if Henry's determination to excel over Francis in all things didn't spring, as did her own husband's, from consciousness that his origins were not all as noble as he would wish. Less than a hundred years before, the Tudors had been ill-educated little squires, while Francis, his rival, came from a line of kings which had reigned in France since the 10th century.

The unwelcome thought struck her that for all this current great show of friendship between Henry and Francis, Henry was unequal to the task of making a true friendship with the man who must make him aware of his own shortcomings. Mary hoped this sudden intuition was wrong, but in her heart she knew it was not. She felt a brooding disquiet as another horse was fetched for her brother and he continued to parade his noble accomplishments.

The entertainments continued unabated. And although the heart had gone out of Mary, she concealed it successfully. Henry, whatever his private feelings of inferiority before the sleek French nobility, on the surface at least, he continued to enjoy himself with gusto. He had always loved to dance and disguise himself and he swaggered boisterously before the elegant French, as pleased with himself as a great spoilt child. Beside her, Mary heard Catherine sigh faintly as her monstrous infant of a husband showed off. And for all her doubts about this show of friendship lasting, Mary could still feel thankful that she had escaped the fate of most princesses. Her impulsive marriage had in many respects given her the best of both worlds. She kept a queenly estate in her own home and was also second lady in both England and France.

Admittedly, the queenly estate that her station demanded brought its own difficulties, particularly over the money it cost to maintain it. Even so, and though she sometimes questioned the strength of Charles's love for her, she realised as she watched the brother kings at their games and studied their worn-out queens, she had much for which to be thankful.

Francis now sported an eye-patch as he had received a black eye riding against the Earl of Devon. This newly-dashing appearance encouraged him to flirt more outrageously than ever, which increased the Madonna-look of his queen.

Playtime was, however, drawing to a close. The two courts attended mass in a semi-open chapel at the end of their historic meeting. Henry and Francis pledged their intention of building a church on the site and even went so far as to decide on a name, 'La Chapelle de Notre Dame De La Paix'. Mary doubted their dreams of church-building would be any longer-lived than the peace that had inspired it, for all the sadness that was voiced on both sides as the meeting broke up and for all that the two kings embraced like long separated siblings whose affection distance couldn't tarnish. For all Henry's show of friendship with Francis, Mary knew that he would straight afterwards ride off for a second meeting with Catherine's nephew, the Emperor Charles. And who knew what the outcome of that would be for them all? Maybe she would yet find her recently-restored French dower income finding its way instead into Francis' war-chests.

CHAPTER NINETEEN

As Mary had feared, peace between the European monarchs lasted no longer this time than it had in the past. Although, along with the rest, Francis had signed up to the League, he broke away from it and attacked the domains of the Emperor. Charles V promptly called upon England to honour her treaty obligations and declare war on France, and Henry, his instincts for war-mongering as finely-honed as Francis', was eager to fall in with the Emperor's demands.

Henry was excited by the thought of pitting his skills against Francis in a real battle. And with Charles V and his vast empire behind him, war became an even more alluring prospect. Victory would be almost assured, he had told Cardinal Wolsey.

Wolsey didn't share Henry's optimism. He reminded Henry that war was a costly business and always uncertain of outcome. It would be better to wait a while, he counselled. Perhaps, in the interim, Francis would listen to the wise advice of his mother and pull back.

Henry stuck out a petulant lip. 'On my honour, how could I deny the Emperor my support? I gave my word as a king.'

He frowned suspiciously at Wolsey. 'Would you have me break it?'

Henry's honour was a creature almost as tender as his conscience; neither could be ignored. 'Indeed not, Sire.' Masterfully, Wolsey put just the right amount of indignation into his voice. 'I would never counsel you to such an action. I merely advise that it would not be good policy to be too precipitate. We should wait and see how this matter progresses. Perhaps,' he added thoughtfully, as if the idea had just occurred to him, 'if England were to offer to mediate betwixt them, it would give time for tempers to cool. If they agreed, England's entry into the conflict could be postponed, perhaps indefinitely.' Henry turned sulky again, but Wolsey, who knew when to offer a carrot, pointed out, 'Such a postponement would give us more time to prepare. If mediation failed, we should be duty-bound to support the Emperor. Honour, as you so rightly say, Sire, would permit no other course.'

Teased from his sulks by Wolsey's words Henry eased his stiff neck and admitted that Wolsey might have a point. 'It is true, as you say, that continental campaigns are costly. Perhaps we should take a little more time to consider what should be done before we rush to do the Emperor's bidding. That which is fast begun oft ends awry.'

Wolsey smiled to himself when he saw how pleased Henry was with the aptness of his little homily. Encouraged in his belief that he had brought Henry round to his own way of thinking on the matter and that he would now be more receptive to his final and strongest argument against war, he added softly, 'Scotland, Sire, is another reason for caution. That accursed country is ever ready to plunge a knife into England's back. Remember how, the last time you invaded France, they entered by the country's back door after we had left by the front?' Henry nodded at this reminder of Scotland's perfidy.

That time they had been fortunate and the flower of Scotland's nobles had died at the Battle of Flodden, their sister, Margaret's husband, King James, among them. Catherine had sent the king's bloody coat to Henry in France.

'They would as lief plunge the knife for the sake of their friendship with France as for their own sake. We would not wish to defend the Emperor's dominions at the possible cost of your own.'

'Of a surety,' Henry murmured.

Reminded of this enemy at his back who would be ready to seize an advantage from any continental adventure, Henry looked to have lost some of his lust for battle. Wolsey encouraged this loss still further. 'Albany, the Scottish regent, is only too ready to do Francis' bidding. He would be across the border into England before our army had advanced fifty miles. It would be essential, Sire, that we secured our back door before we opened the front.' Henry nodded. Wolsey was gratified to see that the fire in the king's belly seemed to have been doused. Scotland, that ever-present bogey, was a useful tool to cool the king's ardor for war.

However, despite the Cardinal's ability to sway Henry, some things were beyond even his abilities to alter. And events on the continent soon forced a rethink. For Francis, too, had trouble on his doorstep. The thoughtless confiscation of Charles Bourbon's lands on the death of his royal wife had turned this powerful noble into France's enemy and his rebellion against his over-lord, the King of France, turned the tide in the allies' favour. Francis now had his very own Albany.

Bourbon's disaffection, together with the Emperor's second visit to England, provided the impetus to encourage Henry and Wolsey to enter the ring. A herald was now despatched to France to make declaration of war.

Once again, to Mary's bitter disappointment, her income from France was in jeopardy. It seemed that no sooner were their finances set on a fair course than the unpredictable political winds that blew through Europe must swamp and overset them. Mary put down her book and shut it. She had told Catherine she was keen to again take up the Latin that she had been taught as a child. Catherine had been delighted and had been full of encouragement. But today, Mary found concentration impossible. She listened anxiously for the clamour that would herald the arrival of the refugees from the French court which was expected imminently. Amongst those refugees was Anne Boleyn, Mary's youngest Maid of Honour from her time as Queen of France. Mary was eager to talk to Anne and learn, first-hand, what news there was from France.

When Anne Boleyn and the others finally arrived, Mary sent a maid with a message for Anne to come to her apartments. Her summons was quickly answered. Smiling, Mary welcomed her to court. Apart from learning of recent events in France that might adversely affect her dower income, Mary was also keen on renewing an old acquaintance. She and her young Maids had shared worrying and dangerous times together. Their experiences at the court of France had created a bond of intimacy which Mary was keen to revisit.

She was surprised to see how much Anne had blossomed during her years in France. Although she was still slim, it was now a slimness of willowy grace where before it had been mere gawkiness. She appeared so polished, so cultured and stylish that Mary could see no trace of the shy and sallow little girl to whom she had given her unwanted gowns. But she was being foolish; how could anyone remain a child at Francis' court?. She laughed and told Anne what she had been thinking. 'But of course you have changed from that little girl whose growth outpaced her gowns. France obviously suited you. But sit down, Anne. I am eager for news of France. Tell me something of the court's doings.'

Her smile gracious, Anne seated herself with the smooth elegance that had so surprised Mary. She still felt disconcerted that the little Maid of Honour of her memory should be such a startling contrast to the Anne who now sat so composedly before her. She sensed from the girl's demeanour that Anne had not liked to be reminded of the shabby and outgrown gowns or of the necessity of accepting Mary's charity. It seemed her little Maid of Honour had discovered a certain hauteur during the process that had turned her from an ugly duckling into a swan. Although on the surface, she was pleasant enough, Mary sensed an underlying resentment and wondered at the girl's ability to so long harbour a grudge over so small a matter.

But perhaps it was not only the matter of the gowns, Mary thought as she encouraged the girl to chat. It would be understandable if Anne was irked that Henry's determination on war had put to an abrupt end her pleasant life in France. She might indeed feel resentment towards Henry's sister that she should have been hurried from France and the only home she had known for many years. Whether such was the cause of Anne's ill-feeling, Mary didn't know. It was, in any case, beyond her power to ease the cause of either resentment. Anyway, it was surely beyond time that Anne returned home. She was no longer a child and must be anxious for her father to find a husband for her.

The renewal of intimacy that Mary had hoped for didn't occur; that intimacy had vanished as surely as the little Maid with whom she had shared it. Whatever the reason for its loss, Mary found she couldn't take to this new Anne. She put away the hopes she had cherished of girlish confidences and of learning whatever Anne might have gauged of Francis' intentions. After no more than half-an-hour, she drew the visit to a close.

Of much more importance to Mary was her anxiety about her husband. For Charles had been appointed to lead an English expedition across the Channel. Originally, Henry's plan had been limited to the capture of Boulogne, which, if it could be achieved, would provide them with another Channel port and give a great boost to the next year's campaign. But Bourbon and the Emperor proposed a more dangerous and ambitious plan; that Charles Brandon should link up with Margaret of Austria's army from the Netherlands and march on Paris, while Bourbon launched his revolt against Francis at the same time as the allies crossed the French frontier.

Mary had been dismayed when, although Henry had been against it, Wolsey had been persuaded by Count Buren, the Emperor's general, that the difficulties of besieging Boulogne would be too great. Despite Henry's misgivings, Wolsey persuaded the king to back this new and more ambitious plan.

War and its many perils filled her every waking hour and she dreaded Charles's departure. As well as worrying about Charles, she had another, underlying cause for concern: what would become of her if she should be widowed a second time? Widowhood would, she knew, free her to once again become a marital pawn in Henry's power-plays.

Charles, of course, brushed her fears aside, so delighted was he to have his chance to prove his worth to Henry that he even attempted to deny his doubts that the new campaign plan was wise. Mary was worried that his desire for glory would make him over-daring and place him in even more peril. Charles had laughed at her anxieties. It was clear he couldn't wait to be off.

Stung, Mary said, 'You seem eager to leave me, Charles. You may find the prospect of war entertaining, but I do not.' She took his arm and pleaded with him. 'All I ask is your promise that you will not do anything foolhardy. The king's favour will be of no use to you if you are dead.'

He sighed, but did as she had asked. 'You make your point, Mary,' he told her. 'I promise not to indulge in any unnecessary heroics.' Solemnly, he crossed his heart. 'But please, no more of your entreaties. They weaken a man.'

Mary held her tongue after that. And at least during the weeks of preparation she was kept too busy to brood, sewing the many banners and flags that the army would take with them to France.

The collection of money to pay for the war, the many preparations required for the transportation of the troops to Calais and negotiations with Bourbon, all caused so many delays that Charles bemoaned the passing of the summer and the loss of so many campaign days, for wars were rarely fought during the difficult winter months. It was not till the beginning of September that everything was in place. Then came yet more delay. Francis had discovered Bourbon's treachery and their ally was forced to flee to Italy, just avoiding capture and arrest as a traitor.

Charles complained to Mary, 'The campaign season will be over before we even leave Calais. How can I win this war if my army is hog-tied by winter's mud?'

Mary, knowing how eager was Charles to head a glorious army and return home in triumph, did her best to soothe his frustrations. But finally the expedition was ready to set out for Calais. Their goodbyes were muted; Mary trying desperately to keep her fears to herself; Charles anxious not to give her cause to revive them.

He held out his arms. 'Come, sweetheart, kiss me and wish me luck. The sooner I get started, the sooner I'll return to you. Do not delay me with more tears,' he warned, as Mary's eyes glittered. 'We've had delays in plenty already. Any more and we will never get to Paris before winter sets in and that'll not please the king.'

Mary sighed and went into his arms. 'I can't help it. I still wish Henry had given the task to someone else. He has enough fighting nobles to choose from, as the good Lord knows. Why did he have to choose you for this dangerous enterprise?'

'I would hope it is because he values my martial abilities.' Charles gazed at her in astonishment. 'By the Mass, Mary, there were any number competing for the honour. Besides, we need the king's friendship. *I* need his friendship. You know full well that there are many about him who still see only my lowly birth. They regard my marriage to the king's sister with envious eyes and if they could do me a hurt they surely would. Your brother's friendship, aye, and his admiration, too, are worth a great deal to me. If I can obtain his favour by winning his wars for him I'll do it, right gladly. You have long known of my ambitions, Mary. You used to be proud of them once. Don't attempt to hold me back. I'll not be put in leading strings.'

Mary kept quiet. She had no alternative. But for him to choose this occasion of their leave-taking to reveal the depth of his ambition increased her fears tenfold. In spite of his promise not to do anything foolhardy, she suspected that ambition would blind him to danger until it was too late.

Taking her silence for acquiescence, Charles's voice softened. 'Let us not part with harsh words, Mary. I want to be able to remember you with a smile, not a frown, when I am in France.' Gently he teased, 'Do you think me, the hero of Tournai, so inexperienced in war that I will act like a smooth-skinned boy? For shame, Mary. I had thought you held me in higher esteem than that.'

Mary had the grace to look discomfited. She attempted a denial, but Charles waved her efforts away. Strengthening his embrace, he demanded, 'Now, are you going to kiss me or not?'

Having kissed her soundly and allowed her a few final minutes of fussing around him, Charles departed. His next word was a message that he had reached Calais safely. The following letter told her that he had set out from there on 19 September, which left only seven or eight weeks of campaigning weather left. Mary knew that must have infuriated him. She then sat back to fret and worry and wait for his next letter.

At first, all went well. At the end of October, Charles wrote jauntily that he had advanced a hundred miles into French territory, crossed the Somme near Bouvain and was within sixty miles of Paris. Proudly, he listed his achievements and how pleased with him Henry would be; English troops had not been so near the French capital for generations.

Mary began to share her husband's pride in his achievements. The excitement in England at fever-pitch, Henry, full of dreams of at last wearing the coveted French crown, enthusiastically agreed to throw in reinforcements to keep the campaign going through the winter. But by the beginning of

November it was clear things were going less well. Charles's next letter told of the early sharp frosts they had experienced. Mary, concerned lest he might take a chill, hurried to her bureau to reply. She urged him to make sure he wore dry clothing, even though she knew in her heart he would spurn to cosset himself when the ordinary soldiers would suffer far greater hardships. Which they did, according to his next letter; a hundred of his soldiers had died from cold and disease. Francis had rushed troops to Paris and its population looked set on making a determined stand in defence of their city.

Clearly, there was to be no easy victory. Charles's dreams of success had turned into a nightmare of bone-chilling weather, sickness and disaffection. The looked-for thaw, when it came, exchanged icy ground for thick, clinging mud. It was now impossible to even pitch a tent and the supply carts of their Burgundian allies were bogged down. His soldiers were mutinous because they hadn't received their pay. Charles berated Margaret of Austria's ministers who refused to risk sending the money for the soldiers' pay from Antwerp so far into France along the unguarded roads. Large contingents of the foreign troops started to melt away, seeing their chance of booty vanishing. Once again, Charles complained, England was let down by allies who had the unfortunate habit of giving up or turning tail at the most inopportune moments.

Mary suspected that, for Charles, the thick mud would be an ill-omened reminder of that earlier time in France when they had waited in fear for Henry's response to their secret marriage. And so it was to prove, for his next letter was clearly penned in the bitterness of ignominious failure.

Without the means to advance, retreat was the only option. As swiftly as conditions allowed, Charles and his Burgundian co-general turned back to Flanders, even as the reinforcements from England were being made ready for dispatch from the south coast.

Henry, all his dreams left lying in the mud of France, at first refused to believe that the campaign was over. He put his mind to feverishly devising schemes to continue with it, but eventually, even he had to accept the inevitable and agree to postpone campaigning till the next year. Such was Henry's disappointment, that the troops were left to linger in Flanders. Charles, to Mary's relief, was recalled home.

She awaited his return with some trepidation, for how could she not be aware of the pinpricks her husband had endured from the high nobles of Henry's court? Low-born, like Wolsey, Charles had not risen like her brother's right-hand man from intelligence and ability alone. For all that many of the courtiers hated Wolsey, they could not deny the man's ability, whereas Charles, it was felt, had risen only by virtue of his friendship with her brother and his marriage to herself. She knew how the knowledge gnawed at him and how much he longed to make one achievement that would force men to look at him with respect that he had earned visible in their eyes. That was why he had wanted so desperately to do well during the French campaign. And it had all come to naught. How bitter must the knowledge be that he would now secure for himself not only further and more savagely-jabbed pinpricks, but had failed also to secure respect as a fighting man and, into the bargain, had certainly ensured the loss of her dower income.

As she waited for him to return, Mary could almost wish that Charles lacked ambition, for it was that which curdled his soul. But, without the ambition that coursed so strongly through him, would she have loved him so well? Perhaps it would have been better for him if she had never done so, she thought sadly when she saw him. He had lost a lot of weight and looked worn and weary when he finally arrived at their apartments after having first been close-closeted with Henry and Wolsey. He was no longer the confident warrior who had set out believing the war was his opportunity to crown himself with glory. But at least he still had the energy for anger. For once, Mary was glad to see it as he flung himself restlessly about their chamber and launched into a torrent of rage on his favourite theme.

'This result is Wolsey's doing. He it was who wanted us to push for Paris. Even the king was against it and warned that we would be obliged to retreat to Flanders. It was too ambitious and sudden a plan and too late in the year. I had feared this,' he reminded her, 'but that meddling prelate must, as always have his own way, thinking to save the cost of a campaign next year by joining now with the Emperor and the rebel Bourbon to bring France to defeat. I had bad feelings about the changed policy, but the king agreed, so I had no choice but to press for Paris. As usual, Wolsey took too much on himself. He's a churchman, what can he know of war and its many difficulties? Better had the king never listened to him. But for Wolsey's ambitious schemes, we might now have had a good base in Boulogne to work from next year. Now, it's all to be done again.'

Mary hated to see him so full of resentment. It brought a resurgence of the old grievances against Wolsey to go with the new ones. To suffer such a failure through no fault of his own must be as bitter to him as wormwood. He so longed for Henry's approbation. Instead, he must be apprehensive that Henry, angry and disappointed at this failure, would lay the blame for it at the door of Charles's generalship. For this, too, he blamed Wolsey. Mary knew not what she could do or say to comfort him. Nor did she know how to comfort herself. There was no comfort to be had for either of them.

Their spirits were at such a low ebb that Mary managed to find consolation in the thought that nothing else could go awry for them. Unfortunately, in this she was proved wrong. One day, she caught the tail-end of a conversation between two courtiers concerning her marriage. Believing their chat to be no more than jealous tittle-tattle, Mary put it from her mind. But then the rumours started in earnest. Tongues vicious against Charles, eager to wound him and not caring that Mary would also be wounded, tattled that their marriage was not a true one.

Stunned, Mary of course had known that Charles's marital history was chequered. Such things were the staple of daily gossip. He had been thirty at the time of their marriage so previous entanglements were implicit. Mary, young and in love, had given little thought to just how tangled his previous love-life had been. She had assumed that he was free to marry her. Why would she not? Charles wasn't a fool. It was one thing and dangerous enough, to secretly marry the king's sister. But to marry her bigamously was altogether too enormous a folly to be even contemplated by any man, certainly not by one who sought the king's friendship above all.

Convinced by such arguments that the rumours must be false, Mary did her best to ignore them. But this was easier said than done. And as his previous love-life was laid bare in all its confusion, Mary was horrified to find the gossips might have the right of it.

She had been a child when Charles had wed the wealthy Anne Browne, the daughter of Sir Anthony Browne. Her, Charles had dismissed on some pretext. He had then married his first wife's close kin, Lady Mortimer, but the church had obliged him to return to his first spouse. She had died in 1513, leaving him with two daughters whom Mary had taken under her wing.

After the death of his first wife, Charles had engaged himself to the young heiress of Lord Lisle, being created a Baron in anticipation of this marriage. But she, on reaching maturity, had declined to marry him. Then, as the cruel gossip-mongers had it, he had been quickly on the trail of another advantageous marriage. Sent on a diplomatic mission to Flanders in connection with Mary's own expected marriage to her betrothed, Prince Charles, he had been much taken with the Prince's aunt, Archduchess Margaret, though whether it was the lady or her rich dowry that most impressed him, the gossip differed. Her brother, Henry, had encouraged his friend's wooing of Archduchess Margaret when she visited the town of Tournai after its capture. The Archduchess had apparently been sufficiently captivated by Brandon - who had at the time just cut an extremely dashing figure on the field of battle - to exchange rings with him. But then, Margaret, fearful of the possible consequences, had desired her ring back. Soon after, Charles Brandon had turned his attentions to another high-born lady—Mary herself. And Mary, spurned by the Prince to whom her father had betrothed her, and having for some time admired the tall and handsome Brandon, had fallen in love with him.

Mary wondered now whether Charles had ever truly loved her at all. Admittedly, it had been she who had pushed for the marriage and Charles who had tried to persuade her to wait. But such caution hadn't characterised his previous behaviour in England when he had been more than willing to kiss and fondle her. Happy, too, to allow romantic thoughts of marriage between them. Even Henry had let Mary go on in happy ignorance and the belief that she would be allowed to marry for love until, with his ambitions for the French alliance, he had insisted she marry Louis. Henry, although he had apparently found it amusing enough to encourage Charles's wooing of Archduchess Margaret, hadn't been willing to lose any advantage to himself when it came to his sister's marriage, even if it cost Mary her happiness.

What price that happiness now? thought Mary. After nine years of marriage and three children, Lady Mortimer, Charles's second wife, whom the church had forced him to abandon, had chosen to remind them of her existence. Apparently involved in an increasingly acrimonious dispute with her family, her one-time marriage to Charles had been recalled and enquired into and the legality of his marriage to Mary herself questioned.

As Charles's colourful past rose up to haunt her, Mary took refuge in her bed-chamber. Heartsick, she paced the room, scourging herself with memories of past events; events that she might have been wiser to examine more closely at the time. Hadn't her brother, on her widowhood, attempted to snatch back the carrot he had so enticingly dangled before her to obtain her agreement to the French marriage? Had he, even then, suspected his friend's marital affairs would not stand too close a scrutiny? Or had it been that Henry, ever one to look for advantage to himself, had simply sought how best he might again make use of her?

And what of Charles? The man she called husband, the man with whom she had gone through three marriage ceremonies? He, too, had attempted to backtrack on his promises. Had this been because his declarations of love had meant so little to him? Or was it because his fear of retribution from Henry was based on far more than their secret marriage?

Mary no longer knew what to think, whom to trust. All she felt sure of right now was that she had been grievously betrayed by those on whose love she should have been most able to rely.

CHAPTER TWENTY

Mary's anguish over her marriage that might not actually *be* a marriage. went on and on. Even in her bed-chamber she could find no respite from the gossips, for when she ordered her women from the room, she spent the solitude tormenting herself with the thought that they would be more able to indulge their gossip in the outer chamber.

Desperate to find some quiet corner in the palace, in her own head, she was driven into the gardens. Fortunately, the weather was calmer than her thoughts, with a bright, though fitful sun that sought to hide itself behind clouds, much as she sought to hide herself from others' prying eyes by seeking out that part of the gardens that she knew to be rarely visited.

To her dismay, as she approached the enclosed arbor, Mary heard voices. She was about to retreat when she realised to whom the voices belonged. It was her brother and Anne Boleyn. Startled, Mary was transfixed. She had heard rumours about her brother and Anne, but had disregarded them. The court ran on rumours as her own recent experiences had brought home to her. She had considered these particular rumours baseless; in her mind, whatever the pre-

353

sent reality, Anne remained the gawky little chit she had known and pitied in France. But now, as she stood in rigid pose, she heard her brother's voice again.

'You play with the heart of so many men, Mistress Anne. I have watched and wondered if the heart of your king dared stray within the orbit of such a bright star.'

Henry's voice thickened with what Mary recognised as desire. 'You have made of me a man uncertain, confused and fearful, Madam. I would only that you would look at me as you look at Wyatt and the other poets of the court. For am I, too, not a poet of passing skill?'

Mary was unable to catch Anne's murmured response, but then Henry spoke again. 'See, I have written an ode to you.'

Taut with a mixture of embarrassment, anger and pity, Mary heard Henry clear his throat and begin to recite his ode, an ode to Anne that clearly came straight from the heart. In spite of her own distress, Mary pitied him. Had she not also felt the pangs of such a love? A love that brought with it the bitter taste of anguish, the green god of jealousy and the uncertainty she herself had felt and which her brother was clearly suffering. But, most of all, the ode spoke of a passion that was, like her own for Charles, all but soul-consuming. Strange, Mary thought, as an image of her parents came into her mind, that such passion, which had passed their parents by, should have so gripped their three remaining children; Henry, with his latest light-of-love Anne Boleyn; Margaret, their elder sister, whose passionate love for Archibald Douglas had now turned to such hatred that she was seeking to divorce herself from him. She had become the mistress of Henry Stewart, the handsome young courtier who was the latest love of her life and whom she would marry if she could.

And me? Why, I still love Charles, whether it be a sin or no, though whether he loves me... Her thoughts broke off as she eavesdropped on her brother. Never had she heard him speak in such an imploring manner to the wife to whom he had in his youth declared himself 'Sir Loyal Heart'. Never had he given the slightest sign that his love for Catherine filled him with a white-hot and burning passion as he did now for the woman Mary knew she must think of no longer as her shabby little Maid of Honour.

Quietly, not even waiting to hear Anne's reply - for what would it be from such as she, a wanton's sister, but more of the teasing and withdrawing that, to judge from her brother's anguished words must have gone before - Mary backed away, out of earshot. And even as it occurred to her that Charles would be furious with her if she was discovered spying on the pair, she remembered her own anguish and the possibility that he might not have a husband's right to chide her.

And as the concern about what Charles might think faded, Mary thought of Catherine. Catherine who had endured so much and always with a smile. How bravely she had borne all the tribulations of her married life. But at least she has been spared my particular pain, Mary reminded herself. No one had ever questioned the validity of Catherine's marriage. That was a unique pain, as Mary was daily discovering, one that Catherine, for all her many sufferings and disappointments in childbed, had never experienced.

As she retraced her steps, Mary hoped that Catherine would be spared the knowledge of this, her husband's latest dalliance. It was but a faint hope. Life at court, especially for the king and his consort, was never private, always there was someone ready to make one aware of that which one would rather not know. Catherine would have been aware of the identity of every woman with whom Henry broke his marriage vows. Had it not been Catherine to whom she herself had turned when she had first become aware of the gossip about her and Charles's marriage?

Catherine had been kind. Always devout and becoming more so with the passing of each disappointing year, she had advised Mary to trust in the Lord and to hold fast to her husband.

Mary had tried to follow her advice. Truly, she had trusted in the Lord at least, if not in her husband, if such he be. Earnestly, had she prayed that God would bring her safely out of these marital storms. But her prayers had come to naught. Here she remained, still not knowing whether she was wife or maid. She lacked Catherine's piety. She had drawn away from the stern teachings of her grandmother and Lady Guildford. Always, they had warned her against lightness of mind, of love of the dance and the dangerous emotions of high passion. She had been brought to her present woeful state by ignoring their teachings of how life should be lived. Perhaps that was why God had been so slow to answer her prayers.

As her lonely footsteps paced the paths, deserted now as a sharp breeze blew from the river and a squally rain began to fall, Mary dawdled. Fleetingly, she considered taking the veil and abjuring a life that had turned its pleasures to pain. But then she thought of her children and what they would suffer if their parents' marriage should prove to be an illicit one. For their sake, she could not remove herself from the torment that filled her nights with fear and her days with shame. She must fight. Fight for her marriage, for the sake of the children. And for the sake of herself also. Deeply as she was hurting, Mary admitted to herself that her love for Charles was not something she could lightly toss aside even should she wish to. He might have hurt her deeply, but she still loved him with all her heart.

With a new resolve, Mary went in search of Cardinal Wolsey. Surely, by now, he must have some news for her from the Pope?

Mary's anguish over her marriage that might not actually be a marriage continued, as the Cardinal still had no good news to tell her. But, with mixed emotions of relief and regret, she, acknowledged that the court gossips found - in Henry and Anne Boleyn - another rich source of titillation to amuse them. The marriage of the king's sister was of less moment to ambitious courtiers than currying favour with the king's latest mistress.

Mary wondered if Anne Boleyn would last longer in her brother's favour than had her sister. It seemed likely. Anne had gained a reputation as a wit; a wit with a sharp tongue when she cared to use it, which didn't endear her to the ladies of the court who were frequently the objects of her clever word-play. It was clear to Mary that the young Anne, like a sponge, had absorbed and retained remembrance of all the subtle and not-so-subtle cruelties Mary had endured during her time at the French court. For she could seemingly make language do what she would, with as much skill as any of the acclaimed poets, only her word selection was the more barbed.

But whatever Mary and the other high-born court ladies thought of her, it was clear that the men saw a different Anne. Her elegance and brittle charm had attracted a string of admirers, as her brother's anguished words had attested. The girl had only to flash her great, dark eyes to have another young courtier fall under her spell.

Caught up as she had been in her own troubles, it had taken Mary's discovery of them in the garden for her to realise - that which the rest of the court well knew - that one of those caught up in the girl's spell was none other than her brother, Henry. If she had thought of the matter at all, she had thought that at thirty-five, Henry must be old enough to be immune to this young woman whom the younger courtiers seemed to find so fascinating. But now Mary knew that her judgement was flawed. Her brother was a man as other men and just as susceptible to Anne Boleyn's charms.

Mary found her gaze drawn to her brother that evening after supper was cleared. And what she observed was only too revealing. For Henry's study of Anne's lissom figure as it swayed seductively in the new dance she had brought home with her from France, seemed all-absorbing. Startled, Mary saw a hunger in her brother's eyes that she had never seen before. It was a hunger she recognised well; was it not the twin of her own hunger for Charles? How well, too, she knew its demands.

In spite of the supper of many courses she had just consumed, an aching hollow seemed to find a niche in her stomach as, still watching Henry, she saw his gaze narrow as it turned to the dumpy figure of the wife seated at his side. It was obvious to Mary and must be so to Catherine herself, that 'Sir Loyal Heart' was loyal no more and was comparing the exciting Anne to the staid Catherine to the latter's detriment.

While she admired her sister-in-law's fortitude, even Mary had to reluctantly concede Anne Boleyn's attractions. From the shining fall of her dark hair under its elegant French hood, to her grace as now she danced the stately pavanne, she was the focus of every eye in the court and knew it. How could Catherine begin to compete with such as she for her husband's love?

As the music ended, Henry was up from his seat and across the floor to claim the next dance, a more lively Spanish pavanne. And as the music started up again, the shimmering banks of candles seemed to flicker only for Anne and Henry. It was clear from his eager attentiveness and the pleading that Mary had overheard in the garden, that Anne hadn't yet succumbed to his desire. But Mary guessed that it would only be a matter of time before Anne followed the example of the long-since married-off Bessie Blount, Anne's own sister, and the others who had followed her into Henry's bed.

Her brother wanted consolation for the loss of the coveted French crown and the continuing lack of a male heir, which he looked increasingly unlikely to get from Catherine. And he wanted that consolation now.

It seemed the rest of the court thought the same, for, everywhere Mary's gaze alighted, she saw the same avid looks, the same speculation. The whole court, it seemed, had eyes only for Anne and Henry. Their concentration verged on the voyeuristic. And Henry? Henry only had eyes for Anne. It was a wonder the heat in them didn't devour her.

Of course, it didn't take long before the court gamblers – who would bet on how soon the sickly would succumb to their ailments or how long a wooing a maid would require – began making bets on how soon this devouring would occur.

However, to everyone's astonishment, not least Henry's, this Boleyn was of a different mettle to the wanton sister Mary remembered from her time in France. One had only to look at Anne's head, held proudly on its long and slender neck to know that she looked for more from life than a quick tumble in the king's bed. To be used and then discarded for a newer, younger toy, clearly held no appeal for this Boleyn.

Mary, with troubles enough of her own, could still find compassion to spare for Catherine. Approaching forty-one, Catherine, unlike Mary, had long since become inured to the many disappointments that life contained. When the ceremonies of the court left her free to follow her own inclination, the queen spent most of her time on her knees.

Mary longed to say to her that this was no way to retain her husband's affection. But with a growing estrangement between her own husband and herself, Mary felt she was in no position to advise another woman on how to best order her marriage. Still, it was true, that for all her brother's professed piety, he enjoyed more lively amusements also, and Anne Boleyn looked as if she promised to be the liveliest of them all. Anne's time in France had not only taught her style and elegance; clearly, in that debauched court which followed Francis' promiscuous example, Anne had learned many subtleties in the arts of courtly love. Her admirers, once caught in her web, desired no escape. Their only desire was to please her and find her dark, hypnotic eyes turn on them with favour.

Henry seemed more tightly caught in these spidery coils of love than any. Strangely, although court intriguers questioned those who had spent time at the French court, no wanton's reputation had followed Anne as it had her sister. If the girl had taken lovers she - and they - had been very discreet about it. Not a whisper of impropriety attached to her.

Mary wondered, as the days passed and her brother's infatuation grew, if this chaste reputation was not more alluring to Henry than her wit. Her brother admired virtue in a woman. But for all his fondness for womanly virtue - whether real or, as seemed likely in Anne's case, skilfully feigned - he would consider it a challenge also. It was becoming apparent that Anne Boleyn was not only an intelligent woman who knew well how to use her God-given and French-polished wiles, but a dangerous one also.

And as Mary thought back over the interview with Anne on the girl's return to England, she found herself wondering uneasily how deep the girl's influence would go with Henry. Had she been unwise to show her dislike for this new Anne so plainly? Mary found herself watching the girl, wondering at her own feelings of dislike. Was it that she, who now had reason to side with a wronged wife, gave all her sympathy to Catherine for reasons that were not entirely selfless? Or was it simply that she was jealous? She had once been considered the court beauty, still was by those who preferred her fair colouring to Anne's unfashionable brunette. But she was now the mother of three children and at an age to be considered a matron. Her love-match with Charles made over ten years before, had, before the legality of their marriage had been questioned, settled into a tame domestic routine.

Now, of course, it was in a state of flux and uncertainty. Mary sighed and for the present forgot about Anne Boleyn as her thoughts again settled on the question of her marriage.

The solution to the vexing question of its legality was no nearer. But as the months passed, Mary had acknowledged to herself that however Charles had wronged her, she still loved him. Had only ever loved him. But her love only increased her pain when she realised that the still uncertain legality of their marriage gave the older nobility of the court another weapon to use against him. Had they truly endured those long weeks of terror in France for a marriage that, in the eyes of the Church, might be no marriage at all? The likely consequences, if so, made Mary tremble for the future, not only for herself and Charles but also for their children. The

church might even force him to return to Lady Mortimer—
had she not been required to relinquish him to his first wife?

Mary couldn't bear to contemplate such a possibility. She
had married Charles, believing it to be a true marriage. She
must cleave to that belief. To do otherwise would send her
spiralling down to a pit that would contain nothing but despair. And that she must avoid at all costs, for the sake of her
children.

The next morning, after walking with her ladies in the gardens, Mary went in search of the man she still called husband. He was in their apartments, fumbling through some
papers. He hadn't heard her entry and when she spoke his
name her voice brought his head up sharply. Guiltily? 'What
are you looking for amongst those papers?' she asked, sus-
pecting she had caught him out in some furtive act that he
didn't want her to know about. Alas, that was the way her
thoughts too frequently ran these days.

'Nothing,' he replied, as he quickly shuffled the papers
together and thrust them in a drawer. 'Just some legal papers. Nothing of any import.'

Mary, her heart full of her own sufferings and those of
Catherine, that other wronged wife, commented sharply, 'I
thought perhaps you might be seeking the dispensation for
our marriage. Have you such a document, Charles?'

This was now an old conversation, well worn, but it did
not stop Mary from raising it once more. 'The whole court
speaks of our marriage. Can you have any idea what I felt
when I at last became privy to that which so closely concerns

me?' She remembered the pain and shame of it as though it were yesterday rather than many weeks ago. 'Why did you never seek a complete and proper dispensation for our marriage?'

This had become another well-worn ritual that, as though to torture themselves further, they went through regularly, as was Charles's reply.

'How could I, Mary, when you rushed me into our marriage in such haste? The thought never entered my head.'

It was his one defence. But it was a stout one, a defence, moreover, that laid the blame for the situation squarely on Mary.

Aware that her impetuous passion for him had helped to bring about the present situation, Mary had been the first to admit her own part in their predicament. But it didn't help that he should constantly remind her of it. 'And afterwards?' she demanded. 'Have not the many years we have been wed since provided ample time for you to seek to set matters to rights?'

Just like Henry, Charles, too, hated being placed in the wrong. As usual, he began to bluster. 'There have been so many things to think of, Mary. First one misfortune, then another. The time never seemed right to question a marriage that seemed so solid.' When he saw that this second, poorer line of defence was availing him nothing, he launched into attack. 'But you gave no thought to the matter, either, Mary, did you? My past life was no secret, yet you rarely questioned me about it. Why did you never broach the subject?'

Mary hadn't wanted to think about the years of Charles's life - and the other women - before she had entered it to claim his heart. The only way she had been able to avoid thinking about them had been to blank them out entirely. Mary was unwilling to admit her jealousy even to herself; to admit it to him was all but impossible. 'Naturally I did not broach the subject. How could I have known the necessity? The past was yours, yours, too, the marriages. It was surely for you to seek answers, not I. Being King Louis' widow I knew that I was legally free to wed. Why should it have occurred to me, young and innocent as I was, to apply for dispensation on your behalf? Even had I thought such a thing necessary, I would have had no idea how to set about it. Such doings are the affairs of men, not women. Or they ought to be.' The affair of one man, certainly, she could have added. She didn't fling the final words in his face, but she thought them and they hung accusingly in the air between them.

'No, but your great friend, the Cardinal knew well how to make such enquiries. Is he not, even now, probing deeply into my affairs at your instigation?'

'What else would you have had me do?' Mary asked. 'What is my position at the moment? I am neither wife nor maid. Our children could be branded bastards.' The words, finally brought into the clear light of day shocked them both. Mary sat down suddenly. 'Oh Charles, what will we do if the Church were to force you to return to your previous wife?'

Charles put on a mask of confidence she knew he must be far from feeling. 'They wouldn't do that,' he assured her. 'Don't upset yourself so.'

'They did before, though, did they not?' she insisted.
'Dear God, what are we to do? Perhaps we should both go to
see Cardinal Wolsey again and plead with him to redouble
his efforts on our behalf.'

A mulish look settled on Charles's face. 'No. I'll not do it.
I will not plead for his help again. Would you really put me
through that once more?'

Before she could say another word, he had picked up his
hat from the bed where he had thrown it and vanished
through the door, leaving her to contemplate going to see
the Cardinal on her own once again. She really couldn't see
why Charles was so unwilling to put himself through another
such interview. Had not Cardinal Wolsey been eminently
practical in his attempts to sort out the sorry mess that was
Charles's marital history?

Mary's thoughts ran back in time, to that first argument
between herself and Charles and the, inevitable, interview
with Wolsey that had followed it. At first, Charles had been
adamant that he would not be forced again into going cap in
hand to Wolsey for help. But Mary had reminded him that
their future and that of their children depended upon it. 'It
is not I who would put you through it,' she had reminded
him, 'but evil necessity. Surely you see that? He has the
knowledge of the law and the Church and would be sympathetic.'

'To you, maybe.'

'To you also if you would only cease to think of him as an
enemy.'

When he had glowered and looked ready to refuse again, she had told him sharply, 'We have no choice, can you not see that? If you will not see him for my sake, at least do it for the sake of our children. Would you see Harry and our daughters branded bastards before all the world?' She had felt giddy with relief when his shamed expression acknowledged capitulation and he had gone with her to see the Cardinal.

Wolsey had been a great comfort to Mary. He had been understanding, and after he had served her a sweetened wine to ease her agitation, he had soothed her worry and advised her to calm herself.

'Such matters can often be smoothed over, your Grace,' he had assured her. 'It may take some time, though. So I must warn you to be patient.'

Dismayed, Mary had asked, 'How much time, my lord? I was hoping to get it quickly settled for it is a distressing situation to have to live with.'

'Indeed. I can see how painful it must be for you. But at least now the wrong is realised we can start to right it.' He accepted her invitation and sat his bulk down beside Mary, his expression thoughtful.

Mary had felt strangely comforted in his presence. His confidence that matters could be put right was reassuring. This intelligent, worldly man would not so lightly have eased her fears if he were not certain he could mend the matter.

The Cardinal had addressed himself to Charles who stood glowering at the door as though ready to depart instantly should the Cardinal utter one displeasing word. 'My lord?' The Cardinal's voice was soft as he invited him to be seated.

Sullenly, Charles found himself a seat against the wall. 'You are sure you set no dispensation request in motion whilst you were in France? We want no complications.'

'No. I did not,' Charles muttered through tight-clenched lips. 'There was neither the time nor the opportunity. Nor did I believe there was the need.'

'All we had time to think of was my brother, King Henry, my lord,' Mary broke in. 'He filled all our thoughts.'

'Indeed.' He smiled at them both. 'I recall the busy correspondence we had at the time of your marriage. But we found the answer to the problem posed then. We shall do the same again.' The Cardinal focused his attention on Charles. 'My lord, you understand I will need to go through your marital history most thoroughly if I am to present a good case. Sometimes, the smallest detail can make a difference.'

Although he had known that this would be necessary, Charles looked so red-faced that Mary thought he might burst with vexation. But before he could, Wolsey spoke again, more firmly this time.

'I am truly sorry, my lord. But it is necessary. Being previously married to the lady's close kin would create a case of affinity, which would possibly dispose of the problem. But we two can go through the details together. There will be no need to further distress your wife, the Dowager-Queen's Grace.'

Mary was grateful that the Cardinal should show such sensitivity and discretion for Charles's sake. For her own, she had no desire to learn further details. All she wanted was to have the matter settled.

Wolsey turned back to Mary. 'You can now leave this matter safely in our hands, your Grace. But I would beg you to remember what I said before about having patience. The Vatican can be slow and ponderous on such matters, it is true, but better that than a hasty judgement that has failed to weigh all the facts of the case. You will be able to rely on their decision when it arrives as the best minds in the Church will have weighed all the evidence before coming to a conclusion.'

Relieved that the problem was now in the capable hands of Cardinal Wolsey, Mary had risen to leave them, thanking him for the trouble they were putting him to. 'It is good of you to concern yourself with our problems.' She managed a rueful smile. 'It seems we are ever burdening you with them.'

'I am pleased to serve your Grace.' He escorted her to the door. 'Pray, try not to worry too much. I feel confident we can resolve this matter.'

'I trust you are right, my lord. The gossip here at court has been very cruel.'

He nodded sadly. 'Alas, there is much jealousy and spite here. I, too, have felt it fall on my own head. Most of it is caused by envy and wrong-headedness.'

Behind her, Mary felt her husband glower as though he felt the dart had been aimed at him. Perhaps it had, and not undeservedly so, she thought. Fortunately, Charles made no angry retort and she left after giving her husband one last, pleading look to encourage his co-operation.

Mary came out of her reverie to realise she was chilled to the bone. The fire had fallen low and she called for a servant to come and replenish it. Charles had told her little of what had ensued between the Cardinal and himself after her departure, though he revealed the Cardinal's delving had been thorough and that Wolsey had intimated that his readiness to assist them was more for the sake of the friendliness that Mary had always shown him than for any concern he had felt for her husband.

Mary, sensitive to the sly looks and carefully muffled sniggers of the court as the weeks progressed to months with still no resolution, retired to the country. There, she found solace in her children. Charles had determined to remain at court, refusing to be hounded away by gossip as he had been by debt. He was, in any case, at this time incapable of affording her any comfort. Their marriage seemed doomed to mutual recriminations. Perhaps her cynical sister, Margaret had had the right of it in her views on marriage. Had she not told Mary that she had been a fool ever to marry Charles? They seemed destined to achieve little lasting happiness from their union. But at least, here in the country, she could find peace of a sort. Her children were growing up fast. Henry, her eldest was now eight, his sisters, Frances and Eleanor, seven and five. Harry was growing into a handsome boy, the pride of her heart. Mary knew she shouldn't have favourites, but he was her first-born and her only son, born after all the worry brought about by her reckless marriage and his arrival had brought her much joy.

Thoughts of her children brought her to the nursery. They all ran to her as soon as she appeared, eagerly abandoning their books. She cuddled them all, but it was Harry who remained by her side, pressing his little body against her.

'Shall you stay here with us now, Mother?' he asked. 'We miss you so when you're at court.'

'Yes, my son.' She smiled fondly down at him and ruffled the thick fair hair that was as golden as her own—he took after her in looks, while Eleanor favoured her father and Frances still bore a great resemblance to her Uncle Henry, a likeness especially evident when she was displeased about something. 'I won't return to court for a while. I want to stay and see what you have all learned since I was last home.'

'I can ride my pony over the ditch now, Mother,' Harry told her proudly. 'Do you want to watch me? It's easy.'

His pride in this achievement brought a sharp rebuke from his sister, Frances. 'Don't boast so, Harry. You didn't find it easy at all. He fell off more times than I can count, Mother,' Francis told her slyly.

Beyond the sly, slighting tittle-tattle about her brother's skills as a rider and her own sudden anxiety that her son might suffer injury, Mary sensed Frances' resentment that she should favour Harry. Mary smothered a sigh. Her elder daughter had a growing tendency to thrust herself forward and to tell tales; unattractive traits in one so young and a girl at that. Mary would have rebuked her, but decided instead to make her displeasure plain by ignoring her. For Frances that would be a greater punishment than any rebuke. Mary turned back to Harry. 'I wish you would take care, my son. You're too precious to risk your neck in reckless folly. Such skills are learned slowly and are learned best if not rushed.'

371

The nursery schoolroom was cosy, with a good fire burning and many candles lighting the room against the lowering sky. Mary discussed her children's progress with their tutor. None of her children were bookish, she knew, all preferring to be outside about physical pursuits, but as long as he instilled in them sufficient education for them to take their places at court, she would be happy.

After a little while, she dismissed the man. Relenting in her decision to punish Frances by ignoring her, she now called her two daughters over to her. 'You know that you're all precious to me, do you not?'

Eleanor nodded immediately and buried her head in Mary's skirts. Frances hung back, resentment evident in the small, petulant mouth that was so like Henry's, and in the jawline that was over-heavy in a young girl. Mary bit back the desire to rebuke the girl. Truly, Frances would test the patience of any mother.

Frances, having failed to reply to her mother's question, showed her preference for her father by asking why he had not returned. 'I so long to see him.'

'Your father had much business to see to for the king,' Mary told her, thankful that gossip about her and Charles's marriage was unlikely to penetrate this far from the court; it would give Frances another reason to resent her. 'No doubt he'll come home 'ere long.' Mary wasn't sure that she would want to see him unless he brought the long-awaited answer from the Papal court.

But Frances wasn't so easily put off. 'Is he with Lady Mortimer, Mother?'

Mary stared at her daughter, shocked that court gossip had indeed penetrated this far. It could only have been some gossiping servant returned with her from court that could have spread the tale. Her daughter's voice had again held that sly note and Mary looked closely at her. Frances was fond of pretending she knew more than she did. Such airs made her feel superior to the brother who was the elder by a year.

But the child was only seven, Mary was forced to remind herself. Even if she had heard some gossip about her parents' marriage, she was too young to understand it, as, to Mary's relief, the child's next words proved.

'I heard she had brought him some troubles,' Francis told her. 'I'm sure my father will be able to help her sort them out.'

Mary hadn't realised she had been holding her breath. She now breathed out on a sigh, thankful to learn that Frances' youth and ignorance of the world had indeed saved herself and her siblings from knowledge that could only bring them pain. She would have to question her ladies and the servants and make sure they talked no more of the matter, at least not in the children's hearing.

'No, he's not with Lady Mortimer, child,' Mary told her now. She kept her voice light as she asked, 'Who's been telling you such things?'

Frances shrugged. 'I can't remember. But I heard tell he once liked the lady, so our Father would be likely to help her if he could, wouldn't he?'

'Never mind about Lady Mortimer, Frances.' Her brother interrupted to return to a subject that he considered of far more importance. 'Mother, will you come and watch me ride? I can go like the wind.' He dragged impatiently at Mary's hand and she laughingly submitted to his importunate pleading.

Mary was conscious of the sullen looks and dragging feet of Frances as she trailed after them. She tried to share her love equally, but Frances made it very difficult. In character, she took after Margaret, to Mary's secret regret. The child looked, too, as if she would develop her Uncle Henry's tendency to be greedy about food. If not curbed, she would become unhealthily plump. Already, she was inclined to pudginess. She had also, unfortunately, inherited more than sufficient of Margaret's character and would bully little Eleanor unmercifully if not watched. Still, Mary consoled herself, Frances was young yet. She might easily grow out of such unattractive traits. Children went through so many phases. Perhaps now she was home to offer the child more motherly guidance, Frances would be less wilful.

The days with her children passed pleasantly for Mary, which was as well. For this period of retirement in the country was made even more necessary by her husband's increasing extravagance at court. Determined to remain by Henry's side, Charles needed to compete on an equal footing with the other nobles. But such competition required much outlay and their income was still greatly reduced. Certainly, it was insufficient for them both to be at court with all its expenses or only for a short while. The requirement that Mary keep regal pomp was even more of a drain when at court. But as the questions about the legality of their marriage had still not been answered, Mary preferred to remain away rather than suffer again from the eternal gossip and speculation. Cardinal Wolsey had spoken truth when he had said she would require patience. The vast machinery of the Vatican was as slow and ponderous as he had warned.

Charles's visits were infrequent and were becoming shorter, so they spent many weeks separated. Even when he was home in the country with her, he told her little of his doings. She had wondered if Anne Boleyn was still high in Henry's favour and had asked Charles, but he had merely nodded and had added nothing more. His taciturnity on the subject had puzzled her until it had struck her that the matter touched too closely on his own past careless infidelities for him to be anxious to discuss it with her.

Henry, her brother, of course, had never been fond of letter-writing; not that he would confess to his own sister about the course of an adulterous love affair. And Catherine, doing her best to ignore it, would be more likely to confide such a humiliation to her confessor than to a letter. But truly, Mary thought, it sounded as if things at court went on much as they always had. The thought comforted her. She was conscious that she had lately become something of a country sparrow, out of sight and out of mind of the court and its doings. It was cheering to think that she was not as out of touch as she had thought. What was it the French said? *Plus ça change, plus c'est la même chose.* That was it. The court was like that. Whatever events might occur there, things remained essentially much the same as always.

CHAPTER TWENTY-ONE

Even in the quiet of her country retirement, Mary learned the latest startling news. The Emperor, without the aid of Henry's troops, had triumphed over the French, overwhelmingly defeating them outside the walls of Pavia. More incredible still, the Emperor had captured King Francis and taken him to Madrid as his prisoner.

News had it that Francis had put up a good fight although being attacked on several fronts; by the Papal troops in Italy, where his forces were driven out; in the north of France, where Henry's troops together with those of the Emperor, had invaded, and at Pavia, where the Emperor's troops had completely routed Francis.

Mary tried to imagine the elegant, proud Francis in the humbled role of prisoner, but it was impossible to picture him thus. How he would hate his situation. And how set-about must be his doting mother that this most shining member of their 'Trinity' should find himself a captive, especially as it seemed likely he would remain one for some time. Because the French army was shattered. Thousands of its men had been killed, among them, Richard de la Pole, the 'White Rose of York', who had dared to lay claim to Henry's throne from the safety of Francis' dominions.

Mary was saddened to think of all the French gallants she had known lying bloodied on the battlefield, food for the carrion crows. Henry, of course, would have his thoughts set on higher things. With France open like a ripe peach, he would be eager to share his ally's spoils and would now certainly look to have his French crowning.

Henry, always keen for witnesses to his glory, penned a brief note asking her to return to court. And Mary, for once putting aside her misgivings about the costs, duly travelled up from her country retreat. But when she reached court and had settled into her apartments, Mary learned that events had overtaken her. After Henry had sent off urgent and eager letters to the Emperor, his flame of hope for a French crown brightly burning, the Emperor had caused the flame to flicker. Catherine's triumphant nephew, Charles V, insisted that he was now penniless and anxious for peace; the time was inappropriate for Henry to seek Francis' crown.

So, the peach wouldn't be plucked after all and Henry's bright flame had died. He had set great store on his alliance with the Emperor, but now he stormed about the palace counting his grievances against him, not least that he had lent him huge sums. How ruefully did Mary think on them, for a fraction of their value would have made a world of difference to her and Charles's financial difficulties. To add insult to injury, the Emperor had cast aside his betrothed, Henry and Catherine's young daughter and Mary's namesake, who, before, had been betrothed to Francis' eldest son.

Odd that she and her niece should, in turn, have both been betrothed and spurned by the same man. As if taking

Henry's money and rejecting Henry's daughter wasn't enough, the Emperor also deprived Henry of any share of the spoils. No wonder her brother's mood cast a pall over the whole court.

As Mary renewed several old acquaintances, she learned that Henry was determined to teach the young puppy of an Emperor a lesson and had decided that the best means of doing this would be for England to come to terms with France. This was glad news for Mary whose income was always in short supply when her brother chose enmity with France over amity. But for all her relief, Henry's feelers in this direction brought the sad news that Claude, Francis' queen, had died. Only twenty-five, she had never enjoyed good health and her strength had been worn down by her many pregnancies, continuing ill-health, and melancholy at Francis' numerous infidelities. Mary remembered Claude's many kindnesses during her own marriage to Claude's father. Though only a young girl, she had graced the throne with her kind heart and her many good qualities. France would, Mary judged, be the poorer by her death as the many epithets her name now attracted attested. Mary mourned her truly. She felt, with Claude's passing, she had lost a valued friend and the last of her youth. But at Henry's court, her sadness was shared by few. Indeed, these days, the court was more lively than ever. For here, Anne Boleyn held sway and she it was who, with her wit, had the overseeing of the many masques and balls. It seemed that Catherine had little say, which was another sadness for Mary. She was further demeaned when Henry created his son by Bessie Blount Earl of Richmond.

Perhaps to discourage any remonstrances from Mary he created her and Charles's son, Harry, Earl of Lincoln. It was rumoured that Henry, who had clearly given up hope of getting himself a son from Catherine, was even toying with the idea of making his son legitimate; the giving of the title would pave the way for such a move.

After her long sojourn in the country, Mary had found herself looking forward to the excitements of court life. But the excitements she had found were far from those desired. Although her dower income from France now looked as if it would be restored to her, the news was overshadowed by Henry's unkind treatment of Catherine. Now he had a lively, attractive mistress and had created his illegitimate son an Earl, Catherine's many failures seemed the more marked. Not only, his actions seemed to underline, had she failed to give him a son, she was also lacking in womanly attractions in that she had become old, stout and unable to join in any of the king's pursuits.

Henry, still only in his mid-thirties, enjoyed dancing and hunting as much as he ever had, often staying in the saddle all day and then dancing all night. With Catherine no longer able to take part there had grown up a band around the king who shared his interests. This band was in the main comprised of the liveliest and most witty of his courtiers. Charles, of course, still as ambitious as ever, must form part of this band. It caused more arguments between Mary and her husband. How could it not, when at the centre of this band was Anne Boleyn, with whom Henry had become besotted. Her little Maid of Honour now queened it over them all.

There was something about Anne that hadn't been present in her plump and sensuous sister; a calculating intelligence that seemed able to warm Henry's fires from the empty furnace of her cold heart. And she didn't lack wily advisers; behind her, was her father and her arrogant uncle, the Duke of Norfolk. Between Anne, her father and her uncle, it seemed they were more than capable of steering Henry in the direction of their desires.

Woe betide Catherine if they succeeded. What future might there be for an ageing and barren queen if her husband spurned her? With her own worries about her marriage weighing heavy the thought wasn't a happy one and Mary went in search of her sister-in-law.

The queen was in her apartments. Still regal and gracious, she was delighted to see Mary. Catherine cast off her sad looks and managed one of the broad smiles that had so frequently wreathed her face in happier days.

Although Mary commiserated with Catherine, the queen's high Spanish pride made it difficult to voice any sympathy; to do so would mean that Catherine must acknowledge her own humiliation. Charles, of course, sided with the king and his paramour. He had tried to insist that Mary refrain from showing any outward sympathy for Catherine, fearing it would anger the king and be damaging to him, but Mary felt that her sympathies were her own to direct where she would. Although she sympathised with her brother in his kingly need for a legitimate son, emotionally,

Mary had always been a woman first and a royal princess second, so her compassion was all for Catherine. Did they not share common troubles? One with a marriage threatened by the power of a ruthless mistress and the other with a marriage threatened by the power of the church.

Even with troubles aplenty of her own, Catherine could still find time to soothe Mary's worries. 'I'm glad you're back at court,' she told Mary. 'You shouldn't hide yourself away in the country so often. There is no need. You can hold your head high as the Mortimer affair is rarely spoken of.'

'Maybe not,' Mary replied. 'But it is very much alive for me. The Pope still keeps me waiting for an answer. Anyway,' Mary forced a cheerful note into her voice, 'Wolsey's hopeful, so I must bide my soul in patience that everything will turn out right.' Although she knew that Catherine was reluctant to discuss her own marital troubles she was always ready to listen to Mary's woes; perhaps, listening to the troubles of others helped her to cope with her own. Mary found it all but impossible not to speak of Catherine and Henry's marriage and she made a sideways allusion to it, hoping to encourage Catherine to unburden herself. 'The court has changed greatly since I was last here and not for the better. I confess I could scarce believe my eyes to see the Bullen woman lead my brother such a dance. However did she reach such heights? I remember her sister, Mary. Although she was a mare who gave many men a ride, she was kind-hearted enough. It is difficult to believe she and her sister come from the same stable.'

Catherine permitted herself a tiny nod and the comment, 'You will find much here now difficult to believe. Sometimes I can scarce believe it myself.'

'There must be some way we can make Henry come to his senses.' Mary had become fiery on Catherine's behalf. 'He loved you well at one time and that not so long ago. Could you not—?'

Catherine gave a laugh that contained little humour. 'What would you have me do, Mary? Flirt and dance with the most handsome of Henry's courtiers to make him jealous?' Catherine lifted her skirts to show her swollen ankles and puffy legs. 'These poor limbs are beyond the task, I fear.' She lowered her skirts and sat back. 'My greatest mistake is beyond my ability to correct.' She directed a courageous smile at Mary. 'I failed my husband in my most important duty: that of getting sons. It must always come between us.'

'You may yet get a son, Catherine. You're still young enough.'

'A child needs someone to father it, alas. The laws of nature remain the same at least, if all else seems to have gone mad.' Catherine lowered her eyes as she confessed. 'Your brother rarely graces my bed these days. So you see, even if I am still capable of getting me a son, the opportunity to do so is seldom there.'

Mary, not knowing how else to comfort Catherine, took her hand and squeezed it tightly. But, in spite of Catherine's revelation, Mary still felt there must be something they could do. She had tried appealing to Henry, but that had achieved nothing. Possibly an appeal to Anne Boleyn's better nature might have some effect. Mary was prepared to try anything if it would ease Catherine's pain, even if she must humiliate herself in the process. She had liked Anne well enough during their shared time in France and had treated her kindly. It was possible that another, more determined, attempt at rekindling her memories of those times would have the desired result. She could at least try. For Catherine's sake, she would lower her dignity and talk to her brother's harlot.

Mary put to the back of her mind her recollection of the new haughtiness Anne had acquired and sent a message to Anne that she wished to see her. She even lowered her queenly dignity to the extent that she became a courtier rather than the courted, when Anne was cool about visiting Mary's apartments.

To her surprise, Anne was welcoming enough, and offered her wine and sweetmeats. But, aware as she was, of Mary's resentment and disapproval, her manner was as cool as her invitation had been.

'Tis a novelty to entertain the Dowager-Queen of France in my chambers,' she remarked, adding slyly, 'though her husband, the Duke, is often here.'

'Indeed,' Mary managed to mutter. With difficulty, she overcame her fury that the woman should try to bait her, put aside her own feelings, and concentrated her thoughts on Catherine's happiness. It was the reason she was here. They were quite alone, as Anne had dismissed her admirers, Grateful at least that there would be no witnesses to what passed between them, Mary tentatively broached the reason for her visit.

Anne's reaction was hot and speedy. She took advantage of their privacy to commit lése-majesty. 'Give up the king, you say? Think you, Madam,' she demanded, 'that I should pay heed to a woman who can't even prove the legality of her own marriage? Perhaps you should straighten your own affairs before you attempt to offer your advice to me.'

Mary's cheeks burned. That Anne should throw that in her face. She clung to the shreds of her dignity as she replied, 'That the legality of my marriage gives cause for discussion is no fault of mine, as I'm sure you know.' Mary reminded herself again that she had come here to talk about Catherine and Henry's marriage, not her own. She tried once more. 'If not for Catherine, will you give up the king and leave the court out of the friendship we once shared in France?'

Anne's scorn stung her. 'Friendship? Is that what you call it? You gave me a few of your oldest gowns, gowns which I had to alter myself, and I am to recall this occasion with gratitude? Nay, Madam, gratitude is not what I feel, nor friendship either. I know you all thought me a plain, ungainly child, but if I had little else then, I had my pride. Receiving your cast-offs didn't make my situation any easier. Do you think the other Maids stopped their teasing because I had a few pretty gowns?'

Mary was chastened enough to apologise. 'I'm sorry. I didn't realise they tormented you so.' How could she have? She had been young, foolish and deeply unhappy, far too concerned with her own woes to notice those of others.

Anne, of course, remembered things differently. 'You were too busy flirting with the dazzling Francis to see what was happening under your nose.' Anne drew herself up. 'But those days are long gone, like the forlorn little maid I once was. Good riddance to them both. So, Madam, don't come here with your queenly airs and your talk of kindnesses. I no longer need your kindness. I have the king's.'

This last was said with such a darting look of triumph that Mary, having no other weapons, was goaded into using the weapon of status, even though, as she spoke, she realised it was unwise. 'Remember, Madam, to whom you speak. You—'

'I know full well to whom I speak,' Anne assured her. 'But mayhap, you would do well to heed your own advice. The Queen of England has already learned to her cost of the power and influence Anne Boleyn, the little Maid of Honour, has here now. Perhaps it is time that the Dowager-Queen of France learned it also.'

'I wish Henry could hear you. I doubt he'd be impressed by your spite.'

Anne gave a careless shrug. 'Complain to the king if you dare. You'll find him unwilling to listen to tittle-tattle about me. I am the virtuous Anne and can do no wrong in his eyes. And virtuous I be, though few in the court acknowledge it.'

Mary was not surprised that Anne should bait her with the name of the king. Henry would have told Anne what had passed between them. She did not need Anne to tell her that Henry would refuse to listen. As his sister, she had felt it her duty to speak to him. It had been useless, of course, as she had known it would be.

It had been early evening, the sun shining on the wooden panelling in his apartments and on Henry himself who had the vain habit of placing himself where the sun's rays could light on him and best display his red-gold good looks and gorgeous apparel.

She had asked to speak to him alone and he had dismissed his courtiers. Nervously, she had asked him if the rumours were true and that he intended to set Catherine aside for her Maid of Honour.

Immediately, he had turned aggressive. 'Has Catherine sent you here?'

Mary denied it. 'I came because I am concerned for you. For Catherine also. I love you both well and would not wish either of you to suffer pain. I warn you, brother, think. Think before it is too late. You may believe it would be Catherine alone who would suffer if she is set aside. But that is not true. You, too, would suffer. You know the people do not like Anne Boleyn. Do you wish to risk losing their love as Catherine loses yours?'

He hadn't liked that, of course. Mary knew how much he valued the love of his subjects.

'I will not lose their love,' he had insisted. 'I will keep their love and get me a son also. You, Mary, have your son already. Would you deny me mine?'

'Many times have I prayed for you and Catherine to have the joy of a healthy prince. It has grieved me sorely that you have no son. But have you never thought that as such is the case it must be God's will that it is so?'

It had been the wrong thing to say. Mary had known it as soon as the words had left her mouth. Henry was prepared to fall in with God's will only when it agreed with his own.

'It is not God's will that I remain without my son. It was the Pope who wrongly gave me a dispensation to marry Catherine. As the Pope has caused the problem, the Pope can right it by agreeing that Catherine should be put aside. I will have my son. And as I haven't got him on the Spanish woman I'll get him on Anne. I don't care what anyone says. I am determined on it.'

There had been nothing more to say after that, but a softly murmured, 'Have a care for your mortal soul also, Henry,' before she walked softly away.

Mary blinked and came back from her unhappy trip down Memory Lane to find that she and Anne had both stood up during their exchange. Now Anne came up close and thrust her face forward to tell her, 'His poor, barren wife is queen in name only. *I* am the true queen now, as all do acknowledge.' She smiled. It was a smile made up of malice and triumph.

Mary felt sick. The pain in her side started up. She bit her tongue lest she call Anne 'harlot' to her face, and bring the power Anne had boasted of down on her own head and that of her husband and children. For now, Mary had to accept that Anne Boleyn *did* have the power to hurt them both. The effort to remain silent almost choked her. Insults burned on her tongue to be spoken. Somehow, Mary got out of the room. She stood in the corridor, breathing deeply while she tried to control her wildly beating heart. Behind her, she heard Anne's mocking laughter. It pursued her as she hurried along the corridors to her waiting litter and, wth her tail between her legs, went home to Suffolk House, their London home.

She had been as foolish in trying to speak to Anne as she had been in tackling Henry. Catherine's unhappiness had spurred her on. Mary had tried to appeal to Anne's better nature, but it was clear Anne Boleyn didn't possess such a thing. Mary could only hope her interference did not damage Catherine's position even more.

Mary had hoped to find solitude to regain her composure. But to her consternation, Charles was there and clearly waiting for her.

He could not fail to recognise her agitation—nor did he. And when she had finally confessed its cause he gave her another tongue-lashing. Mary attempted to defend herself. 'I was only trying to help Catherine. She has need of friends now.'

'She doesn't need friends like you, Mary, to interfere and make her position even more difficult. You are becoming a worse meddler than that accursed Cardinal. Have I spent months gaining the friendship and trust of the Lady Anne only to have you upset all my efforts in a minute? Truly, it is a pity you didn't remain in the country. Now I suppose I'll have to try to repair the damage you have wrought.' With that, he marched past her without another glance, bellowing for his horse.

Upset, Mary kept to her home for the next few days. She feared that Charles was right and that her impetuous importuning of Anne Boleyn would only make Catherine's situation worse. She had been horrified to discover how confident was Anne Boleyn of her power. Her one-time gawky little Maid of Honour now ruled over Mary's husband as surely as she ruled over the king. That Charles should be frightened of offending this slim young woman outraged Mary. Astonishingly, it seemed, if what the court whispers and Anne's own words had claimed were true, she had managed to ensnare her brother without actually letting him possess her. But Anne Boleyn had not spent seven years at the French court without learning Gallic guile; it went some way to explaining how she managed such a feat.

When Mary ventured back to the court, she kept her eyes open and her mouth shut. She saw with dismay that each time Anne rejected Henry's adulterous advances his passion for her deepened. Henry was so caught in the snares of love that he would do anything, agree to anything, if only he could have her. He had long since warned off several of his courtiers who were also enamoured of the lady. He was determined to have her for himself. Whispers flew around the court that Henry had promised her the earth, the moon, the stars, if she would only give in and lay with him. But still Anne refused. She wanted more. As Mary had learned, she wanted to be queen. Worse, Henry had so tired of Catherine that he was now actively hunting round for means to cast her off so that he could marry Anne.

These matters were whispered into Mary's ear in the marital bed she shared with Charles. He had promptly sworn her to secrecy. Mary didn't confess that she had no need to learn the truth of this from her husband; she already had it from her brother. Mary began to fear for her brother, for his crown and even for his mortal soul. Henry's 'Secret Matter' was now common knowledge at the court. Charles was deeply enmeshed in it and committed to Anne and Henry's hopes for their union.

Such a widely-known secret couldn't long remain within the bounds of the court. Soon, it was being discussed in every tavern and ale-house and Anne was abused by the people whenever she ventured into the streets.

Wolsey, on Henry's orders, had set the divorce in motion by setting up a secret court at Westminster which he demanded Henry attend in order to answer the charge of having lived unlawfully for eighteen years with the widow of his own deceased brother, Arthur. Henry's obsession with Anne was leading him down dangerous paths, for he could not lightly repudiate Catherine. Her nephew was the mighty Emperor. He would not allow his aunt to be thus cast off, for all that Henry prated of his conscience and his fear that his marriage was an adulterous one since Catherine had been his brother's wife first.

What consciences we Tudors have, Mary thought. There is Henry, with his mighty conscience over the marriage he no longer wanted; her own pricking conscience concerning her own marriage and the constant humiliations and difficulties Charles suffered because of it. These had caused him to take a grievous dislike to Cardinal Wolsey. Charles had sided with Anne not only because she was the woman Henry wished to marry, but also because Anne, too, believed Wolsey to be her enemy. For Charles, any enemy of Wolsey must perforce be his friend.

Mary had come to find the court less and less to her liking and spent more time in the country and at their London house on the river at Southwark. When she wasn't at court, she would spend long, melancholy hours staring from the window at the river. Although she couldn't see the heads that decorated London Bridge, she didn't need to. In her mind's eye she could see them clearly; they put her in fear for her own family, for this obsession of Henry's could bring the country to a civil war, such was the feelings it aroused, not only in England, but across Europe.

Mary's health had been poor for some time. She suffered greatly from a recurring pain in her side which was exacerbated by her anxiety about the future. What would become of them all if Henry got his wish and set Catherine aside? Would the Emperor invade to restore his aunt to her rightful place? Would he, by force of arms, tumble Henry from his throne? And what of Charles, her husband? If all these events came about, Charles would fall with Henry. He would surely lose his head. Round and round Mary's thoughts went, imagining ever more grim and terrifying events unfolding. She looked down at her hands and saw they were trembling. She gripped each with the other and tried to force them to be still. But, like so much else in her life in these turbulent times the tremors in her hands were beyond her control.

The timing of this spread of knowledge about Henry's desire to marry Anne was unfortunate, as shortly after, Catherine's nephew, the mighty Emperor, captured Pope Clement whilst his soldiers sacked Rome. Thus, the Pope who was expected to agree to Henry's demand for a divorce was in the hands of Catherine's powerful nephew and unlikely to anger him by sanctioning this insult to the Emperor's aunt. Henry was furious at this downward turn in his fortunes. Especially when he realised that the Emperor's capture of the Pope must bring his and Wolsey's secret court to a precipitous close. Henry poured his complaints into Charles's ears and he came home to Mary whenever he could get away and relieved his burdens by telling her all about them.

'The king has become convinced that the Emperor spends his time planning how best to ruin his hopes. He has had King Francis in his power for a year-and-a-half; now he also has the Pope. As if that was not enough, we have learned that Francis has agreed to a Treaty between himself and the Emperor and is to marry the Emperor's sister. Your brother is most displeased.'

'And taking it out on Catherine, I doubt not.'

Charles had the grace to look abashed. He admitted that a furious Henry had confronted the unfortunate Catherine. 'He told her that he felt they had been living in sin for the entire duration of their time together and that theirs was no marriage. He told me that Catherine burst into tears.'

Who could blame the poor queen? thought Mary. Worn down by constant humiliation, told her long marriage was no marriage at all, even Catherine's great dignity must fall before such an onslaught.

'I confess I felt sorry for the poor lady,' Charles told her. 'For all that her stubbornness has vexed the king's hopes.'

Would that Henry would fall out of his obsession with Anne Boleyn, thought Mary. But there was no sign of such a thing. Her brother's days of calling himself 'Sir Loyal Heart' were long gone. His anger against the Emperor and his untimely triumphs rebounded spitefully on Catherine. Mary knew that Henry felt that Catherine and her family had brought him nothing but troubles and disappointments. Not only had she failed in her duty to get a son, but her Hapsburg relatives had, one after the other, let him down. According to Henry, he had been cheated or disappointed of help in his French ambitions in turn, by Ferdinand, Maximilian and now Charles. He had had enough. That his hopes for a divorce should be delayed once more by the actions of Catherine's nephew was the final straw. Henry's grievances didn't make him any kinder to his wife.

Mary sighed. Where would it all end? In civil war and invasion as she feared? She knew her brother. He was not the man to long endure having his wants denied. He had been remarkably patient thus far. But it was clear that Henry's short stock of patience was rapidly coming to an end. And with Anne Boleyn pushing him, who knew to what travails he would put them all before he had his desire?

But Mary's fears about her brother and what he would do were now set aside by an enemy even more deadly than the Emperor.

CHAPTER TWENTY-TWO

The sweating sickness had returned to London. Its evil, clutching fingers groped their insidious way into Mary's home, intent on destruction.

Her beloved son, Harry caught the contagion. Mary was appalled and terrified for him. She had shared the common belief that children didn't get the sweat unless they heard their elders talking about it. It was considered a male disease mostly and an English one; women and Frenchmen caught the contagion as rarely as children were said to.

But Mary had no time to ponder who might have spoken of it to her son and so placed him in its way. She nursed him herself, not trusting anyone else to care for her boy. She wiped his hot forehead as the fever took him and cuddled him close when he shivered. The fever had wracked his little body and left him exhausted. He called piteously for his father, who was from home.

'Where is he?' he asked Mary. 'When shall he come?'

Mary had sent urgent messages to Charles, but with the sickness raging, she couldn't be sure they had reached him. Desperate to soothe Harry, Mary had to calm her anguish before she could reply. 'Soon. I have sent for him. Hush now. Lie still, sweeting. Save your strength so you have some to greet your father on his return.'

Harry quietened and slept a little. But soon the fever broke out again and he lapsed into semi-consciousness, tossing and turning as though trying to shake off some devil. One minute he was burning up, the next shivering with cold. He couldn't long continue like that; his little body would not have the strength. And so it proved.

The crisis came that evening as the shadows were falling. It had been a beautiful day and was turning into a lovely evening. Mary could still see the last, fading sunlight on the drawn curtain. The beauty of the day seemed to mock her. Her son's suffering was the more unbearably poignant that it should occur on such a day when he should be running and jumping in the sunshine.

In another of his rarer lucid moments, he whispered, 'It's getting dark, mother. I don't like the dark.'

'Mama will make it as bright as day, sweeting.' Mary called for candles, masses of them. Soon it was, indeed, almost as bright as day, but Harry still complained of the dark, his voice small and frightened. With the directness of youth, he asked her, 'Mother, am I going to die?'

Mary denied it, to herself as much as to her child. To her shame, her sudden tears at his artless question mocked her denial. She was unable even to protect her child from the cruel knowledge of his own imminent death.

Harry seemed to accept his mortality and find it more easy to bear than did his mother. Exhaustion gave him an unnatural calm. His blue-grey eyes, so like her own, regarded her with a sad, almost fatalistic solemnity. 'Why has my father not come? I do so long to see him once again before I die.'

His resignation to his fate tormented Mary. Again she denied he was dying, this time forcing the tears to remain unshed. She was thankful that Charles returned home shortly after to share her sad vigil. He and Mary sat either side of Harry's bed, clinging to his hands, ready to drag him back from the icy clutches of death.

Charles was as distraught as Mary. She knew how well he loved the boy. But although he loved his son for his own sake, she knew he could never forget that he was the king's nephew also. He had held high ambitions for this rare, Tudor boy of whom the king was so fond. Charles had dreamed such dreams for his son; Mary suspected his hopes had gone as high as the crown, in spite of the birth of the Princess Mary, in spite of his own low birth which would have made his son's acceptance in such a role difficult. Her sister, Margaret also now had only the one son; her other boy by James IV having died before he was two, but Henry had never had the chance to know them as he had their boy.

Mary was glad to see Charles's ambition forgotten for once. When he had finally reached home he had come immediately to the bed-chamber, taken his son in his arms most tenderly and rocked him from side to side as gentle as any nursemaid. He was so affected that he even pleaded with God to only let his son live and he would finish with ambition. 'Would that I could give you my strength, my son,' he had murmured against Harry's sweat-drenched hair.

But, of course, he hadn't been able to do that, so they sat and watched the life drain out of the boy, while the physicians Mary had summoned could only stand and wring their hands. They both knew that the end was fast approaching, but even though neither was willing to acknowledge it, still it came, darkly creeping, so silent they didn't recognise its arrival, an arrival heralded by the tiny smile that appeared on Harry's face and was as quickly gone.

Mary clutched Charles's arm. 'He smiled, Charles. Did you see?' Eagerly, Mary gazed down at her son. She stroked his soft cheek. But his stillness made her draw back in sudden fear. She couldn't bring herself to feel if his heart was still beating; Charles, a soldier with all too much experience of death, did that.

He closed Harry's eyes and turned to Mary. 'He has gone. Our boy has gone.' He broke down then, huge, wracking sobs burst from him and he gathered his son's frail body in his strong arms for the last time.

Strangely, Mary felt unable to shed any more tears. Instead, she sat numbly as though turned to stone. If tears fell they fell inside where no one could see them. She could only gaze, unblinking at her weeping husband. Her boy was dead. The pride and delight of her heart lay still. Soon, he would have the chill of the earth about him. Mary couldn't bear it. Only twelve, he had been about to flower into young manhood. Instead, the sweating sickness had claimed him for the grave. Never again would he ride like the wind. Never again would the sun catch his bright hair and cause her to catch her breath at its golden beauty.

At last Charles's sobs quieted. He leant across the bed to Mary, seeking comfort in questions. 'Why Harry? Why our son?'

Mary had no answers for him. Her body was as still as that of her boy. She didn't notice when Charles, abandoning the attempt to reach her, left the room, calling for her maid. But the maid was also unable to reach her. Shock had made Mary retreat into herself. She had found a sanctuary from bitter reality and none were to be allowed to wrest her from it.

As usual, the court had fled London, retreating before the sweating sickness. For once, Charles had the leisure to spend time with his family. But although he continually attempted to comfort his wife, to get through to her, she paid him no heed. He was at a loss. He did not know what to do when her eyes looked through and beyond him. In the end he gave up and left her to her silent grieving.

The king's no longer 'secret' matter had occupied much of his time before Harry's death. Henry's frustration was making him increasingly vindictive. His desperation for the divorce forced him to push his sympathisers more firmly into his own camp. You were either with him or against him, and Charles had long since chosen his side. Henry expected his followers to treat Catherine as harshly as he did himself. Although Charles loathed this brutal duty, he did it, helped to become inured to it by the very stubbornness of Catherine's will. The sweating sickness brought but a brief respite from such pressures.

'Madam, please. You must eat something for your health's sake.' The voice came from far away and Mary ignored it. But the rough hands that began to shake her could not be so easily ignored. They finally managed to drag her back to an unwelcome recognition that she still lived.

Her maid, Susan, stood by her, her eyes red from weeping. Mary's heart softened at the sight. Susan had loved Harry well and mourned him truly. But Mary didn't want to be cajoled back to life by Susan or anyone else. 'Eat, you say?' Mary now demanded. 'The thought of food sickens me. My health or lack of it is of no importance now that I have lost my only son.'

'You still have two daughters,' Susan reminded her. 'What of them? They need you, Madam.'

'Cannot you attend to their wants, Susan?' Mary wanted only to be left alone with her grief. 'I have lost my son. Can you not understand what that means to me?'

'Of course I do. We all loved young Harry. But now he has no need of us or our love. Your daughters though, do. But most of all they need their mother. Think you, Madam, they have been unaffected by their brother's death?'

'What would you have me do, Susan?' Mary challenged. 'Order dark gowns for them so they may mourn their brother respectably clad?' Mary could hear the bitterness in her voice, but why should she not feel bitter? Life, seemingly every aspect of it, had turned irredeemably sour. Now her maid chose to nag her. Why couldn't the woman leave her be?

'Dark gowns? Nay, my lady. So many have died in the city
I'd be hard-pressed to find someone to make them even if I
dared attempt the search.' Her voice became wheedling.
'Come now, eat some broth to please me.'

Knowing she would get no peace otherwise, Mary submitted to her maid's pleading with ill-grace. And although
she only managed to eat half a bowl of broth Susan was satisfied. She took the half-emptied dish from Mary's grasp and
glided silently from the chamber.

Apart from the whistle of wind through the eaves, the
house was as silent as the tomb. All it lacked was the corpse,
for in spite of Mary's protests, Harry's little body had been
removed in its hastily-constructed coffin and buried. Susan
it was, who had insisted that the coffin and its precious,
golden treasure must be taken away. She had tried to insist
also that they pack up and leave for the country, but Mary
had refused. Now though, no doubt encouraged by her success with the broth, she returned, looking for another victory.

'We must get away from here, my lady,' she told Mary in
a voice that was becoming more insistent. 'London is still full
of the sickness.'

'That again? Why can you not leave me be?' A little of
Mary's old spirit returned. 'This was my son's room. I can
still smell his special scent, still feel his presence, yet you
would have me leave him here all alone. I cannot.'

'You can and you must, my lady. What you feel in this
room is your own longing, nothing more. Harry is with the

Lord. Part of him remains in your heart and always will, no matter where you be.'

'Aye,' Mary had replied. 'He's in my heart. But he's here also. Can you not feel him, Susan?'

Susan had sighed, but had told her patiently enough, 'You shouldn't turn this room into a shrine, my lady. Remember the Lord's words. 'You shall not set up false images?' She knelt imploringly by Mary's side. 'People are dying by the score, by the hundred. One moment they had life and the next they had nothing. You were ill for a time. Do you want the same sickness to claim your daughters also?'

Mary turned away from her maid's entreaties. 'You are cruel, Susan. Can you not let me mourn my son?'

'I could let you remain here and mourn your son. If your desire is to mourn your daughters also. You think me cruel, but the sweating sickness is crueller still. It doesn't recognise a house of mourning and will intrude amongst your grief and cause you more if it is given the chance. You can mourn in the country, my lady, where the air is sweet. Everything's packed. We're just waiting for you.'

While Susan's words had little effect, it took the sight of a man collapsing on the far side of the river to penetrate Mary's resistance. Once, he tried, feebly to rise, but then he fell back and was still. As still as Harry. For the first time this thought did not make her retreat into the numbness she had felt for so long. Instead, it energised her. Susan was right. She had lost her son, but she still had two daughters. What had she been thinking of to let them linger in this unhealthy city with the sickness raging? They must get away.

It was too dangerous to remain any longer. She heard Charles's voice shouting some order to a servant and hurried down to speak to him. He readily agreed that they must leave—had he not been entreating her to agree to this course for some days? Thanks to Susan, the house was pretty well packed up already. All Mary had to do was allow her weakened body to be helped into the waiting litter. The horses were whipped up and they drove through London's near-deserted streets, away from the raging pestilence, to Westhorpe.

It was a place that held many memories of Harry. Too many perhaps, for as she wandered through the rooms, these memories served only to remind Mary of her loss. Harry's doings and laughter filled the place. He had been as lively and full of mischief as any boy. Everywhere Mary's gaze rested she found yet another reminder of her sorrow.

There was the tree he had climbed on his seventh birthday, nearly breaking his neck when he had fallen. There was his first pony, placidly grazing in the field, as uncaring as the tree that Harry was gone.

Even when she looked in the glass she must be reminded. Everyone had remarked on Harry's likeness to herself. Now, it seemed that his blue-grey eyes stared back at her from under the golden hair. For the first time in days Mary acknowledged that hers was not the only heart grieving. Charles, too, felt the pain and now that she had come out of her inward retreat sufficiently to notice him again they began to grow close once more. He became again the attentive husband he had been before Henry's desire for a divorce and

Charles's determination to help him get it had come between them. And as their mutual grief deepened with the days, the importance of the divorce seemed to lessen, its significance in the scheme of things reduced beside the great leveller of death.

Although Mary's grief for her son was an ever-present ache, the shock had receded, but it didn't bring acceptance in its wake. It brought only despair. Even Catherine, fond of her as Mary was, had been relegated to the back of her mind. Her grief was selfish and could spare no compassion just yet for the pain of another.

The days turned to weeks. The quiet of the country was as a soothing balm, gradually it calmed the worst of her grief. Perhaps God would grant them a second son to try to fill some of the hollow space in her heart.

The court had at last ventured to return to London. Charles, much as he loved his wife and truly mourned his son, felt he needed to bring some normality back to his life. He wanted to see fresh faces. Happy, smiling faces. At Westhorpe, the servants still crept about as though they might somehow disturb Harry's ghost. Charles was weary of the unremitting gloom that hung over the house. It oppressed him. Much as he had loved his son, he was now dead. Charles didn't feel, as Mary seemed to, that he should devote the rest of his life to mourning the boy. He wanted to return to court. Mary did not. It was inevitable that their renewed closeness wasn't to last. When some unguarded remark revealed how harsh had been his treatment of Catherine, Mary withdrew from him again. He had hoped she would feel able to return to court once the sickness was over, but, unable to endure a court with Anne Boleyn in it, Mary insisted on remaining in the country. Nowadays, she had little taste for court life, certainly not one where Anne Boleyn was treated as its queen. A court where all who wished to remain in Henry's favour must pay homage to the Lady Anne.

He knew that Mary, with her remembrance of Catherine's many kindnesses, couldn't bring herself to accept the supremacy of her brother's mistress. They had argued about it. In his anger, Charles had revealed he did not share her scruples on the matter. Ambition had demanded he dance attendance on the lady. He had become snappy and irritable, champing at the bit to be back at court.

Mary watched Charles with growing resentment. His sorrow over the loss of their son was, she realised, but a weak thing beside her own.

At last, unable to watch his growing restlessness, Mary turned on him. 'Go then. You are obviously eager to be off. It's plain you have no desire to be here with me and your daughters.' Her angry words brought a matching anger.

'Can you wonder at it?' he demanded. 'You spend more time fondling Harry's old pony than you do me. What do you expect me to do?'

'I've told you. Go back to court and Henry's harlot. You obviously find her and her wicked ways more to your taste than me.'

'At least she's lively and amusing. All you do is mope about the place nursing your grief. Harry's dead. You should try to accept it, as I have, instead of wallowing in morbid thoughts. It isn't good for you to remain brooding in this backwater.'

'This backwater, as you call it, is my home. And yours, though you are so eager to depart from it.'

'You have a home in London,' he reminded her. 'You should try sharing it with me. Your son may be dead, but you still have a husband.'

His harsh words upset her. His voice became softer, 'You should come with me to court. You'll forget your sorrow more easily there.'

'Forget it?' Incredulously, she stared at him. 'I do not wish to forget it. I will mourn my son till the day I die. How could my sorrow be eased at a court where that woman rules? Would you have me fawn over her as you do?' Mary turned away. 'I'll not do it. Catherine deserves my loyalty. My brother might spurn her, but I shall not. I think too much of the queen to seem to sanction Henry's lust for that Bullen whore, which my return to court would surely do. I'm ashamed that you do not feel the same.'

'Then damn you and Catherine. I'm the king's man. First and last. Remember it.'

Soon after, he had flung out of the house, throwing orders left and right. Mary had watched through the bed-chamber window as he leapt on his horse and rode fast for London. He had not paused to say goodbye. A tear escaped and tracked its solitary path down her cheek. I have lost him, she thought. Lost him to Anne Boleyn and my brother. And all because I pushed so hard for him to marry me that I forced him to live for weeks in terror of Henry's vengeance. The act that I thought would ensure my happiness turns out to have been the act that denies me that which I most desire. For Charles had sworn never again to incur her brother's anger. His fawning over Anne Boleyn was the result.

She turned away from the window as Charles disappeared from sight. She sank down on the bed. Oh cruel life, to have come full circle and encircled me in my own machinations. Because although she was indeed, married to Charles – at least, if the Papal Court did finally confirm it – it was Anne Boleyn, not she, who held him fast. It was a bitter realisation. And one she was coming more often to think she deserved.

So ended their brief reunion. It struck Mary, as dreary day followed dreary day, that her family were not destined to long enjoy the pleasures of marital harmony. She had heard that her sister, Margaret, had finally obtained her divorce from Archibald Douglas, her second husband, and was free to marry her lover, Henry Stewart. If Henry had his way he wouldn't be far behind his elder sister's faithless example.

It seemed to Mary that she, too, had lost her husband. Charles was the king's man now, the king's and Anne Boleyn's. The knowledge of their divided loyalties lay between them like an unbridgeable river, with Mary on one side and Charles and the unexplored land of his heart, on the other. Had she ever really known him? Or had he always been capable of the cruelties he and Henry now inflicted on Catherine?

Perhaps it was so and she had been the only one not to see it, for her sister, Margaret, had thought Charles a marital adventurer, ever seeking the richest booty. Whether that was so or not the love she still felt for him made her consider things from a viewpoint other than her sister's. It was possible that she did him an injustice and it was simply as she had concluded on his departure, that, after their terrors in Paris, his sworn determination to help Henry fulfil his desires had simply melded with his own ambition. Together these had wrought the change.

Instead of one, she now had two loved ones to mourn; the old Charles was surely as dead to her as her son. If he had ever existed anywhere other than her own head.

Frances Brandon was cross. She ignored the droning voice of the tutor and instead amused herself in her favourite fantasy of imagining she was the belle at some court masque. How she longed to be there. She had only just started to taste some of its pleasures when the sweat that had killed her brother had broken out and she had been forced to retire to the country to mourn.

Frances had done more scowling than mourning, though her scarce-concealed defiance had barely earned her a rebuke. Her mother was still so tied up in her hand-wringing that she had little energy for chastising her elder daughter.

Though buried in the stultifying tedium that was country life, Frances still heard intriguing snippets of the court's doings. All sorts of exciting things happened there, most of them thought up by Anne Boleyn. The king's mistress might not be over-popular, but she knew how to arrange enter-tainments. Her tutor's voice droned on, disturbing her fanta-sy and Frances frowned ferociously at him. She should be at court. She should take a leading role in one of Lady Anne's cleverly contrived masques. She should be admired and feted as was her due. She was the king's niece and such was her right. Frances' lips formed a thin line as she thought of the mother who had denied her such pleasures. The mother whose dark brooding invaded the entire house, making laughter a sin and worldly longings unnatural and somehow deviant. Frances longed for the day she could escape this gloomy prison and go to court like her father. The reminder of what she was denied made her crosser still, made her want to cause pain. She looked at her little sister, sitting so atten-tively beside her and, on an impulse, she pulled spitefully at Eleanor's hair.

Eleanor's cry brought the intervention of their tutor and he began to berate Frances for her behaviour. Francis ig-nored him and turned from him in scorn; he was a timid man and had already shown himself incapable of reining-in her worst excesses of behaviour. Her sister's acceptance of her lot enraged Francis still further. 'How can you be so placid, Eleanor?' she demanded now as, behind her, unheeded, the tutor twittered on. 'You sit in this drab schoolroom day after day, attending to these boring lessons as though there were nothing else in life.'

The tutor's twitterings were getting on Frances' nerves. She turned on him in a rage and practically screamed at him. 'Be silent. Get you gone. I'll listen to no more of your dreary utterances today.' Frances dismissed the wretched man from her thoughts entirely as she returned to upbraiding her sister. 'Do you not wish to be at court with all its excitements before we are too mourning grey to enjoy them?'

'But how can we go to court, Frances?' Eleanor asked, puzzlement in her pretty face. 'You know how our mother feels about the Lady Anne. Besides, she still grieves for Harry. Do you not miss him? I do.'

Much to Frances' disgust, Eleanor's face puckered in distress. 'Do not start that skriking again or I shall box your ears.' Eleanor's snivellings dried to a few sniffs. At least she could always get this little sister to do her bidding. The thought mollified somewhat, even if their mother seemed unwilling to bend to her will. With a shrug, Frances cast her brother into the realms of the dead, where he belonged. 'It is months since he died,' she sharply reminded the sniffing Eleanor. 'You and mother should give over your grieving. It is high time our mother remembered she has living daughters and not just a dead son.'

To her surprise, her timid little sister rebuked her. 'You're unkind, Frances. Our mother loves us well. Why must you always have such jealousy in your heart? Did you not love Harry?' Eleanor frowned and added thoughtfully. 'You did little enough mourning for him.'

Frances snorted in that unladylike way that her mother had failed to correct. 'Harry? He'd have been well enough, I suppose, if he'd not been the first-born and a boy.' She stamped her foot. 'Why should daughters always have to come second? 'Tis unfair. I should have been the boy. If I was, my mother would not keep me buried in the country, would not prevent me from taking my rightful place at court.'

'But you're not a boy,' Eleanor reminded her, before she picked up the book they had been studying and resumed her lesson.

Francis snatched it from her and flung it to the floor where she commenced to jump on it and damage the delicately painted pictures that adorned the pages. 'Now, mother's pet,' she demanded between each damaging jump, 'will you give over with your stupid reading and pay attention when I'm speaking to you?'

'Frances! Stop that this instant.'

Frances hadn't heard her mother's entry. She guessed the tutor had run to her, telling tales. She scowled at Eleanor's back as her sister hurried to their mother and buried her head in her dress. 'Pick up Eleanor's book, or I will have you beaten.'

Resentfully, Francis did as her mother bid, but the way she threw the book heavily down on the desk showed her defiance and her mother's gaze narrowed.

'Why do you always have to vex me, child? Can you not ever be reasonable and well-behaved like your sister? Eleanor doesn't cause me a tenth of the trouble that you do, yet she's so much younger.'

'Why do you not send me to court, then, mother?' Frances suggested pertly. 'Then I would be out of your hair and not a continual annoyance to you.'

'You, go to court? You'd have to mend your ill-mannered ways, Frances, before I take you to court. Such behaviour would not be tolerated there, so if you so badly wish to go there you would do well to reflect on the matter.'

'But how can I learn of the behaviour expected at court if I am not there to observe it?' Frances demanded sullenly. 'I hate it here, it's so dull. I long to witness for myself the clever masques devised by the Lady Anne and—'

'Be silent, Frances. You are insolent. Continue with such behaviour and you are likely never to go to court, nor be fit to be taken.'

Frances stared at her mother in sullen defiance. She had thought her mother might have been weakening. But then, Frances admitted to herself, she had foolishly mentioned the Lady Anne. The woman was like a red rag to her mother, for they all knew how she hated the lady. Frances thought Anne very stylish with her cleverly designed gowns. She could see why her uncle Henry preferred her to his old and fat queen. Why shouldn't he rid himself of her if he wished? What was the point in being king if you couldn't do what you wanted? What was the point in being the king's niece if you also could not do what you wanted?

'You would not enjoy the court now, Frances,' her mother tried to assure her. 'Your own cousin, Mary, my namesake, finds little enough pleasure there when she sees her mother daily humiliated by that woman. You used to be fond of your Aunt Catherine. Would you wish to hurt her by honouring the Bullen woman? For that is what you would be obliged to do if I took you to court.'

Frances didn't care about that. But she knew better than to say so. If she did, she would be accused of nurturing unnatural feelings.

'I would also have to pay homage to her, as though she were a queen. I'll not do it. I hope, as my daughter, Frances, you would feel shame even to consider it.'

Frances was unmoved by her mother's hopes. She cast her gaze longingly to the window. It was a bright day with a stiff breeze. On such a day she should be out on her horse, flying over hedges and ditches with one of the more daring stable boys, not forced to study for hours in a stuffy chamber.

After giving another lecture on ladylike behaviour, Mary called for the tutor and ordered them back to their lessons. Issuing Frances with firm warnings about what reward further ill-behaviour would bring her, their mother left.

Outside the chamber, Mary leaned back against the closed door, shut her eyes and pressed her hand to her side as the pain that now but rarely gave her ease flared into angry life. Dear God, how her eldest daughter vexed her. Once again the thought sprang into her head that it were a pity God had seen fit to take her son and leave her daughter. It was a wicked thought, Mary knew. Frances was her own child, but she could not like her. From the cradle, her eldest daughter had seemed to know how best to vex her and to take pleasure in acting on the knowledge.

You must try to like her, Mary told herself again, must try to get through to her. The only sound from behind the door was the low drone of the tutor. Satisfied that her re-

413

buke had for the moment subdued her unruly daughter, Mary left them to it and made for her bed-chamber, hoping a few quiet hours would persuade the pain in her side to give her some respite.

She was worried about Frances. The girl was too wilful. In this, she took after her Aunt Margaret, whose own wilful behaviour in the pursuit of her own way had become notorious. Nightly, Mary prayed that Frances wasn't going to be another Margaret. She would have to find a strong man when the time came for the girl to marry. A strong man might soften her and arouse a few tender feelings. For at the moment, the only person capable of causing such emotions in Frances' breast was Frances. Her longings and her self-pity were forever fighting each other for the little tenderness that breast contained. It didn't help that Mary blamed herself for the flaws in her daughter's character. If she and Charles had not married...

Mary sighed. The years of financial problems and their periods of self-banishment from court were resented by Frances who had always been desperate to be the centre of attention. Mary knew the girl blamed her for all the things she felt she ought to have, but didn't have, especially a permanent place at court.

It wounded Mary that Frances clearly cared little that Anne Boleyn ruled over her aunt and cousin, flaunting her scarlet behaviour by wearing scarlet gowns and Catherine's jewels. Frances thought Anne Boleyn exciting. What cared she if her cousin, the king's own daughter, was barely tolerated after taking her mother's side? No, Frances would never share Mary's feelings. She would have no qualms about curt-seying to her Aunt Catherine's usurper. Mary refused to grant Catherine's rival such a triumph and if the only way she could bring it off was by keeping Frances in the country, so be it.

It was some days later. Mary was sewing in her solar when she heard a messenger arrive. He was brought straight to her and when Mary had read the letter he had brought, she was filled with joy that God seemed to have at last listened to the devout Catherine's many prayers.

For the Bullen harlot was grievously sick. And though Mary begged God's forgiveness for her uncharitable thoughts, she felt He would surely understand and sympa-thise with them for Anne Boleyn had ruined Catherine's life and that of her daughter. She had also come between Mary and her own husband, causing more arguments and cross words than even that fraught time after their secret mar-riage. And now, she came between them in an even more damaging way, forcing them, by her very existence, to spend long periods apart, periods when bitterness festered and re-sentment grew. And then there was Frances, yet another problem to lay at Anne Boleyn's door. Perhaps God would be kind and let the sweating sickness that afflicted the lady take her on to the next world. For certain it was that Anne Boleyn had caused grief enough in this one.

CHAPTER TWENTY-THREE

Mary's hopes were dashed when she learned from letters from her husband and friends at court that not only had Anne Boleyn survived her illness, but that her brush with death had placed her even more firmly in Henry's affections. She was now more arrogant and demanding than ever. And even though Henry had sent her from his side on the arrival of Cardinal Campeggio who was expected, with Wolsey, to pass judgement on Henry and Catherine's marriage, it was clear this was simply so that her brother would not compromise himself in Campeggio's eyes.

However, it seemed that Henry and his mistress were not to have things all their own way, for Cardinal Campeggio, who suffered badly from the gout, took to his bed as soon as he arrived. Mary's correspondents hinted that this was caused as much by political expediency as by pain. Pope Clement, that eternal shilly-shallier, had clearly determined not to grant the divorce. He would not act against the wishes of Catherine's nephew, the Emperor. And as Henry's allies, one by one, fell victim to the Emperor Charles's power, the Pope's desire to delay the divorce grant increased.

Of course, the situation was far from pleasing to the Lady Anne. And as Charles, together with Anne Boleyn's uncle, the Duke of Norfolk, had sided with the king and his lady, Anne would expect them to explain what to her must be maddening delays. Placating the lady would never have been an easy task.

Mary learned from several sources that her husband had been forced to soothe her and she burned with resentment for his sake. It seemed the world had gone mad when a chit of a girl could cause such trouble.

It wasn't long before Mary learned by what means Charles had managed to placate his demanding mistress. He had turned Anne Boleyn's wrath over the delays and pointed it in the direction of one they had both had long hated—Cardinal Wolsey. Foolishly, Charles had attacked the Cardinal in Council. But Charles was no match for the Cardinal in argument and had been reminded that it was only through Wolsey's efforts that he had retained his head after his secret marriage. Mary could imagine how little such a humiliation would endear the Cardinal to her husband.

What sad times they lived through, Mary thought. But they were saddest of all for Catherine as, pushed by Anne's spite, the frustrated Henry forced the queen away from Greenwich to Hampton Court and Anne moved into the rooms beside the king that had been Catherine's.

Much as Mary agonised over her husband's difficulties and her brother's understandable desire for a male heir, she was glad, for Catherine's sake, that the queen had had one satisfaction in all this. For although the Legatine Court, with Wolsey and Campeggio officiating to hear the divorce, had finally opened at Blackfriars, it had become increasingly bogged down in petty details, and at the end of the legal term, the case was recalled to be heard in Rome.

Henry, of course, was furious and looked round for a scapegoat. Pushed by Anne and Mary's husband, he settled on Wolsey. He had failed the king over the divorce, failed as arbiter of Europe where even his vast plans for a peace conference had fallen into disarray. Worse, France, the Pope and the Emperor looked likely to come to terms—terms that excluded England.

All Henry's hopes for the divorce would be over if the Pope and the Emperor were united. Wolsey's failure to secure his master's wishes meant that his downfall was only a matter of time. To Mary's sadness, amongst the wolves who began to gather, eager to take a bite of Wolsey's plump flesh, was the man who had more reason than most to be grateful to the Cardinal; her own husband, Charles. Not only had Wolsey interceded with Henry and gained for them her brother's forgiveness, Mary now learned that, in the midst of all his troubles, he had managed to gain Papal confirmation that her and Charles's marriage was legal. He had been a good friend to them in truth and Mary felt ashamed of his treatment at the hands of her brother and husband. Although she was relieved to receive confirmation of the legality of her marriage, apart from lifting one of her worries, it came too late to bring much joy. Of course, it was good that her children no longer risked the taint of bastardy and could now be betrothed without difficulty. But after all the suffering and arguments over the legality or otherwise of Henry and Catherine's marriage, the confirmation that her own was valid seemed small beer indeed, made smaller by the fact that she saw but little of her husband in these troubled times. He was fast in Anne Boleyn's clutches and seldom dared to leave the court in case someone poisoned her against him as he had poisoned her against Wolsey.

Alone in the country with her two remaining children, Mary wondered what would become of them all. Her and Charles's marriage was not setting the country and Europe by the ear as was Henry's. Set aside, their marriage would not attract the wrath of the Emperor. But Henry's wish to set Catherine aside and marry Anne Boleyn would do this and more. And Charles was tangled in the midst of it.

Had it only been two years ago that he had shown her such tenderness at the death of their son? Alas, Mary reflected, such tenderness hadn't lasted. He had been eager to return to court and gain Henry's praise by tormenting poor Catherine. The unrelenting pressures had made him harsh and unfeeling and if Henry didn't soon get his way, who knew on whom his anger might next descend?

Once again, Mary felt she could not remain blameless in all this. Her demand that Charles marry her had led them to this situation. The fear Charles had felt at that time had brought about in him a determination that he would never again fall foul of Henry's desires. Whether this vow meant he had to be kind or cruel, just or unjust, he would follow wherever Henry led, glad to be able to do so. And to what had their great love brought them? Separation and estrangement. The divorce had driven a wedge between them and would continue to do so. Poor beleaguered Cardinal Wolsey had striven to get Papal recognition for a marriage that now hardly seemed worthy of the name. Mary was saddened by the realisation that their marriage could never return to its old affectionate footing. Too much had passed between them for that. And the more she looked back, the more Mary convinced herself that it needn't have been that way and that Henry would have graciously agreed to their marriage once they had returned home and Charles's desperate need to get back into Henry's affections would never have happened.

But it was too late now for might-have-beens. Henry was determined on his divorce and Charles was determined to help him to get it, whatever the cost to Catherine, Henry or their own love and marriage.

Mary's life, her visits to a court queened over by Anne Boleyn, a rare event, had become firmly rooted in the country. There was little at court for her now. Besides, she had no wish to witness her husband's degradation, his ever-more shameful behaviour. The brother, the husband, she had once known and respected were both lost to her. Henry, the big brother she had adored as a child had been over-shadowed by the hydra-headed monster of his conscience. The matter of the divorce touched them all. Touched and left its mark.

Her little niece, Mary, her namesake, had been reduced to rebellious silence over the treatment of her mother. Now on the verge of womanhood, her life had been blighted and Mary's heart ached for her. The bright, happy little girl her father had called his 'pearl', whom Mary remembered with affection, had gone and in her place was a sad-eyed young woman, neglected, ignored and old beyond her years. Bullied and humiliated, she had withdrawn into herself, beyond the harlot's taunts. Most cruel of all, the poor child was not allowed to see her mother lest they encourage one another's defiance.

The shame Mary felt at the behaviour of the men in her family was overtaken only by her hatred of the woman whose black-eyed witchery had so hypnotised her brother that he must draw Charles, too, under her spell. Even Frances had been suborned and was becoming more sullen by the day at her mother's refusal to allow her to worship at the black altar of Anne Boleyn with the rest.

Mary was at a loss what to do with the girl, a difficulty not eased by the fact that they had never been close. Mary had tried to reason with her daughter, to make her understand that she could not, in honour, reside at court as she wished. But Frances refused to accept any point of view but her own. All she thought of was the unfair sacrifice she was called upon to make for honour's sake and her resentment grew with each additional day's sacrifice.

Frances had never been one to meet anyone halfway. She refused to remember the many loving acts of her Aunt Catherine. Instead, all she thought of was the pleasure Catherine's stubbornness denied her. But for Queen Catherine, her reasoning ran, she would be at court, able to enjoy all the amusements.

Mary understood that it was hard for the girl living such a quiet life and she did her best to enliven it, giving banquets and balls for their neighbours, even though her health made such entertainments an ordeal. But Frances was determined to be miserable. Nothing for her would do but the splendours and extravagance of the court entertainments. Mary was forced into the unwilling and painful acceptance that she had born a daughter at once shallow, stubborn and selfish. Clearly, Frances longed to be gone from her home. Mary had looked to put off her eldest daughter's marriage for a year or two yet as she was still young, but, in despair, Mary acknowledged that while she could find no answers to the girl's waywardness, the strong husband she needed, might.

Increasingly unwell with the agonising pains in her side, Mary scarcely had the energy to cope with her wilful daughter. She decided to write to Charles and suggest they got the girl settled into marriage. Marriage and motherhood would surely steady her.

Mary couldn't help the flutter of pleasure she felt when she heard that Charles was coming home on one of his infrequent visits. For all the shame she felt over his behaviour, he was her husband still and she loved him. But his homecoming would be bitter-sweet, reminding her, as it did, of other, more loving homecomings.

She pushed the thought from her mind and set the servants in a flurry preparing his favourite dishes. He had become fond of turkey, which they had enjoyed during the meeting with King Francis when he and Henry had entertained each other at the Field of the Cloth of Gold—how long ago that now seemed.

So the turkeys were caught and butchered and were roasting with a mouth-watering aroma that filled the house by the time Charles arrived home.

Mary felt a frisson of alarm when she first saw him. She was surprised to see how grey he had become. He seemed frayed. But, Mary thought sadly as she greeted him, how could he be otherwise? Was he not in constant attendance on Henry and his demanding harpy? Anne Boleyn on her own was enough to fray any man, but Henry's temper was also becoming increasingly unpredictable.

Worried by the strain he must daily endure, Mary did her best to cosset him. She led him to the solar where a good fire burned and ordered him a mulled ale, a warming drink on a chill day. Gradually, with the draining of the ale, he leaned back in his chair and Mary was relieved to see some of the tension drain out of him.

Later, after supper, as Charles, overfull of good wine, lounged before the fire, he was restored enough to tell her some of Henry's doings. He even managed to make her laugh when he revealed the many and varied ways her brother was trying to get his own way over the divorce.

Goaded by Anne and her tantrums, Henry had produced a bevy of plans over the months to persuade Pope Clement to grant him the divorce, all equally ludicrous.

He had despatched agents to Rome with assorted instructions. He had proposed that Catherine should enter a nunnery and if, as seemed likely, she insisted on Henry entering a cloister at the same time, the Pope was to help him extricate himself from his unwelcome hooded chastity.

Mary laughed so hysterically at the idea of her larger-than-life brother becoming a monk that even Charles, to whom all this must be painfully familiar, also began to splut-

424

ter. The abstinence of such a life, would alone, without the chastity, not be in Henry's capability for more than half a day, Mary knew. His vows would be broken at the first sight of a well-stuffed goose or a well-filled bodice.

Charles said, 'and if the Pope failed to do your brother's bidding, the agents had instructions to investigate the novel notion of allowing the king two wives at the same time.'

Mary shook her head in amazement. And as her well-wined and dined husband emptied another glass of wine, he tipsily confided more information. 'Your brother had the foresight to find examples of multiple partners being permitted and he provided quotes from the Old Testament to back up his arguments.'

Such schemes, must, even to Henry, have seemed unlikely of success. But Mary sobered as she realised that such acts showed her brother's increasing desperation. Ridiculous as Henry's antics were, they were truly no laughing matter; the lines of strain on Charles's face, softened now by the mellow candlelight, bore witness to that. As did his determined burying of his head in his wine goblet.

Mary knew, too, how distressed Catherine was at not being permitted to see her own daughter. But, of course, she had not best-pleased Henry when she had written to the Pope complaining that she would have no justice in England and asked him to transfer judgement on the divorce to Rome—which he had done.

Mary knew better than to ask for news of Catherine; it was one sure way to force an argument and Mary wanted this reconciliation to be a happy one for it would no doubt have to sustain her for many weeks. Her heart softened as she looked at Charles. Sprawled in his seat by the fire, his face highlighted by the flames, he looked more weary than ever. High position and the favour of Henry and Anne Boleyn had clearly brought him little of the joy he had expected; his face was becoming more lined, his hair more grey each time she saw him. Mary wished they could go back and build their life together on a footing more firm than the rocky ground of Henry's goodwill. But she had chosen to snatch at happiness in Paris and they were both now paying the price.

As Mary studied her weary husband, drowsy from the heat of the fire and the quantity of wine he had consumed, and recalled the worn-down content of his conversation she sensed, for the first time, his longing to escape the sticky web in which he had become ensnared. Hope stirred in her breast as it occurred to her he might now be ready to listen to her. It might yet be possible for Charles to extricate himself from the mess of Henry's desires. He seemed more open to the suggestion tonight than she had ever dared hope. Their marriage, which for long after their son's death had seemed a poor thing of snatched meetings and abrupt partings, might again become what it had once been.

Mary rose, moved across to him and knelt at his feet. 'Stay here with me, my love,' she urged. 'Let my brother and his harlot fight their own battles. They have worn you out with their demands.'

As he turned her suggestion over his expression lightened and Mary's hopes rose as she watched him. He was older and wiser now; surely he had discovered that having the king's confidence was not such a marvellous thing. Had he not the evidence of Wolsey to help him see the truth of this? For the Cardinal, for all his ability and greatness and for all the years he had spent serving Henry, was now out of favour.

But Mary's hopes were short-lived. For after draining his wine and refilling the goblet, the light went out of his countenance and she knew he would reject the temptation she had put before him.

'Would that it were that simple,' he told her. 'I am too deeply enmeshed in this thing now. I must continue. Even should the king permit me to ease myself out, Anne Boleyn would not and she rules the king. Even if she were to agree, there is still Wolsey to consider. Should he somehow manage to worm himself back into the king's favour, he would waste no time ensuring I lost it. Too many bitter things have been said and done over this divorce for him to take any other course. No.' Charles drank off the latest goblet and for all that his consumption had been heavy, he seemed more sober than on his arrival. 'This divorce must be brought to conclusion and for my health's sake I need to be at the king's side when it is. Whether it be done with or without the Pope.'

'Without the Pope?' Mary didn't understand. 'If the Pope doesn't agree, there can be no divorce. How could there be?'

Charles gave a world-weary laugh. 'How I envy you your naivety over this matter, sweetheart. Would that I had appreciated more the quiet pleasures of country living when I had the chance.' He leaned forward and caressed her cheek as if he found it difficult to believe a woman could have such softness in her. 'Anne Boleyn's tongue grows sharper by the

427

day. She goads the king increasingly and the rest of us must bear the brunt. You cannot begin to realise how I long for what I once had and failed to appreciate. Does it give you any satisfaction, Mary, to know you were right and I was wrong? Daily I am finding that ambition and power are not as sweet as I thought.

'Wolsey is on his way out; the recall of the divorce to Rome made sure of that. It is only a matter of time now, but I must remain at court to make sure he falls. And although he has retired to his manor of The Moor and the king bade Norfolk and me to take back his great seal of office, the king is still fond of him. It is not impossible that that wily churchman might even now wangle for himself a return to the king's favour.'

Mary had heard about Charles and the Duke of Norfolk's visit to Wolsey. She had heard that the Cardinal had confounded them by demanding to see the written order from the king for the return of the great seal of office. But such had been their haste, they had not thought to obtain it and had been forced to slope off without the seal, much to their mutual fury. Charles had said nothing of this to Mary and she knew better than to remind him of it.

'I still don't understand,' she said. 'If Wolsey should fall there are other churchmen to take his place. Wolsey is not the church, merely one part of it.'

'No. If – when – Wolsey falls, the church falls with him. The Lutheran leanings of many at court, Anne Boleyn included, daily fill the king's head with new ideas.'

Mary stared at her husband in horror. 'But—but,' she eventually managed to burst out, 'that way leads to civil war, the Papal interdict and horror.' The dead would remain unburied, babies unbaptised and the betrothed unmarried. Briefly, Mary thought of Frances and the tantrums that would have to be endured at any suggestion that marriage and freedom from parental restraint might be delayed.

'Your brother says he gives not a fig for the Pope or his interdicts. He thinks to do away with Rome and himself lead the church here in England. Woe betide any priest who tried to defy him by refusing the usual sacraments. Baptisms would still go ahead, weddings, funerals. Your brother would insist upon it, ensuring his will with as many executions as necessary. We are in for a time of great turmoil.'

And all because of the demands of her once little Maid of Honour, thought Mary. Little Anne of the too-short skirts, who, because she prized her 'virtue' so highly, demanded the destruction of the church which had denied her desires.

'Surely, even Henry wouldn't dare to take such a step.' But even as she spoke, Mary knew she deceived herself. Henry would dare much and demand that the rest of the country dare also for his sake. Mary had barely touched her own wine, but now she snatched up her goblet and drank deeply, hoping the sweet Malmsey wine would somehow sugar her thoughts and blur the edges of such madness.

'There are many to guide him that way,' Charles told her. 'I cannot risk not being one of his guides. Anne Boleyn's influence is all now. If I am not with her and her desires I can only be against her. I've been involved too long and too deeply. My defection at this time would be regarded as treachery and the Lady Anne would take special care to ensure that the king also saw it in that light.'

Charles stared dolefully into the now-dying flames as if he saw his future there and liked not what he saw. 'I am trapped, Mary. Don't you see? Trapped by my own actions and ambitions. There is no going back for me. I can only go forward to the end of the road and to whatever destiny it holds.'

'At last, that traitorous cur is dead. Pity he couldn't have lingered a while and we'd have had the pleasure of seeing his fat head on a pole over London Bridge.'

Charles's pleasure at Wolsey's death saddened Mary, for she knew he had been a true friend. It pained her to think of all the humiliations that had chased him to the grave; titles and property had been taken from him; he, who had once thought nothing of entertaining hundreds to banquets in one of his splendid houses, had been forced to beg money from his chaplain to pay his servants' wages. After his fall from grace and his ultimate banishment to his See of York, he and what had remained of his household had no sheets, nor even any beds to put them on.

She remembered his kindness to her when she had feared her marriage to Charles was no true marriage and was thankful death had spared him the ultimate humiliation— execution for treason.

Charles, with the knowledge that Wolsey would now never regain the king's affection, had been able to spare time to come home to Westhorpe and attend to other matters. Their eldest daughter, Frances, was now betrothed. But in spite of Mary's conviction that their daughter needed a strong man, one she couldn't rule, Charles had decided differently and with the king's agreement had betrothed Frances to her cousin, Henry Grey, third Marquis of Dorset.

Like Mary's own husband, Henry Grey had been set to marry elsewhere and had been betrothed to the Lady Catherine Fitzalan. But he had cast aside this betrothal on the death of his father in order to marry the king's niece. History had a habit of repeating itself, thought Mary. Here was another youth who would throw off old promises for ambition's sake. Between her brother, her sister, her husband and her soon-to-be son-in-law, it was becoming quite a family tradition.

Disappointed in the match, she had tried to dissuade Charles from it, but he would brook no interference. Had not the king sanctioned the betrothal? But neither king nor father could sanction for happiness, and Mary foresaw little of this for her daughter. For Henry Grey was a weak-minded boy, not the strong man Mary knew her daughter needed. Moreover, his weak mind was filled with ambition.

Young Henry Grey now resided with them at Westhorpe so the young pair could get to know one another before they were wed. Charles had obtained the wardship of the boy, backed by the king's recommendation, which amounted to a command and he was taken from his mother's keeping and transferred to Charles's guardianship for the remainder of his minority.

It hadn't taken the determined Frances long to gain the upper hand over her betrothed. For once, Frances had made use of a certain subtlety, which would, Mary suspected, be discarded once they were formally married and she had the ruling of the empty-headed young Dorset.

Mary wondered what follies the pair - whose union fused the unhappy combination of greed, ambition and stupidity - might not be capable of together. Because follies there would surely be. How could there not be when her daughter's wilful selfishness would receive no check? Denied the strong husband she needed, Frances' worst traits could only deepen. Mary was saddened that a girl of thirteen could be so full of gall and bitterness. It was yet another thing for Mary to hold against Anne Boleyn. She was grateful she didn't know what the future held, for the here and now held troubles enough.

It was near noon and they were at dinner, just a small family group. This last ensured that Frances should be full of pout. Her betrothed didn't seem to notice Frances' mood; all his attention was for his prospective father-in-law who had so recently returned from court.

'Now the king will obtain his divorce, my lord,' young Dorset opined, with an attempt at the worldly air that was at odds with his youth.

Mary saw him dart a sly glance at the pouting Frances as if he would show off in front of her by displaying such man-of-the-world manners, such clever knowingness. It was the young pairs' misfortune, she thought, that he was not clever at all, certainly not as clever as he thought himself to be.

But Charles was in a benign mood and didn't check the boy. Instead, he smiled condescendingly and pretended to confide in him. 'Aye lad,' he said. 'Wolsey never strove very hard for it, as the Lady Anne suspected. 'Tis a shame we weren't able to shut him in the Tower. What interesting discoveries might we have made if he could have been persuaded to tell us of all his connivings?'

Mary choked on her wine. When she got her breath back, she said, 'You can't mean he would have been tortured, Charles? Not the great Cardinal? He was my brother's respected advisor for many years and always served him loyally.'

'You've lived the quiet life too long. You know little of the court's doings.'

Charles's admonishment was sharp. Was he demonstrating to the young Dorset how best to reprove a royal wife? Her husband had grown proud now he was high in the king's confidence from his own efforts rather than because of his marriage. He had smothered his doubts and thrown himself wholeheartedly behind Henry's desires, so much so, that he felt strong enough to rebuke the king's sister in earnest.

'You were ever over-friendly to Wolsey, Mary. You would be wise to keep such opinions to yourself. 'Tis not a good season for such leanings. The Lady Anne hated him and she will soon be wedded to the king. She'll not brook any with friendly feelings for Wolsey at court.'

'The Lady Anne. The Lady Anne.' Mary was tired of the name. 'Why don't you give her her proper name, Charles? She is the king's whore. How could such as she wear a crown? When I think of poor Catherine and the dignity she brought to—'

'Hold your tongue, Mary. By the Mass, have you gone wit-less? Your brother wouldn't save Wolsey and at the Lady Anne's urging has let even his own daughter know she risks the axe if she continues to defy him. Do you think she would long permit you - king's sister or no - to remain at liberty for speaking thus?'

Mary refused to believe that Henry would allow Anne Boleyn to threaten her. She had to think that way, she found. There were precious few such solaces left to her. To think that she, who had risen to marriage to the King of France, should now have sunk so low that her brother's harlot could think to threaten her... It was not to be borne. 'Henry would let no harm come to me,' she insisted. 'It was you and Norfolk who persuaded him to act against Cardinal Wolsey, no doubt with his mistress whispering hate-filled pillow-talk. It is my belief than when it came to it and had Wolsey not died when he did, Henry would have given the Cardinal his liberty and sufficient income to live nobly. He was never vindictive, not the brother I knew.'

'Times have changed and your brother with them. He is so desperate for the divorce that nothing else matters. The Lady Anne pushes him ever forward to that end. She has no choice. The thing has gone too far. Have I not told you that even his own daughter is treated as of no account? Truly, you are soft in the head if you believe he wouldn't permit his sister to be so treated if Anne Boleyn decreed. Perhaps, when next you come to court you should leave your tongue behind. I well remember the last time you upset the lady. I had to bear the brunt of it for days.'

Mary had all but forgotten the presence of her daughter and Henry Grey during this exchange, but now she became aware of their open-mouthed fascination. Charles was right in one thing at least; it was unwise to speak so openly against her brother's whore. Now she signalled to the musicians to play and firmly suggested the young pair dance. It would not do to have them listening in to any further indiscretions if what Charles said was true.

As they watched the young betrothed pair move down from the dais to the floor, Mary felt her own fear grow as Charles confided the latest court doings.

'The Lady is too powerful now, Mary, for any to go against her. The king does her bidding in all things.'

Charles's words chastened Mary further. She sat back and stared into her wine cup, marvelling that lives that had once been as sweet and promising as had hers and Henry's should have turned so about. How had her brother ever got into the clutches of such a she-devil as Anne Boleyn?

Mary shook her head at the workings of fate and drank deeply of the soothing ruby-red wine. She could only pray that like poor Wolsey who had also climbed high, Anne Boleyn would as swiftly fall. Mary hoped her poor health would allow her to witness the event. It was true that the harlot's temper tantrums were becoming notorious. How much longer would her brother endure them?

Mary knew she was becoming embittered. But that woman had done too much harm for Mary to have soft feelings for her welfare. Was not her own husband as much the Bullen's creature as the king? Was not her poor niece being so tormented and badgered that her health was damaged, her very life threatened? Was not Catherine now queen in name only, soon not to be even that? Harried, old, sick—how much longer could she find the strength to demand her rights and those of her daughter? The happy court that Mary had known and enjoyed as a carefree young girl was no more. Charles's explicit warnings made clear it was a place where there was danger in a word or a look. Fear possessed her as she looked at Charles. What would be his fate if he and Norfolk failed to achieve the divorce? Henry, as he grew older, was becoming less forgiving of failure, and Charles, with his low birth and high-rising attracted jealousy as had Wolsey. Like Charles, the Cardinal had cast off his lowly beginnings, but they had helped to drag him down in the end.

Mary, her sympathy for Catherine overset by fear for her husband, placed a warning hand on his wrist. 'I beg you, tread warily, Charles. The path of those who lead the king's business is not, as you have discovered, strewn with gifts and glories only. If he does not get his divorce after all this, who knows who he might blame?'

Charles's eyes shadowed. But he managed a taut, 'Tired of championing Catherine?'

'No.' But she feared this goal of her brother's would bring about the downfall of many more than the Cardinal before it was achieved. Pray God one of them wasn't her own husband. 'But I am beginning to think the divorce could scarce lead to worse misery than all this striving to obtain it. At least Catherine might find some tranquillity if it is accomplished and she is forced to accept it as fact.'

The mention of Catherine angered him, as it always did. Mary still thought of Catherine as a friend, a beleaguered friend. To Charles, she was a mule-headed old woman who could have saved them all this trouble if she had entered the nunnery as Henry had wanted.

Charles banged his empty wine goblet back on the board. 'It's time I was off back to court.' He shouted to Henry Grey, 'Ride part of the way with me.'

'Am I not to get a kiss, then, Charles? Your departures are always so hasty these days. You're barely here but you're gone again.' Mary's reproach brought him back to her side. He kissed her cheek lightly.

'The king's business demands all my time, Mary, you know that. Have you not warned me of the dangers I might face if I should fail?' Wistfully, he studied her face. 'Would that you were able to keep a respectful tongue in your head towards the Lady Anne, you would be welcome to return with me.'

'Even if such a miracle should occur, I doubt I could manage the journey now,' Mary told him. 'This wretched pain in my side makes travelling difficult.' In fact, it made of it a torture, but Mary had kept the extent of her suffering to herself; Charles had enough problems to concern him, she would not add to them more than she did already. 'The roads are so poor that I'm in constant fear of the litter being overturned. But I shall miss you.'

'And I you, but what would you have me do, Mary? I have to be at court, you know that as well as I do. Would you have me split myself asunder?'

He had taken her last remark as a reproach she saw and was sorry for it. But she had spoken no more than the truth. She *would* miss him sorely. She would have loved to go with him to court, even with the pain that getting there would entail—if the court did not contain the Lady Anne.

'A wife's place is with her husband,' he reproached her in turn. 'Cannot you try a little harder? Now Frances is betrothed, she would enjoy the pleasures of the court as much as you did at her age. 'Tis a shame you scarcely ever take her there.'

'Yes Mother,' Frances chimed in as she and Dorset returned to their seats. 'How am I ever to become the great lady you are forever telling me I must learn to be if I have no chance to study the ladies of the court? I am nearly a woman, soon to be a wife, yet still I am denied. 'Tis unfair.'

It was an all too familiar complaint. And Mary, who would not brook her daughter studying at the feet of her brother's harlot, issued a sharp reminder. 'You are neither woman nor wife yet, Madam. And until you are you will do as I say. Now kiss your father goodbye. You can then escort me to chapel and we will pray for the king's happiness.' And the fall of his harlot, Mary added silently to herself.

Frances scowled. And after kissing her father and watching the departure, she reluctantly escorted her mother to the chapel. Mary was aware her daughter's resentment at the restrictions she placed on her life were growing, but she didn't know what to do about them. It was unfortunate that denying her a place at court should so displease Frances. But the girl was now betrothed and would soon be her own mistress. Mary didn't doubt that she would have little trouble in persuading the young and biddable Henry Grey to reside with her wherever she chose.

Things were moving on apace. Another Thomas, another commoner like Thomas Wolsey, had the ear of the king. Thomas Cranmer it was who had planted the seed that had taken root in Henry's head. The question went: Did England need the Pope? Or did the Pope have greater need of England?

Mary, still in the country, was beginning to feel akin to some sort of poor relation, for Henry, Anne Boleyn, her own husband and many of the rest of the court were off on a jaunt to France. Mary had been invited, but she had turned the invitation down. Her refusal had angered Henry and she was sorry for it. For Charles's sake and for the love that still existed between her brother and herself, Mary would have liked to please him. But she would not join a party that included Anne Boleyn. Her brother had then demanded her jewels to go in her place. Resentfully, conscious of Charles's need to please Henry in all things, Mary had handed them over so they could adorn Nan Bullen, newly created Marchioness of Pembroke for the French visit. But at least she had the satisfaction of knowing that Henry had rebuked the high and mighty Marchioness for the shrill tantrum that had ensued on the discovery that Henry had permitted Mary to refuse the invitation. The news of his rebuke had spread swiftly around the court. It gave Mary hope that Anne Boleyn's power to hold the king was waning.

For all her ill-health, for all her determination not to honour Anne Boleyn, Mary envied the great throng that was travelling to France. How long ago it seemed since she was a young girl, admired for her golden beauty and part of such an exciting journey. Now she was a middle-aged matron and her life revolved around household matters, Frances' growing tempers and coping with the increasing pain in her side. More and more often lately she had been forced her to take to her bed because of it. She had frighteningly little energy these days and what little she had was depleted by pain and Frances' demands.

Charles had written to tell her that Henry and his paramour hoped for much from their French trip. It seemed King Francis was happy to accept Henry's mistress at his court, though Mary doubted his ladies would be so accommodating.

Anne and Henry had been right in their optimistic expectations of their French trip. Even deep in the country, Mary learned how happy they were. It did not take much working out that Anne had finally given Henry his heart's desire and had surrendered her once prized virtue. Truly, she felt, Anne must have been frightened after Henry's rebuke to surrender that which she had so-zealously guarded. She was no longer young, had a tongue as sharp as any fish-wife and had many enemies. Anne had played the long game skilfully and would recognise when the time had come to part with her maidenhead.

'So he has married her, then?' Mary had guessed what might have been the final outcome of the trip to the licentious French court. 'It must have been a very hole-in-the-corner wedding.' As theirs had been, Mary reminded herself. At least, in copying their example, Anne would not now be able to taunt her with a similar reminder.

'It was very quiet,' Charles admitted. 'A secret ceremony. But they're wed right enough. It's not so secret now of course. Everyone could see that the king was bursting to talk about some great event. He's happier than I have seen him in years. Anyway, the news is all over the court and will be all over the country soon enough.'

Mary felt hurt that her brother had chosen to keep her in ignorance of his marriage. She supposed she had only herself to blame. After all, had she not done the same? And it was not as if she would have chosen to attend the ceremony.

'It's funny,' Charles mused. 'They had been getting like an old married couple before. But now it's 'sweetheart' this and 'sweetheart' that. The king can't do enough for her it seems.'

'That can only mean one thing. She's pregnant.'

Charles stared at her. 'Do you think so?'

Mary smiled. Men could be such blind fools. 'Nothing else would make Henry behave so, not even Anne's precious maidenhead. Count on it.'

Charles shook his head in wonder. 'Christ's Blood,' he said, 'I believe you're right, Mary. It could be naught else, as you say.' He looked thoughtful now. 'It must have been when they were in France. Or just after.'

Mary nodded. She had already guessed as much but hadn't confided her suspicions to Charles. 'It'll be an August or September birth, I'd guess.'

He nodded. 'Tis hard to believe after all these years of striving they are finally wed and the lady is pregnant. We can hope for some peace now it is achieved.' Relieved, he added, 'The king is very careful of her, very tender.'

'So was he to Catherine, once. Have you both forgotten that Catherine still lives, is still, in the eyes of the church, Henry's lawful, wedded wife? Henry's long-awaited son, if son it be, will still be a bastard like any other.'

Charles glanced nervously over his shoulder. 'Lower your voice, Mary. Such comments are dangerous.' His words revealed the depth of his fear.

Mary refused to be cowed in her own home. 'It's the truth, whether the lady likes it or no. Nothing will alter that.'

'That's where you're wrong. The king intends to alter it. He's determined on it. He'll not let anything stand in his way, not now. He's all force and vigor. He's nominated Thomas Cranmer to the vacant See of Canterbury. If Rome agrees and he's confirmed as Archbishop, Henry will get his divorce. Cranmer has all but promised the king.' Charles shook his head in wonder as he added, 'You should see your brother, Mary. He's like a boy again, playing pranks and laughing all the while. 'Tis good to see him so joyful.'

Mary said a silent prayer for Catherine, her brother's abandoned queen. Sure it was that Catherine would never enjoy a second youth. She had had little enough joy in the first one. Thinking of Catherine and the many disappointments she had endured over the years, made her comment thoughtfully, 'What if Anne Boleyn bears a girl? What then?'

The suggestion horrified Charles. 'A girl? It won't be a girl.' Grim-faced, he added, 'It can't be a girl. Too much hangs on the birth of a son for that.'

Mary marvelled at his capacity for self-delusion. They didn't want a girl: ergo, it wouldn't be a girl. Had the possibility even entered his head before she put it there? Or Henry's? Catherine would no doubt see such an occurrence as Divine retribution. She wouldn't be alone in the opinion. Mary pushed, 'But if she did carry a girl, what might be the result do you think?'

Charles shrugged. 'Who knows? Though whether the king could – or would – take kindly to another disappointment... It could be the beginning of the end for her. Your brother wants a son and the lady has promised him one.'

She was surprised to hear Charles admit that Anne Boleyn might not be given a second opportunity if she failed to deliver on her promise. Her many enemies would be happy to see her fall. But Charles, who had come home for a break from court troubles, refused to discuss the matter further, though his voice warned Mary that the change of subject matter would not be to her taste. And so it proved.

'Frances will soon be sixteen. It's time she was wed. And if I arrange for the ceremony to be conducted in our London house you'll have to come to court and bring our daughters. The king is joyful, as I told you, and demands that everyone around him is similarly joyful. Once she brings forth her boy there'll be none allowed to spurn her or deny her her place. You'll have to make friends with her whether you would or no. You may as well get used to the idea and get the deed over early with Frances' wedding as the excuse for your presence.'

Mary longed to refuse, but she knew Charles was right . He had soon forgotten the possibility that Anne might have a girl, she noticed. Now, his confidence made Mary, too, forget the possibility.

Later that day, Charles rode off back to London with her promise to follow him as soon as possible. She had waved to him and kept a smile fixed on her face all the while. She had long feared the arrival of this day. Charles was right, of course. If - when - Anne Boleyn had her boy, no one would be allowed to treat her coolly; not even the king's sister. She had longed to refuse to go, but she knew that, in this, she had no choice but to accede to Charles's wishes. Her husband's conviction, her brother's great joy, both made her wonder at her own doubts as to the flavour of the fruit Anne carried. Was it possible that the arrogant Anne, so long triumphant in all things, would fail now? Mary had shaken her head and gone off to speak to her daughters as Charles had suggested.

At least the news had lifted the sullen look from Frances' face. For once, her elder daughter was helpful and eager to do Mary's bidding. She left them and the servants in a flurry of packing, excitedly discussing the wedding and retired to her chamber to rest.

The prospect of the long journey and her likely reception at the end of it made her heart pound and left her breathless. She would be thirty-seven in March and felt every year of her age. And as she eased herself down onto the huge bed, she found herself looking back over the years. She thought of her first marriage, to the aged King Louis and gave a smile at the ironies of life. She had been accused of shortening his life by her love of late nights. She had been young and thoughtless then, but now she could understand to what trials the aged and sickly Louis had been put to keep up with her youthful energy. The Wheel of Fortune had turned full circle in very truth, and now it was she who was the sickly one. She did not feel well enough to make the long journey from Suffolk to London, but then, when did she ever feel well nowadays? Charles would be extremely vexed if she wrote refusing to go. And if her wedding was postponed Frances would become impossible. There was no escaping. She would sooner endure the journey than Frances' tantrums.

Besides, Charles was already en route, his head stuffed with wedding arrangements and pleas from Frances that he buy her various expensive London gewgaws to adorn her on her wedding day. No, the wedding could not be put off and she had to go to court. She must resign herself to it.

Mary had persuaded her physician to empty his bags of his remedies so she might stave off some of the pain in her side during the interminable journey to London. Even so, the roads made the journey a nightmare; the horses seemed to stumble over every rut, jolting Mary in her litter till she almost cried from the pain.

The weather didn't help. It was bone-chillingly cold and she huddled under her fur-lined robes, shivering, the foot-warmer she had enjoyed at the start of the journey to London long since cooled. Frances, as ever, added to the torments of the journey. She was impatient at their slow progress and made her displeasure known to her mother.

'Can we go no faster, mother?' she demanded from her palfrey, which, having spurned the use of a litter, she rode beside Mary. With a scowl, she added, 'my wedding will be over before I get there at this rate. My betrothed will have tired of waiting and organised some stand-in to take my place.'

Mary took the long, calming breath that was so often necessary before speaking to Frances. 'Patience, child. It is unseemly for a young girl to show such eagerness. Dorset will wait for you, of that you can be sure.' In truth, thought Mary, her young kinsman would wait a year to ally himself in marriage with the king's niece. He had thrown off his previous betrothed quickly enough.

Just then, the horses carrying Mary's litter went over a particularly pot-holed section of the road. The horses stumbled and Mary was so badly jolted that she cried out in pain. Eleanor, her other daughter, beside her in the litter and so unlike her sister, asked kindly, 'Are you all right, Mother? Is the pain no better?'

'A little, sweeting,' Mary lied. 'But these treacherous winter roads don't make for easy travelling. I wonder that your father didn't wait and arrange your sister's wedding for the summer.' Mary longed for her warm and comfortable bed at Westhorpe, but it would no longer be there; dismantled, it was even now, on the road to London, just as she was. She began to wish she had defied Charles and never set out on this wretched journey. Frances could just as easily have been married from their Suffolk home. But Charles wouldn't have permitted that, she knew and as for Frances... She was at last to get her wish and go to court. She would have become impossible if she had been denied both court and a London wedding.

So, the gruelling journey continued. Mary swallowed more of her physician's remedies and fell into a drugged doze. Finally, after what had seemed like interminable days on the road, she woke to the familiar clamour and stink of London.

The people seemed sullen. As they travelled through the streets, she heard several angry shouts against Anne Boleyn. Unlike Catherine, Anne had never been popular with the Londoners. But then, she had never thought enough of them to care about their dislike. It was a mistake too late for her to remedy now.

As they reached London Bridge, adorned with its usual human heads, to cross to Southwark, Mary averted her gaze, relieved they had arrived at last. But it was a relief tainted with thoughts of what must follow; her humiliation, like Catherine and her daughter before her, at the hands of Anne Boleyn.

CHAPTER TWENTY-FIVE

Mary sent word of their arrival to Charles, and apologies to Henry for her tardiness, before she retired to her chamber. She was so thankful to sink into bed and enjoy some comfort at last, that she longed to stay there. But she could not forever put off her meeting with the Lady Anne, and after a few days' rest, feeling a little better, she ordered her most becoming gown and allowed Susan and her other maids to dress her.

Henry was delighted to see her. He made much of her and his nieces, chaffing Frances on her coming wedding till Mary feared some ill-natured retort. Of this at least she need have no fear; now that Frances had got her way she was all smiles and sweetness, blushing becomingly at her Uncle Henry's teasing.

Anne, of course, showed none of Henry's delight in her presence. It was clear she regarded herself as virtually Queen now and the gaze she fixed on Mary was haughty and unforgiving. It gave warning that she had no intention of making Mary's capitulation an easy one. But at least her brother seemed determined to overlook her lack of humility to his new wife. His expression told them all that he would tolerate no tantrums today.

Mary sensed Anne wasn't to be so easily cowed. Her black eyes were as bold as ever and her pregnancy, though not yet far advanced, provided the only army she required to defy the king.

'So you have finally come to court, your Grace,' she said to Mary. 'I understand your daughter is to be married. I must congratulate you.'

Surprised at this unexpected conciliatory tone, Mary agreed it was so.

'It must be a great relief to you that the Pope finally agreed to legalise your union with the Duke of Suffolk.' Even as this venomous dart was loosed, Anne was preparing another. 'The taint of bastardy is an evil thing, is it not?'

Mary had resolved before this meeting that she would make no retort that would damage her husband's favour with Henry. But Anne's slur, though delivered in honey-sweet tones, was a slur none the less and one that Mary refused to tolerate. How dare the smug trollop taunt her about bastardy when she carried the seed of another woman's husband in her womb? For all her airs, Anne was yet no truly legal wife to Henry. She was in a weak position to pour forth such insults.

Mary, her voice as honeyed as Anne's, retorted, 'Yes, Madam, you speak truth. The Church has long condemned those who beget bastards. As you say, the truth of my marriage has Papal confirmation.' The question 'has yours?' hung unspoken in the air between them.

Fortunately, her brother had not witnessed this exchange. He had removed himself to the other end of the room and was in the middle of a laughing group of courtiers. Charles, though, had remained at her side. She heard him draw in a sharp breath, and knew she could expect a rebuke when they were alone. But for now, Mary savoured the satisfaction her words had brought. She excused herself from her would-be tormenter and made her way to her brother's side. The courtiers broke ranks and made way for her. 'You look well, Henry,' she told her brother. Henry was wearing a doublet of tawny brocade and did indeed look well. 'That colour suits you. I recall that you had a doublet of similar hue when you were a boy. Do you remember it? The days of our youth, hey brother? Such happy times.'

She turned and found Anne at her elbow. 'Does the king ever tell you of our childhood days at Eltham, Madam?' Let Anne be reminded that Henry had had a life before she had come on the scene and it had been a life he had been happy with. Anne didn't trouble to reply and Mary carried on. 'I was lucky to have such a fine brother. Henry was always very loving and kind to his little sister.' Mary turned with a smile to Henry. 'Now look at us, brother, with growing families of our own. How is my little niece? I would remember me to her. 'Tis so long since I've seen her.'

Henry chose not to recall that his daughter had often displeased him. Instead, to Anne's glowering displeasure, he told Mary, 'She's not so little now, Mary. Only a year older than your eldest girl.'

'Your Mary takes after her father, does she not, Charles?' Mary demanded of her husband. Charles hastened to agree with her. 'Such a bright, knowing child and so affectionate. You must be proud of her, Henry.'

451

Henry blushed a little for shame at his treatment of his daughter, but admitted his pride in her. 'Mary's quite a scholar,' he told her, 'though she can dance as prettily as any.'

'I shall enjoy seeing her dance at her cousin's wedding celebrations.'

'She has become a little wilful of late, sister,' Henry complained, his little mouth pursing. 'I thought to ask your advice.'

Mary laughed. 'I'm no expert on dealing with wilful daughters, Henry. I would that I were. I'll be glad to get Frances married and off my hands. Perhaps you should consider the same for Mary?'

To her surprise, Henry nodded consideringly at this. Mary darted a glance at Anne. The arrogant look was gone to be replaced by a nervous lip-biting which pleased Mary. It indicated that Anne wasn't quite as secure as she would have them all believe. As did the fact that not only had she managed to exclude Henry's light o' love from the conversation, but that Henry hadn't even noticed. She had heard how Anne dominated the conversation at court, organising the masques and other entertainments with that ready wit that had grown sharper with the years. This was one conversation she had been unable to dominate. After all, she could scarcely evince an interest in the king's daughter this late in the day.

Mary commented on the alterations her brother had made since she had last been at court. After her admiration of these changes, Henry insisted he must show her the rest.

GERALDINE EVANS

Eagerly, he took her arm and led her off for a turn around the palace and the gardens, her daughters, Charles and the other courtiers trailing behind them. Only Anne was left behind, but even this Henry failed to notice.

Mary felt an only-too-human pleasure at having trumped Anne Boleyn's ace. Of course, it had helped that Henry had been so pleased to see her that he had deliberately ignored the undercurrents that existed between his new wife and his sister. But it was revealing that he had failed to notice she had not joined the party touring the palace. It indicated that Henry was no longer quite as careful of the lady as he had once been. Still, Mary warned herself, she must make sure she didn't outstay her welcome. She would get Frances married and return home to Suffolk.

She would be glad to go. The noise and odours of London upset her after so long in the fresh and quiet country air. She suspected that Charles would be as keen for her to depart as she was herself. For as soon as they had retired to dress for supper he had indeed rebuked her for her tart tongue and had impressed on her how she was to behave to the Lady Anne in future. Mary knew he would be furious with her if she disobeyed him. He was high in the lady's favour, she knew, but if Mary was to repeat honeyed insults it would not be long before Anne's dislike for the wife spread to the husband. It would be as well for both she and Charles if she were to go home. She would find it difficult to long continue to bite her tongue or find honey with which to coat it.

She had forgotten, too, how exhausting was court life. She longed for some peace. But there was little of that to be

453

found at court. For Mary, the unending round of entertainments were now something to be endured rather than enjoyed. She sat through banquet after banquet feeling faint and queasy, the pain in her side reduced to a dull ache by the combined strength of copious quantities of wine and her physician's potions. With what fellow-feeling she now thought of King Louis. What will-power the old king must have had during their brief marriage. She remembered with a pang of remorse how many nights he had, for her pleasure, sat up late, hours after he would at one time have retired to his bed. He had been kind to her, too, whereas her robustly healthy family were impatient with her. She couldn't altogether blame them. Ill-health was unwelcome at such celebrations.

Henry, though, had been kind. That was a change from the old days. There had been a time, and not so long ago, when he had been at pains to remove himself from sickness and disease. His intolerance had been something of an obsession; he had even sent Anne Boleyn from his side when she had been ill with the sweat. But now, Henry showed he had become quite an authority on ailments and their various remedies. He seemed to find the subject fascinating, Mary discovered, in spite, or perhaps because of, his horror and fear of ill-health. It was a strange interest for a king. But, like her, he was no longer young and must suffer the ailments that middle-age brought. He would know what it was to be at the mercy of the physicians' harsh remedies that were often more to be feared than any disease. Henry told her that he now preferred to treat himself when possible. He had even suggested a soothing potion for her to take and Mary had promised to try it.

The day of Frances' wedding dawned. Mary was glad to find that Henry's recommended remedy seemed to have worked. She was relieved on such a day to have respite from the continual pains.

Frances was at last displaying the nerves of a bride. In her it produced sulks, tantrums and spite in equal measures. And as Eleanor ran into Mary's chamber in tears once again, Mary sighed and wondered what Frances had done now.

'What's this then, child?' she asked Eleanor. 'Tears on your sister's wedding day? Why so? Pray, don't tell me your sister's slapped you again?'

Eleanor shook her head. That was something at least, thought Mary. It would be a relief to get the girl wed. She could feel some sympathy for the fate of Frances' betrothed if the lad wasn't such a fool.

'She's torn my gown.' Fresh tears erupted. 'She said it was her day and that mine was too pretty for her liking.'

Mary soothed her daughter and wiped away her tears. She felt the pain in her side begin to throb at this latest irritation. She strove for calm. Today should be a day for joy, she would not have it spoiled. She remembered her wedding day, or rather days - for she had, between King Louis and Charles, as she had often recalled in the days leading up to this wedding - undergone quite a few. 'Where's Susan?' she asked now. 'I'm sure she'll be able to repair it for you.'

'I'm here, my lady.' Susan bustled into the room. 'Come, child. Let me see.' Susan examined the tear. 'I can soon mend that, sweeting,' she quickly assured the still-tearful Eleanor. 'It's only along the seam and not a real tear at all. I'll repair it and no one will know the difference.'

'But I'll know,' Eleanor sniffed.

Susan took Eleanor off and Mary was left in peace once more. For a fleeting moment she considered ordering a beating for her eldest daughter. It was something she rarely sanctioned, but Frances richly deserved such a punishment. Mary knew she had been too lenient with the girl. However, it was too late now to regret her own leniency. She could scarcely start correcting the deficit on her daughter's wedding day. For the bride and her sister both to have red, puffy eyes would be a sorry start to such a celebration.

Mary stood up quickly. Too quickly, for the room spun and she had to grab a chair for support. These turns of hers were getting worse, she admitted. Only let her get through the ceremony and the banquet to follow.

Thank the Lord. The wedding was over. The bride and groom had been put to bed. Even young Dorset could surely manage the rest without assistance.

Mary retired to her chamber, thankful she had got through the day without further upset. She must try to get some sleep.

Henry was in jovial humour these days. Mary, like the rest of the court, knew that this meant that Henry believed the long-awaited divorce was finally within his grasp.

GERALDINE EVANS

The Act in Restraint of Appeals had proclaimed England's jurisdictional self-sufficiency, and all national cases were now to be heard in England, the validity or otherwise of Henry's marriage to Catherine included, with no appeal to any higher authority, because none now existed. Thus Henry made use of the Pope's servant, the Archbishop, to deny the Pope's existence. Mary felt sure that the irony of it would amuse Henry.

Quicker than a fever, the news spread round the court that Henry's new Archbishop, Thomas Cranmer, had written to Henry, begging to hear and give judgement on Henry's important matter. Henry, of course, had graciously given his consent. After long debate, Archbishop Cranmer announced his judgement on Henry and Catherine's marriage. He declared it invalid as it was impeded by Divine law, which no Pope could dispense. The Archbishop's findings on Henry's marriage to Catherine were revealed late in May and were such a foregone conclusion that Anne, even before his judgement, had confidently started to call herself Queen.

It was clear that even Henry was worried how such a bold move would be received. But by now, only the rough commoners dared to openly deride Anne. At court, most knew better than to cross the lady, and there, there were few murmurings. This gave Henry and Anne such confidence that they were now ready to declare that they had in fact, married in January, four months earlier.

Anne had long possessed Catherine's husband and jewellery; she would now also have her queenly title. Catherine had been brusquely informed that she must surrender her

457

title of Queen and accept that of Dowager-Princess. Thus was she relegated to her earlier role as Arthur's widow, as though all the long years of marriage to Henry, all the tragic still-births and lost babes, had never been.

Catherine's final degradation upset Mary. She had no wish to witness the coronation of her old friend's usurper which was to take place on 1st June, Whit Sunday. It would be as costly and impressive an occasion as could be contrived. Charles had been put in charge of arranging it and although he had expended vast sums from the treasury, they had been insufficient to purchase the cheers of the people. Their sullenness was more marked than ever. Henry cursed with annoyance at his subjects' attitude to his new queen, but they had loved Catherine well for her many charitable interests and they regarded Anne with dislike. To them, as to Mary, the lady was no lady. She was no more than the king's harlot and they did not feel that such a one was deserving of their cheers.

Charles confided that he would be obliged to put paid place-men in the crowd to do the required cheering. But whether he did or not, Mary was determined she would not witness Anne Boleyn's triumph. As Charles had remarked, the lady's position would be undeniable once she was crowned. Anne would be eager for revenge on those who had slighted her. It would be as well not to be available.

So, in a misty blur of sickness, Mary had travelled home to Westhorpe, accompanied by Eleanor, the sulking Frances and sad remembrances of another coronation in happier times.

No one had had to be paid to cheer at Catherine and Henry's joint coronation. Mary was sad for Henry's sake that the Londoners were not prepared to please him in his demand that they cheer his new queen as she made her way to Westminster Abbey for her crowning. He had always been at pains to gain the Londoners' regard, a regard he had held since boyhood. Their sullenness would grieve him. But he had brought the necessity to pay for cheers upon himself, and no matter how much or how often Anne raged and stormed, the Londoners disliked her and her stiff-necked ways and she would be left in no doubt of it. It was some consolation to Mary when she finally reached home and could retire to bed.

The pain was now coming in great waves that left her gasping. Now nothing she did seemed to make any difference. She was so full of pills she wondered she did not rattle. Mary smiled amidst the pain at the thought that at least Henry had had the good sense not to marry Anne until she had proved herself fruitful. It was her ability to bear children that had made her Queen, not her regal character, for that was Catherine's alone. Anne had been unable to steal that from her predecessor, as she had stolen her husband, her royal jewels, and her crown.

Faces came and went in Mary's tortured brain. Some had gone before she could even recall their names. Catherine's sad face lingered as Mary had last seen her; defiant of Henry in spite of her endless humiliations. Poor lady, to have so many years of marriage dismissed as though they had never been, was cruel. The Princess Mary would likely be declared a bastard now, the poor unhappy child. Anne Boleyn could be relied upon to insist that her offspring took precedence.

Mary groaned as the pain caught her again. Everything went black all of a sudden. Frightened, she called out. 'Frances, are you there?'

Mary saw a darker shadow move within the other darkness. It came towards her and Frances' sullen voice issued from within it. 'Yes, Mother, I'm here.'

'Call the physician again, child. He must have something to ease the pain.'

Frances was unsympathetic. 'He has tried all his pills and potions on you already, Mother. He has nothing left to try.'

Frances sounded resentful and Mary had no difficulty in guessing the reason for it. Frances must be thinking that her mother and her imaginary ailments had spoilt her pleasure again. She was now a married woman and shouldn't still be under her mother's ruling—the cry 'unfair' was doubtless even now echoing around her daughter's head.

Mary was sorry to be the reason her daughter was denied the excitement of the coronation. If it had been anyone other than Anne Boleyn there would have been no question of them all remaining in London and witnessing it. Mary knew her daughter thought she had used her ill-health as an excuse to leave London. So, for that matter, did Charles and Henry. They had both been vexed with her, but Mary had at least managed to coax them round.

Charles, of course, in charge of organising Anne Boleyn's coronation, had remained at court, as had Frances' young husband, Dorset—another reason for Frances' resentment of her mother. Mary let out a sigh. The pain chose that moment to give her a brief respite and she breathed gently, scared that even her breathing would set it off again. She opened her eyes to find her daughter's gaze fixed on her, dislike writ plain. All the potions Mary had taken had left her befuddled. Why did her child hate her so? 'Why do you look at me like that, Frances?' she asked. 'Have I done something else to vex you?'

'What have you done, Mother? For you to ask that.' Frances came close up to the bed and stared down at her mother with small, hate-filled eyes. 'You have done what you always do—immured me in the country and prevented me having the pleasure that other girls of my station enjoy. You know how I had looked forward to my wedding. And then the excitement of the coronation. Surely, with it coming but a few short months after my nuptials, we could have remained in London? But no, you must drag me back here with you. I am a married woman now,' Frances reminded her again, 'and would be treated as such.'

Mary turned her head away to hide the tears. Was it so much to ask of her daughter that she comfort her in her sickness? Mary felt weak and strangely light-headed. Not up to coping with another of Frances' tantrums. If only the girl would be as reasonable and loving as her sister. But it was true that Mary and her elder daughter had never got on. Likely, they never would.

She turned back. Frances was again at the window. She gazed forlornly out at the sunshine – that she was cooped up indoors no doubt another cause for resentment - for Frances had always found more pleasure in physical exercise than she had in intellectual pursuits; she was like her father in that.

Faintly, Mary said, 'I did not mean to spoil your pleasure, Frances. I am ill, truly ill, can you not understand that? Can you not show me a little sympathy? You may now be married, but you are still very young and in need of guidance. Who could I have left you with in London? The new Queen? You know well she can have no fondness for the Duchess of Suffolk's daughter. It is said she gives your poor cousin, Mary, such pinches and slaps the child is black and blue. No, you were better to come home with me than to stay and witness the woman taking your Aunt Catherine's place. Married lady or no, I am still your mother and I'll not have you honour that woman for all she now calls herself Queen.'

'My father honours her,' Frances was quick to remind her. 'We both know he desires you to do likewise. Surely, it is your place to obey your husband, Mother?'

'Pray do not lecture me on the requirements of duty or obedience,' Mary forced out through teeth gritted against the returning pain; the respite had been brief. 'I think I can be trusted to know both better than you. Your father is a man grown and makes his own decisions. It is his choice if he chooses to honour Anne Boleyn, the same as it is mine, as a woman grown, to choose not to.'

'Surely, you mean the Queen, mother? For that is what she is. She has been crowned and royally anointed.'

'I know what I mean,' Mary retorted, wishing only that her argumentative daughter would leave her and let her have some peace. 'For me, Catherine is still Queen and always will be, no matter if the Bullen woman is crowned a thousand times. The Lady Anne is a common harlot; an usurper. Likely, if she fails to bear my brother a son, there'll be another to take her place. The Lord knows the court teems with harlots aplenty. She has made many enemies with that sharp tongue of hers. Even your father, who has no reason to love the lady, hopes she'll goad Henry too far one day. If that day comes, then she'll suffer the same fate as poor Catherine.'

'Surely an' you speak treason, Mother?'

'Treason? It is no treason. How can it be, when I am only speaking of Lady Anne Boleyn. She is not the Queen, that title is rightfully Catherine's. You should not be so ready to honour harlots, Frances. It is shameful and reflects on your own character and lack of judgement.'

Mary's lecture did nothing to improve Frances' humour and she scowled. 'My father would say your judgement was wrong in this. You know it well.'

'I think you can trust me to know my own husband best. Would that I could be sure you will be able to say the same for your own.'

Frances' gaze narrowed. 'What do you mean?'

'Oh, nothing, nothing. Simply that he is weak and likely to be easily-led. Such men do not make the best or most reliable of husbands as I tried to convince your father. But you are happy enough with his choice, I think?' Frances nodded. 'Anyway, you will go your own road, I doubt not. I am too late to influence you to the right or wrong way to behave. Perhaps it is possible your husband will do that when he becomes a man.' Mary thought it unlikely. Henry Grey needed someone to guide and influence him and would have no spare wisdom for Frances.

Fleetingly, Mary wished her husband were here to give her some comfort; but then she faced the reality; they were no longer the impetuous lovers they might once have been. Mary gave a bitter, self-mocking laugh. She had felt their great love could overcome anything. How foolish she had been. Charles, when it came down to it, had always loved ambition more. Who was to say that he wasn't right so to love? She had brought him many problems during their marriage, not least the resentment of many on the king's Council as well as a depleted and often unreliable dower income. If she had not pushed him into marriage Henry would have found his great friend a rich heiress; had he not once tried for Archduchess Margaret, for him?

How long she had clung to the illusion that theirs was a great love, a shared love. Yet where was he now, when she was so sick, but off courting Henry's new Queen? There had been early indications enough of what fickle a thing was the love of Charles Brandon. Self-delusion had clouded her vision. But it was clear enough now. Could she not see Charles's love of ambition reflected in her daughter's eyes? It was odd, Mary thought, that she had long believed Frances to resemble Margaret—and so she did in some ways. But she resembled her father more, much more. Charles had shown himself as lacking in sympathy as his eldest daughter. Time made such sad alterations. Charles's own daughters from his first marriage were kinder to her than Frances. It was Frances, always Frances, who must torment her.

The pain in her side stabbed her again. It was stronger than ever now. Frances' embittered face blurred. Mary longed for her dead son and the comfort he would have given her. They were of a kind, she and Harry, sentimental and loving.

Mary lapsed in and out of consciousness all through the long, summer afternoon. The evening shadows were lengthening when she thought she heard her son calling her. Strange that he should do so now, for it had been about this time of day that he had died. She could see his face so clearly. He was smiling. After witnessing the extent of his suffering before his death it was good now to see him looking so happy. Mary's lips turned up in response. He had always been her favourite child, now she gladly acknowledged the fact.

She remembered her bitter grief when she had lost him and fresh tears welled in her eyes. Her vision of the world was still misty, but she could still see Harry as clear as clear. He called her again, arms outstretched in greeting. Mary struggled to reach him through waves of pain. He turned away, thinking, no doubt, that she ignored him. Distraught, Mary called to him. 'I'm coming, Harry. I'm coming, my son. Do not leave me again,' she pleaded on a sob. To her great joy he turned back to her.

She seemed to be floating down a long tunnel filled with light. Harry stood at the end of the tunnel, outlined in a shimmering haze. At last she reached him and embraced him with a happy sigh. Softly, she murmured his name.

After the previous restlessness, Mary's sudden stillness alerted the watchers in the chamber.

Frances abandoned her sullen watching post by the window and crossed to the bed, suddenly frightened; no longer the confident young woman who would have her 'rights'. She gazed down at her mother. She could have sworn she had heard her mutter her brother's name. But no, her mother lay, quiet and still, her golden hair cascading over her pillows. As she would now forever lay.

Frances stood back from the bed and beckoned her sister forward. 'The Queen of France is dead,' she said.

The End

BIBLIOGRAPHY

Chrimes S B
Henry VII

Erickson Carolly
Anne Boleyn

Mackie JD
The Earlier Tudors

Croom Brown Mary
Mary Tudor, Queen of France

Strickland Agnes
Lives of the Tudor and Stuart Princesses

Kidson Peter
The Medieval World

Cunnington C W & P
Handbook of English Costume in the 16th Century

Quennell M & C H B
A History of Everyday Things in England

Scarisbrick JJ
Henry VIII

Howard Alexander
Endless Cavalcade: A Diary of British Festivals and Customs

Seward Desmond
Prince of the Renaissance-The Life of Francis I

Hackett Francis
Francis I

Ridley Jasper
Henry VIII

Williamson David
Kings & Queens of Britain

Chapman Hester W
Lady Jane Grey

Fraser Antonia
The Six Wives of Henry VIII

Cole Robert
A Traveller's History of Paris

Sim Alison
Pleasures and Pastimes in Tudor England

Dunlop Ian
Royal Palaces of France

Ridley Jasper
The Tudor Age

Potterton David (Editor)
Culpeper's Colour Herbal

Starkey David
Six Wives: The Queens of Henry VIII

Perry Maria
The Sisters of Henry VIII – The Tumultuous Lives of
Margaret of Scotland and Mary of France

HISTORICAL NOTES 1

One of the intriguing aspects of England's Tudor siblings is
just how closely-entwined are their lives and those of their
children and grandchildren.

Mary Tudor, the 'Reluctant Queen' of the novel, was the
younger sister of Henry VIII, whom history tells us was to go
on to become the infamously much-married monarch of six
wives, leaving behind him a tangled and disputed succession.

Elizabeth of York, the mother of Henry, Mary and Margaret Tudor, was the elder sister of the 'Princes in the Tow-

er', murdered, so history has it, by their wicked paternal uncle, Richard III, who was slain, in his turn, by the forces of Henry Tudor at Bosworth Field. Bosworth was the deciding battle in the long-running wars between the rival factions of York and Lancaster (The Wars of the Roses, the name given to their battles came from the adopted emblems of each side—the White Rose of York and the Red Rose of Lancaster). The marriage between Elizabeth of York and Henry of Lancaster was meant to finally put an end to this rivalry for the throne.

Mary Tudor's granddaughter (by her and Charles Brandon's daughter, Frances), was the tragic Lady Jane Grey, whose father plotted to put her on the throne in place of Henry VIII's daughter (another Mary Tudor). Tragically, the sixteen-year-old Jane Grey was beheaded, along with her young husband and father, after the plot to oust Henry VIII's eldest daughter failed. Thus, Lady Jane Grey, the 'Reluctant Queen's' granddaughter, was beheaded on the orders of Mary's niece, who was the cousin of Jane Grey herself. The Tudors certainly believed in keeping everything in the family—even executions.

Mary and Henry's elder sister, Margaret, who, in her early teens, had been married to James IV of Scotland in an attempt to put a stop to the interminable hostilities between England and Scotland, was the grandmother of the equally tragic Mary Queen of Scots, who was beheaded by her cousin, Elizabeth I (Henry VIII's daughter by his second marriage, to Anne Boleyn).

Margaret's granddaughter by James IV, Mary Queen of Scots, married, as her second husband, Henry, Lord Darnley.

Lord Darnley was another of Margaret Tudor's grandchildren, this time, by her second husband, Archibald Douglas.

A terrible husband, Darnley – Margaret's grandson by her second marriage - was killed in a plot that implicated Mary Queen of Scots - Margaret's granddaughter by her first marriage to James IV.

HISTORICAL NOTE 2

Henry VII (the father to Mary, Margaret and Henry VIII), had no real hereditary claim to the throne of England. His claim to the throne (and that of his son, Henry VIII), was shaky, to say the least, which explains why Henry VIII was so keen to get a son that he set off on his notorious serial marriages.

Catherine of France, the twenty-year-old widow of Henry V, had fallen in love with a gentleman of her guard, Owen Tudor, and secretly married him.

Edmund Tudor, the son of Catherine and Owen, married the eleven-year-old Margaret Beaufort, the granddaughter of an illegitimate son of John of Gaunt and Catherine Swynford, who had afterwards been legitimised by an Act of Parliament. Just thirteen, Margaret Beaufort gave birth to her only child, a son, who was to become Henry VII.

So what claim did Henry Tudor, Duke of Richmond, have to England's throne? He never clearly stated what it was. Hardly surprising, as the claim was so unsatisfactory. If by hereditary succession from Edward III, through his mother, Margaret Beaufort, there were other claimants with a far better title than he—including his mother, who was still very much alive at the time he ascended the throne as Henry VII.

In any case, the patent which legitimised the children of John of Gaunt and his one-time mistress, Catherine Swynford, had clearly stated that they were ineligible to succeed to the throne.

Equally, he did not claim the throne through the rights of his wife, Elizabeth of York, the Yorkist heiress, as he didn't marry her till three months after he had been crowned king. In any case, she and the rest of Edward IV's children by Elizabeth Grey (including the two boys, Edward and Richard, the 'Princes in the Tower') had been declared illegitimate by their paternal uncle, Richard III, by virtue of Edward IV's pre-contract of marriage to Eleanor Butler.

Henry Tudor did not even claim the throne by right of conquest. Perhaps this was wise, given that his invading army had been composed chiefly of the hated French. The Act of Parliament merely declared that he alone was the rightful king, while Henry himself announced that he was king by just hereditary title and by the Judgement of God revealed by his victory on the battlefield of Bosworth.

HISTORICAL NOTE 3

From my research, there seems to be some confusion as to the actual date that Mary's son, Henry died. Some books I have consulted had him dying around the age of 11 and others had him dying around the age of 18, some nine months after Mary. For the purposes of greater drama, I have taken the earlier date as the date of her son's death.

ABOUT THE AUTHOR

Geraldine Evans is a multi-published author of mystery novels. Reluctant Queen is her first historical.

PRAISE FOR RELUCTANT QUEEN

'A very readable account of a fascinating woman who dared to stand up to Henry VIII and survived. It is thoroughly researched, admirably written and the author's love of the Tudor period shines through.'
HISTORICAL NOVELS REVIEW

'Creatively imagines the private life of Mary Rose Tudor in this richly-textured historical novel. A thoroughly researched, elegantly written historical tale.' **KIRKUS INDIE**

Geraldine Evans is mostly-known for her popular mystery series: Rafferty & Llewellyn and Casey & Catt.
Geraldine Evans has been writing since her twenties and has had eighteen novels traditionally published (Macmillan, St Martin's Press, Worldwide (pb), Severn House, Hale, Isis Soundings (audio), F A Thorpe (lp), but in 2010 took the momentous decision to leave the world of traditional publishing behind and turn indie.

She has also had published articles on a variety of subjects, including, Historical Biography, Writing, Astrology, Palmistry and other New Age subjects. She has also written a dramatisation of Dead Before Morning, the first book in her Rafferty series and a sitcom, Jamjars, which is awaiting offers.

She is a Londoner, but now lives in Norfolk England where she moved, with her late husband George, in 2000.

CONNECT WITH THE AUTHOR

WEBSITE/BLOG: http://geraldineevansbooks.com
Author of the digital, Amazon Category Best Selling Rafferty & Llewellyn and Casey & Catt police procedural series
Author of the digital, Amazon UK Category No 1 Best Seller: Reluctant Queen: The Story of Mary Rose Tudor, the Defiant Little Sister of Infamous English king, Henry VIII
Author of Romantic Novels (Under the pen name Maria Meredith)
Author of two New Age books: Get The Right Guy! and Writers' Woes, How to Avoid Them and Get it Right Next Time, under her pen name Gennifer Dooley-Hart

AMAZON AUTHOR PAGE:

https://www.amazon.com/author/geraldine.evans
WEBSITE/BLOG: http://geraldineevansbooks.com

NEWSLETTER SIGN-UP LINK FOR NEWS, BARGAINS

AND GIVEAWAYS: http://eepurl.com/AKjSj

Geraldine Evans uses **AUTHORGRAPH** to connect

personally with readers.
http://www.authorgraph.com/authors/gerrieevans
AMAZON UK: http://amzn.to/15LoZHh

AMAZON US: http://amzn.to/X3xCIj

BARNES & NOBLE:

http://www.barnesandnoble.com/s/geraldine-evans

APPLE EBOOKS:

http://ibookstore.com/products.php?i=B005MLA1TC

KOBO EBOOKS:

http://store.kobobooks.com/Search/Query?ac=1&Query=ger
aldine+evans&sort=TitleAsc

TWITTER: http://www.twitter.com/@gerrieevans

FACEBOOK: http://www.facebook.com/pages/Geraldine-
Evans-Crime-Author/134541119922978?ref=hl

GOODREADS:

https://www.goodreads.com/author/show/54701.Geraldine_
Evans

GOOGLE+:

https://plus.google.com/105635492037945817182/posts

CRIMESPACE:

http://www.crimespace.ning.com/profile/GeraldineEvans

LINKEDIN: http://uk.linkedin.com/pub/geraldine-
evans/24/550/90a

REDROOM: http://redroom.com/member/geraldine-evans

SMASHWORDS:

http://www.smashwords.com/profile/view/GeraldineEvans